PO

MISSMATCH

W9-AGT-355

a lauren holbrook novel

e r y n n   m a n g u m

MISSMATCH

TH1NK
P.O. Box 35001
Colorado Springs, Colorado 80935

© 2007 by Erynn Mangum

ISBN-13: 978-1-60006-095-3
ISBN-10: 1-60006-095-1

Cover design by studiogearbox.com
Cover image of girl by Johner/Getty
Cover image of coffee cup with writing by studiogearbox.com

Creative Team: Melanie Knox, Susan Martins Miller, Kathy Mosier, Arvid Wallen,
        Kathy Guist

Some of the anecdotal illustrations in this book are true to life and are included with the permission of the persons involved. All other illustrations are composites of real situations, and any resemblance to people living or dead is coincidental.

Mangum, Erynn, 1985-
  Miss Match : a Lauren Holbrook novel / Erynn Mangum.
     p. cm.
  ISBN 1-60006-095-1
  1. Dating (Social customs)--Fiction. I. Title.
  PS3613.A5373M57 2007
  813'.6--dc22
                              2006034502

Printed in the United States of America

4 5 6 7 8 9 10 / 11 10 09 08

To my mom, Susan Elaine Terry Mangum, who holds many titles in my life: Mom, Adviser, Co-conspirator, and, best of all, Friend. I can't even imagine a more amazing mother. I want to be like you when I grow up. I love you!

Acknowledgments

To God. Lord, this book is all for You. What an incredible journey we've had thus far—I can't wait for the rest. Thank You! To You alone be the glory!

Thanks also to:

Mom—I don't have the words! I am eternally blessed to have you as my mother, my encourager, and my friend. Thank you so much, Mom, for all the time, effort, advice, suggestions, and travel you have poured into this whole process. This book is more yours than it is mine. I love you.

Dad for telling me I could be a writer—without ever reading my work! The faith you have in me has made me work even harder. Thank you for providing me with everything I needed to write this story and for celebrating the milestones with me. I love you!

Bryant, who came up with the original title—again, without reading the book! Thank you for encouraging me in this and bearing with me all these years. I love you, brother.

Caleb, who by the sweetness of his heart read this very chick-lit story and didn't hate it. Thank you for going above and beyond your call of duty as my brother! I love you.

Cayce, my favorite sister. Not only did you read my story, correct it, and discuss the characters with me, but you're a much more talented writer than I am. I look forward to reading one of your books someday. I love you!

Nama, my amazing grandmother, who has read my stories from the time I was very small. Thank you so much for calling and e-mailing about the characters: "I still think Brandon's going to marry Laurie!" I love you!

All my extended family and friends—you know who you are. Thank you so much for the prayers, encouragement, and (okay, I'll admit it) the fodder for this story. I'm so thankful for you!

NavPress for taking a chance on an unknown kid, to borrow a common phrase. You guys are wonderful! Melanie Knox, Susan Miller, Kathy Mosier, Kate Epperson, and all who have pushed and stretched this manuscript to make it the best it can be—thank you! You all are amazing!

The Christian Writers Guild for their fabulous writing course, their incredible conferences, and, mostly, their friendship. My mentors, Terry White and Brandilyn Collins—I have grown so much because of you! Thank you!

Wikipedia and WebMD—two priceless online resources!

Starbucks for inventing two drinks that fueled much of this story: The Mocha and the Caramel Frappuccino.

Costco for selling dog food–sized bags of Starbucks French Roast. This book was finished in part because of them.

And Jane Austen. Much of the inspiration for this book came from her incredible masterpieces *Emma* and *Pride and Prejudice*.

Prologue

"Jingle allll the waaay!"

It is one week until Christmas. My soon-to-be-retired boss, Mr. Knox, sighs as I come in the door.

"Don't take this the wrong way, Lauren, but I'd stick to photography."

I toss my backpack in the general direction of the pointless secretary's desk. Pointless because we don't have a secretary nor a use for one.

"Has anyone ever told you how great you are with compliments?" I say.

"Do you mind taking my eleven o'clock appointment?" Mr. Knox asks, tucking his pencil behind his ear, as is his custom. Mr. Knox is in his midsixties, is maybe five foot eight — barely two inches taller than me — and has balding hair the exact color of Nilla Wafers.

I know this because I discreetly compared the two just the other day.

He's also the only person other than my oldest sister who calls me by my full name, Lauren. Most people call me Laurie.

"Sure, I can take it," I tell him, pulling off my gloves and hat, which makes my hair crackle with static.

Mr. Knox is giving me his classic How-Did-I-Get-Stuck-with-Her? look. "Your hair is a wreck, Lauren."

"Once again, the compliments just overwhelm me." I try my best to smooth my hair.

He frowns at the failed effort. "Go look in the mirror. And hurry. It's three minutes until eleven."

The studio is basically a big square building someone added interior walls to in order to make it seem more complex. One corner of the building is the front room with the useless secretary's desk. The four portrait studios are right behind the desk. There's a long hall with one office, a room for people to change clothes, a bathroom, and a tiny employee lounge alongside it. The studio is extremely well-respected—we get business from all over the area.

I half-skip down the hall. It is, after all, one week until Christmas—the most wonderful time of the year!

My best friend and Mr. Knox's grandson, Brandon Knox, is sitting in the employee lounge, guzzling a Coke and staring at the clock.

I poke my head in. "Hey."

He swallows. "Hi, Laur. Two minutes and thirty-three seconds."

"Until what? The Ghost of Christmas Future?"

"Worse."

"I don't know, Brandon. The Christmas Future ghost was pretty scary."

"The Rawleys."

"Okay, never mind. You win." The Rawleys have seven kids who don't know the meaning of the word *discipline*. A part of me wants to throw the book of Proverbs at them each time they come in.

Brandon finishes the Coke and grabs a Dr. Pepper. He's combating the Rawleys the only way we know how—loads and loads of caffeine. "Your hair looks great," he says between swallows.

"Thanks, I'm about to go spray it so it'll stay like this." I riffle my hand through it. "How do you think I'd look as a blonde?"

Slurp. "I prefer you as a brunette."

"Even if my eyes were blue?"

"They're not, so I don't know why we're having this conversation, Nutsy."

Don't ask. It's a nickname dating to the first time we watched *Robin Hood* together.

"Gray is close to blue." I bat my eyelashes at him.

"It is not."

"Is too."

"One minute and eleven seconds."

I grab a can of Dr. Pepper for myself. "You're in my prayers, Brandon."

"I'm in my prayers too." He moans.

I grin at him, duck into the bathroom, and comb down my hair, and I'm back down the hall just as an average-height guy with short, spiky brown hair gelled to perfection comes through the door. He's wearing a nice suit and looks like he could quote me the stock exchange numbers for Procter & Gamble off the top of his head.

Mr. Knox has left apparently, but there's one of his blue sticky notes on the desk. *His name is Nate Kennedy. Hope you fixed your hair.*

"Hi, Nate," I say, smiling nicely. "I'm Laurie. I'll be taking your picture."

"It's for my business cards." He says this very loudly, as if my now-combed-down hair has clogged my ears.

"Oh yeah? What do you do?" I point toward Studio One and he follows me in. I bite back a grin as I see the Rawley's fifteen-passenger van pull up.

"I'm a stockbroker."

Man, I nailed his job.

"Neat."

"I just moved to town. I got transferred h re to Colorado from Arizona." He looks around the small studio, stopping at the bright green piece of paper I have taped to the door. It has my favorite verse written on it: Psalm 37:4.

"Are you a Christian?" he asks.

I plop a chair in front of the camera for him. "Yep."

"Really? Wow, this is great. Me too. I'm actually looking for a church." He sits in the chair.

I go around to the other side of the camera. "Well, you can try my church. They only tar every third visitor, and I think that happened last week, so you should be good."

He starts laughing right away. A nice laugh.

I smile, squint through the lens, and suddenly have a very realistic daydream.

Lexi wearing a white slip dress, carrying a bouquet of red tulips, walking down the aisle to Nate.

Lexi? My older sister? Marrying this up-and-coming stockbroker?

I half-gasp.

"What?" Nate yells.

I decide he cannot lower his voice to save his life. "Come to church on Sunday. You'll like it. I promise."

"Uh. Sure."

Sunday morning dawns sunshiny and bitterly cold. I am standing just inside the front door of my church, shivering. The things I do for my sister's future happiness.

Nate comes through the door and I yell, "Nate! Hi, remember me?"

His face splits in a grin. "Um. Yeah, of course I remember you."

"Good. How was your week?"

"Fine."

He looks like he's going to go on into the service, so I need to distract him. Lexi has no sense of punctuality at all.

"Tell me about the stock exchange. I've been thinking about investing."

"Really? Well, that's good because right now . . ."

My brain stops there and I keep eye contact and nod occasionally just so he thinks I'm still paying attention.

The door opens.

Remember those movie scenes where the hero and heroine finally meet and there's this huge swell from an orchestra?

You're not going to believe this, but it does happen!

The door opens; Lexi pops her incredibly gorgeous head in and doesn't even glance in my direction as she half-runs to the sanctuary, pushing her earrings through her ears as she jogs.

"Lex!"

She turns, and right then is when the music director, David, starts strumming a sweet song on his guitar.

Nate blinks at her, taken aback. Lexi is beautiful—long, long, long honey blonde hair, huge gray eyes, a perfect smattering of freckles across her adorable nose.

"Hey, Baby," she says to me. She smiles politely at the starched gent next to me. "I'm Lexi Holbrook, Laurie's sister."

"I'm Nate." Swallow. "Nate Kennedy."

They shake hands.

I grin. Electricity is zipping through the air and it isn't just from my again static-clung hair.

"You're welcome to sit next to us," Lexi says, like I knew she would.

"Sure. I'd like that."

They don't even make sure I'm behind them as they disappear into the sanctuary.

I try very hard not to burst into a happy song and dance. Well, moderately hard anyway.

"Laurie?"

I whirl, midtwist.

Brandon comes down the hall, frowning. "What are you doing?"

"Brandon, darlin'," I drawl, grinning exuberantly, "I have discovered my life's work."

"It's not coffee drinking, is it? How many cups have you had today anyway?"

"No, it's not coffee drinking." I wave my hands around. "Eight months, Brandon. Maybe less."

"Eight months until what?"

I grin in the direction of the sanctuary doors and then smirk at Brandon. "First Corinthians 7:36," I tell him, opening the door.

He whips his Bible from his coat pocket, flips to the passage. I'm halfway in the sanctuary, the congregation is singing, and I can *still* hear his yell.

"'They should get married'? *Laurie!*"

Chapter One

Twelve Months, Three Weeks, and Nine Hours Later

There comes a time in every woman's life when she desperately desires to be married. At least, this is what I have always been told by my father. I am beginning to doubt his word on the subject. I am officially, as of one week, twenty-three years old and haven't the slightest inkling of matrimony *or* desperation.

I didn't feel desperate at my friends' weddings or even at my sister's wedding, which took place just a few hours ago. My father did, however.

"I can't believe Lexi's getting married." This is all Dad said during Lexi's six-month engagement. To be honest, I'm glad the day finally came so Dad can maybe get over it and move on with life.

I shouldn't be so optimistic.

"I can't believe Lexi got married."

The only change in the conversation is the tense.

Dad is in his favorite chair, the red one with the plaid stripes, staring bleakly at the floor where Lexi's dog, Muffin, blissfully chews the designer coffee table legs unhindered. Dad's gray hair is still combed nicely from the wedding, but he's changed into a pair of khakis and a polo shirt.

A fire is roaring in the massive fireplace, and all the lights in the house are off except the one lamp by Dad's chair.

"Dad, come on. You've got to move on now. Lex is married, to a wonderful guy I might add, and that's that." I lounge on the limited edition leather couch, still in my maid of honor gown. Lexi always dreamed of a fancy, black-tie-only wedding. Fortunately Dad could afford it. Dad told me he didn't sell his Internet company just to sit on the millions of dollars, and Lexi told me to stand up straight every four minutes so I wouldn't wrinkle the two-thousand-dollar dress.

I'm having fun mashing as many wrinkles as possible into the hateful fabric.

"Laurie-girl."

Dad turns woeful gray eyes at me, and I suddenly have the impression of staring at a humanized basset hound.

"Yes, Dad?"

"Don't ever get married, Laurie-girl. I don't think I can take you leaving me."

I laugh. "You have nothing to worry about, Dad. Even if I did want to get married, which I don't, there aren't any good men around anymore anyway."

"I feel the same way about women." The voice is not my dad's.

I roll my eyes. "Can't you ever knock?"

Brandon strolls into the room like he owns the place. He stops by Dad's chair. "How are you doing, sir?"

"Not too good, Brandon."

"I was afraid of that." Up to this point, Brandon hasn't even turned in my direction. Now he winks at me. He is still in his tux, the tie undone, and his straight, short brown hair is no longer combed neatly. Brandon is tall, and his lankiness just makes him look taller. The tux kind of rounds him out a little bit.

He's still talking. "Lexi's absence will be keenly felt, I'm sure."

"Oh brother." I adjust my position so that I can attack the left side of the dress. "Why are you here, Brandon?"

He hands Dad a box. "I found these after the wedding. I thought you might like them, Mr. Holbrook."

Unopened tea bags fill the box. Dad smiles for the first time that day. "Thanks."

"For Pete's sake." I groan. "Dad, Lexi hasn't lived here for four years! It's not like you saw her every day. In fact, you'll probably see her more now. Lexi and Nate's house is two blocks away."

Dad nods, his face easing back into a sad frown. "I guess, Laurie-girl."

I close my eyes.

"So what big plans do you have for this evening?" Brandon sits at the other end of the couch from me, kicking my bare foot.

"None." I twist away. "Dad wants to rest."

"The wedding wore me out. And there's a bad cold going around." Dad puts a hand to his forehead. "I hope I didn't catch it."

When I was in fifth grade, my teacher asked my class to describe our parents in one word. Mom passed away when I was eight, so I only had to depict Dad. It was the easiest assignment I have ever had. One word: Hypochondriac. The hardest part of the assignment was spelling it.

Brandon's mouth twists in a pitiful attempt to not smile. "Don't worry, Mr. Holbrook. I'm sure you're safe."

"I don't know. I'm going to go make some tea. Would either of you like some?"

I know what kind it will be. Lemongrass. *Blegh.*

"No thanks, Dad," I say cheerfully. "I feel fine."

"You got your mother's immune system. You should be thanking God for that every day," Dad says solemnly.

I nod.

"None for me either." Brandon smiles. "I had a glass of orange juice before coming over."

"Smart boy. See, Laurie-girl? You should take a few lessons from Brandon."

"I'll try," I say, this time not as cheerfully.

Dad leaves the room. Brandon waits until Dad is out of earshot. "He's not doing very well," he whispers.

I groan.

"I guess you knew that." He pauses. "How are you doing?"

"I'm fine. Lex is happy, Nate is happy, and I'm happy because I'm the one who introduced them." One week before Christmas. How romantic is that?

He brushes it off. "Luck."

"Not luck. They're perfect for each other."

"Yes, but don't attribute that to yourself. God would have had them meet eventually on their own."

Brandon takes great pride in minimizing the things in which I take great pride.

"Say what you want. But I know I'm partly responsible for the wedding today, and I'm proud of it."

"Laurie, I wish you wouldn't do that," Dad says, coming back from the kitchen.

"What's that, Dad?"

"Tear families apart."

I blink. Brandon starts laughing and tries to cover it with a cough.

"Dad, I didn't tear any families apart, I joined them together."

"A wedding is a very sad thing for every family. Did you see Nate's mother today?" He shakes his head mournfully.

"She was bawling," Brandon says.

"Exactly." Dad points at me. "Tearing families apart." A faint whistle floats from the kitchen, and Dad leaves again.

I can't get mad at Dad. But I definitely can at Brandon.

"What is the matter with you?"

"What?"

"Telling him Nate's mom was bawling." I whack his tux-shrouded shoulder. "Good grief, Brandon."

He laughs.

Brandon Knox has been my best friend since second grade. We met on the playground during an intense game of Fox and Hound. After we both ended up with bloody noses and spent the next three hours together in the nurse's office, it was fated—we would either be best friends or best enemies for life. There are times when I wonder if we're really the latter dressed up as the former.

He's been there for all the major events in my life. When my mom died. When I had braces. Graduation. Both of my sisters' weddings.

It can make me sappy if I think about it too long.

"Where are you coming from, Brandon?" Dad comes into the room with a steaming mug filled with thick, pale sludge.

"Adam and Laney's. Actually, they told me you weren't taking this well."

Laney is my sister and older than me by three years. Lexi is one year older.

"Laney." Dad jumps on her name. "How is my girl?"

"Dad, you just saw her three hours ago."

Dad ignores me. "Is she taking the wedding well?"

"She's doing great. She was a little busy when I saw her. Jess was crying hysterically, Dorie was throwing her dinner, and Jack was spitting up." He points to a red spot on his wrist. "Spaghetti."

I start laughing. "Ah, the joys of motherhood."

Brandon grins.

Dad doesn't see the humor in it. "Does she need help?" Worry creeps into his tone.

"Not anymore. Between me and Adam there was an adult for each kid. So Adam cleaned up Dorie, Laney took care of Jack, and I tried to distract Jess."

"I bet your mother feels the loss of Adam as much as I feel the loss of Laney and Lexi," Dad says.

Brandon shrugs. "Mm. I think Mom was just glad he'd found a nice girl to marry."

"She's a strong woman, then." Dad takes a sip of his tea. "Well, kids, I'm going to bed. Laurie-girl, you should as well. You don't want to catch the cold."

"I'll be up soon."

Dad nods at Brandon. "Good night, son."

"Night, Mr. Holbrook."

He disappears up the stairs.

I start working on the front of the dress.

"What in the world are you doing, Laurie?" Brandon is staring at me, his eyebrows bunched together.

"Wrinkling this."

He starts laughing. "You are a stubborn, pig-headed, know-it-all woman."

I crunch more of the silky material against the sofa. "Yeah, well, we all have our little faults. You're opinionated, meddling, and devious, and I still let you stick around." I pause. "Don't ask me why."

"That's why I like you, Lauren Emma Holbrook. You're not afraid to tell me what you really think of me."

"Anytime, Knox."

He gets quiet and I look over at him. "What are you thinking about?"

Brandon blinks. "Oh. Nothing."

"Yeah, right. Give it up." He has his classic off-in-Never-Never-Land look. His eyes are usually a light brown color, but when he's deep in thought, they darken considerably. It makes it easy to know when he's stopped listening to me.

He stretches. "Adam and Laney."

"Translation: Chaos."

He smiles. "No, just about the two of them. They're happy. Really happy. Even in the chaos."

I stop messing up the dress for a minute. "So?"

"So don't you ever envy what they've got?"

This is what our friendship is like: No pretenses.

"Sometimes," I admit. "Not the whole husband thing, you understand. Just the contentment."

He nods. "I mean, we both know they aren't perfect." He snorts as he laughs.

"Yeah. But they accept it. Is that what you're talking about?"

"Yeah." He plays with his class ring. "I think Nate and Lexi have it too."

"Any good marriage should." I go back to wrinkling.

"Sometimes I wonder—"

"Uh-oh."

"What marriage would be like," he finishes.

I immediately start shaking my head. "I don't. I am perfectly happy here. I'm not missing out on anything. I have everything I could ever want or need. Dad dotes on me, I have a good job, and then there's you, of course."

"Yeah, but, Laur, things change. One day you might wake up and I'll be married with a couple of kids, you'll have to take care of your dad instead of the other way around, and whatever." He shakes his hands around as he talks, trying to pull the words from the air, I guess.

For a moment, just the tiniest millisecond, I worry.

Then I get over it. Nothing is going to change. Life is comfortable right now. Brandon is kidding.

He looks serious.

I shrug him off. "Well, I'll stress about that when it happens."

"Laurie's lifelong motto." He yawns. "I should go back to my place."

"You mean you've had your own place this whole time? Heck, I thought you lived here." I smile at him. He's relaxed back into the sofa, head lolled, completely at ease.

He grins and he is the same old Brandon again. "Good night, Laurie," he sing-songs.

I stand, relishing the way the dress creases in all the wrong places. "Night, Brandon."

He watches my pleasure and shakes his head. "Lauren Holbrook, you are one of a kind."

"Yes, thank you."

"See you at work tomorrow."

"Bye."

He lets himself out and I go upstairs. It's Sunday night. Work begins again tomorrow. Life will once again fall into its perfect pace.

I change into my pajamas, fall into bed, and am asleep almost as soon as I touch the pillow.

Almost.

Do I envy what Laney and Lexi have?

Nah.

And then I go to sleep.

Chapter Two

I wake up at eight when my alarm goes off.

Ugh.

Sometime in my prewedding madness yesterday morning, I must have hit the tuner on my alarm clock. Loud trumpets and twangy guitars burst from my clock like a Mexican hat-dancing quartet has taken up residence in my bedroom.

May it never be so.

I hit the alarm clock with the sudden strength of a heavyweight boxer and throw the covers off.

I dress casually because I'm twenty-three years old and I can. People who come to The Brandon Knox Photography Studio expect my coworker, Ruby Palmer, who is thirty-three, to look coordinated and professional because they know she is officially An Adult. People look at me in my jeans and sweater and brush it off because I look like just A Kid.

I take advantage of my youth.

I've been working for the studio since I was a sophomore in high school, at first mostly as a gopher for Mr. Knox, who still owns the place. The older I got, the more I fell in love with the photography process, and Mr. Knox started training me to take the photographs instead of doing my half-secretarial, half-hold-the-screaming-baby job. Brandon's been there since he was about eight. He manages the place now while his grandparents take extremely long trips to exotic places.

It takes me five minutes to get dressed and thirty minutes to fix my hair. I am a stickler about my hair.

Downstairs, Dad holds his lemongrass tea in one hand and his blue indigestion medication in the other.

"Good morning, Laurie. Did you sleep well?" He pops the horse-sized pill in his mouth and swallows it without blinking.

Here's what I don't understand: Horse-sized indigestion pills. It seems like if you're having indigestion, swallowing a pill the size of Massachusetts would be a little difficult.

I answer his question while pouring a cup of coffee. "Yes, Dad. How did you sleep?"

He exhales sadly. "Not as well as I would have if Lexi had been home."

"Dad, Lexi hasn't lived here for four years." If I'm not careful, this can become last night's conversation minus our buffer, Brandon. "What is on your schedule for today?"

"I thought I'd go see Laney."

Bad idea. "Dad, I think Muffin is due in for a veterinarian visit today. Would you mind taking her? I'm working all day today."

He pauses for a second, mulling it over. "Good thinking, Laurie. Lexi wouldn't be happy if Muffin keeled over while she was on her honeymoon."

"Thanks, Dad." Relief.

"Who are you taking pictures of today?"

"Unless we have any last-minute cancellations, we have the Rawleys, the Carters, the Jacksons, and Linda and Greg." *Oops.* I regret the last two names the moment they slip out.

Dad perks up. "Linda and Greg? Linda Myers and Greg Halloway? Why are they getting a picture taken?"

Oh brother. I shove a piece of toast in my mouth. With Dad's dismal view of marriage, it is my only hope of continuing to have a peaceful breakfast. "Weww, Dwad, Winda an Gweg awe gwetting—"

"Laurie, don't talk with food in your mouth. That's rude."

Thank You, Lord. I take my time chewing. A lot of time. I swallow. "Sorry, Dad. Whoa, look at the time. I need to run."

"You don't want to be late."

"Nope, because that would give Brandon license to fire me." I jump up from the table.

"Brandon wouldn't fire you, Honey." He smiles up at me. "Have a good day."

I run for my shoes and backpack and climb into my new Tahoe. All Dad's retirement money and no one to spend it on . . . except me.

See why I'm never getting married?

I drive the five minutes across town to the studio. Brandon's grandfather started the studio about thirty years ago. Brandon's wanted to run it since birth, and last January, Mr. Knox half-retired. Now Brandon runs the place, while Mr. Knox just owns it. It's grown a lot in a year, and Mr. Knox was even nice enough to let Brandon change the name to The Brandon Knox Photography Studio. Now he has four photographers, including me, working for him and is in the market for a secretary.

"You are this close to late." Ruby holds her thumb and forefinger a hair's width apart.

"But I managed to avoid lateness yet again." I sling my backpack into my cubbyhole. I hate carrying a backpack. I am constantly forgetting it. But when the alternative is a purse—well, a purse is just not my style.

Ruby just looks at me and shakes her head. Ruby Palmer has no sense of humor at all, thrives on punctuality, and eats Slim Fast bars for lunch.

If this is what happens when you turn thirty-three, I am never growing up.

She is always dressed stiffly. Or maybe it's just her posture that makes her look stiff. Honestly, you'd think she has a board tied to her vertebrae the way she stands. She has very boring past-the-shoulder-length, mousy brown hair and pretty eyes that could be prettier if she'd just smile occasionally.

There's a part of me that wants to toss a neon-colored scarf around her neck and jump about singing. It's hard to maintain a stiff composure when there is someone dancing around you and you're wearing neon.

Brandon walks in. "Morning, Ruby. Morning, Laurie."

"Good morning, Brandon."

"Hey."

I notice Brandon is seven seconds late, but as the boss, I guess it's his right because Ruby keeps her mouth closed.

"Where are Ty and Newton?" Brandon plops a file folder on the desk and hangs up his coat on the tree by the door. Ty and Newton are the closed-mouthed photographers here. They don't speak to me. Apparently I'm too loud for their tastes.

"In the back," Ruby says to Brandon. "The Rawleys showed up early. Again. It takes both Ty and Newton to corral their kids."

Brandon grins. "How many kids this time?"

"My count? Eight. You never know, though. With all the movement, I could have miscounted." She shakes her head and then smoothes her hair.

The Rawleys have consistently added a child to their family every year since I can remember.

"Laurie, you've got the Carters; Ruby, you take the Jacksons."

"Yes, sir."

My answer is a halfhearted, "Uhh." Brandon does this just to spite me. The Carters like to be photographed with their two cats. I detest cats.

"Oh," Brandon says suddenly. "And Laurie, I just heard that Tina Braxton and Kyle Medfield got engaged. They'll be coming in for pictures at three."

"Tina?" I yell.

Brandon does the funny twisting with his mouth meaning he's hiding a grin. "Yeah, Tina. You remember Tina."

My chin is super-glued to the carpet. "She's eighteen. She's hardly legal. I mentored her through seventh-grade English as my senior extra-credit project."

"Did she pass?" Ruby asks.

"No," Brandon says.

"I can't believe she's engaged!"

"Well, you know, sometimes it just happens. A guy meets a girl. They like each other. Then they love each other. Then they decide to get married." Brandon shrugs. "It happens."

"Yeah, but not to children." I'm not really upset they're getting married. It is more the fact that Tina is eighteen and has already been proposed to.

No one has ever proposed to me.

I wouldn't accept him if he did. It would just be somewhat flattering.

What's so great about Tina Braxton anyway? Sure, she's beautiful, kind, and a good Christian, but what other qualities does she have?

Plenty. I sigh.

Brandon notices my silent pity party and levels me with a stare even Tina Braxton would shudder at. *We'll talk later,* it says.

Oh joy.

He picks up the appointment book. "I had a call about the ad I put in the newspaper. Hannah Curtis will be coming by to interview for the secretary position about four fifteen."

"Who's Hannah Curtis?" With a name like that, I'm picturing a fiftyish woman, probably with no sense of humor. The only person here who does actually laugh is Brandon, and he can't get too goofy because he has to remain bosslike.

Brandon glances at a yellow sticky note he's holding. "She just moved here about a month ago. I haven't actually met her in person, just talked to her on the phone on my way in. She seems nice enough. We'll see."

The bell over the door jangles and the Carters come in.

With Bonny and Betty, The Cats Boisterous.

"Hi!" I say with a cheeky smile. "Good to see you again! Oh, and Bonny and Betty are looking well!"

Three o'clock marches around much too quickly. I hardly have time to gather my composure after the family reunion mob leaves before Tina and Kyle walk in.

A radiant Tina and Kyle.

Oh brother.

"Tina." I tip my head to one side. "You look fantastic."

"Hi, Laurie." Her voice is whispery, fairylike. "This is my fiancé, Kyle."

Kyle shakes my hand. "Nice to meet you, Laurie."

Tina sparkles. Perfectly smooth, chocolate-toned complexion. Perfect brown eyes. Perfect caramel-highlighted black hair.

Perfect, perfect, perfect.

Never have I felt so blah in all my life.

Kyle looks proud he snatched her up first. His black hair is short and fairly curly. Brown eyes. Muscled. Tall. Pretty darn cute.

Brandon materializes beside me, and I can read the glint in his eyes.

This couple is going to hang on the studio waiting room wall.

Where they can mock me day and night.

Wait a minute. What am I thinking?

I *am* Lauren Holbrook. I have a good job and a father who would give me the state if he were able. . . . I have everything I could ever need or desire.

That's right.

"Right this way. We'll be in Studio Four. You'll get three clothing changes during the session. . . ."

It isn't so bad. Tina sweetly informs me they will be married in four weeks. Kyle smiles like a model in *GQ*.

I wave good-bye to them and turn to face Brandon.

"So how was the charming couple?" His eyes are sparkling at me because he knows the answer.

I push my fingers into my face. "Charming. Too charming. My cheeks hurt from smiling."

"Loosen them quick. I need you to be—"

"Charming?" I keep massaging my cheeks. Any blush I had previously applied is now gone.

"For lack of a better word. Yeah. Charming for Hannah Curtis. Got it?"

I salute. "Yes, Captain."

"Good."

Hannah Curtis arrives at four fifteen on the dot. I watch Ruby tensely count the seconds, ready to pounce if Hannah is a microsecond late.

A petite blonde with big, round blue eyes and a figure boasting good genes and lots of exercise walks through the door. The room is immediately filled with a fog of her citrusy perfume.

Surely, surely, *surely* this isn't Hannah Curtis.

"Can I help you?" I ask.

"Yes." The blonde brushes her shiny locks away from her even shinier lips. "I'm Hannah Curtis. I'm looking for Brandon Knox."

"Sure." I paste on a terse smile. "I'll take you back to his office."

"Thank you."

I march down the long, carpeted hallway to Brandon's office. Peach-Faced Barbie follows along as best she can in her toothpick heels and knee-length skirt.

"Brandon." I burst through his door. "This is Hannah Curtis."

Brandon stands, his eyes widening. "Oh." His voice is much lower than normal. "Hi. I'm Brandon Knox."

"Hannah Curtis."

I just said that, idiot.

I need to leave before my mouth starts working without the controlling presence of my brain.

"I'll leave you now." I feel very unfeminine in my loose-fitting jeans. Especially next to Hannah with her legs arcing gracefully from beneath her dress.

Who does she think she is? It is January, for Pete's sake!

"No," Brandon suddenly erupts. "Stay, Laurie."

Now I feel like an unfeminine collie. *Sit, Laurie. Stay, Laurie. Good girl!*

"Yes, sir."

This brings Brandon out of his ogle fest. He breaks his gaze with Hannah and starts staring at me. Only this isn't the same Gosh-You're-Beautiful gawk Hannah received. This is a What-the-Heck-Is-the-Matter-with-You? stare.

Good old Brandon. Always boosts the ego.

"Have a seat, Hannah," he says softly. I get a nod toward the chair next to hers.

"So." Brandon folds his hands together on his desk in the typical bosslike gesture. "You're here about the secretarial job."

Secretarial job? No, I heard you needed a plumber, Mr. Knox!

"Yes." She also weaves her fingers together on her lap.

"Do you have your résumé with you?"

Nah. Who brings a résumé to a job interview?

"Yes, right here." Hannah pulls a crisp sheet of paper from her purse. How does she manage this? Her purse is half the size of the paper, yet the paper isn't folded!

Whoa. We're dealing with a pro here.

Brandon peruses it, the familiar wrinkle between his eyebrows appearing. Hannah and I smile stiffly at each other in silence.

Finally, I break it. "So you just moved here? "

"Yes." This is it. No explanation, nothing!

"From where?"

"Los Angeles." Then she does this flip thing with her head that says clearly, *I do not want to talk to you of all people right now.*

I watch the way the light bounces off her hair and know she is absolutely the wrong person for this job.

Of course, Brandon is reading and misses the whole of it. By the time he looks up, she is Miss-Heaven-Help-Me, I'm-Too-Sweet.

"Looks good, Miss Curtis." He sets the paper on his desk.

She waves one manicured hand. "Oh, please, call me Hannah."

"Fine. Hannah, you seem very qualified for the job. We can offer you eight dollars an hour."

She half-tosses her hair again, only this time instead of looking snooty she gives off an innocent and sugary air. "Sounds fine, Brandon."

"Great! I'm glad. Laurie here can fill you in on all the particulars.

Answering the phone and the like."

I manage a brief smile. "Sure can."

"Okay!" She is annoyingly perky. "When do I start?"

He shrugs. "How about tomorrow?"

"Good! I'll be here!" Okay, bubbly enthusiasm is starting to grate on my nerves.

"Nine o'clock. It was nice meeting you, Hannah."

She sends him a saccharine smile. "Same here. Bye now."

Brandon and Hannah stand. I follow suit. "I'll walk you out." I will like nothing better than locking the door after her.

"No, Laurie. Stay here."

There's the collie thing again.

"I'll walk Hannah out," he says.

I wait until his office door is closed before flouncing in my chair. I need chocolate. And fast. Preferably loaded with caffeine. Whoever invented chocolate-covered coffee beans is a genius deserving of praise.

The door opens and Brandon is back.

"Don't get up."

Aha. Here is the Brandon I know. "Yes, Brandon? Did you need to speak with me about something?"

"What is going on?" He leans on his desk in front of me.

I try tossing my hair like Pantene Pro-V Barbie, but I guess you have to be blonde to pull that off. "I beg your pardon?"

"You don't like Hannah."

"You are so observant."

"Why not?" He spreads out his hands in confusion.

"She's rude, she's conceited, she's immature, she talks like a Barbie doll." I tick the points off on my fingers. "Shall I continue?"

Brandon pushes himself on top of his desk. "You're jealous."

"No, I'm not."

"Yes, you are." He crosses his arms. I can still smell the orangey perfume.

"Why would I be jealous of *her*?"

"Oh, I don't know. She's beautiful. She's intelligent. She's pretty."

"You've mentioned her looks already, thank you."

His mouth curves in a patronizing smile. I hate it when he smiles like this. It makes me feel like I'm four years old.

"Come on, Laurie. Be nice to her, okay? You will have to work together."

"Thanks to you."

"That ad has been in the newspaper for the past three weeks. I'm getting to the point where I'm willing to hire any bimbo who can type."

I stand. "Looks to me like you just did."

"Laurie—"

"Good night, Brandon."

"Don't be like this, Laur." He sounds sincere, but I don't feel like talking with him about this.

I take great pleasure slamming the door in his face.

If I wasn't already sure, I am now. I'm never getting married. Especially if men want brainless Victoria's Secret models for wives.

Well, it suits me. It will just be me and my Hershey bars from this day forward, 'til death do us part.

Chapter Three

Dad is waiting for me when I get home. "Are you all right, Honey?" He closes the garage door.

"Fine, why?" A package of candy bars is safely ensconced in my coat pocket. Dad doesn't like me pigging out on chocolate. He'll worry about my love life, or lack thereof, and then worry about my upcoming marriage, or lack thereof.

"Brandon has called four times to see if you've gotten home okay." Dad shows me the phone in case I don't believe him.

"I'm sure he has." I sweep past Dad. "I don't want to talk to him right now. I just want to go to my room and forget everything related to work for a few minutes, and Brandon Knox is definitely related to work."

The phone rings.

Dad reads the number on the caller ID and looks at me.

I smile haughtily. "Tell him I've decided to take up squid fishing in Borneo, please."

Dad closes his eyes. "That's not very polite, Laurie."

"Politeness has ceased to be a virtue. I'm going to my room."

I hear Dad exhale and answer the phone as I climb the stairs. "Hello, Brandon."

The great thing about my room is that I designed it myself. The walls are cream colored, and I have a bunch of fun lamps everywhere instead of an overhead light. There's a bed, a desk, a photograph wall, and, best of all, a perfectly squishy recliner situated very snugly by a TV. It makes for a primo spot for a pity party.

"Ah." I settle into the chair. Out comes the chocolate, in goes Sandra Bullock and Bill Pullman.

Life is good.

I have finished three Butterfingers and a Milky Way and I'm halfway through a bag of M&Ms before the predictable knock comes.

I know who it is. Dad. Concerned about his daughter. Worried she's contracted a horrible mental illness salved only by excessive chocolate and romance.

Good old Dad.

"Come in!"

Brandon walks into Forbidden Territory. Sandra Bullock and I react at the same time. She gapes, I frown.

Brandon takes in the candy wrappers and the chocolate left to be devoured.

"You're turning into a psycho." He's changed from his work clothes into loose-fitting jeans and a USA T-shirt.

I pop another handful of M&Ms in my mouth. "That's okay, all the great photographers were said to be crazy. Leave me alone."

He doesn't listen. What else is new?

"Whatcha watching?"

"*While You Were Sleeping.*"

"Mm." He sits beside the chair and picks up one of the Milky Way wrappers. "Got a second?"

I pause the movie, making sure he hears my annoyed breath.

"Is this about Lexi?"

"Lexi?" What does my sister have to do with this?

"Yeah. Her getting married and all. Leaving you with your dad. Does it make you want to get married?"

I stare at him. "Brandon, you're the psycho."

"So why are you up here all by yourself watching a romantic comedy and scarfing down candy bars?"

Come to think of it, why am I so depressed? This is the thing about chocolate. Once you've eaten so much, you forget what the problems are in the first place.

I try to shrug my way out of it. Brandon just looks at me.

"I don't know."

"Is it because of Hannah?"

"No." And it isn't. Who cares about stuffy Hula Barbie anyway? Just because I'll have to work with her for the rest of my life . . . "I'm ready for a change. Laney's married, Lex is married, Dad's . . . still Dad."

Brandon covers a grin with his fist.

"I'm ready for something to happen to me." I finger an M&M. My life is so predictable now. I hate predictability. The last time I felt sponta-neous, I was introducing Nate and Lexi.

Brandon keeps pressing. "Like . . . ?"

"Something different. Something unusual. Something . . ."

"Barbie-like?"

I give him the glare. Full wattage.

He laughs so hard he falls over. "Oh, Laurie," he says, wiping tears from his eyes, "you crack me up."

"Yeah? Well, you need someone to crack open your head and make sure your brain is still in there."

"Hey, you're the one turning into a schizophrenic on me."

This is what Brandon and I have done for years: Trade insults.

"Yeah, but a cute schizophrenic."

"A chocoholic schizophrenic." He throws the wrapper at me and stands. "I should go. Got work in the morning."

"Ugh."

He sticks a finger in my face. "You'd better be there too, or it's your head on a silver platter."

I groan. "Do I really have to train Barbie?"

"Yes."

"You hired her. Why can't you train her?"

He smiles at me sardonically. "I don't have the time."

I shove another handful of M&Ms in my mouth. "Bad excuse."

He pats the top of my head. It's the collie thing again.

"Sleep well, Nutsy."

"You too."

The morning comes much too soon. I fall out of bed and half-consider wearing a skirt. Just for a millisecond. Ditching the idea, I reach for another pair of jeans. I am Lauren Holbrook, and I will set my own fashion statement, not follow Aloha Barbie's.

Here is what I like to do: Sing in the car and watch the other drivers' expressions.

I get a very good expression from a guy in a forest green Honda. It makes me wish I had my camera. This is the problem with being a photographer. You make money taking pictures you don't want to take and when you find one you want to take, you don't have a camera. It is one of nature's laws. I call it Holbrook's Law.

I get to the studio a good fifteen seconds early, much to Ruby's chagrin. The only joy she finds in her day is ragging on people who are late.

Career Barbie shows up at nine o'clock, one minute, and eleven seconds.

Ruby is so pleased she almost swallows her tongue.

"Here at The Brandon Knox Photography Studio, we strive for excellence in everything. Which means we show up on time for work. You are seventy-one seconds late."

Hannah's wide blue eyes widen a fraction more, but only for a moment. "Of course. I apologize. I will be on time tomorrow."

Rats. She handles it like she does this weekly.

"Good morning, Laura." My nose informs me she felt flowery today. My left eyelid is shaking from the sheer force of scent around her.

"Actually, it's *Laurie.*" I smile close-lipped. "Ready to start training?"

"Yes. Let me find a place for my purse."

"Right here in the cubbyholes behind the desk. I already marked you a spot."

It took every ounce of self-control to mark it "Hannah" and not "Disco Barbie."

Actually, make it Malibu Barbie. She is again wearing a short skirt—it's still January—with a flower pattern on it, a sleeveless tank top, a see-through sweater, and heels adding four inches to her height.

When I got out of the car this morning, the temperature gauge on my dashboard read thirty-one degrees. The weatherman last night warned about snow and ice for today.

And I'm working with a brochure for summer in Hawaii.

Hannah stashes her purse, and I show her the phone. "Three lines. More than we will ever need or desire. This is the hold button. This is the speaker button. Sometimes Brandon wants to use the speaker rather than the handset."

"Okay."

"We answer it like so." I pick up the handset. The dial tone buzzes in my ear. "Hello, The Brandon Knox Photography Studio." I replace the handset. "Ta-da!"

Hannah doesn't break a smile. "Okay."

"Brandon, Ty, Newton, Ruby, and I will give you our schedules at the beginning of the week of the days we can and can't be here, and you fill in the calendar with appointments based on those."

"Okay."

I spread out my hands. "And that's about it."

"Okay."

"Oh! There's paychecks. I'll show you those later." I'm praying it's much later. Now my right eyelid has joined in the trembling. Hannah needs to learn the art of moderation when it comes to perfume.

"Okay."

I blink repeatedly, rubbing my eyes. "Got questions?"

"Where's Brandon?"

"He may not be in this morning. Who knows? I'll let you get accustomed to the desk. Besides, there's the Creightons pulling up now, and I've got them."

Bless the Creightons.

Brandon saunters in at ten thirty just as I wave good-bye to the Creightons. "You're late." My voice hisses.

"Wanted to avoid the bloodshed," he whispers back. Then, "Good morning, Hannah! How are you doing today?"

Beach Girl Barbie *can* manage a smile for Mr. Knox. "Just fine, Brandon," she coos. "How are you?"

"Peachy." Brandon winks at me and continues the saunter to his office.

It was a stroke of luck I left a Milky Way in my car last night. I am going to need it today.

"Want to eat lunch with me, Brandon?" Hannah asks this as Brandon walks by about eleven forty-five.

"Uh, sure." He turns to me. I am digging out a peanut butter sandwich with a side of Krispy Kreme from the mini refrigerator under the desk. "Want to eat with us?"

It doesn't take a subsonic missile inspector to note the look of *ugh* written on Bridesmaid Barbie's pretty face.

"I'd love to." Not because I want to but because I feel I should.

Brandon and I sit in the chairs in front of Hannah's desk, and she sits behind it. Not even ten seconds go by before Brandon invites her to our Wednesday night singles' class.

Oh brother.

I have no doubt where Hannah will fit in our singles' class.

There are three groups of singles: Those who will marry soon, those who will marry eventually, and those, like me, who will never marry.

Blonde, beautiful, blue-eyed, high-heeled. Hannah will have a diamond ring and a date in June in six months, no less. First group, all the way.

Her blue eyes alight with joy at the prospect of two dozen good-looking, available guys.

Then again, the fact they're Christians could be a problem.

"Are you a Christian, Hannah?" I ask.

"Well," she giggles, "I'm not a heathen."

Brandon and I don't laugh. "Have you ever invited Jesus into your life?" Brandon asks.

Hannah tries the shrug route. "Not really."

"Then please come Wednesday night." Brandon surprises me. "The teaching is awesome."

"I'll try to be there."

My shock is apparent on my face, I guess, because Brandon levels a swift kick to my shin bone.

"Ah!" I yell.

"Bless you." Hannah hands me a Kleenex.

I get home feeling mentally exhausted. My only consolation is I have the day off tomorrow. I walk into the living room.

"Hey, Sweetie." Dad is sitting in his chair, reading an investment magazine. There's a low fire in the fireplace and it smells woodsy, a combination of the fire and Dad's aftershave. A heavenly combo after today's Flower Overpower.

"Hi, Dad. What did you do today?"

He smiles whimsically. "I went to see Laney."

Uh-oh. Laney is going to have my head.

"Uh, how's she doing?" I cover my mouth in a fake yawn. *Think, Laurie, think!*

"Good." His face creases in a frown. "I think she was tired, though. She didn't move from the couch."

"Oh."

This can be good news or bad.

"But the kids are doing well. Lively as ever." Dad lifts his mug of lemongrass tea. "You know how children are carriers of every type of influenza in the books."

"Uh-huh."

I need to call Laney.

"I'm going to go change into my workout clothes, Dad." Not like I work out, but "workout clothes" sounds so much better than "sweats."

"Okay, Honey."

I race up the stairs, shut my bedroom door, grab the cordless phone, and walk into the adjoining bath. Dad has been known to listen at doors.

"Laney?"

She laughs. "You are predictable, Lauren. I told Adam you were going to call between 6:10 and 6:20. It is 6:13." She gets serious. "Did Dad notice anything weird?"

"He said you sat a lot." I sit on the edge of the tub.

"I told him I was tired."

I nod, then remember I'm on the phone. "Yeah, he told me."

"So he doesn't know." Her voice fills with relief.

"Not yet anyway. How long are you going to not tell him?"

She lets her breath out. "A couple more weeks."

This is what my sisters do: Dump their problems on me and then tell me not to let Dad know anything.

I hate being the youngest.

And I love being the youngest. I get away with more.

"I got to go, Laney."

"Love ya, Lauren."

I hang up and throw on my change of clothes.

My head is halfway in the sweatshirt and halfway out when I have a vision.

Ruby arrayed in white, her hands filled with flowers, her usually solemn brown eyes bright with joy. Walking down an aisle to . . . Nick?

Ruby Palmer marry Nick Amery? Nick's my oh-so-single singles' pastor in charge of our Wednesday night class. Ruby is in the second group of singles. She is a waiter.

It will work out perfectly. Ruby, thirty-three, without a discernable smidgen of humor. Nick, thirty-four, more fun than a kid at Christmas.

A match made in heaven.

I told Brandon I wanted something more in my life. Matchmaking is as good a sport as any, I suppose.

I finish pulling on the shirt and hop down the stairs two at a time.

"Don't do that, Laurie. I don't want you to slip and fall. Hospital stays these days will kill you."

I skip over to Dad's chair and kiss the top of his head. "Fear not, Father," I say dramatically. "I have reason to live."

Ruby Palmer will become Ruby Amery in seven months or less. I give you my word.

Chapter Four

Our Wednesday night class takes place in Nick Amery's home. He bought the house three years ago, mostly because the group grew too big to use his apartment and he felt the call to settle.

I make sure I am there early. I bring a big pan of my homemade box brownies for dessert afterward. There is little in life that bonds two hearts together faster than homemade brownies.

"Wow, Laurie, you're the best," Nick exclaims when I set the pan on his kitchen counter.

"No, I'm not. These are box brownies, but don't tell anyone else. A snap to make. You should see Ruby's chocolate lava cake. No box, no mix, just a recipe card. Now, that's talent." I am casual.

"Mmm." Nick opens the lid.

I slap his hand. "Why don't we ask Ruby to bring the lava cake next week?"

He blinks and looks up. "Wait a second, who?"

"Ruby," I annunciate. "My coworker? Chef extraordinaire?"

"Oh, got it. I think I met her at church once." Nick frowns thoughtfully. "She hasn't been coming to this study long, has she? Medium height, brown hair?"

"That's her." And about fifteen other girls in the study.

His frown deepens. "She's not . . ." His voice drops a little lower. "She's not the most friendly, Laurie."

"She's just not very good around crowds," I say. "One on one is much more her speed." I smile brightly as I see the lady of the conversation come in. "That's her." I point toward Ruby.

Nick is looking at her, head tipped slightly to the right. "You know, she looks kind of like . . ." he pauses, voice quiet.

"Kind of like . . ." I parrot.

"Hmm? Oh, no one. A girl I knew in middle school."

"Oh." I say this very casually, but my brain is a mass of happy jumping beans. *They knew each other!* This is all happening so perfectly I immediately look around to make sure I wasn't transported to an animated Disney movie. "So should we ask her to bring the lava cake?" I ask, once I'm reassured I'm still in real life.

"Sounds good to me. Chocolate and Bible study make a winning combination."

So do you and Ruby. I smile wide.

He gives me a strange look and then says, "Laurie, I've been thinking. You need to lead the junior high girls' group at church."

"Junior high? Girls?"

"Yeah. Pastor Ed asked me to come up with some suggestions for leaders and I thought of you. Linda Myers is leading it now, but she's getting married and doesn't think she can still swing it."

"Hormones?" I'm aghast.

Nick grins. "You'll love it and you know it. I'm going to tell Pastor Ed you said yes, okay?"

"You would be lying. I haven't said that word yet tonight." A thought pops in my head. "You know who would be great? Ruby. I work with her, you know. She's great with the teens who come in for pictures."

I lie not. She is.

"Ruby, huh? You two could do it together."

I shake my head. "I still haven't said the word, Nick."

"You will. And I'll be there when you do. Ruby, huh?" he says again, a thoughtful look in his eyes.

Ping! Score for Cupid!

"Yeah, Ruby."

"Huh. Well, I guess I'll ask her."

During this conversation, singles of all ages and sizes are piling into Nick's living room, dumping books, Bibles, coats, and gloves on the floor.

Nick looks longingly at the brownies. "Guess we'd better corral in the forces." He drags his eyes off the pan and surveys the room.

We have a very unpredictable attendance—about two dozen regulars, and the other dozen are sporadic. I look around and count three married couples, three engaged couples, several seriously dating, Nick and Ruby, and about five singles.

Our singles' class is not truly a singles' class.

Nick leaves to mingle.

"Hey." Brandon comes over and gives me a hug.

"Hey."

He watches me cut the brownies. "Did you have a good day?"

"Fabulous."

Yet another odd look comes my way. "Your day was fabulous?"

I nod. "Yes." I say this right at the unfortunate moment that Nick is passing by again.

"Aha!" Nick yells, sticking his finger in my face. "You said yes!"

I close my eyes and fight nausea. I have been avoiding junior high since I finally got out of it.

"What was that all about?" Brandon asks after Nick leaves again.

"The end of my fabulous day." *But wait!* There is still the inevitable meeting over chocolate occurring sometime in the next two hours.

Sunlight shines again.

I smile.

Brandon stares at me. "You're up to something."

"My lips are sealed."

"Uh-huh." He reaches for the brownies and gets the same hand slap Nick received. "Well, if it involves me and someone female in gender, forget about it. You are not going to set me up."

Set Brandon up? The thought is preposterous. "You?" I snort. "You and who? Beachfront Barbie?"

His mouth twists in a poor attempt not to smile.

"Hi, guys."

A girl with a blonde ponytail and a face void of makeup, wearing a fleece pullover, jeans, and hiking boots stops beside the kitchen counter.

I smile nicely. "Hi." My brain scrambles. I do not know this person.

Brandon saves me. "Hannah! You came! That's great!"

Hannah? This natural beauty is *Hannah*? Polka-Dot Barbie owns a pair of leg coverings?

I blink several times in succession.

"Hi, Hannah," I stumble.

"Forgive Laurie." Brandon doesn't pull his eyes from our exquisite coworker. "She's like this when we let her loose around chocolate."

Hannah giggles, and it isn't the high-pitched squeak I heard all day yesterday. This laugh is actually pleasant.

Something fishy is going on.

"Want to find a seat?" Brandon asks her.

"Sure."

They disappear into the throng.

I watch them dissolve with a sigh. It's not just friendship in

Brandon's eyes.

It's admiration.

And how quickly admiration grows into love.

A twinge akin to jealousy catches in my side. If Brandon gets serious with Boardwalk Barbie—

Hannah. Her name is Hannah, Laurie.

If Brandon gets serious with Hannah, our friendship will become like yesterday's oatmeal. Guy-girl friendships don't work when one of the guy-girl gets married to a different guy or girl.

She is going to steal my basically-brother.

"Let's get things started!" Nick yells just in time. The pan of brownies is poised to disappear down my tightening throat.

I sit on the floor beside Luke and Holly, Engaged Couple Number 4.

There is one thing to do: Hannah needs to fall in love with someone who doesn't have a photography studio named after him.

I glance skillfully around the room. Who are our eligible bachelors here tonight?

There is Andrew. Thirty-five and counting. *Too old for Hannah.*

Marvin. *Nah.*

Nick. *Taken and doesn't know it.*

My eyes settle on Stephen Weatherby. Twenty-nine. Med student. Ambitious. Charming. And quite good-looking, now that I look at him.

Perfect.

The Plan is falling into place. Hannah will become a Christian. Stephen will begin to admire her many high-heeled qualities. Brandon will be forced out, leaving me, Lauren Holbrook, his longtime best friend, to be his best friend forever and ever.

Amen.

Nick stands and reads from 1 Corinthians. "Love is patient, love is kind. . . ."

Fitting.

I am twenty-three years old, and I have heard this passage eight times in my five years in the singles' class.

Stephen sits in a folding chair, his guitar on his knee. "Let's go to the Lord in worship." His fingers strum down the strings.

Three praise songs and two hymns later, Nick again stands. "Most of us are single because we're waiting for love."

Not this one.

"What we need to realize is God has called us to be single *because* of His love. He wants to show us love that can truly fulfill us."

Nick teaches for thirty minutes. We take prayer requests. Pray. Dismiss.

Opportunity number one.

"Ruby!" I yell.

Ruby comes over. "Hi, Laurie." She looks confused at my calling. We're not close friends, in case you didn't guess.

She's still wearing her work clothes and looking frightfully uncomfortable. Unexpectedly, I feel a little sorry for her. This Bible study can be a bit overwhelming the first couple of times, particularly if you don't like people to begin with. This is only Ruby's third time coming, though she comes regularly to church.

Confession: First time she came, I wanted to cry with the sheer injustice of having to see her for an entire twelve hours.

I smile warmly at her now, and her confused look just gets deeper.

"Ruby, Nick has a question for you." I snag Nick's sleeve as he passes by.

"Oh yeah, that's right." Nick smiles a little awkwardly at her and repeats his proposal of teaching the junior high kids.

Ruby nods. "Of course I'll help."

"That was fast." Nick grins.

"And cooperative and helpful," I say. "You're making me look bad, Ruby."

She smiles. *Smiles!* The corners of Ruby Palmer's mouth actually lift!

It is a miracle. I have worked with this woman for the last three years and gone to church with her for the last year, and I can count on one hand how many times I've seen her smile. I am blessed just to witness it.

Must keep her smiling. I start jabbering. "Nick and I were talking about that chocolate lava cake you brought to the studio around Christmas. He was wondering if you could bring it next week."

She nods again. "Sure. It's not that hard."

"It would be for me." The point is to make her seem like a gourmet. "Ruby, Nick wants us to teach together, but would you mind doing the majority of the teaching? I'm still kind of young to be leading it."

The key is for Nick to see how mature Ruby is. He's looking at her, eyes narrowed, expression contemplative. Sort of how I look when I'm trying to discern whether I should get the House Blend or French Roast at Starbucks.

"Not a problem," she says. "When do we start?"

"Three weeks," Nick says. "I've got the curriculum for you."

"Good. Do you want me to pick it up?" She smoothes her plain hair behind her ear.

Nick shakes his head. "I'll bring it by the studio for you."

She smiles. Again! "Thanks."

He smiles, slightly shrugging, the contemplation over, I guess. "No, thank *you.*"

Then they smile awkwardly again.

If I weren't so happy, I would probably be puking. *Score is Cupid: 2, Disinterestedness: 0.*

I leave Nick and Ruby to chat about their newfound love for each other and go to pry Hannah away from my best pal.

"Hey, Laurie."

Obstacle. Not good. Stephen Weatherby stands directly between me and the goal.

"Hi, Stephen. How are you?" I ask because, darn it, I was raised to be polite.

He grins at me, fingering his guitar strings. "Good. Work is crazy, but life is going well. How about you?" Stephen is an intern at the hospital. He's going to be a doctor.

"Oh fine. Nothing new in picture world."

He laughs for about two minutes.

This is not good at all.

I peek over Stephen's shoulder and see Brandon and Hannah in a very serious discussion. His mouth is moving rapid-fire, and she's nodding continuously.

If I know Brandon, and I know him very well, he's giving her the gospel message point-blank. Brandon doesn't mince words when it comes to evangelism.

"—make them?" Stephen asks.

I blink. "Oh, sorry, Stephen, what did you say?"

"I said, these are good brownies, did you make them?" He repeats this louder. I guess he attributes my lack of attention to the deafening noise in the room.

"Yeah, but they're from a box."

"They taste better than any box brownies I've ever had." Stephen smiles, his eyes darkening.

Uh-oh. Yep, there it is. Shining in bright neon lights from the scoreboard. *Score is Cupid: 3, Disinterestedness: 1.*

This is not The Plan. *Hannah* is supposed to be catching young Dr. America's attentions, not me.

What is wrong with Stephen anyway? I've known him almost all my life. His mom and my mom were good friends. Why, oh why, oh why did he choose this night to pick up a conversation?

"Thanks," I answer him.

I catch Brandon's wave. He marches over, Ski Trip Barbie behind him. "I'm going to give Hannah a ride home."

Stephen smiles at Hannah. "Hi. I'm Stephen Weatherby. I don't think we've met."

Oh good. A good development. Finally.

Hannah smiles her pretty smile. "Hannah Curtis. Nice to meet you."

They shake hands.

"Where are you from, Hannah?" he asks.

"California."

"Oh, well it's good to have you here." Stephen turns slightly from me and more toward Hannah.

I'm not offended in the least.

I look at Brandon. He watches the exchange between Hannah and Stephen, a short smile on his face.

"Uh, excuse us." I grab Brandon by the bicep and push him into the kitchen.

He yanks his arm away. "What are you doing?"

"Here. Have a brownie." Maybe with his mouth full of chocolate, he'll be more receptive to The Plan.

He takes it suspiciously. "What is going on?"

"I just think that Stephen and Hannah wanted to talk privately for a few minutes." I set the brownie knife in the near-empty pan. "Stephen went to school in California for a few years. They can talk tourist talk."

Brandon swallows. "Laurie."

"Don't say it, Brandon. I know what you are thinking."

He takes another bite. Swallows. "Did you make these brownies?"

"Yep."

He licks his lips. "They're good."

"Oh. Thanks."

"I mean it. What did you put in them? These aren't your normal brownies."

I cut another square for him. "You're right."

Brandon's eyes widen. "Let me guess. Cyanide?"

"Nutmeg, you idiot. You would all be dead now if it were cyanide."

"Hmm." He finishes the brownie. "Good decision. Okay. I'll see you at work tomorrow. I'm taking Hannah home."

"How did she get here?" I set the knife in the pan and cross my arms over my chest.

He pauses. "I have no idea."

"Well, unless she broke her foot sometime between verses three and four, I think she can safely drive herself home. She's not a little kid, Brandon."

He makes a noise deep in his throat. I've known him long enough to know it means, *You're perfectly right, Lauren Holbrook; I just don't want to admit it.*

Nick and Ruby are sitting at the kitchen table eating brownies. *Ping! Cupid: 4.* The other team doesn't count since the only one who scored is me.

She laughs at something he says.

This is not a Normal Occurrence.

Brandon apparently follows my gaze because he gasps. "Is that Ruby Palmer over there?"

I "mm-hmm" sappily. "Yep."

"The same one who works with us?"

"Yep." I can't keep a proud smile off my face.

"Laughing?" His tone gives away what he thinks. He stares at me for a second. "Laurie." Now his tone is accusing.

"Yes, dear Brandon? Would you like another brownie?"

He just shakes his head at me.

"Give it seven months," I say. "Seven months and we'll hear the bells tolling for Mr. and Mrs. Nicolas Amery."

I smile at them like the proud matchmaker I am. *Nick and Ruby Amery.*

I like the sound of that!

Chapter Five

"All right. Hold a second, don't move! Good! Now, say 'spaghetti!'"

Three voices mutter "spaghetti" through clinched smiles. Father, mother, fifteen-year-old daughter.

"Say, 'Dad, I'm eloping with Dave from chemistry class!'"

The girl bursts out laughing. *Click* goes the camera.

I love being a photographer. You get to make people say stupid things for a living.

"And you're done." I pull the computer mouse from the ledge beneath the camera, click the *close* and *send* buttons, and get the computer ready for a new family.

The dad stretches. "Thanks, Laurie."

"You're welcome. Hannah can get you situated in a viewing room and you can pick the poses and we'll have the prints done by tomorrow at four." The speech rolls off my tongue as naturally as possible. "See you tomorrow!"

The door closes after them. It is ten minutes until three, and I still have four appointments left.

I pick up the props in the studio and go to find a Dr. Pepper before the Fentons show up.

"Laurie, come here for a sec," Brandon calls from his office.

Reverse my steps. Slink into his office. Flop into chair.

"Cut with the drama, Laur." Brandon sits on his desk. "I need you to do me a favor. Hannah's car is in the shop, and I picked her up for work. Nick called; he needs help moving a neighbor's furniture, and I have to leave early."

I can hear the favor before he says it. "And you want me to take her home." I bite my bottom lip. "Fine." Better me than Brandon anyway.

"Good! Thanks."

"I'd better get time and a half for this. You made me miss my caffeine break." Brandon's neon clock shouts "Three o'clock!"

He points at me with his pen. "Caffeine has been said to shorten life spans."

"If I'm going to die, Brandon, I want to die happy." I close the door on his laugh.

Four families crowd the waiting room. Two have sobbing babies. Five kids under the age of five run wildly around in circles. Eight adults yell simultaneously: "Sit down! Be quiet! Behave!"

Hannah's perfect blonde hair is beginning to frazzle. For the tiniest minute, I feel sorry for her.

"Fentons!" I yell, the minute of pity over.

A brown-haired couple stands, grabs three of the little kids by the arms, and drags them kicking and screaming over to me.

"Hi." Fake smile. "I'm Laurie."

"We're the Fentons," the man says, breathing hard.

"We'll be in Studio Two. Follow me, please."

I pray the entire distance to the studio.

Six o'clock does not come soon enough. I stare with Hannah at the wreck compromising the waiting room.

We keep a few toys on hand to distract the kids. They are strewn over the entire room: On the chairs, on the tables, on Hannah's desk. A quite distinct jelly-coated handprint mars the front of it.

Hannah looks at it, exhaustion written on her beautiful face. "Should we make a copy for the police?"

Humor. Bubblegum Barbie has a sense of humor?

"A copy!" I start laughing hysterically.

Hannah giggles.

I am laughing so hard I have to sit down. Then I can't breathe, so I stretch out on my back, tears rolling down my face.

I calm somewhat and roll to my side. Hannah is on the floor as well, wiping mascara-coated tears from her cheeks.

We make eye contact.

She grins.

Bad move.

We both start wheezing, crying, choking on the bubbles of mirth overriding our systems. "A copy!" I gasp for breath. "For the police! Look out, Hannah! We've been *jammed*!"

Hannah whoops. "I can see the headlines now: 'Police Searching for Jelly-Fingered Mobster.'"

"In diapers!"

"The Jelly-Fingered Rugrat!"

It is in this state Ty, Newton, and Ruby find us. Ty and Newton merely mutter under their breaths, step over us, and walk out.

Ruby stops. "What on earth?"

I roll to my stomach, inhaling the musty scent from the carpet. "Hi, Ruby." My body convulses in half breaths, half laughs.

Hannah snorts, breathes hard, and giggles again. "Hi, Ruby."

Ruby smiles at us.

Miracles never cease.

"What is going on?" The bark is gone from Ruby's voice.

"We're just . . . we're just . . . haaaaaww!"

I can't help it. Tears fill my eyes again; my lungs sear with every breath. Hannah joins me. Ten seconds later, Ruby kneels beside me on the floor without a clue what *she* is laughing about.

After another fifteen minutes, we peel ourselves off the floor and decide the mess can wait until tomorrow.

Then we go to dinner.

Here's what I think: Hannah Curtis and Ruby Palmer make very good dinner dates.

I suggest Vizzini's, an Italian place just a few blocks away. We are stuffing our faces with breadsticks twenty minutes later.

"So." Ruby twirls her fork in her spaghetti. "How old are you, Hannah?"

"Twenty-one." Hannah smiles at me. She's cried all the mascara off her lashes and yanked her hair back in a half-hearted knot, and though she still wears her chopstick heels, I can't see them under the table. Plus, either my nose has grown accustomed to her perfume, or she's wearing a lot less.

She seems almost . . . *normal.*

I never thought I'd say that about Preppie Barbie.

Ruby grins as well. Her brown hair has fallen from the perfectionist waves she creases it in every day and is now soft and accessible around her cheeks. Her eyes are bright, her movements not dictated by the clock for once.

Ruby Palmer seems almost normal too. I figure it's Nick in her case, though. Love tends to make normal people crazy and crazy people normal.

"You're twenty-three, right?" Ruby directs the question to me.

"Yep."

"You and Brandon seem pretty close," Hannah says.

Ruby answers for me. "They've been best friends since they were babies."

"Well, second grade anyway," I correct.

"Must be neat to be that close with a guy and still be just friends," Hannah says.

I hear something more than just speculation in her voice, but I don't push it. "Yes and no. Guys are weird."

Ruby chokes on her spaghetti. "You've got that right." Her eyes spark with glee. "Weird and uncanny."

"And smelly," Hannah says.

I snort loudly. I don't usually snort when I laugh, but when it comes to either snorting or spitting a big mouthful of ravioli at Ruby, I decide to go with the snort.

Ruby's eyes twinkle. She is enjoying this far too much. "And unclean."

"Sloppy."

"Primitive."

"They're just weird," I declare. Ruby and Hannah voice their agreement.

"I'm glad you came to Bible study," I tell Hannah. "Are you going to come again?"

"Um. Sure. Probably. I don't know."

Ruby starts laughing. "Oh, very decisive, Hannah."

Hannah grins. "Okay. I'll go."

When I went to work this morning, Hannah and I weren't really even on speaking terms, and I didn't know Ruby could talk about anything other than tardiness.

When we leave the restaurant at eleven thirty, we leave friends.
I like having friends.

I arrive home to a cop car with its lights flashing.

Oh no. My mood goes south immediately. I throw down the emergency brake, jump from the car, and run inside.

"What's going on?" I yell the minute I open the door.

"Laurie!" Dad grabs my shoulders and presses me to his chest. "Laurie, Laurie, thank God!"

A uniformed cop shuts his notebook. "Well, guess that's that." He leaves.

Dad pushes me back to arm's length. "Where in the world were you? I called and I called and I called, and you never answered."

Guiltily, I look at my cell phone. Yep, it is still in silent mode from Bible study last night. "17 MISSED CALLS" shouts from the screen.

"I'm sorry, Dad. Ruby and Hannah and I went to dinner."

"You and who?"

There is no mistaking the incredulous gasp in Brandon's voice. He stands from where I didn't see him on the couch.

"You went to dinner with the human stopwatch and Princess Barbie?" His mouth is wide.

"Yes, I did." I have to admit I feel proud I put that expression on Brandon's usually blasé face.

Dad's shoulders slump and his wrinkles show more tonight than I've ever seen them. "You okay, Dad?" I wrap an arm around him.

"I'm stressed from the evening's events."

I pat his shoulder. "Let's get you to bed."

Fifteen minutes later, after changing into my pajamas, I go downstairs and Brandon is *still* here. It is now twelve fifteen in the morning.

"Go home, Brandon."

"Let's talk for a few minutes." He points to the seat beside him.

I sit grudgingly. "What?"

"Did you learn anything today?"

This is what Brandon thinks he is: My conscience.

"No." I do not feel cooperative at the moment. I am tired, my ribs are sore from laughing, and I do not want to hear from Jiminy Cricket.

"Laurie."

I *hate* it when he draws my name out like that.

"I stereotyped Hannah and Ruby. But so did you. I've confessed and moved on."

He smiles. "I'm glad you had a good time."

I send him a small grin. "Thanks, Brandon."

He smiles again, stands, and pats my head like the collie I guess I look like. "Sweet dreams, kiddo."

I climb into bed, exhausted, at ten until one. And I have to work tomorrow! I promise myself this will not become a routine and collapse on the fluffy mattress.

My alarm goes off at 4:20 a.m.

I jump out of bed like my sheets have turned into a sea of shrieking eels. Once my heart stops pounding in my ears, I realize it isn't a man shrouded in black holding a knife over my bed who spoke; it's Dan Jenkins, the early morning deejay for KGHT, the local soft rock station.

I didn't set my alarm for 4:20.

I turn off the radio and flop back on the bed.

But sleep eludes me.

Here's what I am going to do: Build a bonfire and sacrifice my alarm clock.

Three sleepless hours later, I roll off the bed and stumble into the bathroom. A ghost of a woman meets me in the mirror, and I nod hello before brushing my teeth.

At ten until eight, I fall down the stairs and collapse at the breakfast table.

"Laurie? Honey, are you okay?"

"Coffee." My voice is rasping like an eighty-five-year-old. "I need coffee."

Dad pours the coffee like he works in a New York City Starbucks at rush hour. "Here. Drink."

I slurp the thick black drink down to the bottom in one breath.

"More?"

"Please."

By the third cup, I'm beginning to regain my strength. Dad stares at me like I'm the Spirit of Christmas Present as I unglue my head from the table and get it firmly attached to my shoulders again.

"Much better. Now for breakfast. Sorry, Dad. I had a rough night. Dan Jenkins woke me up at 4:20."

"Funny. I don't remember hearing the phone ring."

"He wasn't on the phone, he was on my alarm. Long story." I slap two slices into the toaster.

"How late are you working tonight, Laurie?"

I stop spreading peanut butter on the toast. "Same as usual, I think. Six."

Dad takes a sip of his lemongrass tea. *Blegh.* "Would you like to go on a dinner date? Just the two of us?"

I almost point out it is just the two of us every night until I see the hope in his eyes. Poor Dad. I get so busy with work and friends I don't give him enough attention.

"Sure." I smile. "I'd love to, Dad. Wow! A real date. This is the first in a long time."

Dad's eyes light up. "Wonderful. This will be fun, Laurie-girl. I have something to tell you, anyhow."

Now I am curious. "What?"

"Dinner, Honey. I'll tell you at dinner. You'd better eat quick if you want to make it to work on time."

I walk through the doors of The Brandon Knox Photography Studio at exactly 8:59 and twenty-seven seconds. Ruby will be proud.

But Ruby isn't at her usual post.

"Ruby?" I yell.

Hannah's head pops out from under the desk. "She took the day off."

"No, I mean Ruby *Palmer*."

Hannah grins. "That's what I said. Brandon told me this morning. Ruby wanted the day off for something or another. A Nuggets game?"

"I wouldn't have put Ruby in the basketball fan category." I walk around the desk to shove my beat-up backpack in the cubby. My backpack is my one possession I'm rarely without. I got it in the ninth grade, and it used to be a dusky gray, but I'd call it more of a splotchy gray now. Nine years of rain, sun, and that time I accidentally went through the car wash with the back windows open have left their mark on it.

I get a big surprise when I turn from wrestling the bag into the cubby.

"Hannah!"

She blinks those beautiful blue eyes. "What?"

"You're wearing jeans!" I am flabbergasted. Completely.

She flips her pony-tailed head. "I didn't think you should be the only one who gets away with it."

I congratulate her. "You have broken through the Career Woman Mold."

Hannah sits in her swivel chair. "I got asked out on a date tonight."

"Oh yeah?" I love the conspiratorial feeling. "So did I! Who is yours with?"

She gives me a strange look. "Brandon."

This rocks me back on my heels. Brandon asked her out? On a date? Just the two of them?

What is Brandon thinking? Sure, I like Hannah well enough . . . as a *friend*. She isn't a Christian, for Pete's sake!

I sit right there on the floor behind her desk. Maybe we aren't talking about the same Brandon.

Fat chance.

She rubs her hands together, a worried expression on her gorgeous face. "I haven't told him yes or no yet. I don't know what to do, Laurie. Who is your date with?"

"My dad." I rub my thumbnail. "About Brandon."

Her eyes round in worry. "I don't want to hurt his feelings, Laurie. I like Brandon. A lot."

So far it sounds like a winning combination to me.

"So what's the problem?" I ask.

She twists her hands around and around each other before finally throwing them in her lap. "He's my boss!" It comes out as a moan.

I blink. Then blink again.

Whoa.

Brandon Knox picked a girl with *sense.*

Never thought I'd say *that* about Gold-Plated Barbie, either.

I push myself to my knees and pat her shoulder. "Gotcha. Want to know what I think?"

She nods miserably.

"I think he's a first-class, grade-A, no-doubt-about-it idiot."

Her mouth drops. She covers it. Then she giggles.

"He should know better than that. First, because the Bible clearly states that Christians and non-Christians should not be dating. Second, because he *is* your boss. And third because . . ." I whirl my hand in the air, at a loss for words.

"Because just *because.*" She hugs me. Hugs me! "Thanks, Laurie. I'm glad you work here."

I stand purposefully. "Mr. Goodness-Gracious-I-Live-in-an-Empty-Bachelor-Pad and I are going to have a serious heart-to-heart. Excuse me, Hannah."

I march down the hall, my footsteps eaten up by the carpeting. For once, I wish the floors were linoleum or wood. I need the sound effects now.

Boom . . . boom . . . boom.

Executioners tread here.

I don't bother knocking on his office door.

"Brandon Michael Knox."

Brandon looks up from his desk, a smile peeking on his lips and then racing for cover when it sees the smoke from my burning pupils.

"Hi, Laurie." He is clearly going over everything he has said to me in the last twenty-four hours and analyzing it, trying to figure out what caused the appearance of the Wicked Witch of the West.

I stop in front of his desk. Hands on hips. Eyes in Sniper Mode. Ready to ping him with the smallest indiscretion.

"You asked Hannah out?" I enunciate each individual word.

He blinks. His jaw drops. "Uh, who told you?"

"Hannah."

Obviously, he didn't plan on this little development. He squirms. "Okay, Laurie, before you get mad—"

"Too late."

"You need to know I was asking her out to discuss what we talked about at Bible study." He looks at me hopefully.

What does he expect me to say? *Oh, Brandon, bless you for your kind and Christ-centered heart! I am a fool to have assumed you wanted to do anything but witness to the poor lost soul!*

I gape at him. "Brandon, how stupid do you think I am?"

"Not very."

"Then why on earth did you just feed me that blatant lie?"

He sits back in his chair. "Uh . . ."

I point at his heart. "You need to do some serious soul-searching, Bud."

And I leave. Quite pleased with myself, actually. I didn't preach or rant. I kept myself cool and confident through the whole confrontation.

I *am* Lauren Holbrook, after all. I have a reputation to protect.

"What did he say?" Hannah's eyes are wide with trepidation.

I shrug. "Nothing remarkable. Lots of 'uhh.'"

"You're the best, Laurie."

I nod graciously.

The chime over the door jingles, and Hannah and I look over. A model for *Today's Best-Looking Guys* walks in, pulling his shades off his face.

Stephen Weatherby.

My memory isn't perfect, but I don't recall seeing him in the appointment book.

"Hey, Stephen," I say casually. "What's up?"

"Hi, Laurie. Hannah." He walks to the desk and looks at me, a smile spreading across his chiseled face. "Can I talk to you for a second?" He directs the question to me.

Uh-oh.

The Plan is crumbling before my very eyes.

"Sure," I say weakly. I look at Hannah, who is grinning unabashedly at me. "When the McKenzies get here, tell them I'll be right with them."

"Will do." Hannah's eyes flash in sheer delight.

Who would have thought Prom Queen Barbie enjoyed watching human sacrifices being led to the altar?

I follow Stephen outside.

Chapter Six

Stephen walks down the sidewalk and stops in front of Wong Hu's, a cheesy Chinese place run by a bunch of Swedes. This could be the reason for its cheesiness, I suppose.

"Laurie," Stephen fiddles with his sunglasses.

"Yes, Stephen?"

"I was wondering if . . ." His voice trails off and he looks off into the distance, fidgeting.

I suddenly feel sorry for Dr. America.

"If?" I encourage.

"If you'd like to join me for dinner Tuesday night?" He finally finds the courage to look me in the eye.

Oh brother. Now the question: Do I say yes and please his ego? Or do I say no and break his heart?

Dad's words, spoken so often during my childhood, float back to me on a very unwelcome cloud. "Always be pleasing and accepting, Laurie-girl. Never be rude or impolite."

Darn it, Dad.

"Sure, I'll go." My voice is quiet. I feel the need to add, "as a friend," but I don't think Stephen hears me, he is so busy smiling.

"Great, that's great," he gushes. "So I'll pick you up here or at your house?"

"Here's fine."

"Great! Uh, want to go to Vizzini's or Halia's?"

I shrug. "Vizzini's."

"Great! I'll be here. Six o'clock?"

"Fine."

He grins. "Great!"

I have to smile. He is pretty cute in all his excitement. I hope I don't disappoint him. I'm not the most enthralling date.

"See you later!" he calls, slipping his shades back on and again reverting into the cool, collected young doctor.

"Bye." I step back inside the studio. Hannah almost makes it back to her desk. "Spying?" I greet her.

"Observing," she corrects. She grins. "So when's the wedding, Laurie?"

"No wedding." I shake my head vehemently. "We're going as friends. I am not the marrying kind."

She snorts. For being Rhinestone Barbie she can do it pretty well. Not as well as I can, but pretty well.

"He did not look like he had just asked a friend to dinner," Hannah states.

I feel the call to defend myself. "He knows I'm not ever getting married."

"Really?" One perfect eyebrow slips up under her bangs.

Doubt descends like brownie batter sliding off a baking spoon. *Kerplunk.*

Sure, Stephen knows. I mean, like I said, I've known the guy for forever. Not very well, but I've known him. Surely he's heard about my stance on marriage.

Surely.

Hannah watches my private battle, and her other eyebrow disappears. My private battle is apparently not so private.

"Surely he knows," I tell her.

"Uh-huh." It is not a convinced "uh-huh."

The chime on the door rings and the McKenzies walk in, carrying two-month-old Amber and holding five-year-old Zach's hand.

"Hey, guys," I greet them and lead them to Studio Three.

When twelve o'clock ticks around and neither Hannah nor I have seen Brandon again, Hannah begins to feel sorry for him.

"Don't do that. Prince-Not-So-Charming deserves every word I said to him."

Hannah doesn't look convinced. "He at least needs to eat."

"Did he bring his lunch?"

She opens the fridge under her desk. "If he did, it's not refrigerated."

She looks so worried, I capitulate. "Fine," I grouse while grabbing my backpack. "I'm going to Bud's anyway. I'll get him a hamburger. Do you want one?"

She purses her lips. "Do they sell hot dogs?"

"Yep."

A five-dollar bill appears from the pocket of her jeans. "Lots of relish."

Shoreline Barbie likes hot dogs?

I can walk the three-minute trek to Bud's with my eyes closed, I come here so often. I push Bud's door, and four hundred catlike screeches sound from the hinges.

I wince. "You might want to oil that door," I tell Mikey, the son of Bud.

Mikey grins, showing the full extent of his braces. "But then what could you criticize?" This kid knows me too well. He grins at me. "What does your ladyship desire today?" He takes his place behind the cash register.

"Two hamburgers and a hot dog. Lots of relish on the hot dog."

His red eyebrows climb on his freckled, zit-infested forehead. "Okay." He grins again. "What did he do to you?"

I glare at him. "First off, buddy-boy, that's none of your business. Second, hamburgers are hardly a comfort food. And third, I'm buying for Brandon and Hannah."

"Who's Hannah?"

I grab a chunk of napkins. "Our new secretary. You've probably seen her in the parking lot. Blonde. Thin. Blue-eyed."

Mikey's eyes widen. "Oh! You mean the babe in the blue Taurus?"

"Smart and observant. Mikey, what other improvements are you hiding?"

Mikey bats his eyes at me. Braces have been good for him. He is developing a nice smile.

He totals the order. "Four bucks, eight cents. Minus the tip, of course."

I pull out my wallet. "Here you go. Four dollars." I count out the change into his hand. "Six, seven, eight cents." I slide the billfold back in my backpack. "Don't eat the yellow snow."

He makes a face and hands me a white paper bag. Already grease is marking it.

"See you Monday, Laurie."

I need to stop being so predictable.

"Yeah, yeah." I smile at him as I go outside.

The bell chimes over the door when I step inside the studio. Hannah has the phone to her ear.

"Actually, Mr. Holbrook, she just came back. Want to talk to her?"

Hannah hands me the phone. "It's your dad."

"Hi, Dad." I set the paper bag on Hannah's desk. She grimaces at the grease stains, pulls four paper towels from under her desk, and puts the bag on them.

"Laurie, Honey, you forgot to turn your cell phone off silent again."

"No way." I dig in my backpack. "Oh my gosh, I never turned the ringer on. Sorry about that! It is being turned on. Now."

"I wanted to tell you that I'll pick you up from work tonight and then we can get your car after dinner. Does that work?"

Bless Dad's heart. He is so excited about this dinner.

"Sure, Dad." I grin. "That works great."

"See you at six, Sweetheart."

I give the phone to Hannah, who hangs it up for me. "Did you find your hot dog?"

She nods, nose wrinkling. "Do they soak these in oil before cooking them?"

"Sure do. Bud's trademark. That's what makes them *fresh*." I pull my hamburger from the bag. "Here's your change. Has The Bachelor emerged yet?"

She shakes her head, her mouth full of hot dog.

"Guess I'll take this back to him then."

Here's what I am: A nice person. Mostly.

"Brandon!" I pound on his office door, then open it.

Brandon sits at his desk, fingers steepled, face pensive. He watches me walk over without changing his expression.

"Lunchtime." I set the bag squarely on his desk, grease and all. "Eat."

He moans. "Laurie . . ."

"Brandon . . ." I follow suit.

He rakes his hands through his hair. "What have I done?"

I have to admit I feel sorry for the guy. "Nothing that can't be fixed. If it makes you feel better, Hannah had more sense than you anyhow. She didn't want to go out." I go around the desk and pat his shoulder.

He sighs. "I'm glad you work here, Laurie."

I pause midpat. "Can I have a raise?"

"No."

"Just checking. Eat up. Lots of nutrients in there. Grease, oil, grease, and . . ." I snap my fingers repeatedly. "What else? Oh! Oil."

A smile twitches in the corner of his mouth.

"A perfect specimen from Bud's."

Brandon pulls the burger from the bag. "How's Mikey?"

"Obviously still eating his pop's food. A colony of acne relatives are living on his face." I watch him rip the paper off the hamburger. "I have a date tonight and Tuesday."

Brandon nearly swallows his tongue. "*You* do?"

He could be more flattering. "Yes, me," I say with a growl. "Why is that so hard to believe?"

"Well, who asked you?"

"Dad." Brandon's face relaxes for a moment. Only a moment. "And Stephen Weatherby."

His mouth drops open. It isn't a pleasant sight with the half-chewed burger lolling around in there.

"Stephen?"

I nod. "Yeah."

"Weatherby?"

Nod again. "Uh-huh."

"The doctor?"

"One and the same."

Brandon stares at me. "And you said yes?" He is incredulous.

"Sure I said yes. He's a doctor. You don't say no when a doctor asks you out."

"I thought you weren't ever getting married," he accuses.

I avoided his eyes. "Stephen knows that."

"Then why did he ask you out?"

The question could be strung up in the air with blazing, brightly colored Christmas lights.

"I . . . don't know," I falter. "Maybe just to catch up on old times?"

Brandon rolls his eyes. "Uh-huh. Right. Well, give my regards to the poor man."

"Doctor's aren't poor men." I turn on my heel and walk out.

Brandon has to be wrong.

He *has* to. Stephen only wants to chat about the good old days in elementary school.

After lunch I photograph six families, four of them with kids under the age of five. So the day passes relatively quickly. My headache, however, does not. I am taking aspirin when Dad shows up.

"What's wrong, Honey?" The bell over the door chimes as he enters.

I swallow the pills. "I'm attempting to convince the little elves with jackhammers in my head to take a break."

Dad frowns. Hannah smiles.

"Hi, Mr. Holbrook. I'm Hannah. I talked to you earlier on the phone."

"Hello, Hannah, nice to meet you."

"Good night, Laurie. Have a good dinner," she says.

"Night, Hannah."

Dad watches her leave. "Ready to go?"

"Sure am."

I follow Dad out to his Mustang convertible and manage to cajole him to put the top down. We drive the six minutes to Vizzini's in silence, the cold wind whistling through my hair and drying out my eyes.

Once we are seated, Dad hands a twenty to the waiter, a tall, skinny guy with a gold name tag reading "JACK," and asks that the breadsticks keep coming and the water glasses stay full for the next two hours. JACK is quite happy to oblige.

"So. What's up, Dad?" I ask this after Dad finishes blessing the two plates of spaghetti in front of us.

Dad smiles. "You're a wonderful daughter, Laurie. I really have enjoyed all the time we've been able to spend together since your mom died."

I frown. "Are you going somewhere, Dad?"

Dad folds his hands on the table. "Yes and no."

This is what I don't like: Beating around the bush.

"What are you saying, Dad?" The tiniest smidgen of worry skitters up my spinal cord.

He grins at me. "Actually you are the one who gave me the idea."

Already this is sounding bad.

"Remember when you told me to tell Brandon you had taken up

squid fishing?"

I blink. Once. Twice. Thrice. "You're going to take up squid fishing?" I ask very slowly.

I expect a chuckle, a laugh, a hand slap, and then a profuse answer telling me how absolutely ridiculous this is.

Dad shrugs.

Not good at all.

"Not squid fishing, per se. Just regular fishing. All I've done since retiring, Hon, is hang around the house. I'm going stir crazy!" He waves his hands. "I want to do something outdoorsy for a change. My friend John did, and look at him now."

John is the poster child for *Game & Fish*.

"Yeah, but, Dad." I scramble. "Think of all the diseases you could catch from the water!"

Dad nods. "I have considered that. But I went to that new hunting store today and found these." He slides a box across the table.

"'Purification tablets,'" I read.

"Yep. Those, my dear, will kill any bacteria in the water."

I have a vision of a U-Haul backing up to Lake Michigan and depositing four hundred pounds of these Alka-Seltzers into it, the lake suddenly becoming crystal blue bottled water.

I set the box down. "You're serious about this."

His eyes are sparkling. "I'm planning a trip for the month of March."

"March. Dad, that's in like six weeks."

"I know." He reaches across the table and takes my hand. "I was hoping you could go with me."

I look in Dad's eyes, and every excuse I have crumbles. Fishing is not my thing. I will take electricity and running water over a grimy, scaly, squiggly fish any day. Up to this point, I figured Dad agreed with me.

"Okay," I mutter. How bad can a long weekend fishing be? It's not long enough to die of boredom. A cozy, short trip to some hole-in-the-wall lake, catch a few bass, go home.

Sounds fairly easy.

Dad's elation shines in his face. "I'll start getting the supplies this week."

"Well, don't overdo, Dad. I mean, we probably have enough food at home. And sleeping bags." I twirl my fork in my spaghetti.

"Not for a month we don't, Laurie."

My fork stops centimeters from my mouth. Dad has good timing. A millisecond later, spaghetti would have been rocketing out of my mouth and splattering all over Dad's white shirt.

"A month!" I can't help it. I yell.

JACK comes running. "Is everything okay?" He twists a dishtowel around in his hands.

"Fine, fine," Dad says, seeing my jaw is stapled to the fake wood table.

Still wringing the towel nervously, JACK leaves.

Dad looks at me. "Laurie?"

"Where?" It's the only word I can form.

"A place by the Sacramento–San Joaquin Delta. A little town."

I blink. "For a month."

Dad's eyes are shining in excitement.

Drat my guilt complex.

"Fine." I sigh. "I'll go if Brandon will give me that month off."

He could have been jumping up and down. "Good! Ah, Laurie, this will be so much fun! Just the two of us, the open water, the rustic cabin on the river. . . ."

"Running water?" Incredible.

"Of course running water. And electricity. What did you think?

We'd sleep in a tent?"

I shrug.

"No, this is a cabin. You don't even have to fish with me if you don't want to. The scenery is gorgeous. Bring your camera."

"March," I say again.

"Yep. Temperatures in the fifties and sixties."

I twirl my fork around, contemplating. How bad could it be? A month of relaxation, picture taking, and fish for dinner.

"How are you doing?" a voice murmurs near my ear.

I jump. A meatball flips cleanly off my fork and lands *splat*, right in my lap.

JACK stands there, water pitcher in hand. His expression registers horror.

I can see it coming before it happens, yet my brain doesn't work fast enough. "Oh my gosh," JACK says, "I'm so sorr — "

Swosh! The water sloshes out of the pitcher, rinsing the meatball and soaking my jeans.

A normal person would have screamed and jumped up.

I am not normal.

I sit there. Exhale. Take the dishtowel hanging from JACK's apron and mop it up, all the while being stared at by not only the whole restaurant but also two men with their mouths wide open.

"Oh my gosh," JACK says again.

I give him the towel. "Ready to leave, Dad?" I chirp.

"Sure, Honey."

Dad sets a couple of bills on the table and gives JACK a withering look. I smile at him. "Have a good night."

I put my coat on, but it doesn't reach low enough. A big circle of water and a few flecks of spaghetti sauce mar the entire front of my pants.

How embarrassing. Mostly for JACK, I think.

Dad opens the door for me and a blast of cold January wind hits my pants and immediately freezes them solid. Sitting is going to be an issue.

"Here, Honey." Dad opens the car door.

"Th-thanks, Da-ad." My teeth chatter. Being wet outside in January is miserable.

"Oh dear. You'll catch your death. Get in."

He drives to the studio to pick up my car, coming very close to breaking the speed limit. My dad always drives ten miles under. He's the old guy in the Mustang no one feels they can pass. Never ceases to drive me nuts. I follow him home as best I can.

"Get out, get out." He grabs my arm and hustles me into the house, into the living room, and onto the couch, where he pulls out a big afghan Laney made and wraps it around me mummylike.

"I'll make you some tea." He disappears before I can protest.

Lemongrass. *Blegh.*

Coffee sounds good. Vanilla coffee. Lots of sugar. Whipped cream. Steaming, warm, sweet.

"Here you go." Dad passes me a mug full of thick, pale sludge. It smells so strong my eyes start watering.

"I put honey in there because I know you like things sweet."

What is it with putting honey in drinks to sweeten them? Just put in God-given sugar for Pete's sake.

"Thanks," I say, because I'm nice. I take a sip and gag, but disguise it as a cough, which is a bad idea.

"Oh land. You're coughing now. This is not good. Not good at all." He leaves the room and comes back with his hands full of antibacterial room spray, hand gel, and wipes. He sets to work immediately, wiping down door handles, spraying the nose-tickling stuff in my face, and smothering my hands with the goop.

Yuck.

Friday ends with a hot bath and then another round from the sanitation department of my household. I get in bed and don't move the whole night — mostly because the glop didn't dry completely and is now stuck to the sheets.

Chapter Seven

Monday morning I wake up feeling convicted.

I *hate* it when that happens.

Stephen Weatherby has to know how casually I'm approaching this. Period. No exceptions.

I slide out of bed and pludge to the bathroom.

Here's what I like to do: Make up words. Pludge: (*v*) The half-walking, half-dragging of oneself. Designated for sleepiness, laziness, and Laurie-ness.

I brush my teeth and decide to skip the hair regimen. I believe pony-tail elastics exist to show the kindness of God.

Dad is halfway through the paper, and my breakfast is on the table.

"Morning, Honey. Are you feeling better yet? Here, take this." He hands me two caplets of vitamin C, three immune-building pills, and a mug of muck.

"Thanks, Dad."

Even though this is the fourth cup of gag-me stuff I've had in the past four days, I still swallow it with difficulty and wash it down with four cups of coffee and two bowls of Coco-Odies.

Coco-Odies: The only cereal where you can actually OD on

chocolate. I'm pretty sure that's how the name was picked.

"Bye, Dad."

"Have a good day at work, Laurie-girl."

I walk into work at nine o'clock and fourteen seconds, cringing, my ears preparing themselves for the verbal lashing I have coming.

"Morning, Laurie."

"Hey, Hannah."

I look around. "Where's Ruby?" I ask. Again.

Hannah brushes her hair out of her eyes. "She's getting Studio Two ready for . . . never mind."

Ruby comes around the corner, tugging self-consciously at her hair. "Laurie. Hi."

Her *hair*! I gaze in inanimate wonder at the short, sassy bob cut and highlighting done on Ruby's used-to-be-plain, past-her-shoulders hair.

"Ruby!" I exclaim.

"Do you like it?" She pulls on it again. "I'm not sure. It's really short."

"I love it," I gush. "Love-it-love-it-love-it. Wow, Ruby. When did you get it done?"

"Friday afternoon."

So while I dealt with Prince-Not-So-Charming, Ruby Palmer turned herself into Cinderella.

The chime over the door jangles and is immediately followed by a long whistle, totally inappropriate if you ask me. Ruby seems to appreciate it though. She blushes four shades of pink, and grins.

"Wow, Ruby. Holy cow, you look great!" Brandon says. "Did you get contacts?"

Ruby's eyebrows go up as she shoots a look of *men!* to Hannah and me. "Uh, Brandon, I didn't wear glasses to begin with."

He is in confusion. "You didn't? Well, something's different. Get a new outfit?"

"Nope."

Ruby doesn't intend to give Brandon any help at all. Good for her.

He looks closely at her. "Gosh, Ruby. I give up. What's different?"

"Think hair, Brandon." Hannah's voice brims with sheer, unabashed glee.

"Oh!" Brandon yells. "Your hair's different. Looks amazing, Ruby."

"Gee, thanks." She rolls her eyes to me and looks out the window. The blush starting to recede jump-starts back into place.

I follow her gaze. Nick Amery.

"You know, he seems a little . . ." she says, fiddling with a lock of hair.

"A little what?" I ask. "Weird? Funny? Pastoral?"

"Familiar," she says, ignoring my suggestions. "Like from a long time ago. Maybe junior high."

The "Wedding March" sounds through my brain in reckless abandon. I try really hard to keep a grin off my face.

Well, moderately hard anyway.

"Nick! Hey, what's up?" I whip the door open for him, since his arms are laden with books.

"This is the curriculum for . . ." His eyes land with a resounding *smack!* on our lovely, newly transformed Ruby.

"For . . ." she urges him.

"Uh, right. Uh, for the, um, the junior high girls' group, uh, that is, for the Tuesday night meetings with the girls' group." Nick swallows. "Wow, Ruby. Hi. You look . . . uh, beautiful."

She blushes darker. "Thanks, Nick. That's . . . sweet."

I glance at Hannah, who looks like she just swallowed Dad's lemongrass tea. *Blegh.*

I'll admit it. I probably would have the same reaction to their gushiness if I hadn't been the one to arrange it. As it is, I am giddy.

The hair is a nice touch on Ruby's part.

"So what have we got here?" I step in for the sake of Hannah's stomach.

"The curriculum." Nick shoves the books in my face. "There's two leader's books and two student editions so you can see what the kids are doing. And here's the handouts. We use an NIV Bible, just so you know."

I nod and transfer the books to Hannah's desk. *Romans in Review.*

This is a pet peeve of mine: Alliteration. Preachers do this all the time. For example, my pastor's points in the sermon on Sunday? Conduct, Condition, and Consider.

This curriculum is going to grate on my nerves. Splashed underneath the title on all the books is *Realizing Romans Remains Really Relevant.*

Do people honestly talk like that?

"As you can see, we're going through Romans." Nick hands me the last book.

Ruby is still fiddling with her hair. "In two weeks now, right?"

"Right," Nick says. "Our middle school group is pretty small, so you'll have sixth through eighth graders."

"Works Well With We," I say.

I guess people really do talk like that because only Hannah and Brandon give me weird looks. But Nick and Ruby are involved in a stare contest and aren't listening.

"Ruby, I have a question for you," Nick says suddenly.

I'm rooting for "Will you marry me?" But I think it might be a bit soon for that.

Nick continues. "Did you by any chance go to Hamilton Middle School?"

Ruby's mouth drops open. "So that's how I know you!" She grins. "I thought you seemed familiar. We had the same homeroom, right?"

Nick's grinning as well. "I think so. Ruby Palmer." He says her name all reflectively, shaking his head. "Man, I had the biggest crush on you in the seventh grade. What happened to you?"

I didn't think it was possible, but her blush darkens even more. "My family moved the beginning of my eighth grade year. I moved back after college. Wow. Good to see you again."

"Yeah, you too."

I'm *really* trying not to burst into a happy dance.

Nick checks his watch. "Well, I got to go. See you guys Wednesday."

"The Hernandez family is here, Laurie." Brandon is watching the parking lot.

Lunch rolls around and I go to Bud's, where Mikey greets me with a smug smile.

"Well, look who is here," he says airily.

"Stuff it, Buddy."

"That would be my father. I'm Mikey. Nice to meet you."

I eat at Hannah's desk.

"Tell me about your church," Hannah says in between bites of her hot dog.

I blink. "We're nondenominational."

"No, I mean *about* your church," she says. "What are the people like? Do most of the people in the singles' class go there?"

"Yeah. Nick teaches a class Sunday mornings too. The people are great. I've been going there all my life." I watch her eat for a second. "Want to come this Sunday with Dad and me?"

Her face brightens. "Yeah. Yeah, I'd like that."

I lick mustard off my finger. "Are you coming Wednesday?"

"Yeah, I think so."

I finish my burger. "Let me know if you need a ride."

"Hey, Laurie?" Hannah asks, right as I toss my wrapper in her trash can and stand.

"Yeah?"

She fiddles with her hot dog. "Right. So I went to get a Bible the other day."

I try to control the elation on my face so as not to scare her off. "Oh yeah?"

"Mm-hmm." She takes a deep breath and throws her hands up in frustration. "There's like thousands to choose from and they all have these weird initials on them and some are leather and some are hardback and some are pink and if that's not enough, you have to choose size and shape and if you want an index or not. And what on earth does red lettering mean? Because I picked one up that said that, and I didn't see any red letters." She lets out an aggravated huff.

I smile at her. "How about I go with you?"

"Would you? Laurie, that would be great." She smiles a huge smile.

Hannah is definitely making some serious progress.

Ruby and I each take our curriculum home with us. I look through the books to see what I'll be teaching.

Lesson 1: Apostleship.

This could be deep.

The front door opens. "What's up?"

"Hey, Brandon."

Brandon sits on the sofa. "I thought you might want to catch a movie or something tonight."

I balance my chin on my hand. The invite has come many times over the years.

Over the years. Like a flash of my camera, I realize my dear friend has grown up.

Sometime in the past seventeen years, his shoulders broadened, his face lost the baby fat residing on his cheeks, his eyes took on something other than the innocent seven-year-old glint.

It makes my stomach hurt to see it. What if what Brandon said a week ago comes true?

"One day you might wake up, and I'll be married with a couple of kids."

One of my ducks in a row bearing Brandon's name skirts out of line.

I have a feeling chocolate isn't going to help this problem.

"What's wrong?" Brandon's forehead creases in a frown.

"You're . . . old."

He starts laughing. "Wow, what a compliment!" He stops. "You're not laughing."

"Come on, Brandon, I'm serious." I close the curriculum.

"Laurie, I'm only twenty-four. That's not that old. What's gotten into you? I've never seen you like this before." His voice gets quiet.

"We're growing up. I mean, you're twenty-four. You have been able to buy alcohol legally for three years." I am finding it difficult to put my thoughts into words.

He smiles gently. "Well, Honey, don't worry about that. I'm not going to buy it."

"We're not . . . little kids anymore."

His mouth twists in an *aha* expression. "I see. You're thinking about what I said last week."

I nod. "Yeah."

When we were little, Brandon and I talked about how someday we'd each get married and have both of our families get together every weekend.

Suddenly the *someday* is missing. Brandon can get married right now. He can have a family right now.

My stomach feels hollow.

His look softens. "Kinda scary, isn't it?"

"Uh-huh."

"I've been doing a lot of thinking."

The tone of his voice doesn't bode well with my state of mind.

"About this, you know, getting older, growing up." He leans farther into the couch, expression pensive. "I've been reading the Bible this past weekend and praying a lot. When I asked Hannah out and you corrected me? That kind of started my thinking. I'm not sixteen anymore. I should be figuring out what qualities I want in a wife, not just dating for the sake of dating. You know?"

I nod.

"I've gotten . . ." He grasps the air for the word. "Dissatisfied with my relationship with God. Know what I mean?"

No, I do not. A relationship with God is something I have, am happy about, and think about on Sundays, Wednesdays, and for the few minutes I'm doing my devotions in the evening.

"No."

"You'll know eventually."

"Brandon."

"Laurie."

"Let's just go to the movie and pretend we're fourteen again. Okay?"

He smiles, but an odd expression crosses through his eyes. "Sure, Nutsy. Let's go. There's a great new sci-fi flick out."

"I was thinking more along the lines of romance and comedy."

It's an old argument and one we recycle on our way. We buy tickets, find a seat, poke fun at the previews, and soak in the dark, buttered atmosphere.

But my mind doesn't revert into its usual half-dead state during the movie.

I'm not sixteen anymore.

Chapter Eight

I pick up the phone. Take a deep breath. Dial. 5 . . . 5 . . . 5 . . . 4 . . .

I hang up.

"I can't do this," I exclaim to Hannah.

She sets her brand-new Bible on her purse and then sits at her desk with her hands folded smug as ever under her chin. "You can, and you have to."

Rosebud Barbie *would* make sense.

I heave my breath out. "You're sure you don't want to do this for me?"

"And you would learn what from that experience?"

I smile hopefully. "Good friends are hard to come by?"

Hannah quirks her eyebrow up. "Yes, they are. Come on, Laurie. It can't be that hard. You dial, you listen to it ring, you tell Stephen quite firmly and rationally that you can't go out, you hang up. What's so difficult about that?"

"I don't know." I groan, banging my forehead on her desk. "Ow."

"Laurie."

"Do you have any chocolate?"

Hannah rolls her eyes. "Is that your lifelong motto?" She reaches down and pulls open the bottom drawer of her desk. Digs way in the back. Her hand reappears with a stack of Milky Ways.

"Oh bless you, bless you, bless you."

"Don't tell Brandon I have them. He'll probably freak about mice."

Two of the candy bars disappear in two point eight seconds flat. A new world record, I imagine.

"Okay. Now. Call him," Hannah says, pushing the phone back toward me.

I dial again. My pulse rockets so fast I know I soon will pass out.

Good grief. What is the matter with me?

Three rings pass in an interminable amount of time. Fourth ring.

"Hey."

I open my mouth to blurt out my speech.

"You've reached Stephen Weatherby. Leave a message. I'll call you back."

BEEEP!

I hold the phone for several moments before slamming it down in confusion and shock. Hannah rolls her eyes.

"Wimp," she accuses me.

I bite my tongue. I haven't been called that since the fourth grade when I wouldn't play dodgeball for fear of breaking my glasses. Well, I played. I broke my glasses. I sliced a nicely sized cut across my eyebrow and ended up with ten stitches and a bandage the size of Alabama covering my face. Dad nearly had a heart attack.

The days before contacts.

Ruby walks in. "Hey, girls. Want to join me for lunch today?"

"Yes," I say immediately, thankful for the interruption.

"Sure. You can help me talk some sense into Laurie," Hannah says.

"I've tried that before. It didn't work." Ruby grins, tugs on her hair again, and disappears into Studio Three.

The bell over the door jangles and Dr. America walks in. Again. He's wearing jeans and a semi-nice blazer, looking very collegiate. His blond hair is combed just-so, but when he pulls his shades off, his eyes are solemn.

Hannah smiles sweetly first at Stephen and then at me. "Don't worry, Laurie, the Jackmans won't be around for another twenty minutes."

The corners of Stephen's mouth lift in a half smile, but his eyes don't lose the seriousness.

"Could we talk?" he asks.

Uh-oh. I have a foreboding feeling in my little toe about this conversation.

Once again, I follow him outside.

"What's up?" I ask, trying to be nonchalant.

"Uh, it's about, uh, tonight," Stephen stutters. "I've been doing some thinking and well . . . you see, I'm leaving for California soon for a two-year fellowship that very possibly can turn into a long-term job."

"Okay," I say slowly.

"And I like you. A lot. But I don't think it's fair to either of us to start, um, dating right now." His voice drops to a near whisper. "Understand?"

I smile. My chest eases.

"I've been trying to call you," I say, deciding honesty is the best policy. "For the same conclusion, but different reasons."

His forehead creases. "I don't remember the phone ringing."

"I hung up a few times before it could ring."

He smiles. "Why?"

"I didn't want to hurt your feelings. It was really sweet of you to ask me out." I turn on my full-wattage grin. "Can we stay friends?"

I have always sworn I will never use that line, but it slips from my mouth like a smallmouth bass from a fishing basket.

Great. Our fishing trip is five weeks away, and I'm already using fishing analogies.

"I'd like that," Stephen answers. He grins in relief, gives me a hug, and walks to his car. "See you tomorrow night at Bible study."

I go inside.

Hannah taps her pen on the desk impatiently. "So?"

"So we aren't going out. Stephen doesn't want to have a relationship when he's leaving in a little while."

She is incredulous. "You are the luckiest person alive."

I'm not sure how to respond to that. "Thank you."

I wake up on Wednesday without the help of my alarm. I love the days I have off from work.

I pull on a pair of sweats and go downstairs. Dad has a map of California spread out in front of him and is tracing a path with a highlighter.

"Morning, Hon. Cinnamon rolls will be done in a few minutes."

I love my dad.

I give him a hug. "Thanks."

Today is going to be a lovey-dovey day, I can tell. I've had lovable feelings about two separate things now.

"What's on your plate today?" Dad caps the marker.

"I'm going to go see Laney."

He nods approvingly. "Good."

"What about you?"

"Figured I'd check out the sportsman stores in town." Dad says it offhandedly, but I see his excitement.

I grin. "When you find one you like, let me know. I'll go with you next time."

"Deal."

I get to Laney's about ten.

Dorie answers the door. She's five and my only niece. I spoil her like crazy, and she provides childlike wisdom to my chaotic life.

"Auntie Lauren!" She flings herself into my arms.

I catch her before she falls. "Whoa there, girl. Rein it in." I chuck her cheek. Dorie is the cutest girl in the world. Brown wispy hair. Brown eyes. Chubby cheeks. She wants to work at a car wash when she grows up and live on a cherry tree farm.

She's talented, beautiful, and imaginative.

I might be a tad bit biased though.

Jess and Jack, twins at age three, barrel around the corner and each take one of my legs. "Lauren! Lauren! Lauren!"

With Dorie in my arms and a kid wrapped around each leg, it takes me a good five minutes to get to the kitchen. Laney is at the kitchen table, peacefully drinking a cup of coffee.

My sister amazes me. She gets married at twenty, has Dorie a year later, handles twin infants and a toddler, and still manages to be happy and cheerful.

I want to be like Laney when I grow up.

"Mom, Mom, look who's here!" Jess screams.

"Gosh, I wonder." Laney looks up with a grin. "You guys greet Lauren so quietly."

"Subtlety is their dominion." I untangle the boys and set Dorie down.

"Hey!" Jack yells. "We got new shoes!"

"Let's show her!"

The kids run from the room. The term *run* is used loosely. Chubby legs, socks on a wood floor, and no coordination doesn't make for fast runners.

Laney grins. "There's more coffee in the pot, if you want some."

"It had better be decaf. How are you feeling?" I pull a mug from the cabinet.

"Good. Really good. Much better than with the boys. And of course it's decaf."

Laney is pregnant.

I am ecstatic.

"Can I tell Dad?" I pour the coffee and inhale. Vanilla. Laney has good taste.

"Not yet. I'll tell him when we're there for lunch next Saturday. Speaking of which, what can I bring?"

"Nothing. I'm picking up barbecue. And paper plates. No dishes. Less work." I sit opposite her.

"Lexi's coming, right?"

"That's the plan."

Laney smiles. "I'm glad they went to England."

If I ever get married, I want to marry a British guy. Dark curly hair. Dark eyes. Tall, stately, refined. But with a sense of humor. Mr. Darcy, in other words.

I nod. "Me too. Lex promised to check out the guys for me."

"I'm sure Nate will appreciate that."

"You're five weeks along, right?"

"Yeah."

"This one should be a girl."

Laney's eyes sparkle. "I'll do my best." She pats my hand. "Though really, Sweetie, I have absolutely no say in it."

"No. Really?"

She rolls her eyes. "Anyway, you'll have to pray harder than Adam. He wants it to be another boy so he can start his own baseball team."

I laugh. "Sounds like your husband. It's taking the kids awhile to put shoes on, isn't it?"

Laney smirks into her coffee cup. "Two of them still aren't sure how to do that, Lauren."

"You're a cruel mom."

"Thanks. So what have you been up to lately?"

"I'm teaching middle school girls."

She nearly gags on the coffee. "What?"

"Not school subjects. We're going through Romans. At church."

"Oh." She draws the word out. "Got it. So how's it going? I love that book, by the way. Romans is my favorite."

I lean my elbows on the table and study my oldest sister. Laney and I have always been this way. I can tell her anything, and I know it will never get repeated, not even to Lexi.

I think about the brief skimming I've done of the curriculum. "Do you think God is sovereign?" I ask.

"Yes." She says it purposefully, without even a doubt.

"Why?"

She doesn't answer me for a second, just looks. Finally she smiles. "Read Ephesians 1," she says.

Clumping sounds come from the hallway then, and I turn to see Dorie in ballerina shoes and Jack and Jess in brown hiking boots on the wrong feet.

They all three grin at me, and a warm, sickly sweet feeling blooms in my chest until I think I will cry.

I laugh instead. Give them all a hug. Tell them how great they look.

Jess kisses my cheek as I leave, a good sloppy wet one still there when he pulls away.

I like it so much I don't wipe it off.

Chapter Nine

The night is cold and chilly, and judging by the dark, ominous clouds billowing over the horizon like a field of evil mushrooms, I know we are in for quite a snowstorm.

I follow the bubbly written directions to Hannah's apartment. She lives a good fifteen minutes out of my way, but I figure, what the heck? I can be nice.

I pull into the parking space beside her Taurus. Undo my seat belt. Almost turn the car off, but she comes pattering down the metal steps and opens the passenger door. A blast of cold air follows. "Hi!" She grins, breathless, her cheeks turning pink from the cold, her long blonde hair swishing out from behind her in a ponytail.

To have that kind of easy charm . . .

I turn my mind from my envious thoughts. "Hey, Hannah."

"How was your day off?"

"Good. Fun. I went to my sister's. How was your day on?"

She closes the car door and buckles her seat belt. "Fine." She pulls her brightly printed scarf a few inches looser and grips her new Bible I helped her pick out.

"Did you hear about Peter and Nancy?" Hannah says as I back out.

"No." Gee, for being on the job a week, she's sure immersed herself quickly in Brandon and my little circle of friends.

"They're engaged! Isn't that wonderful? They came in for pictures at two. They are so cute together! They said they'd be here tonight."

Peter and Nancy. One more couple in the singles' class. I sigh. They are two of those people you know will end up together one day. It should not bother me so much.

But it does. My mood turns in the general direction of Central America.

Couples, couples, couples.

I am only twenty-three years old. Yet, if this is the Magical Winter of Couplehood, I have missed the horse-drawn carriage.

Is it just me, or is everyone getting married?

"Laurie?"

"I'm fine."

"No, you're not."

"Yes. I am."

Hannah turns in her seat and stares at me with those all-seeing blue eyes.

I throw one hand up, as the other clutches the steering wheel. "Fine. Fine, fine, fine. I am not — "

"Fine?"

"Yeah." I rub my forehead. "I'm just tired, I think. This fishing trip will be a good break. One month of Trout, Trees, and Tranquility. No commitments, no schedules. Just plain relaxation." The trip sounds better and better.

Hannah smiles at me.

"And best of all, no more engagement announcements!" I laugh in pure, unadulterated joy.

Hannah shakes her head. "Good grief, Laurie. You're only twenty-three. And a confirmed bachelorette. Or have you changed your mind?" There is a distinct matchmaker-like tone to her voice.

That position is filled, thank you!

"I have not changed my mind." I'm firm and matter-of-fact. My mood becomes one of resignation and strength. I may be a confirmed bachelorette, but who is to say I can't be a Cute, Charming, and . . . what's another C word? Coquettish confirmed bachelorette?

I pull onto Nick Amery's street and park beneath the barely glowing streetlight. Spooky. I have deep fears about this street. I never let anyone female in gender walk out to her car by herself. I always go with her. And Brandon goes with me.

Cute, Charming, Coquettish, *and* Courageous.

Hannah grins as she gets out of the car, obviously recognizing my mood has lifted and my attitude is back in place.

Bless Hannah.

We run the short jaunt to the open garage door, squeeze past the avid game of pool going on, and go in through the kitchen.

The scent of baking chocolate and percolating coffee hits me square in the nostrils as I go through the door, and I become a Pliable, Pathetic, Pitiful addict.

"Hey, Laurie. And . . . Hannah, right? Good to see you," Nick says.

"I smell chocolate." I stick one gloved finger in the air as I declare this blatantly obvious fact.

Nick starts nodding. "I'm sure you do. Ruby made—"

"And coffee," I interrupt.

He's still nodding. "Ruby has the lava cake in the oven and the coffee, uh, making."

"Percolating, Nick. It's called percolating," Ruby says from behind him. "Hi, girls. Laurie, I recognize that look. Fear not, young one. The chocolate will be ready in thirty minutes. The coffee in five. In the meantime, snack on these." She hands me a package of Oreos, her eyes twinkling.

Given chocolate, I once again become the new me. Cute, Charming, and whatever that other stuff is.

"Thanks, Ruby." I shove two Oreos in my mouth. "You're an angel."

"I know."

It isn't Ruby who speaks, however. It's Nick. Ruby turns the color of her Christmas-red sweater. Nick does too, actually, which makes it even funnier.

I *hate* it when something like this happens and my mouth is full. I have a witty comment for it too.

But, alas and alack, the moment is lost. Ruby excuses herself to the coffeepot, Nick to the rest of the group, and Engaged Couple Numbers Four, Five, and Seven walk into the bustling kitchen.

Apparently, the little seventh-grade crush Nick had is back in full bloom. I can't help the grin.

I hide the Oreos under my coat and go to save a seat on the sofa. But the seats are already gone, so I resign myself to the floor.

Slyly, I slip an Oreo into my mouth.

"I saw that," a voice whispers from behind me. I jump, whirl, and face someone I don't know sitting on the couch behind me.

I swallow. "Saw what?"

He narrows his eyes at me. He is pretty good at it too, considering he is male and all. Males aren't good when it comes to eye rolling, speaking with their eyes, or narrowing them.

"The cookie." He points. "You've got Oreos under your coat."

"Are you the chocolate police?" I immediately close my eyes. This is not the most intelligent comment I have ever made in my life. Good grief. How is it I can be completely at ease with Ruby, Hannah, Nick,

Brandon, and any female and be so totally whacked-out with anyone else of the male species?

He looks at me like I'm a kid Dorie's age. "Uh, no."

I don't know what else to say. Apparently, neither does he. So he sits in complete silence and I sit in crunching silence. I may be embarrassed, but I have never been too embarrassed to eat Oreos.

Not in this lifetime.

Ruby comes over with a mug full of steaming coffee. A fluffy mound of whipped cream floats on the top.

"Here you go, Honey."

Honey? Did Ruby Palmer just call *me* Honey?

I guess I'm beginning to rub off on Ruby. At least someone finds me Cute and Charming.

"Thanks." I grin, touched. "You even put whipped cream in it."

"And sugar. And milk." She shakes her head. "Basically, it's a liquid candy bar."

"May the Lord bless you and keep you, and may His face shine upon you." I am in blissful ecstasy, the guy behind me forgotten.

Ruby laughs. "I'd better leave before you quote the whole benediction." She looks up. "Oh hey, have you met my brother Ryan?"

I turn around and encounter Mr. Narrow Eyes again. "Uh, sort of," I fumble. *Cute, Charming, and Coquettish. Remember?*

"Ryan, this is my friend, Laurie Holbrook. Laurie, this is Ryan Palmer, my younger brother."

"Hi." I manage a charming smile.

He looks at me and then smiles back. "Hey."

Ruby leaves.

"So do you go to school here?" he asks.

"Nope. I work."

"Neat."

I pull the bag from under my coat, balancing Ruby's coffee creation on my knee. "Would you like an Oreo?"

Ryan suddenly grins. He has rather plain brown eyes, but they sparkle conspiratorially. "Can I have the bag?"

"I don't know you that well yet."

"Trust me."

I go against my better judgment and hand him the Oreos. He lifts the pillow resting against the arm of the sofa and tucks the bag behind it. "There. Now the bag won't rustle every time you lean forward."

"Genius." I appraise him. "You must have done better on the logical section than I did in the career placement tests."

"What career did they place you in?"

"Gluing the corrugation to cardboard boxes."

He laughs. A nice laugh, actually.

"What about you?"

"Interior design." He makes a face. "I dumped the results and went for a major in construction management. How about you? What was your major? Are you in the box-making industry?"

"No. My friend Brandon Knox's family has a photography studio that I've been working at since I was fifteen. Since that's what I wanted to do anyway, I just kept working and didn't go to college." I pause for a second, then grin. "It's where Ruby works."

"So you take pictures, huh? Like families and stuff? Like what Ruby does?"

"Yep."

"Say cheese? The whole bit?"

I nod.

"Cool. Sounds like a nice job."

I can make a comment about the crying babies and bratty teens, but I don't want to whine. Besides, Hannah is sending me suggestive smiles from the other side of the room, and quite frankly, I want to end this conversation before she gets any ideas about Ryan and me.

"It's okay." I help myself to an Oreo.

He leans forward, hands clasped between his knees. "Have you lived here long?"

"My whole life."

"Wow. I was born here, but I just moved back last week. Mostly because of Ruby but also because I found a good job."

"In construction?" I am in amazement. Construction isn't exactly a booming industry in this little Colorado town.

"Yeah." Ryan smiles shyly.

Oh brother.

"Okay, guys, let's get things started," Nick announces, saving me from the awkward part of the conversation where I'm supposed to say, "Well, hey, want me to show you around?"

Hannah sits on the floor beside me. She doesn't say anything, but she lifts her eyebrows and gives me a mocking grin.

Ruby sits on the other side of me. Smiles sweetly at Nick and then affectionately at her brother. Then knowingly at me.

Knowingly? What does that mean?

I feel like a square of Saran Wrap. See-through.

Nick takes his authoritative stance at the front of the room. "A couple of announcements before we get started, guys. Peter and Nancy here have some news." He nods to Peter.

Peter takes Nancy's hand possessively. "We're engaged."

Everyone oohs. The singles like me ooh politely. The singles soon to be married ooh excitedly. The couples already married ooh perceptively.

"We're getting married on May 11."

Nick nods. "Other news? Uh, Holly? Your wedding is the what?"

"Tenth of February," Holly supplies.

"Right. And you're looking for a couple of volunteers for serving and cleaning up at the reception."

Holly nods. She's twenty-three, same as me. Well, almost. She's got long, straight, thick, white blonde hair and a teensy, tiny waist and always looks like she walked off the cover of *Cosmo Girl*. We grew up here together, but it's always been one of those "Hi, how are you? Fine, thanks. Well, bye" friendships. We never clicked. She always seemed decades older than me.

Never more than now.

Luke sits beside her and slips his arm around her shoulders, kissing her lightly on the temple. She dimples.

Nick watches them with a strange glint in his eye.

I know exactly what he is thinking: *Gee, that would be nice.*

The matchmaker inside me rises to the occasion, and I look over at Ruby gazing at Nick. *Seven months or less*, I vow to myself.

Thirty minutes later, the buzzer on the oven goes off, and Ruby gets up to rescue the lava cake from all of the salivating bachelors in the house.

"Man, it smells good," Nick says when he is done preaching. "Let's eat."

He is the first one over there. Hannah and I exchange a What-Do-You-Know? glance as he starts helping Ruby serve it instead of digging in.

"Hannah, have you met Ruby's brother, Ryan?" I ask, turning slightly to include our young guest.

Hannah smiles. Ryan smiles. I smile.

"Nice to meet you," they say at the same time and laugh politely at the jinx.

Ryan looks over at Nick. "What do you guys know about him?"

Hannah shrugs. "Ask Laurie."

I tick the points off on my fingers. "He's nice. He's a good teacher. He's very polite."

"He seems to like my sister."

I like the protective gleam in his eyes. Good brothers always have protective gleams in their eyes when it comes to their sisters.

I stand up to go get some lava cake, not realizing my backpack has wound around my legs during the teaching. That's what happens, I guess, when you play with the strap throughout the lesson.

When I try to take a step, I go crashing down to the floor, landing hard on my shoulder.

"Oh my gosh!" Hannah and Ryan, the new Speak Twins, exclaim together.

My fall does garner the attention of the whole Bible study.

I sit up, tossing the offending backpack behind me, muttering that I'm okay.

I will have a nasty bruise tomorrow.

"Wow," Ryan says, helping me stand up. "Are you okay?"

"Fine."

"Nice landing, Holbrook." Brandon walks over with a bowl of steaming chocolate.

My stomach growls loudly.

Brandon grins at me and passes me the bowl. "Eat."

Wow. Now two people have given me chocolate in one night.

Either this is the last night of my life, or I look exceptionally pathetic tonight. I lick the chocolate off the spoon. "Thanks."

Ryan looks at Brandon curiously, and I feel the call for an introduction. They shake hands politely.

This has been a polite night.

After Bible study, I walk outside to snow.

Lots and lots of big, fluffy snowflakes drift peacefully from the sky like they have nothing else in the world to do. I *love* lazy snow. It's so much better than the teensy, tiny snowflakes that blaze down from the heavens like they are on a life-or-death mission to annihilate the planet.

"Wow, look guys, it's snowing!" I yell.

A few people stick their heads out. "Cool," they say, uninterested, and go back inside.

"But it's good snow!" I yell again.

No one appreciates the simple things in life anymore. I get a few shrugs.

Brandon comes outside holding a coffee mug. "Relax, Laurie. It's only frozen water dumping down." He goes back inside.

I look up, letting the snow hit me in the face, saddened by all the work the snow is doing with no one even noticing.

"Whoa! It's snowing!"

Hannah waltzes outside, holding her gloved hands out, a huge smile on her face.

There is hope for that girl yet.

"It's so pretty!" she exclaims.

"I know, I know!" I shout back, even though we are standing two feet away from each other.

She sticks her tongue out. "I heard the first snow of the season always tastes and packs the best," she declares.

"I think so. The rest of the time it tastes grainy and is so powdery it doesn't pack."

I grin at Hannah.

Will wonders never cease?

Instead of immediately turning off the light after I've changed into my pajamas, I sit in bed and pull out my Bible.

Ephesians 1, Laney said earlier today.

I start reading, and when I finish with the chapter, I pause.

Wow.

Is it possible to have been a Christian my entire life and not really have even thought about God's sovereignty?

I turn the light off and snuggle down in the covers. My eyes are shut, my breathing relaxed, but there's a tight spot right below my stomach.

I have a lot to think about.

Chapter Ten

It's Monday night. I hold my peppermint mocha closer and sigh dreamily.

Richard Gere and Julia Roberts are about to kiss for the first time.

I live vicariously through my movies. It's a hobby, a habit, and a way of life.

Bob, the soon-to-be ex-fiancé, is jabbering on as Richard and Julia are swept up in the moment. The phone rings just as Richard gets close enough to kiss her.

You would think he is about to kiss me by the way I react. "Arrg!" I yell, slam the snowman mug down on the coffee table, and jerk up the extension beside me on the couch.

It is against proper etiquette to interrupt the hero kissing the heroine. Movie or not.

"Yes?" I answer it. The snowman on my mug flies for cover from the heat in my voice.

"Uh, Laur?"

"Uh, Brandon?"

"Are you okay?"

"Are you deaf?"

Apparently, he does not know how to respond to that one because he avoids an answer by employing the ask-another-question tactic.

"What are you doing?"

"Watching Richard and Julia kiss."

He knows me too well. He doesn't even question that statement.

"Can I come over?"

Huh. Brave boy.

"Only if you let me finish watching them."

"Okay. Bye."

I rewind until Julia is walking down the aisle toward Richard in her skirt and denim jacket again.

Richard stares at her.

She stares at him.

He leans forward . . .

Ding dong!

"ARRG!"

"Hey, Laur."

"Were you outside when you called?"

He doesn't even a take step back from the wrath of the Wicked Witch of the West. Just saunters in like he owns the place, sits in the chair beside mine, and frowns at the movie.

"Yup."

"Shut up," I say in no uncertain terms. "Do not speak, do not mutter, do not breathe, don't even think."

Once again, I rewind and press the play button. Once again, Julia walks down the aisle. Once again, he stares, she stares, and he leans forward.

They kiss.

I smile.

Brandon gags.

"This isn't healthy." He snatches the remote and pauses the emotion onscreen.

But not offscreen.

"Brandon!" I scream.

"Nutsy." He tosses the remote in the air, catches it, and blows across the top as if it is a gun and he is Clint Eastwood. Then he hits the eject button and *Runaway Bride* pops out of the DVD player.

"You said I could finish watching this!" I jump up.

"I changed my mind," he says easily. "Let's go for a walk."

I am dubious. "A walk."

"Yes, a walk. As in, get your coat, Laurie."

"I don't want to walk." If being difficult were an Olympic sport, I would be on the medal stand at this moment.

"Well, you're going to." He eyes the mug with the hidden snowman. "How many cups have you had so far?"

"One."

"Liar."

"Five." I blink innocently at him. "It could be hot chocolate, for all you know."

"For all I know? Nutsy, it was I who went with you in fourth grade to talk to Principal Carlson about putting the instant cappuccino maker in the lunchroom. Trust me. I know it's hard caffeine and nothing but in that cup." He shakes his finger at me throughout this little speech.

I stick my tongue out at him. "It was not fourth grade."

"Fine. Sixth. Get your coat."

I do what he asks, not because I want to but because if I don't, we'll be having this conversation all night, and I'm tired.

"It's dark outside," I announce.

"Really? Oh my gosh! What ever shall we do?" he yells in fake abandon.

I pull one sleeve of my coat on. "There's a good chance of snow."

"Wear gloves."

Two sleeves on. "Dad will say I'll catch my death."

"Your dad is at the church."

I zip up the coat until it is squashing against my thyroid. "If I get sick and die, it's your fault."

"Fine. I'll arrange your funeral. Let's go."

He opens the front door, and the icy cold Colorado air has both the scent of snow and of someone's fireplace.

I inhale hard and suddenly I'm not mad anymore. Take warning: Frosty air can do that to you.

Or maybe it's the five cups of peppermint mocha.

Either way, the Wicked Witch moved north and became the Good Witch.

Brandon inhales and exhales hard, his breath standing out against the frosty air. "Cold winter nights will do you good every time."

"Where are we going?" I ask.

"I don't care."

We wander in the direction of the little park a few blocks away from my house. Brandon is quiet most of the way.

Then he suddenly bursts.

"What do you think about God's sovereignty?"

I look at him, blinking, a tad weirded out that he and I are both thinking about the same thing. "What do you mean?"

He twists his hand around as if the words are floating in the air. "Do you think God planned everything beforehand? Or do you think we have some choice?"

"As in, if I go to college it's because God planned it, not because I chose it?"

"Right." His voice carries a sense of relief. "What do you think?"

It is my turn to use the ask-another-question ploy. "What do *you* think?"

He quiets again. Shoves his hands in his pockets. Bites his lip. "I don't know. I'm confused."

I've never known Brandon to be confused about anything. Brandon is my conscience. My decision maker. Ever since I can remember, he's had an exact plan for his entire life.

Which is probably why these words scare me a little.

"Maybe you should, you know, talk to Nick or something," I say, fidgeting. "Or Laney." Laney seems to understand it. Much more than the snippets I'm mulling over.

"I'm going to. I'm meeting Nick tomorrow for coffee. I just wanted to use you as a sounding board before I went."

It isn't the first time I've been his sounding board.

"You mean like Romans 9 kind of stuff, right?" I ask.

He looks at me. "Sovereignty isn't just in Romans 9. It's throughout the Bible."

"Yeah, I know."

"So you never told me what you think."

"I don't know, Brandon. It's . . . it's kind of a hard concept." I pause. "If God's in complete control, why do bad things happen to good people?"

"Laur, if Romans 3:23 is correct, there are no good people."

I concede. "True."

There is a long silence. I push my gloved hands into my coat pockets. I look up at the moon, and I suddenly feel very, very small and insignificant.

It is not a nice feeling.

I shrink closer to Brandon, which makes me feel even smaller. I can see my breath and I'm smelling someone's fire, but it doesn't bring any comfort.

Something deep in my gut is still amiss.

If I have the power to change something, doesn't that take power away from God? And in Ephesians 1:19, Paul said something about God's incomparably great power.

"Hey, Brandon?"

"Hmm?"

My thoughts are jumbled. "For God to be God, wouldn't He have to be sovereign?"

"My thoughts exactly, Laur."

Silence again. We reach the park.

"So what else did you want to talk about?" I ask, needing to change the subject.

He shrugs.

"Do you think Richard and Julia will get together in the end?"

He gives me a look that makes me wish for a camera. I giggle.

"You need a life, Laurie."

I spread out my hands. "I have a nice life."

"Because I'm in it."

"Oh, you're a funny boy. I think I'll keep you around as my court jester."

He frowns. "Do I have to wear those little shoes with bells on them?"

"Why not?"

"Sneaking up on you will be harder."

"Then I'll live longer."

He knuckles my head, and after we get home, we both have a peppermint mocha. I cave in and we watch *Rocky*.

It is just like we are fourteen again.

But my gut continues to stay off-centered.

Tuesday morning I walk into work, and Tina Braxton and Kyle Medfield are there.

Perfect, radiant, and two-dimensional.

They smile down from their place of honor on the main wall across from the receptionist desk.

I moan.

"Morning, Laurie."

"Hey, Hannah."

She frowns at me. "You look blue."

"I'm wearing red."

"Wearing red makes you blue?"

"No. What are they doing here? I don't remember another session for them." I hook my thumb toward the picture.

"Like it, huh?" Hannah rolls her eyes. "I know, I know. It's a great pick-me-up during the day. I can sit here and think, 'Gosh, I didn't put on any makeup this morning; I must look awful.' And then I get to see *that*."

Tina's eyes sparkle just so as she looks at me, and I know the portrait somehow embodies the spirit of that evil queen on *Snow White*.

Who is the fairest of them all?

"You, Tina," I say, bowing from the waist, arms outstretched.

"Uh, Laurie?"

I frown. Either Hannah's voice is significantly lower since last I saw her, or we have a stranger in our midst.

I whirl.

Ryan Palmer stands there with the expression of someone who has just seen a smoked salmon stand up and sing "The Star-Spangled Banner."

There I go with those fishing analogies again.

"Ryan . . . hi," I stutter. "How are you?"

"Were you really . . . ?" He stares at me another second, and I guess he recalls the Oreo fiasco because he doesn't finish his thought.

"Is Ruby here?" he asks.

I shrug. "I don't know. I just got here myself."

"She's here," Hannah says. "Studio Four."

"Thanks." Ryan gives me one last look and walks down the hall. After he disappears in the studio, Hannah dissolves.

"That was hysterical!" she screams, gasping for breath between the extremely overdramatic gales of laughter.

"Good grief, Hannah, it wasn't that funny."

"He looked at you like . . . like . . ."

"Yeah, yeah. Shut up."

She grins at me instead. Her blue eyes are spotlighted by the powder blue sweater she wears, and though I can't see her legs behind the desk, I'm fairly certain she's wearing jeans again. Her hair bounces around her shoulders in reckless waves.

Forget Tina.

How is it I end up working with the fairest of them all?

Ryan and Ruby come out of Studio Four, Ruby's arm casually around her brother's waist, his around her shoulders.

"Are you coming tomorrow night?" Ruby asks Ryan.

He sends me a sidelong look. "I think so. I'm supposed to guard the chocolate."

I cross my arms over my chest. *Hmph.* Well, there are ways to get around guards.

"Got a pistol?" Hannah asks.

"No, but I'm fairly good at darts," he says. "Think those will work?"

Rats. Now it's an armed guard. Still plausible. Look what happens in those all-too-realistic movies like Disney's *Robin Hood.* Three armed guards, a locked gate, and a talking snake. And Robin still manages to get all the gold, all the captives, and his life. Not to mention the girl. And to stray from the subject, exactly how long did Maid Marian's ring last? Flowers don't make good engagement rings.

Anyway, chocolate will be a cinch after all that.

"Bring the darts," Hannah instructs. "Ever seen any Old West movies?"

Ryan bursts. "Are you kidding? John Wayne is my favorite actor."

Obviously, we'll need some time to work with Ryan on his choice of actors.

"Remember the strongboxes?" Hannah goes on.

"Yep."

"Bring at least one. You can lock up the chocolate and then stand guard with the darts."

Ryan laughs.

Suddenly, a dart hits me square in the forehead.

Cupid is at work, apparently, and letting me know.

Hannah.

Ryan.

Already they have something in common—Old West movies, bless their future children's hearts.

Ryan will be easy. Hannah, beautiful and intelligent, can steal the heart of a cold-blooded shark.

Mental note: Talk to Dad. Tell him not to mention the fishing trip again until a week before. This is getting ridiculous.

Hannah might be harder. But hanging around a bunch of Christians is apparently rubbing off on her. The salvation issue may not be a problem soon. I'm hopeful, anyway.

But if looks mean anything to her . . .

Just keep him smiling. He might be plain to look at, but when he smiles, his whole face lights up. Pretty cute. Like watching a little fourth grader's expression when he climbs to the top of the monkey bars for the first time.

Plus, he has nice teeth. And pretty eyelashes.

This can work.

"So, Ryan," I butt in, "what are you doing for lunch today?"

He blinks a few times. "Probably eating."

"Want to join us? Brandon owes us lunch out, and you're officially invited."

"Well . . ."

"You aren't seriously going to turn down free food," I lecture. "At Vizzini's? Come on, Ryan. The future reputation of bachelors everywhere is resting on your shoulders."

He smiles. *Good. Keep smiling.* "Uh, sure, I'll go. I guess."

I am ecstatic. "Great! Twelve thirty work?"

"Sure." He squeezes Ruby. "See you at twelve thirty, then."

"Okay." Ruby masks her confusion quite nicely. She has come a long way.

Ryan leaves.

I leave the room a microsecond later. Better to explain The New Plan to Ruby in private, away from Hannah's nosy ears.

I crash open Brandon's office door. To his credit, he doesn't even look up. "Hey, Laurie."

I cross the room and take a seat on top of his desk. "How'd you know it was me?"

"Deduction. Ruby and Hannah don't bang doors. So it was either you or a robber, and I didn't hear screams out front." He smiles, leaning back in his chair. "What's up?"

"Here you go."

He takes the money with a frown. "You're giving me forty bucks?"

"For lunch."

"I'm buying lunch?"

"Yes."

He morphs into principal-mode. "What did you just do?" Folds his hands on his desk, straightens his shoulders, cools his eyes.

Brandon picked the wrong career. He's pretty good at playing principal.

"Well, you're taking us out to lunch today."

"I am." His voice is flat.

"Yep."

"Who is us?"

"You, me, Ruby, Hannah, and," I clear my throat, "Ryan, possibly Ty and Newton."

"Ryan?" he jumps on the name. "Who's Ryan and why are we taking him?"

I make it sound innocent. "You met him Wednesday. He's Ruby's brother."

He nods. "Good enough. Why are we taking him?"

I clamber to the far-off corners of my brain. "Well, he was standing there when I asked everyone to lunch, so I had to include him."

Brandon leans farther back in his chair, crosses his arms, and gives me the expression that says, *How stupid do you think I am?*

"How stupid do you think I am?" he asks.

Man, I nailed that look.

"Is that rhetorical?"

"I know you're not setting Ruby up with her brother."

"Gee, you're a genius."

He ignores me. "And you're staying single, so the obvious choice is our lovely Miss Curtis."

I feign shock. "What on earth gave you that idea? Honestly! The thought of me setting Hannah Curtis up with Ruby's brother—"

"And paying me forty bucks to do it." He waves the bills in my face.

I still his hand. "The future happiness of two people is worth even more than forty dollars to me."

He rolls his eyes. "Bless your kind and generous nature."

"How'd it go with Nick?" I ask. Brandon's meeting with Nick about the sovereignty issue was this morning.

"Good. Great." He lets his breath out and thumps his Bible, which is near my left shoe. "I think I understand a little more."

"Want to share?"

"Later. Let me gather my thoughts first, okay?" He smiles at me and taps my knee with his pen. "Get back to work."

I smile at him, climb off his desk, and start to leave.

"Hey."

I stop. Turn. Smile the full 120 watts.

"Yes, Brandon dear?"

"Don't give me that look. Listen, I have absolutely nothing to do with this matchmaking. All right? I wash my hands."

"Agreed."

"Hey," he says again as I turn the doorknob.

I turn again.

He grins boyishly. "If you bring brownies again, can you put in whatever you put in that last batch? Those were good."

I laugh and leave. I must be rubbing off on Brandon because that is my next plan. After lunch, Ryan will be coaxed to come for an early dinner before Bible study tomorrow night. Brownies are on the menu.

Following will be Hannah's conversion, his imminent proposal, and her exuberant "yes, of course!"

I can almost hear the voice from *Field of Dreams*.

"If you arrange it, wedding bells will come."

And by Jove, I'm going to arrange it.

Chapter Eleven

"Say, 'Cupid rocks!'"

I believe in mixing my personal and business lives.

Four-year-old Delaney repeats me and then kicks her two-year-old brother, Davis. "You're supposed to say it!" she lectures him.

Davis's eyes fill and his lower lip protrudes. "Sowwy, Duh-waney." He blinks repeatedly and sticks his thumb in his mouth.

"Whoa, whoa, guys." I come to poor Davis's rescue. "Uh, how about we don't say anything? Smile!"

Delaney and Davis finish a few minutes later and I watch them leave, praying blessings over the head of Davis, that he might live to age three.

"Ready for lunch?" Hannah asks from behind me.

I turn. "Is Ryan here yet?"

"No, but he should be any minute."

Ruby steps out of Brandon's office, followed by the manager of the studio. "So anyway, I told them to come back next week for a reshoot."

"Sounds fine." Brandon pulls on a jacket.

"Ry here yet?" Ruby asks.

I shake my head. "Nope."

"Good. I'll be right back." She disappears into the bathroom.

"Vizzini's, I'm assuming," Brandon says.

"You assume correctly," I tell him. "Best breadsticks this side of the country."

The bell jangles over the front door and I turn. "Hi, Ryan. Wait a minute—"

Nick is before me.

"Hi, Nick," I revise.

"Nick! Glad you could make it." Brandon shakes Nick's hand. "We'll be heading out as soon as Ryan gets here."

Nick turns to greet Hannah.

Well, well, well. Another matchmaker joined our midst.

"Brandon, you have become what you have mocked," I whisper.

He sighs. "Being around you as much as I am, it was inevitable."

"I know."

Ryan comes inside, pulling his leather coat tightly around him. "It is freezing cold out there."

"Hi, Ryan," Nick says.

"Nick, right? Good to see you again." Ryan turns to Hannah. "Hannah, you're going to want a heavier coat."

Hannah tugs on her lightweight sweater-jacket. "I'll be okay, I think."

Ryan stares at her for a second before muttering something under his breath and stripping off his coat.

"Here." He hands it to her. "It's beat up, but at least it's warm."

"Ryan, I'm not going to take your coat."

"Yes, you are."

My elation at the exchange must show on my face because Brandon elbows me hard in the ribs.

I yelp.

I *hate* it when people look at me with that weird wrinkle right between their eyebrows. It makes me feel like I have suddenly converted into a Turkish dwarf with sideburns and an accordion.

Ruby comes down the hall, and everyone's attention is diverted. She has taken to spiral curling her hair in the past two days and it looks great.

"Nick," she says, no surprise in her voice. "Good to see you. Hey, Ry."

She has obviously been tipped off Nick might come. Brandon doesn't relish moments of sheer shock like I do.

Hannah takes Ryan's coat.

"I can carry five in the Tahoe," I say. "Counting myself."

"Ruby and I can go in my car," Nick says.

Ruby blushes prettily. I nod. "Good. Let's go."

Nick ends up behind me as I pull out of the parking lot. Vizzini's is a mere six minutes away in the heaviest of traffic, and I want to give Nick and Ruby plenty of time to fall in love. So I go ten under the speed limit.

Nick can't pass me without making Ryan think the guy driving his sister is a speed demon. And Ryan and Hannah are too busy chatting in the backseat to notice they can see every blade of dead grass we pass.

Brandon, however, is not.

"Why are you driving like your father?" he asks in a low voice so as not to interrupt the conversation revolving around John Wayne and appaloosas in the back.

I try to sound oblivious. "What do you mean?"

"You're driving thirty miles an hour. It'll be time for dinner before we get there."

I pat his hand resting on the console. "Don't worry, I know what I'm doing."

"I know, and that's what scares me."

Ten minutes later, we are all safely in the restaurant.

And who should be our waiter but JACK?

"Hi," he gapes when he sees who he is seating. "You're back."

Surprise reigns in his voice. I nod mutely.

"Right . . . right this way, please."

After JACK seats us, gives us menus, and leaves, Ruby leans forward. "Laurie, I didn't know you had something going on with the cute waiter guy."

"Me neither," Brandon says.

"There's nothing going on with the cute waiter guy." I lower my voice. "He just dumped a pitcher of water in my lap last time I was here."

Ryan and Hannah burst out laughing. Ruby smiles, sympathetic.

"How come these things always happen to you?" Nick asks.

"Because she's Laurie, Nick," Brandon says. "Her name means 'Bringer of Pandemonium.'"

JACK slinks back to the table. "Have you decided?"

Everyone orders.

He leaves as quickly as he comes.

Brandon watches him go. "Poor guy. I think a hefty tip is in order."

"Have you seen *El Dorado*?" Ryan asks.

"Whoa! Halt the conversation." Ruby raises her hand. "No John Wayne talk, please. I'm begging here."

"And I'm seconding the begging," I add.

Ryan grins at Hannah. "Guess we'll have to talk later."

"Speaking of later," I say skillfully, "I was thinking maybe we could all have an early dinner at my house tomorrow before Bible study." Wow, that was smooth.

"Great idea, Nutsy. I'm in," Brandon says.

Nick watches Ruby. With interest. A lot of it.

"I can make it," she says.

"Me too," Nick says immediately. Hannah and Ryan both nod.

"Nutsy?" Ryan and Nick say together.

I close my eyes. "Brandon."

Lunch passes with a lot of laughs. Meanwhile, The New Plan is carried out with talent and ease.

By the time we leave a 30 percent tip for JACK, I'm convinced Ruby and Hannah will have a double wedding.

I go home that night crafting the second phase. Attraction has been accomplished.

Check mark for Tuesday.

Phase Two Title: Cultivate, Consider, Commit.

Subpoints: Ruby and Hannah will both Cultivate their ever-blossoming relationships with Nick and Ryan. Next, marriage Consideration will arise for the two pairs. And finally, we have a Commitment on both sides and a date in June.

Which leaves me plenty of time to help plan both weddings while still accounting for my month of fishing in March.

"Hi, Honey," Dad says when I come in the house.

A gorgeous fire crackles in the fireplace; Dad is settled in his chair, glasses in place and a book cradled in his hands.

He looks peaceful.

I love my dad.

"Hiya, Pop." I slouch into the love seat.

"How was work?"

"Niductate."

Niductate: (*adj.*) Nice, neat, and productive.

Dad, aware of my word fetish, doesn't do anything but smile at me.

"How was your day?" I ask.

"Good. I picked up some more fishing lures."

Lure.

"Aha!" I yell, shattering Dad's serenity.

"What?" he shouts.

"That's what I need! A lure!"

"Honey, I think you're beautiful just the way you are." Dad relaxes back in his chair. "Don't go changing yourself to attract other people."

"No, not *allure*. A lure. Two words."

"Are you going to go practice fishing?"

I grin. "I sure am."

I use a highlighter and underline Ephesians 1:11. "In him we were also chosen, having been predestined according to the plan of him who works out everything in conformity with the purpose of his will."

According to this, God's plan and purpose cannot be thwarted, because everything conforms to His will.

I bite my lower lip and stare at the verse for a long time before turning out the light.

Wednesday morning I wake to my alarm at seven fifteen. I set it an hour earlier than usual so I can make my Supercalifragilisticexpialidocious Brownies.

The sacrifices I make for the future happiness of my friends.

Now I'm out forty bucks and a crucial hour of beauty sleep.

I mix the concoction vowing if either party doesn't marry, I'm going to bestow a rain of fiery chastisements on their heads.

Brandon, Hannah, and Ruby all show up at exactly five thirty this evening. I think it is sad how Ruby has trained us to be the Punctual Picture Party.

Brandon, in typical fashion, doesn't ring the doorbell, doesn't knock, just barges right in.

I swear I am going to get a deadbolt for that door. One of these days he's going to walk in and I'll be in my underwear.

Fortunately, I got dressed good and early.

"Where's Ryan and Nick?" I ask.

"Nick called, he's on his way." Ruby hands me the salad she made.

I smile sweetly. "He has your number?"

She blushes. "Well . . . he . . . I . . ."

Hannah pats her arm. "Why don't I take your coats?"

I'm more than curious about where she's going to put them. This is the first time Hannah has been to my house.

I grab her arm on her way down the hall. "First door on the right."

"Thanks."

Nick shows up just as the threesome heads to the kitchen.

He looks awful.

I don't let him inside.

"Whoa, Nicky." I shove him back onto the porch and close the door behind me. "What the heck happened to you?"

His hair, normally smoothed down with gel, curls Shirley Temple–like all over his head. Which, by itself, is pretty cute. But his eyes . . .

Blegh.

"Laurie." He swallows.

"Did someone die? Were you in a wreck? What happened?" I push him down on the bench.

He cradles his head in his hands. "Laurie, Laurie, Laurie. I can't do this."

Confusion is setting in. "What? Dinner?"

"No." He looks up, eyes tortured. "Ruby."

I stare at him. "What are you talking about?"

"She's beautiful."

"Okay. With you so far."

"She's so sweet and charming and godly." He shakes his head, looking off in the distance. "She even cooks!"

I'm totally lost. "Nick, I'm not seeing the problem."

"Laurie, look at me!"

It is my firm belief in Pit-of-Despair times like these that honesty is always the best policy.

"You look awful."

His shoulders sag farther. A feat I thought impossible. "Thanks."

"Listen, you can borrow my comb and some spray gel."

"She's amazing, Laurie."

I blink. "Who is?"

"Ruby!"

"So why are you so upset?" I ask. My temper is beginning to play hide-and-seek, and at the moment, it is lost. My voice has more than a little bite to it. It is cold, I'm wearing a lightweight long-sleeved T-shirt and no shoes, and I know I'm getting frostbite on my nose.

Nick stares at me bleakly. "I think . . . I think I . . ."

Suddenly, frostbite or not, I want desperately to hear what he has to say.

"Go on," I urge.

"Oh, Laurie," he whispers. "I think I've fallen—"

"Hey, guys."

ARRG!

It is all I can do to not clobber Ryan over the head with a wicker chair and stuff his body under the porch so Nick can finish.

Nick sobers immediately. "Hi, Ryan." His voice is normal, eyes start to clear. He rubs his hands over his face, blinks a few times.

I smile close-mouthed at Ryan. The moment is lost. I can no longer tell Nick to just go propose. Not with Ruby's brother standing there.

Reality is disappointing.

Any good movie would have gone like so:

NICK: Laurie, I have fallen in love with the most beautiful girl in the world.

LAUREN: Tina Braxton is already taken.

NICK: I do not know this Tina. I speak of Ruby Palmer, the most beautiful girl in the world.

LAUREN: You love Ruby?

NICK: Yes. (*tearfully*) I love Ruby.

LAUREN: Then go tell her so.

NICK: You are a genius, Laurie. Excuse me, I need to ask the most beautiful girl in the world the most important question I will ever ask.

LAUREN: You should.

NICK: Before I go, Laurie, will you be Ruby's maid of honor and allow us the unending delight of naming our future daughter after you?

LAUREN: With pleasure.

Instead, Nick and Ryan walk into the house and I follow. My toes are blue, my hands are ice, my face is stiff, and I distinctly smell the lasagna I put in earlier burning in the oven.

Reality stinks.

"Hey, Nutsy! I think dinner's getting toasty!"

I collect myself and walk into the kitchen. Hannah, Ruby, Nick, and

Ryan all sit at the table. Brandon leans against the counter. "You couldn't pull it out?" I ask him, politely because of our guests, but dangerously because he rests on quicksand.

He gives me a saucy grin. "What, and miss that look?"

This comment elicits chuckles from the table, silent yet tangible wrath from me. I pull the casserole out of the oven and a bowl of packaged salad from the fridge. "We're doing buffet style, folks," I announce, tossing a loaf of French bread beside the lasagna.

Nick hasn't looked at Ruby yet. Ruby looks at him both confusedly (probably because of his hair) and with that wrinkle between her eyes.

He studiously avoids her.

The tension between the two causes a major rift in the natural progression of a thing called conversation.

Silence fills the kitchen. Everyone lines up politely, fills their plates with food, and settles at the table. All in perfect silence. Ryan prays shortly over the food. We all start eating.

I pinch Brandon hard on the bicep. "Say something." I hiss this quietly.

"Uh, yeah, so did anyone catch the Nuggets game this afternoon?" he shouts.

Hannah's mouth works in a hard attempt to not burst out laughing. Her eyes are brimming with mirth as she grins. "Brandon, that's the worst excuse for a conversation I ever heard."

He raises his eyebrows. "Okay, you try."

"I will." She smiles prettily. "Today was my day off and I went and got a puppy."

My mouth drops open. "Aw! What kind?"

"Just a mutt. From the pound. She's little bitty. Six weeks old."

"Aw!" This time, Ruby and I exclaim together.

"What's her name?" Ruby demands.

Hannah shrugs. "I don't know."

"You don't know?" I gasp. "The poor dog doesn't have a name?"

"I was thinking something like Bitsy."

"Bitsy?" I echo. "Oh, Hannah. You can do better than that."

"Much better," Ruby chimes in.

"What color is she?" I ask.

"Brown."

"Like a taupe or a chocolate?" Ruby asks.

Brandon grins. "Now see, there is a question that no male in his right mind would ask."

We ignore him.

"What about Cocoa Bean?" Ruby suggests.

Ryan wrinkles his nose. "Cocoa Bean?" he echoes. "Gag, Ruby. Can you imagine standing in the yard yelling that?"

"Yvonne," Brandon says.

Everyone looks at him.

"What?" I ask, on behalf of the others.

"What about Yvonne?"

I blink.

"Louisa?"

Ruby presses her lips together.

"Doreen."

Hannah gags.

"Boyce?"

By the time dinner is over and we're all pulling on jackets to leave for Bible study, everyone, even Nick, is laughing and suggesting names.

I grin at Brandon as I pull my coat on. To borrow an *Anne of Green Gables* phrase, we're such kindred spirits, I don't even have to say thank you.

I ride to Bible study with Hannah. I'm balancing both of our Bibles in my lap and she's talking nonstop about the book of John, where I told her to start reading.

"It's just so weird to think about," she says, quickly glancing over her shoulder as she changes lanes. "I'm looking forward to the study tonight. I just have like this desire to read and study the Bible that I've never had before. Isn't it weird?"

I only grin at her.

I climb into bed Wednesday night, exhausted. The study was excellent. Nick pulled his act together long enough to teach a fabulous lesson regarding—what else?—the sovereignty of God. Hannah soaked it up.

I reread Ephesians 1 and decide God is definitely trying to teach me something. My stomach is still grappling with the whole sovereignty issue, but I'm getting used to it.

Thursday morning I roll out of bed and land on my to-do list.

Here's what I hate: To-Do Lists. I resent the fact that I cannot function properly without one.

This particular list is scribbled on the back of a napkin from Vizzini's.

Things I Must Do, Yet Do Not Want To:

- Make the bed
- Order the barbecue for Saturday family lunch
- Get Ruby to confess how she feels re: Nick

I climb into my clothes, leave my hair down because I decide the *au natural* look is in, and walk downstairs to face the scent of lemongrass tea head-on.

"Honey, I think we should order the barbecue today," Dad says when I sit at the table.

"On my list," I reply.

He smiles at me. "I like your hair like that, Laurie-girl."

Dad is always good for a compliment.

I arrive at the studio at five after nine. Ruby meets me as I come in the door. "You're late," she announces, a bit testily.

"You're right." I frown as I study her. She looks awful. Her hair is yanked back in a short little ponytail haphazardly teetering on the edge of falling out. She doesn't have any makeup on. And she is wearing a fairly wrinkled cowgirl shirt and jeans.

Jeans!

Hannah smiles tersely at me from behind Ruby.

"Are you okay?" I ask Ruby.

Hannah shakes her head vehemently, mouthing, "No!"

"I'm fine," Ruby says in a biting tone. "I'm just ticked that you're late. Laurie, you know we're supposed to get here *on time*. I needed your help, and you weren't here to give it."

I pull my coat off. "Well, I'm here now. What can I do?"

"Nothing!" she yells, tossing her hands in the air. "I already did it!" She exhales loudly and rubs her face.

Something is definitely wrong.

I study her. "Is this about Nick?"

Dumb question. I watch Hannah flinch and cover her eyes dramatically.

Ruby opens her mouth, then closes it. Then she opens it again. "What? No, it's not about Nick! This has nothing to do with Nick! This is completely about . . ." Her voice trails off and she sinks into one of the chairs in front of Hannah's desk.

Her face gets very white, and tears fill her eyes.

"Girls," she whispers. She rubs her face again.

I sit beside her, dropping my backpack on the floor. Ruby stills her hands over her eyes and just breathes in and out slowly. Hannah raises her eyebrows at me over Ruby's head, and I try hard not to break out into a huge grin. There seems to be a distinct possibility I can mark off number three on my list in the next few minutes.

I'm not going to miss this for the world.

Ruby mashes her lips together, starts to speak, then stops again. "Do you think," she says, finally. "Do you think there's a chance that Nick . . ."

Stops again.

The silence in the room is so loud it's reverberating in my eardrums.

If she doesn't finish this thought, I am seriously going to paint leopard spots on my body, move to the Far Reaches of the Jungle, and spend the rest of my life swinging from vines and not seeing another human as long as I live.

She looks at me so pitifully I come close to crying myself.

The dam breaks.

"I just . . . I don't understand him," she bursts. "Some days he's so understanding and nice and I wonder if he likes me as more than a friend. And other days, he seems so out of reach and avoids me like I have the Bubonic plague." Her voice cracks.

Hannah gives her a Kleenex.

"You'll think I'm crazy." She wipes under her eyes. Her voice drops to a decibel below a whimper. "But I think I . . . sometimes I think he . . ."

"Hi, girls."

Ryan lives life on the edge.

Hannah and I whirl, prepared to kill any and every person, animal, or insect that dares to intrude on this conversation.

Had he not been Ruby's brother, and had she not been in such a delicate mental state, I truly believe Ryan would not still be with us today.

I have such an iron grip on the desk my knuckles pop in protest.

"Hi, Ryan," Ruby says softly, clutching the Kleenex. "What are you doing here?"

"I'm on my way in to work and stopped by to see what was happening here." Ryan looks constructiony. He wears ten-gallon boots, heavy-duty cargo pants, and a big red-and-black-checked flannel shirt, and he's chomping gum. His brown hair scatters all over his head like he got up and forgot how to brush it.

He looks so hopeful and sweet and innocent that I can't stay mad at him.

I melt.

I smile at him. "Well, we're just having some girl talk."

His eyes widen. "And I interrupted. I'm sorry. I . . . Ruby, are you okay?"

There is that ever-so-cute protective gleam in his eyes again. I hope Hannah is noticing it.

Ruby starts waving her hands erratically. "Fine. Just fine. I think an eyelash or something got in my eye. Don't worry about it. Actually, I'm going to go try to get it out. Excuse me."

Ruby disappears in a hurry.

Hannah gives me a What-Do-We-Do-Now? look.

I shrug back an I-Have-No-Idea. Do we go comfort Ruby and perhaps hear the on-the-tip-of-her-tongue confession? Or are we polite and talk to Ryan? Or do we split up and have one talk to Ruby and one talk to Ryan?

I'm casting my vote for Lauren Holbrook, Counselor Spectacular, to speak with Ruby Fair, and Hannah Curtis, Beautiful Secretary, to woo Ryan the Builder.

I open my mouth to speak the plan.

"I'll go see if she got the eyelash out."

Rats. Hannah beats me to the punch. She runs down the hall, knocks once on the bathroom door, and disappears inside.

I lean back against the desk and study Construction Sam in front of me.

"So." He says this tucking his gum in the back corner of his mouth.

"So," I echo.

"Guess you guys aren't very busy this early."

"Nope."

Ryan grunts once, either in acknowledgement of my answer or to fill the silence, I'm not sure.

Here's what I am: Shameless.

"Well, this is Hannah's second week on the job. What do you think of her?"

Ryan sits beside me at Hannah's desk, picking at a callous on his left index finger.

"Uh." He swallows.

I prod. "What?"

"Well . . . I mean, I don't . . . I haven't been around her very long." He is still fiddling with his finger. Beginning to bug me.

I try to ignore the picking. "Okay, so first impression. I'm garnering info for her file."

Ryan smiles at me. "The opinions file?"

"Yep."

"I think she's a good secretary. Ruby likes her, anyway. Says she's prompt." Ryan rolls his eyes. "You know Ruby."

"Trust me, I do."

He chuckles. Keeps picking.

Tolerance level for this is dropping drastically.

"So you give Hannah your stamp of approval?"

He looks at his hand for a second and then shrugs nonchalantly. "Yeah, sure. Why not?"

A little too impersonal. Obviously, I have been slacking on the job.

Pick. Pick. Pick.

I can feel my breathing coming faster as I watch him play with the callous. There are only a very few things that really get under my skin.

Things That Beyond a Doubt Get Under My Skin:

- Picking at calloused skin, scabs, or bites
- Popping knuckles
- Licking the top of the spray cheese bottle
- Leaving a glob of toothpaste in the sink

As you can see, picking a callous is at the very tip-top of my list. Which will explain my next action.

"CUT IT OUT!" I scream. Slap my hands over both of his and still his insolent finger.

He looks at me, blinking and wordless.

I once heard Laney tell me Barbie's boyfriend, Ken, would always be the perfect male—because he didn't speak.

News flash to Laney: I have my hands on a perfect male.

He stares at me like I'm Gonzo from the Muppets tap dancing with a flowerpot on my head.

Then he grins.

It is at this unfortunate moment that Ruby and Hannah reappear. They both stop at the end of the hallway, mouths open, eyes wide.

I just know a squalling baby octopus is about to land on my head.

And then I realize what they are staring at.

Ryan is smiling. At me.

And we are holding hands.

Chapter Twelve

I yank away like Ryan has suddenly begun channeling the spirit of the Dread Pirate Roberts.

There he goes blinking again.

Hannah and Ruby switch from shocked expressions to giddy-pleased expressions. Wait, why is Hannah giddy? Shouldn't she be frothing with jealousy?

"We didn't mean to interrupt." Ruby is all smiles now.

Ryan stares at me confusedly. "You didn't interrupt anything."

"No, nothing," I say emphatically.

"Uh-huh." Hannah smiles. I search her face and see nothing but absolute delight.

"Well, um, I should go," Ryan stutters. He stands.

Poor guy. I feel sorry for him. It is all my fault we are in this situation, and he gets to share the blame. If I know Ruby, he'll never hear the end of it.

"I'll walk you out."

I might regret doing this in five minutes.

I sneak a look at Hannah and Ruby as I follow Ryan out. Strike the first comment.

I *will* regret doing this.

He walks to a blue Chevy pickup and stops by the driver's door.

"Uh, Laurie?"

I shove my hands into the pockets of my jeans. Sigh.

"Yeah, I know."

"Do they think that we were . . . ?" He ducks his head and looks at me.

I nod. Vigorously. "Yep. That's what they think, all right."

"Oh boy," he says, digging his keys out of his front pocket.

"Look, Ryan, this is all my fault. I'm sorry. I get carried away sometimes when something bugs me, and you picking at that—" I point harshly to the infidel finger "—was definitely bugging me."

He grins abruptly. "You mean like this?"

Pick. Pick. Pick.

"ARRG!"

He laughs, and I have the sudden image of Ryan at age five.

Poor Ruby. It's a miracle she turned out so well.

"Stop it." I smack his hands. He does, still grinning. "Look, I'll explain to your sister and Hannah."

"Don't even bother. It won't do any good. Ruby's been trying to set me up with someone nice since I was in seventh grade."

Now it is my turn. "Oh boy." I let my breath out. "What should we do?"

A strange mix of mischievous evil and absolute insanity crosses Ryan's expression.

Uh-oh. I have a very bad feeling about this.

"What if we pretended we were really interested in each other?" He winces. "I mean, not like I'm not interested in you right now . . . it's just that we could make them think we were . . . I didn't mean that . . ."

Okay, now this is fun.

I grin unrepentantly. "You mean you don't like me?"

He closes his eyes. "I'm normally not this smooth."

"Good. I'd hate to think I was the only klutz in this group."

"What do you think?"

I look at him. Ryan is nice. Sweet. Christian.

It will throw a major kink in my plan of Hannah and Ryan together, but really . . . well, she did seem pleased, didn't she? She definitely wasn't *mad*.

Ryan is Ruby's little brother. Could it possibly tempt her toward the altar if her baby brother is falling in love?

And plus, it will put a look like no other on Brandon's face.

What do I have to lose?

"I accept." I shake his hand.

His face splits in the cute little-kid-on-the-monkey-bars smile. "This will be great. Okay. First, I have to ask you out in front of at least one of them."

"Nick," I decide. "He'll tell Ruby, who will go ballistic."

"Genius. When should our date be?"

"Wednesday. Right before Bible study. We should walk in carrying a cup from the same place."

"You're ruthless."

"Ah, don't I know it. So Sunday you'll ask me out?"

"Sunday." He smiles again and squeezes my shoulder. Then he gets in his car and I walk back inside.

Hannah and Ruby both stand by the door, arms crossed, eyes twinkling. "So," Ruby draws the word out. "My brother has expressed his interest, I see."

I blush in an innocent, Oh-Gracious-I've-Been-Found-Out look. "You guys are crazy," I protest lightly. I go around them and to the appointment calendar.

"She's blushing," Hannah says.

Ruby hums her agreement. "And avoiding the subject."

"She likes him," Hannah sing-songs.

"Who likes him?" Brandon asks, walking in and shedding his coat.

"Laurie likes Ryan," Ruby announces.

"I do not!"

"And he likes her," Hannah purrs.

Brandon's eyebrows climb on his forehead, and his lips get very tight. He makes a *hmm* sound in the back of his throat.

It is all I can do to not burst out laughing.

Poor Brandon. I am mean.

"Could I see you in my office, please?" He jerks his thumb down the hall.

I follow. Once the door closes behind me, he whirls.

"Lauren Holbrook, you amaze me." He leans against the edge of his desk, crossing his arms over his chest.

"Why?"

"I thought you weren't getting married."

Haven't we had this discussion before?

"People change sometimes, Brandon. Besides, it's not like I'm marrying the guy. I only just met him, for Pete's sake!"

"What about Hannah? I thought you were trying to set her up with Ryan."

I shrug. "Guess I had an *Emma* moment."

Brandon stares at me quizzically.

"Never mind." I know better than to tread the thick, muddied waters of explaining romantic comedies to a "shoot 'em up, blow 'em up, clean 'em up" movies kind of guy.

"Look, Laurie, I just don't want either of you to get hurt." He pulls me into a hug.

Aw. Unexpectedly, I start getting choked up. Add to that the humongous load of pure, solid guilt landing with a resounding *oomph!* on my back.

"Thanks, Brandon," I sniff, rubbing my face on his shirt.

He pushes me back, grimacing. "Here." Hands me a Kleenex.

I blow my nose, quite loudly, and he grins. "I must admit, though, I pity the poor man."

"Shut up." I miss the trash can by two inches.

"What's with the hair today?" He pokes it for good measure.

"I was tired this morning."

"Uh-huh. I can tell. You look like you brushed it with a fork."

"Worked for Ariel."

"Doesn't work for you. I like it better straight."

I sigh. Between my dad's compliments and Brandon's insults, it's no wonder I'm the emotional roller coaster I am.

At three forty-five, after six families, a cheeseburger, three Dr. Peppers, two lattes, and four Milky Ways, I finally get around to ordering the barbecue.

"Smith Valley Barbecue." I can hear the buzz of people talking and laughing and little kids yelling behind the exhausted female voice.

"I need to place an order for Saturday."

Smith Valley Barbecue is the best in town, and it's no secret. Just the fact that I have to put in an order two days in advance attests to this.

"Okay, go ahead."

I rattle off the order.

"What's the pick-up time?"

"Eleven thirty."

"Name?"

"Laurie Holbrook."

"Phone number?"

I give her both my home and cell numbers.

"Thank you."

Friday night I open my Bible to Philippians 2 and I'm about to turn back a few pages to Ephesians 4, where I left off, when the word *purpose* catches my attention. I back up to verses 12 and 13. "Therefore, my dear friends, as you have always obeyed—not only in my presence, but now much more in my absence—continue to work out your salvation with fear and trembling, for it is God who works in you to will and to act according to his good purpose."

Here's what I don't like: Working out. I figure I'm twenty-three and my metabolism is plenty high without anything extra, so why mess with a good thing?

So if I don't know how to work out physically, what on earth does it mean to work out my salvation?

Saturday I wake up to my alarm clock and come very close to tears. My day—one of my only days for sleeping in—is ruined.

All is lost.

Here's what I like: Overdramatizing.

I pludge down the stairs in my pajamas. Dad sits at the table, calmly reading the newspaper.

He looks up. "Morning, Honey. Coffee is in the pot."

"Mmm."

"Lexi called. She and Nate will be over about eleven."

"Mmm."

"And I changed the cartridges in all the wall units. Kids, you know."

I slump into the chair with my coffee. A few years ago, Dad got the brilliant idea of getting plug-in air fresheners and replacing the liquid with a home-based solution of air sanitizer, germ purifier, and a tart, tangy scent I believe is Pine-Sol. I don't want to know. This is the reason people walk into our house and get that weird wrinkle above their noses.

Four cups of coffee later, I'm on the fringe of waking up. Dad looks at the clock over the oven. "Come on, Laurie-girl. We've got an hour and a half to get things ready."

Not sure what we're getting ready. This is Lexi and Laney we're talking about. They only used to live here.

"I'll go fix my hair."

He nods, sipping his lemongrass tea.

Yucky.

As disgusting as lemongrass tea is when you're awake, it's triple gross when you're half-asleep. The aroma wafting to your nose. *Blegh.*

I wonder if I can move my bedroom to the back corner of a Starbucks.

As I blow my hair dry, I try working on my wide-eyed look of amazement. It will come into play:

1. When Laney announces Baby Number 4, christened "Lauren Junior Knox"
2. When Ryan Palmer asks me out in front of Nick on Sunday
3. When Mr. Darcy proposes next week

It is a good thing I am not a spy. I don't possess the gift of fine theater.

Lexi and Nate ring the doorbell at eleven sharp. That's Nate for you. Lexi is like me, as in "Time? What's time?" Nate can be a drill sergeant.

I open the door and immediately get a huge hug from both of them at the same time.

"Whoa!" I yell.

Lexi laughs and pulls back. "Honey, we've missed you." She bends down to rub a ballistic Muffin's ears.

I grin at Nate. "Yeah, yeah. Sure. Lex, when it's my turn for a two-and-a-half-week honeymoon, I guarantee I won't miss you."

Nate grins at me. "Good girl."

Lexi is beautiful. Of the three of us, she got most of the looks. Laney's pretty, but Lexi is gorgeous.

Nate's nice-looking, but it's more in the "Hi, I'm Nate, young and upcoming stockbroker" look. Short brown hair parted precisely. Brown eyes. He's taller than Lexi, but not by much. Dresses like a magazine photographer could show up on the doorstep at any moment.

They walk over to greet Dad, and I'm closing the door when Laney and Adam pull up in their Explorer.

Dorie races up the steps to give me a hug.

I squeeze her tight, smelling her watermelon-scented shampoo. "Hey there, Favorite Niece."

"Hi," she exclaims. "Look, I grewed a whole fourth of an inch. Auntie Lexi!" She spots my sister and runs for her.

Jess and Jack are next inside, one held by Adam and one held by Brandon.

"Hey, Laurie," Adam greets me, kissing my cheek. "You look great."

"Thanks. Where's Laney?"

"Right behind us." Adam sets Jess down, who immediately grabs my leg. "She's primping, or whatever women do."

He rolls his eyes. Adam and Brandon could be clones.

"Hiya." Brandon smiles, releasing Jack, who grabs my other leg.

Standing is becoming an issue.

"Hey, boys." I pat the top of their blond heads awkwardly. Circulation slows in my legs.

Brandon watches them, grinning, and then grabs my arm. "Auntie Lauren! Auntie Lauren!"

Laney walks in. "Okay, you can all play with Lauren later." She chucks each of the three monkeys on the cheek.

Jack and Jess move on to Lexi's legs, and Brandon wraps an arm around my shoulders. "Well, Nutsy, here we are at the first non-wedding-related, official family lunch of the new year." He says this in broadcaster-like tones.

I shake my head at him. "Oh brother."

"Tell me, Lauren Holbrook, how do you feel about this situation?" He shoves an invisible microphone in my face.

"Difficult to say." I give my best impersonation of Elizabeth Bennett. "Will there be dessert involved?"

"Most definitely."

"And coffee?"

"A staple in this household," Brandon assures me.

"Then I feel wonderful."

All the members of the family above the age of seven sit in the living room. I hesitate to use the word *adults* because that wouldn't include Brandon or me. In this family, adulthood is not reached until after matrimony.

I still hold a place of honor at the kids' table.

"So how was the honeymoon?" I ask.

Nate grins boyishly. "Great. Europe was gorgeous, but it paled in comparison to my bride."

Lexi blushes.

My appetite packs up and leaves. Must change subject. "And what about the European guys?" I look at Lexi.

She starts laughing convulsively. "I found you someone, Baby."

"Oh boy." Nate covers his face.

"Tell me, tell me," I beg.

Lexi brushes her hair out of her face. "Okay. So we're in London and we stopped to get something to eat at this little sandwich shop. Hole in the wall, really. And the waiter— "

"I like waiters," I interrupt.

"And the waiter was very good-looking," Lexi says, embellishing with her voice. "I mean, *very* good-looking. Anyway, Nate hadn't gone in with me because he wanted to take a picture of the place, so I decided this was my chance to pick up someone for you, Honey."

Nate sighs.

"I went up to the counter and ordered two sandwiches and opened my wallet and slid your picture out accidentally— "

"Accidentally, my foot," Nate says.

"And I asked him what he thought of you."

"You didn't." Brandon shakes his head.

"Yes, I did," Lexi says proudly. "And he said, 'Yeah, she's pretty cute.'" She says this in a perfect Texan accent.

"Lex, that's not an English accent."

"Baby, I know. This guy had moved to London from Texas. I went all the way to Europe to find you a husband, and all I got was some American guy who can make a mean turkey sandwich."

I exhale dramatically. "I seem doomed to singleness, I guess."

Brandon shoots me a sideways look. "What about Ryan?"

Uh-oh.

Five heads turn and ten eyeballs stare. I shrink against the sofa. I suddenly feel the rare and specific need for the security blanket I had when I was five.

Brandon, meanwhile, grins in total ecstasy.

Here's what I am going to do: Kill Brandon Michael Knox, resurrect him from the dead, and kill him again.

Chapter Thirteen

(Scene: Semi-darkness. The house is lit only in candlelight; the family is gathered around a roaring fire.)

BRANDON: (*with evil intent*) What is this I hear about you and
   Ryan, Laurie?

FAMILY: (*in unison*) Yes! Tell us, O Fair One!

LAUREN: (*an innocent blush upon her cheeks*) Why, whatever do
   you mean?

BRANDON: (*menacing*) I think you know.

*(Suddenly, the front door blows open with the force of one's hand and
   the whistling wind. Snow gathers in the entry)*

FAMILY: (*in unison*) Harken! Who comes at such an hour?

RYAN: (*enters*) I do!

(He goes to Laurie and kneels at her feet)

LAUREN: Do not fret, I can tie my own shoes.

*(As he kneels, he pulls a velvet box from his pocket. A single solitaire set
   in platinum sparkles)*

LAUREN: (*gasps*)

RYAN: Laurie, my love, will you marry me?

LAUREN: Of course, my pet.

(*Rapturous, the couple kisses*)

FAMILY: (*in unison*) What a wondrous day! Declare a national holiday!

Okay, so it isn't the most realistic, but anything would be better than what does happen.

I blush furiously, Brandon grins cockily, Lexi and Laney look like a pair of pleased pigeons, Nate and Adam exchange "hmm" glances, and Dad's poor face crumples.

The clock in the living room chimes eleven thirty, and I have an excuse. I take it.

"Oops, got to go get the barbecue."

I jump to my feet, shoot Brandon a withering look, grab my coat and keys, and hightail it to the car.

Sad fact: I didn't make the track team at school. It was a devastating blow.

Sadder fact: My sisters—one pregnant, I might add—beat me to the car.

"That's okay, guys, I can get it. Go spend time with Dad."

"You know, Baby, half the fun of coming home is seeing you." Lexi climbs in the passenger seat.

"Yeah and Adam is wanting to spend some guy time with Dad. This is a good chance to let them," Laney voices from the backseat.

Mental note: Do not ever try to pull one over on Lexi and Laney. They are too smart for me.

"Fine, fine," I grouse.

I barely have the key in the ignition before Lexi begins.

"So . . ." She draws her voice out.

"So," I copy.

"Who is Ryan?"

"He is a guy," I answer.

"Is he cute?" Laney asks.

"Is he a Christian?" Lexi says.

"Is he nice?

"What's he like?"

"How did you meet him?"

"What color are his eyes?"

"WHOA!" I scream, throwing my hands up.

Lexi sends me a big-sister look. "Baby, keep your hands on the wheel. Well?"

I sigh. A sister is wonderful, and I totally support the concept of one. However, *sisters*, plural, are conniving, scheming, and can only be tolerated by the strong of heart.

Of course, they're also sweet, adorable, generous, and have never done anything remotely mean or cruel to me.

"One question at a time." I must keep a straight face. I must play the game.

"Is he cute?" Lexi asks this.

Tough question. "Yes." I am unsure. "In a way, I guess. He's cute when he smiles."

Laney's turn. "Is he a Christian?"

"Yep."

"Okay, now that the essentials are out of the way," Lexi says. "Tell us how you met him."

"He's Ruby's younger brother."

Laney frowns. "Ruby?"

"The woman I work with."

"Right," she says. "Oh hey, Adam mentioned something about

Brandon hiring a secretary."

"Hannah. I like her—now. I didn't at first."

"Getting back to the point," Lexi interjects. "I didn't mean how did you meet him, I meant *how* did you meet him."

I nod slowly. "Ah. He came to Bible study. He saw me sneaking Oreos. Then he came by to see Ruby the next day and saw me prostrating myself to a photograph."

Laney and Lexi have known me since I was conceived. They don't even blink at this comment.

"So then, uh, I'm not sure what happened." I'm beginning to fumble a bit here. Do I fabricate a romantic story to satisfy my sisters, or do I tell the partial truth and have them think I'm an old fuddy-duddy?

I ponder this, and the car is silent.

"Well, I certainly am not sure what happened," Lexi finally exclaims. "What happened?"

I lick my lips. "Uh, right, we went out to lunch and dinner with a group—uh, me, Brandon, Hannah, Ruby, and Nick—and he was really nice and then he came by the studio again and Ruby and Hannah weren't around and he just uh—"

"Kissed you?" Laney asks excitedly.

"Asked you out?" Lexi says in the same tone.

"Uh, no that was later." I twist uncomfortably in my seat.

"Good grief, Lauren, what did he do?" Laney bursts out.

"We just talked."

"About what?" Lexi demands.

Hannah. "Just stuff."

"And then?" Laney insists.

"I walked him out and he asked if we could go out sometime."

"And you said yes?"

Rather than joyful, I will describe Lexi's voice as a mixture of incredulous and curious.

I shrug. "Well, yeah."

"Why?" she asks, same tone.

"He's nice."

I watch Laney roll her eyes in the rearview mirror. "Lauren, for pity's sake, just tell us how you *really* feel about this guy. I mean, are you sure you're not dating him just to date someone?"

I pull into a parking spot at Smith Valley Barbecue. Turn off the car. Shift to my sisters.

"No." My voice is quiet. "I really like him. He's funny and inventive and sweet. He seems to have a genuine love for Christ that is really attractive. He has this great relationship with Ruby, and sometimes he gets this protective look on his face when he's talking about her. He works in construction, and he's not quite as tall as Brandon, but he's got these huge shoulders. He's got a lot of callouses on his hands from working with them all the time, but they are good hands, you know? And his eyes are actually almost plain, until he smiles, and then they light up like a little kid's."

I let out a breath. I didn't mean to say that much. Sometime between Ryan being sweet and his eyes sparkling, my nerves calmed and I even stopped planning my speech.

Oh land.

Lexi looks at me, smiling. "Oh, Sweetie. I'm so glad. Laney and I have been praying for Ryan for years."

"I beg your pardon?" Nerves jump into hyperdrive.

"We have," Laney says. "Ever since you were about twelve, Lex and I have been praying for your future husband."

"Okay, hold up," I say. "I'm not marrying him! Yet. If at all."

"Don't you love him?" Lexi asks.

I can't even answer for a second. "What?" I finally blurt.

"Of course she does," Laney answers. "Did you just hear that speech? Sounds like love to me. Come on, girls. Junior is hungry and so am I. And that barbecue smell coming in through the doors isn't helping."

Laney and Lexi hop out and walk to the front of the restaurant, chattering happily.

I follow dumbstruck, my mouth permanently glued into an expression of sheer shock.

Love? They think I *love* Ryan Palmer?

I barely know the guy!

I don't know his favorite color or his favorite book or favorite movie.

Heck, I don't even know his middle name!

A massive headache descends from the doorway of the restaurant. I believe it falls from the mistletoe still hanging there.

How tacky. It has now been a month since Christmas.

"Baby, what's the order under?"

"Laurie," I answer dumbly.

"Laurie," Lexi repeats to the twenty-something male who is salivating over her. She calmly taps the counter with her left hand, displaying her very prominent diamond solitaire.

"One minute." He stares at the ring and turns away.

We are back in the car a moment later. I, still in a trancelike state, buckle my seat belt.

"So when do we get to meet him?" Laney asks. They switched seats, and now Laney is in the front.

"I'll make a deal." My wits begin to return. "I'll let you meet Ryan when you tell Dad you're pregnant."

Laney rolls her eyes at me. "Hardy-har-har. It just so happens that we're going to tell him today."

"I'll believe it when I see it."

Lexi leans forward so she can see Laney. "It's true, Cakey. Why do you keep putting it off?"

Laney gives Lexi a frustrated look. "You know Dad. He'll go ballistic. Remember when I was pregnant with the twins? He wouldn't let me move from the time I began showing." She rubs her hands on her stomach. "I just think the longer I prolong it, the better."

"Or the worse," I say. "Dad's feelings might be hurt if you keep putting it off and he finds out all of us know."

"Well, act surprised today, okay?"

Lexi gives me a look, but nods. "Okay, Cake."

Side note: Lexi has a thing about calling people by their real names. She abstains from it like it would give her a rash. Ever since I can remember, I have been Honey, Baby, Sweetie, Butternut, or, my personal favorite, Doll-face. I have a vast array for Lexi to choose from.

Laney, on the other hand, has always been called Cake by Lexi. The birth of the nickname occurred many years ago. The story goes that Laney, then four, wanted to make our mom a cake for her birthday, and since she couldn't read the recipe, she ended up with something resembling Play-Doh, except with chili powder. She's been Cake or Cakey ever since.

We get back to the house with the food, and the boys do a grand job of consuming everything in sight.

"Dad," Laney says after the kitchen is cleaned, "can you come into the living room?"

We troop in.

"Okay." Laney is smiling with that maternal glow. She looks beautiful. Her brown-blonde hair is curling in gentle tendrils around her face, and her gray eyes are sparkling with tears. Adam takes her hand.

"Daddy, I'm pregnant," she says softly.

I have known for about three weeks. And still, I start crying when she says it. So does Lexi, and the tears stop building up in Laney's eyes and are allowed to free-fall. Then Dorie starts crying because her mom is, and Dad gets choked up as he pulls his firstborn into a huge hug.

We are a big, blubbery mess.

Then we start laughing. And we cry again. And laugh again.

They don't leave until about ten thirty, carrying sleepy kids out the door. Laney and Lexi hug me, and Brandon gives me a wink.

I fall into bed that night exhausted and read a short chapter in Ephesians. Rolling to my back, I stare up at the ceiling, looking at the one remaining glow-in-the-dark star I glued up there in second grade.

Tomorrow is Sunday and the first day of February. Morning will come swiftly, then the inevitable scramble, and then Bible study.

Small groups!

I sit straight up in bed. "Oh no!"

Junior high girls. Tuesday nights. Apostleship.

I'm supposed to have studied the first chapter by Monday so I can talk over it with Ruby. All I've done so far is just briefly skim it.

I fall back in bed. Tomorrow's schedule is thus planned out.

Chapter Fourteen

Sunday school begins promptly at nine o'clock on Sunday mornings. I slide into an empty chair on the left side of the room at 8:57, thoroughly worn out. My alarm clock is on the fritz—again—and decided to go off at 4:27.

I'm dressed nicely because I was raised to dress well for church. Dad always, without fail, wears a tie, and since I sit next to him at the worship service, I don't want to look like he took pity on a poor homeless kid. I wear brown corduroys and a white top.

Just as Nick moves toward the front of the class, Ryan drops into the seat beside me.

"Hey," he smiles.

"Wow, you clean up well, Construction Sam," I whisper, since Nick is beginning his "welcome to class" speech.

"Same to you, Patty Photographer."

He does look good. Carpenter-style khakis, a button-down shirt, and heavens! His hair is actually combed!

He winks and turns toward the front.

"Everyone, we're beginning a new book this week. Turn to Romans, please."

Man. Either God really wants me to read Romans, or I am living in a parallel universe.

"Romans 1," Nick continues. "'Paul, a servant,' and we'll stop there for today." He looks up from the Bible, grinning.

Nick teaches for thirty minutes on those three words, and I find myself taking notes furiously. Obviously, this is a book Nick adores like a clown fish would a coral reef.

Here we go again.

"Paul, a servant," Nick finishes. "We need to consistently examine our actions for signs of service. Ladies and gentlemen, we are at a time in our lives when we have the greatest chance to really serve. And as such, we have a responsibility to God for how we use this time. Service to others or service to ourselves?" He closes his Bible. "Let's pray."

Class dismisses, and people begin to gather their Bibles, coats, gloves, and hats. I stay where I am and so does Ryan.

"So." He lounges in his seat. "How was your family lunch yesterday?"

"Good. Laney finally told Dad she's pregnant."

He angles one eyebrow up. "How far along is she?"

"Seven weeks on Wednesday."

He nods. "Laney is the one with twins, right?"

"Wow, Ryan. You're good. What have you been doing, researching?"

He grins. "Well, I figure I should know at least a little about my"—he clears his throat—"future wife."

"I suppose I have no secrets left."

"Nope."

"You're making me look bad, Ryan." I turn slightly so I can see him better. "How do you take your coffee?"

"Black."

I make a face. "Yuck."

"Deal with it."

"What's your middle name?"

"William."

I test it out. "Ryan William Palmer."

"That's the name."

"And it's a good, solid name." I look down at my hands. "Um, Laney and Lexi want to meet you."

"Oh yeah?" He sounds amused. I glance up. His eyes are sparkling with absolute glee.

"You're enjoying this way too much."

He covers the grin with his fist. A huge scab mars three of his knuckles.

"Ryan!" I exclaim, grabbing his hand. "What happened?"

"It's nothing."

"It looks terrible. You need to put some peroxide on that." I touch the scab gently.

"Thank you, Dr. Laurie."

"How did you do this?"

"I was being stupid and careless."

I give him a look. "Well, stop doing that. You're going to make me a widow before I'm even a wife." I set his hand in his lap.

He smiles at me. "Have I mentioned how pretty you look, Miss Holbrook?"

What is this? My cheeks start to burn.

He tips his head at me. "I like your hair like this."

"Curly?"

"Yeah. And long. You should keep your hair long."

I nod. "Will do."

Nick finishes chatting with Engaged Couple Number 3 and walks over to us. "Hey, guys." He looks from me to Ryan with a slight wrinkle between his eyebrows.

"Hi, Nick." This is getting fun.

"Hey." Ryan oh-so-subtly slides his arm around the back of my chair.

Nick's eyebrows rise slightly. "Did I miss something?"

"What are you talking about?" I ask innocently.

He points at both of us. "You two. Are you . . . ?"

"Are we . . . ?" Ryan copies Nick's tone. He is clearly not giving Nick any help at all.

I like this guy more every minute.

"Dating?" Nick finishes.

"What?" I laugh.

"Well, it's just that you guys seem pretty . . . uh, comfortable, with each other."

"Oh, Nick," I protest.

Ryan shifts and looks at me. "That's not a bad idea, though."

I blink at him. "What? Dating?"

"Yeah. Do you want to go out with me?"

I fight every urge to look at Nick. "Seriously?"

"Sure. Why not? I like you. Maybe Wednesday?" Ryan's eyes are twinkling, and a stubborn smirk curls his mouth.

Have I mentioned how cute he is when he smiles?

"Well . . . I guess . . . I guess I can do Wednesday. Before Bible study."

He grins. "That's what I meant. Pick you up at five?"

"Uh, sure. Okay."

During this conversation, Ryan slips his arm off the back of my chair, and it rests around my shoulders casually. I look up at Nick, who has the expression of someone watching canned tuna play ring around the rosy.

"What were you saying, Nick?" I smile.

He blinks and jerks slightly. "Nothing. We should get to the service, folks."

"Right behind you." Ryan watches Nick pick up his Bible and notebook, and leave.

The moment his back is out of sight, I start giggling. "Ryan, that was perfect!" I exclaim, smacking his arm.

"You're not a bad actress yourself, Laurie."

We stand and he picks up my Bible. "Want to go get something to eat after the service and maybe plan out Wednesday night?"

I don't answer at first. Instead, I study him as we push through throngs of people to get to the sanctuary.

Laney and Lexi are here today. They can meet him. Dad can put his mind to rest that I am, in fact, dating a Christian.

Dating?

Are we even technically dating? The whole thing is a ploy.

But, spear me, I like the guy. He's carrying my Bible for me, for Pete's sake!

"Sure," I tell him.

"Great. Think about where you want to go."

"Someplace with dessert. All this scheming is making me want chocolate."

"Ah, then I have the place for you. I hope it's open on Sundays." He picks a row of chairs and lets me enter first. "Here." He passes my Bible. "Be sure and save a seat for your dad."

"And my sisters. And their families." I pull off my coat and scarf and drape them along the row. He watches me, opening his mouth to speak, then closing it. "What?" I demand.

"Nothing. When do the shoes come off so you can save those last two seats?"

"Shut up and give me your coat."

He hands me his beat-up leather jacket that barely passes for a coat.

Lexi sidles up beside me. "Baby, thanks for saving seats."

I read her look even before she opens her mouth. "Lexi, this is Ryan."

Ryan stands immediately and shakes her hand, then Nate's.

"I've heard a lot about you, Ryan." Lexi smiles coyly.

"You work in construction?" Nate says, setting his and Lexi's Bibles on two of the saved seats.

"Yes, I do."

"What are you doing this Saturday?" Nate asks.

Ryan shrugs. "I don't think I have plans."

"Great! Want to help me lay out a new porch?"

"A porch?" I look at Nate, incredulous. "Nate, it's thirty degrees outside. And you want to build a porch?"

"Sure. That way it's done when it's time to sit out there with lemonade."

Ryan laughs. "Sure, I'll help. What time?"

"Say eleven?"

"Laurie, you can come too," Lexi says.

Uh-oh.

Now here's a nice little domestic scene. The men outside pounding a porch together, the women inside making hot chocolate. I can see this one coming.

Nate will give the standard You-Hurt-Her, You'll-Be-Fish-Bait speech in between hammer blows, while Lexi gives the standard Play-Hard-to-Get-or-Wind-Up-with-a-Lousy-Diamond lecture.

Afterward, thoroughly humiliated and ragged, Ryan and Laurie will drive away contemplating both the monastery/nunnery option and the Guess-We-Could-Elope-and-Move-Far-Far-Away alternative.

I open my mouth to give any sort of excuse to keep from being there on Saturday.

"Why don't you come, Laurie?" Ryan says. Only it isn't a command, as Brandon would have done.

"Okay," I hear myself saying. "Saturday."

"This is a big mistake," I protest to Ryan later as he opens his car door for me.

"What are you talking about?"

"Saturday. Building a porch. Making hot chocolate. Speeches."

Ryan looks at me like I've been bowing to Tina Braxton again. "Beg your pardon?"

"I just know we're going to regret this. And where are you taking me, pray tell?"

"The other day I was on lunch break and I drove past this little place. I only had like half an hour, so I went in." His grin broadens. "You're going to love it."

A moment later, he turns on a side street and stops in front of a corner building with a big sign painted on the windows: Merson's.

"Who's Merson?"

He shrugs as he opens the front door for me.

A blast of warm air followed by the knee-weakening scent of freshly baked gingerbread and roasted coffee hits me in the face.

I inhale. "Lead me in, O Favored One."

Tables are arranged sporadically throughout the little restaurant. A long counter stretches along the back side, and—get this—a ceiling-to-floor glass contraption stocked with every kind of dessert imaginable fills the entire back wall.

I could kiss Ryan.

Struck speechless, I stare in open-mouthed wonder at the sight.

"Can I help you?" a tall, skinny guy with a shock of badly high-lighted blond hair asks.

Ryan glances at me and I guess realizes I'm still in shock. "I think we'll need a few minutes," he says.

"Sure. I'll be in the back. Just ring the little dinger here when you're ready." He bangs an old-style gold desk bell a few times as an example.

Meanwhile, I'm in paradise.

I find my voice.

"Chocolate pie, chocolate cake, chocolate pudding . . ."

"Laurie, you skipped the rhubarb pie, banana cream pie, and bread pudding." Ryan points to the case.

I make a face. "Yucky. Blegh. Gross."

I look at the menu suspended above the counter. Search. Find.

"I know what I want."

He grins at me. "You want to do the honors?"

I take great pleasure in slamming the dinger a few times. The guy comes around the corner, rubbing his hands on a dishtowel, his eyebrows raised.

"Dealing with a master, I see." He tucks the towel in his apron. "What can I get you folks?"

Ryan looks at me. I clear my throat. "I would like a slice of your chocolate pecan cheesecake and a cup of very hot coffee."

"Room for cream?"

"Absolutely, if it's just milk."

He nods, smiling. "And for you?"

Ryan purses his lips. "Key lime pie. And coffee, as well."

"Room for cream?"

"No, thank you."

He scribbles down the order on a piece of paper and punches in the numbers on a calculator. "Six dollars and sixty cents."

Ryan pays while I take the tray to a table by the window. "Thanks, Ryan." I sit and pull my coffee over. It's good—better than good.

He pockets his wallet and sits opposite me. "You're welcome. Though I feel like I'm abetting your sugar addiction. This isn't a very healthy lunch."

"I didn't feel like being healthy today anyway."

He hands me a fork. "When have you ever felt like being healthy?"

"Last week. I ordered a salad."

He gasps dramatically.

"Yes, I know. It was a pivotal moment in my life. Especially since I didn't order dessert with it. That is how you balance meals out, you know."

"Actually, I don't know."

I fork off a creamy bite. "See, if I had wanted to be healthy, I would have ordered a salad, then gotten the cheesecake, because since I ate the salad, I would then be able to eat the cheesecake guilt-free." The cake melts in my mouth and I decide where I want to die.

Ryan is still talking. "Have you ever felt guilty about eating dessert?"

I nod. "Only once. I was at Laney's house and there was this big chocolate cake on the counter, so I got a hunk of it and ate it only to find out that Laney was going to take it to her Bible study. I felt guilty then."

He laughs. "I liked meeting your sisters."

"They liked meeting you."

"This pie is excellent. Want some?"

I lick my fork clean and take a little piece. Sour! I smack my lips. "Ack! All the saliva in my mouth has vanished!" Drain the rest of my coffee.

Ryan shakes his head. "You're not dramatic in the least, are you?"

"No, sir. I'm demure." I bat my eyelashes.

"More coffee?" Man-in-Apron asks, pot poised.

I smile up at him. "I like you."

He pours it, laughing.

"What's your name?" I ask.

"Shawn Merson."

I point. "Like the Merson on the door?"

"One and the same. And you are?"

"I'm Laurie. This is Ryan."

He nods politely. "Well, I'm glad you came. Hope to see you around more often."

"Oh, trust me, Honey. You'll see me more often than you'd like to."

He grins and leaves.

Ryan looks at me. "You have the talent for making friends."

"Yes, but keeping them is a different matter."

"Ruby likes you."

"Correction. Ruby *tolerates* me. We haven't reached the liking stage yet."

Ryan angles his head. "I don't know, Laurie. She was ecstatic when she saw us holding hands at the studio."

"Yes, well, I've sometimes worried about Ruby's brain. The lack of sugar can cause serious mental issues, you know."

Ryan shrugs. "She seems pretty coherent to me."

"Appearances can be deceiving."

"Can I taste your cheesecake?"

"Of course."

He takes a chunk from it, avoiding the nuts, I notice. "You don't like pecans?"

"Not at all." He sticks the fork in his mouth, grimaces, and swallows a lot of coffee.

Didn't we just do this?

He gasps. "You like things *really* sweet."

"Thus the reason I've never gotten a cat."

"I meant the food, Laurie." He leans his elbows on the table. "Have you ever had a pet?"

"In second grade I babysat a parrot for a man I met in the grocery store."

"Second grade?" Ryan is incredulous.

"Yes, second grade. What the man didn't tell me was that it was a permanent babysitting job because he moved and left the bird."

He starts laughing. "What'd you do with it?"

"I kept it for a while. But it only knew three words and two of them I wasn't allowed to say. Dad found someone who would take it, and we gave it to them."

Ryan grins. "Did you like having it?"

"What I remember of it, I did. But Dad and Laney cleaned the cage, so my memories probably aren't the full story. Lexi has a dog that we watch on occasion. Dad isn't a big pet person."

We decide we will go to Vizzini's for the Big Wednesday Date.

"Bye, Shawn!" I call as we leave.

He waves at me from behind the counter. "Bye, Laurie. See you later."

Ryan drops me off at my house, and I change into my favorite sweats and open the curriculum.

Lesson 1: Apostleship
Read Romans 1:1-7.

I do it.

I settle into the couch, Bible in my lap, the curriculum spread out on the cushions.

I rub my head. Why did I ever consent to this?

Woe is me.

The first question in the curriculum catches my eye.

"Paul was set apart by God. Do you believe everyone is set apart?"

"Hey, Laurie!"

"In the living room!" I yell.

Brandon saunters in, carrying two extra-large coffees. He hands one to me, smiling. "Hey there, stranger."

"I love you, Brandon, you know that, right?" I take the coffee, pop off the plastic lid, and inhale the scent.

"I know. What're you up to?" He makes himself comfortable on the other sofa.

"Small-group prep for the middle school girls. I need to have it done by tomorrow." I sip my coffee. It isn't quite as good as Merson's, but it isn't bad. I look at him. "Do you believe everyone is set apart by God?"

"Would that be the same question as do you think everyone has a purpose defined by God?"

Purpose. The word sets off a dinger in my brain, taking me back to those verses in Philippians. I think about it. "I guess so," I answer him.

"Yeah, I believe that." He cradles his coffee against his chest with one hand and gestures with the other. "It's the whole sovereignty of God thing we were talking about earlier, Nutsy."

I nod and make a note in the margin of the book, praying we are allowed to mark them up. *Sovereignty of God.*

"So what do you think I'm set apart for?" I chew the end of the pen.

"Coffee. Chocolate. Photography." He shrugs. "Marriage, probably."

"Okay, hold up on that one."

"Junior high girls."

"I'm not getting married."

"Romantic comedies."

"Furthermore, I think you know that—"

"Taking care of your dad." He pauses. "And I heard from Ruby who heard from Nick that you and Ryan are going out on Wednesday."

"Yeah, well." I rub my forehead, trying to come up with a good reply.

Okay, never mind.

"So what's your defined purpose?" I ask.

"Photography. Management. Baseball games."

"Taunting, ridiculing, and bringing coffee to poor, lack-of-caffeine-stricken young women."

"And Arnold Schwarzenegger movies."

I wrinkle my nose. "He talks like he's got a mouthful of rock candy."

"I thought you liked accents."

"Pretty ones. Australian, for example."

He stands and pats my head.

I bark.

Rolling his eyes, he walks toward the front door. "Get to work!"

I sit with my pen, lips pressed together. Set apart. It's a cool concept, really. God works everything, including my life, to the purpose of His will.

I smile and start writing.

Chapter Fifteen

Ryan holds the door for me as I climb into the passenger seat of his truck. It's Wednesday night, and we've just finished eating at Vizzini's.

"What's the best way for me to get to Nick's house from here?" he asks, climbing behind the wheel.

I point, which is useless because we're still in the parking lot. "Take the first left and the next right."

"Left?"

"Right."

Here's what I will not grow up to become: A driving instructor.

Ryan promptly takes the first right.

I look at him. "What are you doing?"

"You said right."

"I said left."

"No, I said left and then you said right."

"I was affirming the left."

"The left doesn't need affirmation, just confirmation," Ryan grouses, making a U-turn.

"Is that a declaration?"

"Laurie!"

I hold my hands up surrender-style. "I'll be quiet."

We pull onto Nick's dimly lit, mass-murderer-hiding street and park behind a forest green SUV that belongs to the male half of Engaged Couple Number 6, nowhere near the street light and about forty blocks from Nick's front door.

Just goes to show what Ryan knows.

Ryan opens my door. I grab my Bible and his arm and hustle him up the cul-de-sac to the front of Nick's house.

"What's the hurry?"

"Fearsome creatures lurk in these parts."

"Here?" Ryan looks around. "This looks like a nice area of town. Needs better lighting."

"Shh." I hold my finger to my lips. "You have to scurry inside or they'll come out and eat you."

"Lead on, Gretel."

I open the front door and meet the deafening roar that generally accompanies the gathering of twenty or more singles in a very small house.

And, by my quick calculations, more have joined our midst, because I don't recognize a third of them.

The couch is overflowing with bodies, the chairs are all occupied, and the floor is filling fast.

"Grab a piece of carpet quick," Ryan yells in my ear.

"Roger."

"Actually, it's *Ryan*."

I squish on the floor beside a blonde beauty wearing jeans, a white turtleneck, and a powder blue fleecy vest.

"Hey, Laurie," Hannah greets. Her smile widens. "Ryan."

Ryan plops to the floor, banging his elbow hard against my shoulder.

"Ow," I protest.

He grimaces, rubbing his elbow. "Sorry. Hey, Hannah, how are you?"

"A bit crowded."

"Uh-huh."

A long pair of khaki-clad legs bumps into my knees. "Sorry 'bout that," a collegian-looking guy says.

I smile rather than try to reply.

"Where are all these people from?" Ryan asks.

"Who knows? Former felons, repentant hookers, clean drug dealers." I shrug. "There are a lot of options."

"Hey, isn't that Tina Braxton?" Hannah asks, pointing past three pairs of jeans and one skirt.

I can recognize The Queen anywhere. "Yep."

"Where's her gent?" Hannah scans the crowd.

I crane my neck but can't see past anyone's waist. "I don't know; wait until Nick makes them all sit down."

Above the roar, a loud voice shouts. "All right! Everyone find a seat!"

Everyone begins the desperate search for a place to plant their heinies.

A Guy in a Blue Shirt falls backward. Sadly, a much smaller Girl in a Red Shirt is behind him. Providentially, the staircase is behind her, so they don't fall very far.

Blue Shirt picks himself up by grabbing the banister and turns to help Red Shirt.

"Sorry, I'm so sorry," I see him mouth. He probably spoke out loud, but from my position it is hard to tell.

"That's okay," she says, blushing.

Well, what do you know.

Blue Shirt pauses and helps her gather her Bible and then situates himself on the staircase right beside her, talking incessantly. Red Shirt is nodding, smiling, blushing, and nodding.

What exactly, pray tell, are they going to relate to their kids one day?

"No, actually, dear, I met your father when he knocked me flat at an overcrowded Bible study for singles, where we then became Engaged Couple Number 12."

Gee, how romantic.

Whatever happened to the good ol' Knight in Shining Armor encounter? Distressed Damsel gets saved by Shining Knight? None of this Damsel in Distress gets sacked by Shining Knight.

It's enough to make you want to stay single.

The stairs fill faster than a tuna barge in the middle of trout season. The floor becomes the next victim, and by the time everyone has found a resting spot, I'm convinced it is going to be our final one.

Ryan and Hannah are basically on top of me, a guy's knees are wedged between my spinal vertebrae, I inhale a mouthful of the girl's hair in front of me every time I take a breath, and all feeling in both of my feet ebbs into the deep recesses of Nick's carpet.

Singles' class is not the place for claustrophobics.

Stephen Weatherby, Cool, Collected, and Calm, despite the ensuing crisis of forty-nine people losing feeling in their limbs, sits in the one lone chair in the front. The chair does not have a reserved sign on it. However, no one touches it, and this is why: Lone chairs in the front of the class are predestined for musicians, and everyone who has ever been within fifty feet of a singles' class knows this.

Stephen lays his guitar over his right knee and balances it with his forearm. "Great to see all of you here tonight. Let's begin with a word of prayer."

Nick usually says the opening prayer, but looking around, I don't see him anywhere.

Stephen prays a short, honest prayer and rubs his pick down the strings.

Four songs later, Nick appears from the kitchen. His hair is combed, his clothes are pressed, his Bible is in its rightful place under his arm.

But his eyes are bloodshot, red-rimmed, and splintery.

I close my own eyes in pain.

Where is Ruby?

"Open your Bibles with me to the beginning of 1 Corinthians 14, please," he says, clearing his throat. The rustling and *tha-whopping* of sheets of paper follows. Nick coughs into his elbow, blinks repeatedly, and starts reading. "'Follow the way of love and eagerly desire spiritual gifts, especially the gift of prophecy. For anyone who speaks in a tongue does not speak to men but to God. Indeed, no one understands him; he utters mysteries with his spirit. But everyone who prophesies speaks to men for their strengthening, encouragement and comfort.'"

He settles his Bible in the crook of his arm and looks up at all of us. "I see three things in this passage I would really like to expound on. First, that in our pursuit of love . . ." He pauses, a thought-frown settling between his eyebrows. "Be it a brotherly love as talked about in 1 John or a romantic love as spoken of in Ecclesiastes 9:9, that this pursuit should be characterized by strengthening each other in our walks, encouraging each other to godliness, and comforting each other with the truth found in the Word."

Nick teaches for thirty minutes, not looking much better at the end than at the beginning. As he calls for announcements, I almost feel the need to explain to the visiting masses that Nick does not typically look like he's been on a drinking binge in the garage before coming in to preach.

The moment the closing "amen" is said, everyone erupts from their seats like a school of fish in front of a shark. Everyone, that is, except Ryan and Hannah, who stay right where they are, pinning me down.

"I liked that lesson," Hannah says, swiping at her hair until it falls behind her ears in perfect waves.

I nod quickly, pointing to the kitchen. "It was good. How about a snack?"

"I liked the singing too. Must have a choir visiting." Ryan stretches, but doesn't move.

"You know, I sensed chocolate when we came in." I'm grasping now for any excuse to get them to move. "Let's get up and find it."

"Come to think of it, the singing was better this week," Hannah muses.

Ryan nods. "Told ya, it's a choir."

"Maybe," Hannah says slowly. "Maybe everyone's just more talented than we are."

"GET OFF!" I scream, jumping to my feet and pushing them to the floor.

To quote one of my favorite children's poems:

Oh! Somewhere in this favored land the sun is shining bright;
    The band is playing somewhere, and somewhere hearts are light.
    And somewhere men are laughing, and somewhere children shout;
    But there is no sound in Singledom—Loud Lauren has snuffed it out.

I may have doctored that just a little. My apologies to "Casey at the Bat."

The screaming is a bad idea for two reasons: First, because all forty-nine people shut up suddenly and stare directly at me; and second, because the feeling in my legs is still lost somewhere in Nick's carpet and I promptly collapse right on top of Ryan.

I right myself and smile sheepishly. "Sorry, claustrophobic."

No one laughs.

The talking and mingling gradually make it back to their original volume. I cover my face.

Ryan pats my shoulder, whether to comfort me or to disguise his laughter, I can't tell. Then he gives me a shove and I tumble off his lap.

Hannah grins at me unrepentantly. "You do know how to make an impression, don't you, Lauren Holbrook?"

I fall into bed later and tug the covers up around my waist as I lean against the pillows, Bible on my lap. How do I consistently do stupid things? You'd think that at some point the Clumsy Actions Vault inside my head would run empty and I'd mature into a twenty-three-year-old young woman rather than staying a twenty-three-year-old kid forever. *God, how come I can't be more graceful?*

I flip the pages to where I left off in Ephesians 4, take one look at the verses, and immediately start laughing. Hard.

My door opens suddenly. "Honey?" Dad asks, worry filtering through his eyes. He looks around, noticing the TV is off and I'm sitting on my bed with my Bible. The worry blossoms in his expression. "What are you doing?"

"Just my devotions, Dad." I temper the giggles and smile reassuringly. "Sorry to wake you up."

"You didn't. I was going past your room to get a cup of tea." He gives me a long look and slowly backs out. "Good night, Sweetheart."

"Night, Dad."

I look back at the Bible. "Be completely humble and gentle . . . until we all reach unity in the faith and in the knowledge of the Son of God and become mature . . . then we will no longer be infants . . . we will in all things grow up into him who is the Head, that is, Christ."

Whoever said the Bible is not relevant for today or that God no longer speaks is insane.

Ruby meets me at the door on Thursday morning. "Hey, Laurie." Her eyes brim with . . . laughter?

She heard about my Grand Exhibition. "Who told you?"

"Hannah."

"Figures." I drop my backpack into my assigned cubbyhole. "Where were you?"

"My Aunt Barbara is getting married again on Sunday. I didn't have anything to wear, so I went shopping." She makes a face.

I look at her. "Were you successful?"

"No. What are you supposed to wear to your aunt's sixth wedding?"

"I don't have any aunts."

"Consider yourself blessed." She shakes her head. "Not really. Aunts are great—when they're not getting married six times. And making me buy yet another dress."

"You still should have come last night. I could quote verses on materialism."

Ruby sighs. I dig a Milky Way out of one of my hiding places and start nibbling on it. Ruby watches, frowning. "Didn't you just have breakfast?" she asks.

"Yeah, but I'm still hungry."

"Well, what did you have?"

"Coco-Odies."

She looks from the candy bar to my waist and lets out an exhale that sounds more like a growl. "How do you stay so thin?"

"High metabolism. And you're avoiding the subject."

Hannah comes out of Studio Two holding a talking Pooh bear. "Can I have this?" She cuddles it close.

"No," I say to Hannah. "We missed you last night, though I doubt you would have found a place to sit," I tell Ruby.

"Please? I love Pooh."

"I told you, Laurie, I needed a dress."

"He's so cute and squishy and cuddly," Hannah coos.

"Yeah, but you could have shopped on Saturday."

"But I decided to shop last night."

"And he has that squishy voice. So adorable!"

"And found nothing!" I aim my finger at Ruby. "You're avoiding Nick!"

"I am not!"

"Remember that time when he went to go look for the land of milk and honey?"

"You are too! You're scared that he'll reject you to your face."

"That is not true!"

"It was my favorite episode of all."

"Just give him a chance, Ruby!"

"He was doomed to failure."

Ruby and I stop and look at Hannah. "What?" we ask in unison.

She tears sad, beautiful blue eyes away from the yellow bear. "The land of milk and honey. He was doomed to fail there."

"Who was?" Ruby asks slowly.

"Joshua?" I say.

"Winnie-the-Pooh!" Hannah frowns. "Who's Joshua?"

"Like in the Bible." I watch the blank expression in her eyes and shake my head. "Never mind."

"So can I have this?" Hannah presses her face against Pooh's.

Ruby watches her, her face creasing in growing disgust. "You don't even want to know what a little kid did to that the other day."

Hannah's expression changes immediately. "I'm done." She goes back into the studio.

Ruby looks at me, her arms crossed across her chest. "Listen, Laurie, I appreciate the concern, I honestly do. But there's nothing there for you to be concerned about." She waves her hand in the air.

The bell over the door rings right as I open my mouth. She glances up. "That's my nine o'clock," she says to me and then walks over to greet the clients, smiling.

I open the door to Bud's at ten after noon. Mikey lifts his head from wiping down a table and grins.

"Hey, Laurie."

"Hiya, Mikey."

"Give me a sec to finish."

"One."

"Funny."

He sprays the table with the solution in the bottle hanging from his belt loop, then rubs over the surface with a cloth.

"Okay." He dumps the cloth by the register. "Can I try to predict the order?"

I nod. "Go ahead."

"Two cheeseburgers, two onion rings, and two milkshakes?"

I bite my lip. "Uh, I think you meant one cheeseburger, one order of French fries, and a Dr. Pepper."

"Yeah, that's what I meant." He grins at me. "Three dollars and seventy-six cents. Minus the tip."

"Of course. Here's three bucks . . . seventy-four, seventy-five, seventy-six cents." I tuck my wallet back in my backpack. "Look both ways before crossing the street."

"I'll try to remember that." He bags the order and hands it to me. "Have a good day, Laurie."

I polish off the burger during the walk back to the studio, go past Hannah's desk, where she and Ruby are having an animated discussion over carrot sticks, and open Brandon's door.

"Hi, Han," I greet him.

"Hi, Leia. Thanks for the knock."

"You're welcome. Want some fries?" I shake the bag in his face.

He leans back in his chair, spinning a pen between his fingers. "Sure." He smiles.

I take a seat on his desk and pass him the bag. "Whatcha working on?"

"Well, right now I'm working on finances, which should be somewhere under your left ankle."

I nod and sip my drink. Gag. "Ugh." I gasp, hacking. "Mikey must've mixed the lines again. This is definitely root beer."

Blegh.

Root beer ranks up there with lemongrass tea. Even the name is nasty. Root beer. Yuck. Sounds like someone hollowed out a tree branch, pureed what he found, bottled it, and made a killing.

"Can I have it?" Brandon asks.

I napkin off my tongue. "Be my guest." I sputter on the paper shreds sticking in my mouth.

Brandon watches me, his expression curling into a blend of disgust and curiosity. "You are gross." He takes a long drink and sets it purposefully on the desk. "I'm glad you stopped in, actually, because there is something I wanted to tell you."

I wrinkle my nose. "Is it good?"

He sighs. "Does everything have to be good?"

"Yes. Yes, it does. Otherwise it would be bad." I look at him pitifully. "I don't need bad news today. I'm afflicted in spirit."

He rolls his eyes. "Sure you are. And anyway, just because news isn't good doesn't necessarily mean it's bad. It could be neutral."

"Since when is anything you say neutral?"

He covers his face. "Okay, okay. You win." Holds out a hand. "Mark the back side of your house with another tally."

"I will." I shake his hand in a peace gesture.

"Good grief, Laurie."

"So what's your news?" I scoot closer on the desk.

"Watch it, Nutsy, you're crunching the forms."

He leans further back, has a swig of the Gross Stuff, and smiles at me. "I just had a phone call from Laney."

My mouth drops. "Oh my gosh! Oh my gosh, her ultrasound! It's today!" I grab for Brandon's desk phone.

He stops me. "She's not home anymore. She's taking Dorie to dance."

Affliction of soul forgotten, I hop to my knees and grab Brandon by the collar. "What did she say? What?"

"Well, there was good news." He says this slowly and deliberately.

I grab him more tautly. "What?"

He grins at my impatience. "First, get off the desk, Laurie, you're making a mess."

I jump off the desk, and my hip lands with a harrowing *smack!* against the stupid potted plant he keeps there so the office will have a homey feel. I fall to the floor and bounce back to my feet.

Brandon, now standing, gapes.

"What did she say? What did she say?" I beg.

"Didn't that hurt? Aren't you mad? Won't I get another lecture about plants and the outdoors?" Brandon steps over, eyes big.

"Yes, yes, yes. Later, though. After my bruise has had time to darken and grow in size. Now, Laney!"

I again have him by the collar. His mouth curls in his hiding-a-smile smirk.

"Like I said, there's good news." Again said slowly.

"What? What?"

He pauses for a long minute. "They're almost positive that it is indeed human."

He bursts out laughing. I tighten my grip. "Brandon Michael Knox!"

He puts his hands around mine, which are attached to the gills of his shirt, if there is such a thing.

"Okay, okay, sorry. There was news," he says, leisurely.

"Brandon!"

"And, much as I would love to tell you, Laney made me promise I wouldn't."

"What!"

He rips my hands away from his shirt collar. "So sorry, Honey, I'm worthless to you."

"Not entirely. There is still the matter of paychecks." I pace his office. "You know the news."

He nods, grinning like Ricky Ricardo after Lucy broke the news that she was pregnant with Little Ricky. I used to think Ricky's smile was so cute. Now I know.

It's annoying.

I keep pacing.

I poke my finger at his chin. "And you won't tell me?"

"I swore."

"Swore what?"

He holds up his fingers like a boy scout. "I would protect her secret 'to the pain.'"

"Laney's words?"

"Yes."

"Aha!" I stop, finger in air, triumphant. "*The Princess Bride*. Laney never quotes that scene unless it's a really big secret."

He shakes his head, pushing his hands into his pockets arrogantly. "Sorry, kid. You're out of luck. Now, get out so I can get some work done."

"Hey!" I brighten. "What if I offered to buy you a cheesecake?"

"Out, Laurie." He pushes me toward the door.

I scramble. "With strawberry topping. And whipped cream."

"Out."

"And one of those little mint leaves?"

He opens the door and not-so-gently shoves me into the hallway. "Now you're reaching."

"Brandon?" I say quietly.

He pauses shutting the door. "Yes, Laurie?"

I stick my bottom lip out and make Bambi eyes. "My hip hurts."

Slam!

I turn and sulk down the hallway dejectedly toward the two Peeping Thomasinas.

"Wow." Hannah is blinking. "That must have been something."

"Yeah," Ruby says. They both sigh sadly.

"We missed it," Hannah says to Ruby.

"We're idiots, Hannah. We should just assume that any time Laurie walks into that office and closes the door, and there are raised voices heard inside, something of interest is going on."

I fall into the chair beside Ruby. "Ha ha."

"What happened?" Hannah takes the last carrot stick and then tosses the plastic baggie in the trash can.

"Oh, Laney called and told Brandon something exciting and he won't tell me and I'm never speaking to him again." I lift the edge of my shirt.

"Ouch!" Ruby's eyes narrow at the blackening mark on my body.

"Yeah. I hope Baby Number Four appreciates what I'm going through for her."

"Or him," Hannah ventures.

I shake my head vehemently. "No, it's a her. Has to be. Laney and I already worked out the details."

Ruby tugs on her hair. "Did you let God know?"

"Yes."

"Well, Sweetheart, I hate to tell you this, but it's going to be a boy." Ruby grins at me, her eyes softening, and I see the unspoken message that we're on good terms. She pushes her heels off and crosses her legs at the ankles. "Know something?" She looks at her feet. "My mother always told me that a lady keeps her legs crossed at all times and it's nonnegotiable when she's wearing a skirt. And then I had a photograph session with Dr. Metgars, and *she* told me that crossing your legs leads to varicose veins."

Hannah finishes clearing her lunch. "So it's either be a lady and have stripy legs or be a slut and have pretty legs?"

"Not necessarily. See, that's what I thought at first too. And then

I discovered this." She turns forward in her seat, sits up straight, knees together, and slips her left leg behind her right one.

Trouble is, her right knee locks into place and her left leg is already way past the healthy target range for crossed legs.

Ruby screams as she topples to the floor.

"Oh my gosh!" Hannah laughs.

I lean over to help Ruby untangle her skirt from her collar button.

"So the third choice is to be a bruised stripper?" I ask.

Ruby smacks the back of my head, grinning. "Be a lady and keep your mouth shut."

Chapter Sixteen

I make a slight detour on the way home. Park on the street, walk up the three steps to the front door, and find the blue ceramic frog, christened Bill, in one of the flowerpots.

I pull the key from Bill's innards and unlock the door.

"Hey!" I shout into the quiet house.

"Auntie Lauren!" Three little kids yell from somewhere in the direction of the kitchen.

"Hey, Hon, we're eating!"

I walk into the kitchen holding Bill. Everyone is sitting around the table eating spaghetti. Both of the boys have morphed into meatballs, I assume, because sauce covers them from the hair down.

"Hiya." I kneel beside Laney's chair.

She smiles at Adam and looks at me. "What's up, Lauren?"

I give her a look. "You know exactly what's up."

Dorie finishes swallowing, hops out of her chair, and grabs me around the neck, planting a big wet one on my face.

"Hey, Favorite Niece." I hug her back. "How are you?"

"Guess what? Guess what!"

"What?" I touch her button nose.

"Mommy's having twins!" Dorie exclaims.

I sit right there on the kitchen floor.

Laney bursts into laughter and tears as she looks at me.

"Really?" I'm quiet, my mouth widening in a smile, my eyes starting to tingle from the incoming blubber-fest. *Tear ducts, ready!*

"Really," Laney whispers. *Tear ducts, fire!*

I push myself to my knees and give her a hug around her middle, pressing my face into her stomach. "Hi, babies." I kiss them through Laney.

Laney brushes her fingers through my hair. "I like your hair like this, Lauren."

"Thank you." I sit back, clear my throat, and resume business. "Boys or girls?"

"It's still a little early to tell."

I look at Adam. "Five kids."

He fakes a long sigh and looks at his kids gravely. "I know. And see, I always thought we were a maximum four-kid family."

I look seriously around the table. "Guess you'll have to get rid of one of them."

Jess's mouth drops open, spaghetti lolling around inside. "But, Daddy," he sniffs, getting teary. "Can't we stay wif you, please?"

"Yeah," Jack says. "I will make my bed now."

Adam leans next to my ear. "I could get some chores out of these kids for the next eight months."

"You're a cruel man, Adam Knox."

"Runs in the family."

I roll my eyes. "Don't I know it. Look what your brother did to me today."

I show them my bruise.

"Ouch," Laney says. "Get some ice on that, Lauren, it's swelling."

"I'm going to when I get home."

She raises her eyebrows.

Uh-oh. Dad.

I wince. "Then again, maybe not. Man. I want a minifridge/freezer for my birthday, okay, Laney?"

"I'll remember that. Get some ice, Honey."

I stand. "Okay, well I'm going to go. Call Dad so that he knows about the babies when I get home."

"Already did, Laur. I called everyone except you because you were at lunch and I couldn't remember your cell number."

I open the freezer, fill a plastic bag with ice, and write my number on her to-do list. "There you go."

"See you later!" Laney calls.

Dad is waiting when I get home. "Did you hear, Laurie-girl?" He clutches the phone and grins as I throw my backpack in the general direction of the stairs.

"About Laney?" I ask.

"Twins!"

"It's great." I smile sentimentally.

Dad lifts his eyebrows. "I hope she takes care of herself. Remember how sick she was with the boys?"

I go to the kitchen, frowning. "She wasn't sick, Dad."

"Yes, she was. She threw up every time she ate."

"Morning sickness. She was done with that in like two weeks."

"And then she didn't move from the living room chair."

"You wouldn't let her, Dad."

"Of course I wouldn't! She didn't need to be moving." His eyes brighten. "You know, I was just reading an article about childbirth in my magazine. Wait right here."

He disappears from the kitchen. I stir the chili that slowly simmers on the stove. *Medical Mysteries and Common Occurrences.* Not only is the title entirely too long, but the magazine also twists every decent doctor's words into a vicious cocktail of horror, shock, disillusionment, and sheer stupidity of medical staffs.

Dad returns holding it, the glossy cover displaying the picture of a young woman holding a baby the size of her thumbnail.

He pulls one of the kitchen chairs out, sits, and flips through it. "Here it is. 'Pregnancy and Problems: The Bobbsey Twins of the Twenty-First Century.'"

Oh brother.

"'In a culture that idolizes medical knowledge, training, and proper healthcare, there is a terrifying new culprit toward the obstetric ward—the cold shoulder. In the doctors' quest for answers to diseases that plague adults around the country, newborns often get the smallest straw of the medical staff.'"

Dad looks up, his eyes wide.

I stir the chili.

"'Deborah Kyle of Kentucky states that her experience with the obstetrics was nothing less than horrible: "No one believed I was in labor. I gave birth to Kylie two minutes later in the waiting room." Kylie died later from lung failure due to the nurse not properly clearing out her airway after birth.'" Dad covers his mouth with his hand. "Oh my."

After sipping the chili, I add more chili powder. "Look, Dad, who knows where they find these people. That's probably not even a true story. I mean, who really names their child Kylie Kyle?"

He points to the magazine. "But it's written right here."

"People write things that aren't true."

"What decent person would do that?"

"Exactly."

We sit to chili a few minutes later. "Less than a month until our trip, Laurie-girl. Are you excited?"

I nod, mouth full. "Yes. One whole month of nothing but relaxation, seafood, scenery, and no human beings around save for my wonderful father."

Dad waits until I put a big spoonful of chili in my mouth. "There will be more people around."

I start hacking. "I beg your pardon?" I ask.

"We're staying in a cabin, Honey. Along the shoreline with a bunch of other cabins."

"Oh." I wipe chili from my chin. "Well. I can deal with that. I'll just avoid them."

Dad frowns disapprovingly. "You don't want to be rude, Laurie."

"I won't be rude. Just the silent stranger." I toss my hair over my shoulder. "I'll be *mysterious*. Guys like that, I've heard."

Dad puts his spoon down. "Laurie-girl, I wish you wouldn't talk that way. You promised you'll never marry."

"A promise I intend to keep, Dad."

"What if someone comes along and asks you to marry him?" Dad frets.

"Well, I'll say no."

He blinks. "You can do that?"

"What?"

"You can say no to a man proposing?"

"Of course I can."

He picks up his spoon again, satisfied. "And all these years I thought your mother married me because women weren't allowed to tell a suitor no."

━━◈━━

Friday morning Construction Sam walks into The Brandon Knox Photography Studio two minutes after I do.

"Well, hi there." I drowsily tug my gloves off. It is thirty-two degrees and overcast outside. I hate mornings like this. Mornings that are cold, gray, and soggy are supposed to happen on the weekend or on a day off. That way, you can sit in your favorite chair with a vanilla coffee and a good book. With a roaring fire in the background. And your dog's head resting on your feet.

Sigh.

It is going to be a long day. I'm going to have to work hard to keep last night's verses in the forefront of my brain today. "Be very careful, then, how you live— not as unwise but as wise, making the most of every opportunity."

Ryan smiles and hands me a large coffee he's hiding behind his back. "Thought you might need this today."

I grin. "How did you know?"

He looks at me pointedly. "You're Laurie."

I take the coffee and give him a one-armed hug. "I think I'll keep you around." Coffee in one hand, I can easily make the most of every opportunity.

His arm wraps around my waist. "That's the plan, right?"

I sip the coffee. "You even put sugar in." A sappy, sticky feeling blooms in my chest.

"And milk." He points to the coffee.

"You gave me coffee with milk and sugar in it."

He looks at his boots. "Uh, yeah."

I notice something. "Hey! Where's your coffee?"

"I drank it on the way over."

"So you're not staying?"

"There's a thing called work, Laurie."

"You know, I've heard of it."

He glances around at the dark studio. "You the only one here?"

"Well, unless Ty and Newton have evolved into night vision goggles, then yep, I guess so." I sip and smile at him. "This is really good coffee, Ryan. You put just the right amount of condiments in."

He raises his eyebrows. "Condiments?"

"Yes. Sugar, milk, and ketchup."

Ryan laughs. "I came over here for a reason."

"You didn't just come to see me?" I stick my bottom lip out.

"Sadly, no."

"And bring me legal addictive stimulants?" I wave my coffee in his face.

"Most definitely no."

"What's up?"

His brown eyes sparkle in the adorable little-kid smirk. "Do you want to go get dinner tomorrow night?"

"Sure."

He grins. "Really?"

"No, wait a minute. Let me think." Long swig from the coffee. "I don't know, Ryan. I mean, when was the last time you had your driver's license revoked?"

He frowns in thought. "Four months ago?"

"For?"

"Yeah, four."

"No, I meant, why did you have it revoked?"

"Drug possession, intoxicating a minor, knocking off a bank."

"Oh, you're a funny boy."

He leans against Hannah's desk. "Can you still come?"

"I don't know. My dad might get mad."

He tips his head. "Wasn't that a line in a song? Like a Christmas song, maybe?"

I lean beside him. "I'll come."

He smiles at me. "I'm glad." Then he reaches over and pats my shoulder. Awkwardly. Like he is petting a crocodile at one of those farms. I've done it. I know what it looks like.

I start laughing. "What was that?"

"What?"

I pat his shoulder. "I'm so sorry that your pet cat died, Ryan."

He turns toward me. "What do you want me to do?"

"I don't know. But we can't keep this façade up if you *pat* my shoulder after you ask me out." I pat his shoulder again for emphasis.

"Sorry, I'm new at this whole fake-dating thing."

"Well, me too, but I still know enough that you don't *pat* someone's shoulder after asking her out!"

"Will you get off the patting?"

"Is oo a cute wittle puppy?"

"Laurie!" He twists away from my hand. "Good grief, woman, I'd better get a reward for this."

"I'm sure you will get several jewels in your heavenly crown."

He exhales quite loudly and dramatically.

Long pause as he looks at me. "Can I hug you?"

"Honey, you brought me coffee this morning. Do you have to ask?"

I set my coffee on the desk and he gives me a hug.

It is actually a nice hug—no patting involved.

Be still my heart!

"Much better," I smile after we pull away.

He winks and turns. "Have a good day at work, Laurie."

"Bye, Fido."

"Ha ha ha." He holds the door for Hannah on his way out.

She walks in with eyebrows raised. "Soooo," she draws the word out. "I see we had a little early morning rendezvous with *Mister* Ryan Palmer."

I glare.

She looks behind me on the desk. "With coffee, I see." Pulls her coat off while I search the available air for words.

"He was in the neighborhood."

Ouch. Never, never in my dullest dreams have I ever resorted to an excuse so lame. I shall curse this moment forever.

Hannah stares at me like I just said fish sticks come from fish.

"Laurie, please," she says, groaning. "That's a Mr. Rogers comment."

"Okay, bad. I know. I have cursed this moment."

She sits behind her desk and clutches her hands together in anticipation. "So? Tell me! Tell me! Tell me!"

"What? What? What?"

"What happened?"

I try playing dumb. "When?"

"Just now, idiot."

"He brought me coffee."

"How sweet!"

"Yeah." I smile, sappy as ever. Drill a hole in my side, syrup is coming.

Hannah steeples her fingers on the desk while I sit in one of the chairs. "Any particular reason? I noticed there is none for Ruby, Ty, Newton, Brandon, or me."

"Well, he is a poor construction worker." I take a long sip in front of her face, just to slightly rub it in. "Maybe he could only afford two cups of coffee."

"And dinner?"

Nosy, that Hannah.

I haughtily ignore her. "I believe I have a nine o'clock appointment today."

"You're avoiding the subject!" Hannah sticks a finger in my face.

Ruby walks in, shaking her curls and shivering. "It's snowing, girls."

I groan.

"I thought you loved snow," Hannah says.

"I do. From my house. With a fire roaring in the background and hot chocolate in my hands and my favorite book open in front of me and a blanket in my lap."

Ruby giggles. "And your dog's head on your feet."

"Hey, that's it exactly!"

"You've got coffee." She gestures to the cup.

"Guess where it came from," Hannah sing-songs.

Ruby pulls her scarf off and looks closely at the cup. "Looks like . . . Merson's? What's Merson's?"

"Little restaurant. Good coffee. Nice owner."

"From Ryyyyy-an," Hannah finishes her song.

Ruby blinks. "Ryan brought you coffee?"

"Yeah, well, he just dropped by to uh . . . yeah. Anyway, my nine o'clock appointment is late, I guess, but that's good because I need to set up the studio." I'm making a run for it.

"Ryan brought you coffee," Ruby repeats.

I stop halfway to Studio One. "Yes," I reiterate.

Ruby smiles, nostalgic. "He brought you coffee. You know what that means, right, Laurie?"

"He knows I'm a deplorable addict?"

"My baby brother likes you." Ruby lets out her breath slowly, smiling again.

"Uh, right. Well, like I said, got to go." I bolt for the studio and close the door behind me.

Whew.

I turn on the computer, sure Ryan planned the whole bringing me coffee thing to completely embarrass me in front of his sister.

I have got to learn how to play it more cool.

Chapter Seventeen

The bell over the door jangles just as Hannah and I finally sit down to lunch at two.

I look over, ticked off that someone would dare interrupt my affair with the turkey sandwich. Healthy? Yes. At the moment I don't care what it is as long as it's edible. I'm starving.

Turkey sandwich forgotten. Nick stands fidgeting just inside the door.

"Hiya, Nick." I wave.

Nick smiles, the corners of his mouth twitching. *Nerves*. Whatever he has come here to do will take guts — of this I'm sure.

"Hi, Laurie," he stutters. "Hannah."

"Hey," Hannah calls out in a friendly voice. "Got an appointment?"

"No, no. Uh, actually, I was wondering . . ." He stops, looks down at his shoes, looks back up at us, at his hands, the carpet, us, the ceiling, the back wall, us.

"Nick?" I interrupt before his poor neck passes out from exhaustion and his head falls off.

"Yeah. Right." He lets out a long breath. "Is Ruby here?"

"Yep," Hannah answers. "She's in with a client, though, in Studio

Two. Should be done pretty quick. Want to wait?"

He doesn't say anything for a long minute before finally walking forward and collapsing into the chair beside me. "Sure, I'll wait."

I watch his foot bounce up and down, up and down, up and down before finally leveling a good swift kick to his ankle.

"Ouch," he exclaims, probably more surprised than hurt.

"Sit still," I command, lifting my One True Love to my mouth. My stomach growls in protest.

Two o'clock is too late for lunch.

"Laurie." Nick says this suddenly, right as the soft, honey-smelling bread brushes my lips.

My stomach downright yells.

I set the sandwich back on the paper towel, clenching my back teeth together. Turn and look at Nick. "Yes?"

"This will sound crazy," he blurts. "But I need to practice on something other than my mirror."

"Whoa." Hannah waves a hand. She finishes chewing.

My stomach says: *"Look, Hannah's eating and talking. Can you not do the same?"*

I say: *"No, I am not talented in that way."*

"Practice what on Laurie?" Hannah continues, chewing dispensed with.

My stomach gestures toward her in a perturbed manner.

"My speech," Nick says.

"To whom?" I pat my stomach sympathetically.

"Ruby," Nick says.

Hannah raises her hand. "Does it include kissing? Because Laurie's already taken."

Nick chortles. Whether in laughter or in shock, I know not.

My stomach doesn't find that scenario very pleasant either.

"No, uh, kissing." Nick gasps, reaching for his shirt collar.

"Are you sure you don't want to just wait for Ruby?" My eyes are pleading. Practicing a speech such as the one I figure is coming on a person other than the one for whom it is intended is never a good idea. Look what always happens in the movies. If only the hero abstained practicing on his childhood best friend, the heroine would never get upset and never move to Baltimore to fall in love with a different guy, the hero would never have to chase her down and stop her halfway through the wedding, and the movie would be a good hour or more shorter.

"Practice makes perfect," Nick quotes.

"Not always," I tell him. "One time when I was eight, I won this sticky hand at a carnival and I wanted to try to hit Brandon in the back of the head with it, so I practiced and practiced and practiced, and when I finally got good enough, the hand wasn't sticky anymore, so it didn't work."

Hannah laughs and whirls around in her desk chair, her shoulders shaking.

Nick stares at me. "Okay. But this is just a speech."

"Listen to me, Nick. Do you really want Ruby to move to Baltimore and be walking down the aisle toward a different guy and you have to run after her?"

He blinks. "What?"

"Just answer the question."

"Uh . . . I . . . no, no, of course not."

"Good. Then don't practice the speech. Go in there fresh as the morning dew and win her heart."

A wrinkle appears between his eyes. "How'd you know I was going to ask her out?"

I look over at Hannah, who still has her back toward us. Her shoulders jerk suddenly and her hands go toward her face.

I put my hand on Nick's shoulder. "Nicky, I just knew, all right? So. Straighten up. Breathe in. Make the most of the opportunity. March in there with a smile. And find out if June 15 works for her, whether she wants it indoors or out, and what her colors are. Hannah and I can take care of the rest."

He frowns. "See if what works in June?"

"Just ask her, okay?"

My hands close around my sweet sandwich and once again lift it to my lips. I bite into it, moaning in sheer pleasure.

Nick watches me with a strange look on his face. Opens his mouth as if he is going to say something, then closes it.

The door to Studio Two swings open. "Thanks for coming," we hear Ruby call out.

"See ya," a nice-looking man and a pretty woman call back.

I kick his leg again. "Go, Nick. Now."

He takes a deep breath, lets it out quickly, jumps up, half-trips to the studio door, and knocks once on the doorjamb.

"Did you need something else . . . ?" Ruby's voice trails off. "Nick."

"Hi. Can I talk to you?" His voice sounds fairly calm, but his left hand is trembling behind his back.

Aw. My pastor is cute in love.

"Sure," we hear her say after a moment's pause.

Nick walks in and promptly shuts the door.

I glance at Hannah, who grins back at me. In one accord, we race around the desk and plant our ears against the door.

". . . wanted to apologize for the past week." Nick's voice is muffled.

"For what?"

"The past week."

Hannah covers her mouth, her eyes sparking dangerously.

"I mean, apologize for what during the past week?" Ruby asks.

"My standoffishness. I was confused." He exhales harshly.

She pauses. "Confused about what?"

"Us."

"Oh." Ruby's voice is much different now.

"Do you think we could . . . that is, would you consider . . . uh, do you think sometime we might be able to . . . go get something to eat . . . um, together?" Nick clears his throat.

I press my head harder against the rough wood grain. Ruby copies Nick and clears her throat as well. "Yeah. That would be nice, actually."

"Really?" Nick says quickly.

I can hear Ruby's smile. "Yes. Really."

"Wow." Nick breathes. "I mean, thanks, Ruby. I . . ."

Suddenly everything goes quiet.

Hannah peeks at me, mouthing, "What do we do now?"

I shrug. I can feel the grain of the wood impressing a nice design on my ear. It will never be the same. Neither will my back. Kneeling in this position is not something I do every day.

I hear Ruby gasp. "What was that?" She's breathing hard.

My chin hits my knee. "He kissed her!" I mouth excitedly.

Nick is out of breath too. "I'm sorry, I'm sorry. I shouldn't have . . . oh boy. Ruby, I didn't mean to . . ."

Again, silence.

"Good grief." Hannah hisses this in my ear.

I don't really know what happens next. One minute we are crouched against the door, the next we both spill onto the concrete floor of the studio.

"Ow!" Hannah howls.

I just moan. Look up to see Ruby's Told-You-So expression.

"Hi." I sit up and rub my head, which implanted itself into the cement.

"Hello, girls." Ruby raises her eyebrows.

Even with her schoolteacher tone, I notice the two bright pink spots on her cheeks and the extreme sparkle in her eyes.

I grin unrepentantly. "Sorry."

"You are not," Ruby says.

Nick stares at me. I smile at him. "Well, sounds like it went well. We'll just, uh, finish lunch. So, have a nice chat, you two."

I scoot out of the room, dragging Hannah with me, and shut the door.

Hannah starts laughing the minute the door closes. "Oh, Laurie! It happened! It finally happened!"

"I know!"

We hug each other in a congratulatory celebration.

"Girls!" Ruby yells from inside the studio.

"I think Bud's is calling." I scramble to my feet.

"Right behind you." We grab our coats and are out the door before Ruby gets the studio door open.

We run down the sidewalk to Bud's, whip the door open, and collapse into the first open table we find.

Mikey watches us, frowning. "Just pull a bank job, Laurie?"

"Better than that," I grin.

"Knock off a casino?"

Hannah giggles. Mikey turns red.

"Hey, you haven't met Hannah. Mikey, Hannah. Mikey is Bud's son and my secret pal."

Mikey shakes Hannah's hand. "Nice to meet you."

"You too, Mikey."

"So, what did you do?" he asks me.

"Ruby is kissing Nick in Studio Two." I laugh in pure excitement. My blood is doing cartwheels through my veins and I feel *alive*.

I am born to be a matchmaker!

Mikey gasps. "*Ruby?*"

"Ruby," I affirm.

"Ruby Palmer." He is unbelieving.

"One and the same."

"Holy cow," he says, leaning against the counter. "Wow, Laurie. I mean, I always figured the first one of the four of y'all to start kissing someone in the studio would be you."

"Hey!"

"That's not an insult, Laurie," he soothes. "Wow. Ruby Palmer."

"Kissing Nick." I grin, giddy.

"Who is Nick?"

"He's our singles' pastor," Hannah answers.

Now I'm ecstatic for two reasons: Ruby kissed Nick, and Hannah just called Nick "our" pastor.

Miracles happen every day.

"He's the guy in the ugly sedan," Mikey says, using his hands to put two and two together.

I nod. "Yeah, that's him."

"He needs a new car."

"Well, no one's perfect."

Mikey points out the window. "Hey, isn't that—"

Uh-oh. Big Trouble.

"Brandon!"

"He's back?" Hannah swings around to look out. "Oh man. Laurie, what are we going to do?"

I don't answer. Just burst through the door and hightail it to Brandon's car.

He opens his door, staring at me warily. "What happened? What's flooded or on fire or broken?"

I'm out of breath. "Nothing, nothing. Nothing."

"Then why are you rushing out of Bud's?"

"Exercise." I huff. "It was my New Year's resolution."

"You don't make resolutions." Now Brandon is beginning to jog toward his beloved studio. I follow like a little lost dog with my tail cut short and my ears cut long. "And you don't exercise!"

"Look, Brandon, honestly, nothing is wrong. Everything is right. Really right!" I grab his arm to make him stop.

He pulls me along with him. "The camera broke, didn't it?"

"Nothing broke. Stop, Brandon!" I command.

He freezes.

I take a deep breath and step in front of him. The story comes flowing out. "Nick came in this morning to talk to Ruby and they went into the studio and closed the door and he said he was sorry and she said that's okay and then he kissed her—"

Brandon holds up his hands, silencing me. "Whoa. Ruby kissed Nick?" He is incredulous.

"No, actually, Nick kissed Ruby."

"I thought you said they closed the door."

I look at him.

"Wait, who am I talking to? Never mind." His mouth stays open. "Nick kissed her?"

I nod.

"What did Ruby do?"

"I don't know. Right about there is when she opened the door."

Brandon rolls his eyes. "And found you. And if I'm guessing correctly, also Hannah."

"Sadly, yes."

"And they are still in there?"

I nod again.

He lets his breath out slowly. "Wow."

"That's the word of the moment."

"I mean, really. Wow!" His expression suddenly changes and he stares at me long and hard, eyes narrowed and cold. "Lauren Holbrook."

"Brandon Knox."

"You didn't . . . I don't see how it's possible . . . you didn't *make* them fall in love, did you?"

I let my mouth drop open in shock. "Me? How could I even think of toying with something like love?"

"You did it."

"Mmm, I think God did it." I pause, considering my next words. "I may have sort of arranged a few things."

"Oh man, oh man, oh man."

"It's my destiny." I slit my eyes at him, deepen my voice. "Who am I?" I put a hand to my chest. "I'm Cupidwoman!" I poke my finger in his chest. "And plus, I believe you helped, Mr. Acting-So-Innocent."

He finally smiles. Knuckles my head. "Crazy, you are."

"Yeah, well, to each his own. Want a burger?"

"Sure, I'm starved." He wraps an arm around my shoulders and walks me back to Bud's. "I guess you've completely corrupted Hannah by now."

"Well, corruption is in the eye of the beholder."

"That's beauty, Nutsy. Beauty is in the eye of the beholder."

Hannah stands guiltily as we open the door. "Hey, Brandon."

He gives her a look over and then smiles. "You're forgiven."

She sighs. "Thanks."

Mikey takes his rightful place behind the register. "Can I guess? Three hamburgers, one order of French fries, two onion rings, and three milkshakes?" Okay, turkey sandwich definitely forgotten. I'll take a burger and a milkshake over lunchmeat any day.

Brandon nods. "Sure."

Mikey rings the order up. "On the house. Best excitement I've had all day."

We go back to the studio at three. A horrible thing, appointments are. I open the door, shushing the bell, tiptoe in, and wave Hannah and Brandon in behind me.

Studio Two's door is open.

How can I resist that? I peep inside.

Ruby and Nick sit side-by-side on two folding chairs, talking quietly. He holds one of her hands in both of his, slowly rubbing his thumb over her knuckles.

I motion to Hannah, who peeks in as well, turns, and makes doe eyes at me. Then she tiptoes back to her desk, yanking me with her, and whispers, "Aw" in my ear.

"I think we've got company," Ruby says loudly.

"Oh boo for you!" I yell back.

"Do not mess with these ears, Lauren Holbrook." They appear in the doorway a moment later. Ruby smiles at me. "I know you have the Hendersons at three."

"Forget the Hendersons." I grin cheekily. "What's happening with you?"

"Not nosy at all, are we?" Nick is looking at Ruby like she is a ruby.

Hmm. Bad wordplay. He looks at her as if she is the most beautiful thing he's ever seen.

Aw.

Hannah creeps up beside me and nudges my shoulder. I nod slightly.

There's nothing like two people in love to make you feel (A) happy, lovey-dovey, and dreamy or (B) positively lonely.

"Want to get dinner tonight?" I whisper to her.

"Please," she says with a nod.

"I don't have any more appointments, so I'm going to take off." Ruby gets her purse and coat.

It takes every ounce of self-control for Brandon to keep a straight face and wish them a nice afternoon. I know, because I watch his fingers tighten into fists and his knee bounce.

Wesley and Buttercup leave the building.

Hannah and I leave promptly at six.

"Where are you taking me again?" She climbs into my car.

"Merson's. Desserts, coffee, cute little tables."

"Drive on."

We are through the door a few minutes later. Shawn Merson looks up from the counter and grins.

"Hi, Laurie. I saw Ryan this morning."

"Shawn, this is my good friend Hannah." I blink. *Huh.* I think I just said Aloha Barbie was my good friend.

It's funny how quickly things change.

He shakes her hand, smiling. "Take your pick of the tables."

The restaurant isn't crowded. We choose a table in the back corner near the desserts.

An order pad appears in my peripheral vision. "Know what you want?"

I smile at Shawn. "A dinner salad with ranch and a slice of chocolate cake, please. And coffee."

He looks at my blonde companion. "And for you?"

"Sounds good. I'll have the same." Hannah's ogling the Retirement Center for Desserts.

Shawn doesn't even write it down. He grabs the coffee and comes back, filling the mugs on the table. "You two are way too easy."

"Well, you could drizzle caramel sauce over my cake," I say.

"Ooh!" Hannah shrieks. "Yeah! And sprinkle pecans on top."

Shawn rubs his chin where an end-of-the-day blond fuzz is hatching—an entirely aged habit for one so young. "That actually sounds good. I might have to add a new dessert to the menu."

"The Lauren-Hannah?" I suggest.

He shakes his head. "Too long a name. How about turtle cake?"

"Inspired by Laurie and Hannah?" I smile sweetly.

He grins. "You got it."

Shawn leaves and Hannah leans her elbows on the table. "So, Ruby and Nick."

"Soon to be Engaged Couple Number 13," I say with a sigh.

I may be happier than a clam at high tide, and I may have arranged the match myself, but when you're twenty-three years old and you watch every available single person in the entire singles' Bible study get snatched up before your eyes . . .

Well, it gives a new dimension to chocolate cake.

Hannah is sympathetic.

I fiddle with the salt shaker. "Ever wonder what it's like, Hannah?"

"What?"

"Being one-half of a couple."

Hannah lifts her head, surprised. "Don't you know? Aren't you and Ryan a couple?"

It is on the tip of my tongue to blurt out the whole thing and be done with it.

However, there are several things to consider:

1. Ryan would probably like to know if I were going to blow our cover.
2. It's been kind of fun.
3. He brought me coffee this morning!

"Well," I fumble. "I mean, a *serious* couple. Like Nick and Ruby. Or Holly and Luke. Or Nate and Lexi. Or—"

"Tina and Kyle?" Hannah grins.

"Honestly, Hannah. Tell me the truth. Would you really like to spend the rest of your life with a guy like Kyle?"

"You mean sweet, very good-looking, charming, and successful?"

"Uh, yeah."

Shawn sets two plates of moist, heavenly smelling cake on the table in front of our salivating faces. The salad becomes an afterthought.

He steps back and wipes his hands on the dishtowel over his shoulder. "All right, then, ladies, can I get you anything else?"

I can't tear my gaze away from the gorgeous cake. "Shawn, I'm having a thought."

"What's that?"

"Psalm 34. Verse 8. 'Taste and see that the Lord is good.'"

Hannah starts laughing. Shawn gives a little "heh" and leaves.

Hannah levels a look at me over her cake and resumes our previous conversation. "Let's just say if a guy like Kyle asked me to marry him, I would more than consider it. You wouldn't?"

I stick my fork in the cake. "Heck, no."

"And why not?"

"The boy is perfect! I couldn't live with someone who was perfect! I need at least a few flaws to balance my own."

"Really?" She grins evilly. "So what are Ryan's flaws?"

"He's conniving."

Hannah starts laughing. "*Ryan?* Little Ryan? Conniving?"

"Sure. Appearances are deceiving, Hannah."

"Well, he can't be very conniving compared to you."

"Very funny. I don't know, Hannah. I mean, I barely know the guy." I pray for us both and take a bite of my cake. *Mmmm.* "I want to die here."

Hannah smirks. "Eat enough of this and you might."

Chapter Eighteen

The doorbell rings at exactly ten o'clock on Saturday morning, just as I'm pouring coffee into the jumbo-sized thermos. It's a cold, cloudy, gray day, and once again I'm not able to stay home and enjoy it.

Dad looks up from his paper. "Finish getting your coffee, Honey. I'll get the door."

I hear the door squeak. "Hello, Ryan."

"Hi, Mr. Holbrook. How are you doing?"

"Oh fine, fine. Come on in. Laurie's in the kitchen."

"She's out of bed?"

"I heard that!" I yell.

Ryan comes into the kitchen smiling. "Lexi run out of coffee?" He notes the size of the thermos.

I yawn, covering my mouth with my arm. "You can't be too careful."

I've only been up for about thirty minutes, skipping the hair regimen in favor of peaceful slumber. Thus the reason my hair looks like I got out of the shower and brushed it with a wire whisk. I'm wearing my favorite pair of jeans—they're super-soft and faded perfectly from countless washings—a red long-sleeved T-shirt, and my sneakers.

I give Ryan a once-over. He wears jeans, a blue T-shirt under a long-sleeved plaid flannel shirt, and hiking boots, and his brown hair curls in reckless abandon all over his head. Obviously, Ryan skipped the hair regimen as well.

At least we match.

He's grinning at me, and I decide he's laughing at my hair. "Ready?" he asks.

"Yep. Let me grab my coat."

He picks up the thermos for me. "Nice to see you again, Mr. Holbrook."

I hug Dad around his neck. "Bye, Dad."

"Have a good time." Dad walks us to the door. "Wear your coats and tell Lexi hi for me."

"Will do. Love you."

He squeezes my shoulder. "Love you too, Laurie-girl."

We step into the frigid morning air, and Dad closes the door after us.

"Brr!" I say, shivering. "I want the thermos. And where is your coat?"

"In the truck. Didn't you get the memo? Coats aren't cool anymore."

He opens the door for me. "Oh well," I say. "I was never cool to begin with."

He climbs in behind the wheel and looks at me. "I hesitate to ask this, but how do I get to Lexi's?"

"Turn right, go down the road for about two blocks, turn left, and you're there."

Ryan starts the truck. "We could've walked."

"And risk frostbite? I think not." I crank the heater up.

"Here." He hands me a take-out coffee cup from Merson's. "This should tide you over for two blocks."

I take it, touched. "That's so sweet, Ryan."

He shrugs, but his cheeks redden.

"I think I like you." I wrap my hands around the cup, inhaling the steamy, strong scent.

He doesn't look at me. "It's mutual, kid."

We rumble down the street, and I direct him to the cute little ranch house. He pulls into the driveway.

He turns off the engine and looks at the house. "So this is Nate and Lexi's home."

I sip the coffee, nodding. "Isn't it adorable? Hey, word of the wise. Don't look in any of the cupboards. And keep an eye out for Muffin, their sadistic dog."

"Ankle biter?"

"Worse. Terrier."

He winces. "Got it." He comes around and opens my door, taking the thermos. We hurry up the porch steps. "Hey." He stops me before I ring the doorbell.

"Yeah?"

The little-kid smile appears. "Thanks for coming with me, Laurie."

"Thanks for the coffee, Ryan."

I ring the doorbell. Lexi answers it so fast, I know she was waiting by the door. "Hey, guys." She looks beautiful. It's not fair. I know she's been up for maybe ten minutes. Lexi doesn't have any makeup on, and her hair hasn't been brushed, but she could walk off the cover of *People*. Her gray eyes are sleepy-looking, but sparkling.

I squash the jealousy. "Hiya, Lex."

"Lexi." Ryan smiles and pushes me inside.

She returns the smile. "Nate's out back already. You're a sweetheart for doing this, Ryan. What's in the thermos?"

"Laurie's lifeblood."

She starts laughing. "I like you, Ryan."

"Where's the back door?"

She points the way. He squeezes my shoulder and then leaves. Lexi turns raised eyebrows in my direction.

"So cute in the early morning too," she whispers.

"Thank you." I sip the coffee.

She rolls her eyes. "Want some coffeecake?"

I perk up. "Homemade?"

"Of course."

"Did you have to ask?"

She wraps an arm around my shoulders as we walk to the kitchen. "I thought while the boys were out back we could maybe look at some decorator magazines and figure out my color scheme."

I nod, watching her cut a hefty slice of coffeecake.

Lexi makes the best coffeecake. It's actually Laney's original recipe, but Lexi adds nutmeg to the mix. Totally different zing to it. This is where I get my culinary talents—from watching my big sisters make a hundred different cooking mistakes and then not copying them.

I sit at the kitchen table, wave to Nate and Ryan through the window, and eat a big hunk of the cake while they watch.

Ryan makes a face at me.

Lexi sits beside me with her coffee. "So how's it going with the two of you?"

I frown, chewing. "The two of who?"

"You and Ryan."

"Oh. Fine."

"Fine? Honey, people who have been married for ten years are *fine*. You're young, unmarried, and in love. Find a different adjective."

I drink my coffee, thinking. "Swell?"

She chokes. "Never mind. Real romantics, you and Ryan."

"You know me." I take a forkful of cake. "Lexi?"

"What's up, Baby?"

I pause, figuring out my question. "How did you know Nate was the right guy? I mean, like, how did you know he's who God had for you?" My words are faltering because I'm unsure of what I'm asking. I know how I knew Nate was right for Lexi. I not only introduced them, I kept pushing them toward marriage.

Lexi sets her coffee down and lets out a deep breath. "Wow. You're one for early morning surface conversations, you know?" She crinkles her forehead, looks out the window, and watches Nate heft one-half of a board over his shoulder. Ryan grabs the other side.

"Well, I don't really know, I guess." She waves her hands around. "I just remember one day waking up and thinking, 'I'm going to marry Nate.'" She shrugs and picks up her coffee again. "There wasn't a sign in the sky or anything. I just had a peace when I would pray about our future together."

"Helpful, Lex."

"I'll try to do better next time, Sweetie. Ready for swatches?"

We spend the next two hours arguing over whether the living room should be cranberry and beige or cranberry and sandstone. We're sitting on her sofa, legs tucked up underneath us. I have a huge mug of Lexi's cinnamon coffee in my hands, and there's a roaring fire in her fireplace.

It's nice and cozy. I look over at Lexi as she yammers on about how much she likes cranberry and beige together. Her hair is falling over her shoulders, and she's using her hands animatedly as she talks, pointing to an interior design catalog.

I love my sister.

"I'm starved!" Nate yells as he opens the door, letting in a blast of cold air that makes the fire shudder.

Ryan comes in behind him, shutting the door. The fire breathes a sigh of relief.

Lexi hardly glances up from her magazine. "You have got to be kidding. It's barely noon."

"Hey, we're doing hard construction work outside," Nate protests. He comes around the sofa, wraps his arms around a shrieking Lexi, and kisses her neck repeatedly.

"Get off me!" she screams, arms flailing. "You're sweaty!"

I hope she isn't too attached to the cranberry/beige option, because the color card disappears into the couch cushions.

Ryan bends over, resting his arms on the couch, and taps my shoulder. "See, this is marriage." He says this quietly into my ear.

I giggle.

Lexi pushes Nate off with her legs and huffs loudly. "All right, all right. Lunch will be ready in ten minutes." She grabs Nate's hand and pulls herself off the couch. "Come on, Mr. Muscles, you can help."

Nate flexes for her, Lexi dissolves into laughter. "Into the kitchen," she commands.

Ryan watches them go, then comes around the sofa and settles into Lexi's vacated spot. "What are you looking at?"

I sip my coffee. "Color swatches for this room." I hold up my color choice. "What do you think? Cranberry on that wall and sandstone on the other three."

He glances at the walls. "Uh, yeah."

"You don't care in the least, do you?"

"Do you like it?"

"Yes."

He leans back, nodding. "Then I like it too." He eyes my coffee enviously.

I pass the mug to him. "How's the porch building going?"

He sips, grimaces at the sweetness, balances the cup on his knee, and rakes a hand through his curly hair. "It's going okay."

"Aha." I cross my arms smugly. "You got the fish bait speech."

"Come again?"

"You know. 'You hurt her, you'll be fish bait.'"

He grins. "Yep. Except in my case it was ground beef. What about you? Gotten a speech about me yet?"

"Honey, we've been too busy arguing over sandstone or beige."

"I'm not even going to comment on that one." He drains the cup.

"I guess I'm done with the coffee."

"Guess so. Laurie, I haven't known you too long, but I've known you long enough. You've got enough coffee in the kitchen to feed the Israelites escaping from Egypt."

I nod toward the mug. "You realize that had milk and sugar in it."

"I was thirsty."

I watch him for a minute. "You think I'm going to get a ground beef speech about you?" I ask incredulously.

"No, I think yours has something to do with diamonds."

Now I'm impressed. I tell him so.

"Well, I do have an older sister, Laur."

"Did you ever give a ground beef speech?"

"No. Ruby's a few years older. By the time I realized that boyfriends were bad, she'd moved out." He flicks my arm. "What about you?"

"I didn't resort to speech so much as action."

"Do I want to know?"

"Ask Lexi. She can tell you the harrowing tales of having a baby sister."

"Lunchtime!" Lexi yells from the kitchen.

Ryan pulls me off the couch and I lead the way.

Lexi gestures to the island counter. "Informal, yes, but filling."

"Works for me." Ryan's salivating over the rolls, deli meat, and cheeses.

Nate slaps Ryan on the back. "You know, girls, Ryan and I make a pretty good team. We'll have to do this again."

Ryan gives me a sidelong wink. "Sure. What about next weekend?"

"Really?" Nate pounces. "Great! Next week we can make porch chairs."

Ryan cuts open a roll. "I don't know that the porch will get finished today, Nate."

"Two weekends from now?"

Ryan laughs. "Okay, sure."

"Nate!" Lexi scolds. "The poor boy is never going to have any free time."

"What?" Nate protests. "He can hang with me, we can build stuff, and then he gets to come inside and stare at two of the prettiest girls this side of Mississippi." He smacks Ryan's back again. "I never knew how much I missed having a brother. Or even a dad that got into building stuff."

Lexi shakes her head. "Sorry, Ryan. I think you've just been adopted."

"Hey, I think it's great too. I never had a brother either."

Smack!

Ryan's shoulder blade has to be getting sore from Nate's constant pounding.

Nate grins wider. "See, Lex?"

Whap!

I decide to step in for the sake of Ryan's back. Who knows? Ten years from now, after all this hitting, he may not be able to play horsey with his little daughter.

I move behind Ryan, holding my plate.

"Oh, go ahead in front of me, Laurie." He motions to the sandwiches.

"No, no. You're the one who's been working all day."

"Yep, that's right!" Nate gets ready to smack Ryan again and then realizes I stand there. He pats my shoulder.

Ryan's foot nudges mine in a silent "thank you."

We sit at the table, Nate says a prayer, and then we dive in.

"So, Lexi," Ryan says. "First, this is great. Second, I hear that you've got some stories about Laurie torturing your boyfriends?"

Lexi finishes swallowing and bursts into laughter. "Ryan, those stories are better saved for after your honeymoon."

"Why?"

"Because you might change your mind after hearing how cruel she can get."

"Hey!" I yell.

Lexi looks at me. "Well, he might."

Nate nods. "I had to wait until I was married, Laurie. So does Ryan."

I give Ryan a Bambi look. "Don't believe them, dear. I was a perfect angel."

"Uh-huh."

"I was!" I protest. "How can you think otherwise?"

"A certain image of you prostrating yourself to a picture in your studio comes to mind."

Nate coughs.

"Other than that," I tell Ryan.

He tips his head. "How about Oreos?"

"Okay, I'm done pleading innocence." I get a bag of potato chips from Lexi's pantry.

"So, Lex, do you want porch chairs or a chaise lounge?" Nate asks.

"Maybe I should be asking which Ryan would prefer."

Ryan shrugs. "No difference in difficulty, just design."

Lexi peers out the window. "Can I request a table as well?"

"Sure," Nate says. Ryan covers his mouth, his eyes twinkling.

"Okay," she says finally. "A table, four chairs, two chaise lounges. Please."

I pat Ryan's arm. "Hey, this is familiar." He glowers at me. I grin. "Nice knowing you, buddy."

"Too much?" Lexi asks, her face crumpling.

"No, no, not at all," Ryan jumps in. "Just don't expect it by Monday or anything."

"But by summer?"

He nods.

We leave at four. Ryan opens the truck door for me, promising Nate he'll be back next Saturday. Lexi and I decide to paint then.

"Beige!" she yells as I climb into the truck.

"Sandstone!"

Ryan starts the truck, waves, and pulls out of the driveway.

"Sore?" I ask him.

"Mmm . . . a little."

I glance at the clock on the dashboard. "It's still early for dinner. Want to come watch a movie?"

"Sure. Wait a minute. What movie?"

"You and Brandon. Sheesh. No faith at all."

He shoots me a glance. "I heard at least fifteen separate references to fifteen different chick flicks made by you and Lexi during lunch today."

"And wouldn't you like to have known what we were talking about?"

"No. I'm content to just stare cluelessly like Nate."

I laugh. "Thanks for helping him like that. It meant a lot to him."

"Anytime, Laurie."

"Sounds like that's what you promised."

He steers into my driveway. I hop out and unlock the front door. "Dad?" I call.

No answer.

I check the garage; his car is gone. Going back into the kitchen, I rinse out the coffeepot.

"Want some?" I ask Ryan, who comes in through the hallway.

"Uh, sure. You're going to live a short life, Laurie." He is shaking his head.

"Ah, but a good life."

I push the button and the machine starts whirring. "Chocolate?" I offer.

He sighs. "Look, Laur, I'd really like you to be around in thirty years. Don't eat the chocolate, please?"

There is the little-kid-on-the-playground smile.

I exhale dramatically. "Just five M&Ms?"

"Three."

"Four?"

"Deal."

I get the bag, grouchy. "You're trying to change me."

"Not change, exactly. Just prolong you."

I scowl. "What movie did we decide on? *Ever After*?"

"Heh heh." He opens the video closet. "Wow. You have a lot

of movies."

"It's a dollar and fifteen cents to rent one, if you like."

"Funny, Laurie. Hey! *The Dream Team*. I haven't seen this in ages." He pulls out the DVD. "Let's watch this."

I know how to negotiate. "I don't know, Ryan," I say slowly.

"Five M&Ms?"

I shake his hand. "You got it."

I push the DVD in and grab the remote, settling on the right side of the sofa, tucking my feet underneath me. Ryan takes the left side.

"How poetic," I mutter as the movie starts.

"What?"

"Our first movie together is *The Dream Team*. Fitting, considering our ploy, don't you think?"

He shakes the couch he laughs so hard.

I walk into The Brandon Knox Photography Studio Monday morning, brushing snowflakes from my hair and grinning broadly at Hannah, who is sitting at her desk, yawning.

"Good morning, Hannah," I sing, half-tossing, half-shoving my backpack into my cubby. "Isn't it gorgeous outside?"

"Mmph."

"Hey," I say, leaning over to peer into her face. "Today is a happy day. No mumbled answers allowed."

"And why, pray tell, is this a happy day?" She starts guzzling coffee from a very boring stainless-steel thermos.

"Nick and Ruby are together!" I spread out my hands and do a little dance. "It's a wonderful day!"

The bell over the door rings. Ruby walks in.

Maybe *walk* is too strong a word. Perhaps *shuffle* is a better verb for how she enters. Her hair is fixed, her makeup is on, her clothes are ironed, but she just looks . . . slumped over. Like four of those bags of brown sugar Matthew bought Marilla in *Anne of Green Gables* are slung over her shoulders.

I stop the happy dance and give Hannah a concerned look before turning back to Ruby, who is staring out the window.

"Um, Ruby?" I ask.

She jerks and turns, like she didn't know Hannah and I were here. "Oh," she says in a dull voice. "Sorry. I didn't see you. Morning."

This may be bad to ask, but I'm going to ask anyway. "Why'd you miss church yesterday? And how's Nick?"

Her bottom lip immediately relocates to between her teeth. She gives a little shrug and shakes her head.

"Did something happen?" Hannah asks from behind me.

Ruby falls into one of the chairs in front of Hannah's desk, covering her face. "We went to dinner. Twice."

There is no excitement, no sense of happiness in her voice.

I'm starting to feel panicked worry slicing between the tendons in my fingers. I sit beside her, my foot bouncing. "You didn't enjoy it?"

"Dinner?" Ruby questions, lifting her head. "Dinner was fine. I had a salad the first night. Chicken Caesar. The dressing was too anchovy, but it was fine. And I had barbecue the second night. With a side of cole slaw and some biscuits."

"No, Ruby, no, I meant the company, not the food." It is never a good sign when a girl talking about her date starts with a rundown of the meals.

Long sigh from her. "Oh."

Hannah's eyebrows are Velcroed together, a frown on her pretty face. It's her turn to send me a worried look.

I look back at Ruby, who is staring at Studio Two's door with an intensity I've never seen in someone staring at a plain wood door. I follow her gaze, just to see if I'm missing something.

Nope. Door is still plain, light-colored wood.

"Ruby?" I ask.

"They were the most awkward dinners of my life!" she bursts, raking her hands through her hair. "Every conversation felt stilted and just . . . just *weird*. By the end of the second date, I was wondering what on earth we had in common other than both of us being human!" She stands, hands twisting over, under, around each other. "I have to do something. I'm getting the studio ready."

She leaves, going into Studio Three. Hannah opens her mouth to speak, but the door closes behind Ruby.

"She's not supposed to be in that studio today," Hannah tells me.

I let my breath out. "This is not a good development, Hannah. They're perfect for each other. I know that, you know that."

"Maybe they aren't, Laur. I mean, you just heard Ruby."

I give her a look. "Hannah. Have you not been paying any attention these last few weeks? There's obviously a definite like there. He kissed her, for Pete's sake!"

"Seems kind of hopeless," Hannah says dolefully.

"Okay." I brush my hands together businesslike. "We need a plan of action."

She stares at me blankly. "A plan of action?"

"For Nick and Ruby."

"What are you talking about?"

I stand and pull a notebook from my backpack. "You are a novice at this, aren't you?"

I open to the first page in the book and uncap a pen from

Hannah's desk.

"First, we must put them on outings that make them see the deeper person sooner."

"Such as?"

"Oh, you know. White-water rafting, serving in homeless shelters, mountain climbing, or lawn projects."

Hannah frowns. "I can't see Ruby rafting or climbing a mountain."

"Hey, I couldn't see Ruby smiling, and look at her now. I'll research what's around here during my lunch break."

I write: *Deeper dates=Deeper relationship.*

"Next, we must push them to settle quickly. Mostly Nick at this point. He needs to recognize that Ruby is the perfect one for him."

Hannah covers her eyes. "I don't want to know."

I chew on the pen cap. "Who do we know who's Nick's age, a good actress, and sneaky?"

"I'm new in town, remember?"

"Well, keep an eye out."

Find the Other Woman.

"And finally, we need to convince both of them that they are extremely lonely. Hannah, you'll have to figure out what kind of ring Ruby wants. I'll coach Nick on proposal methods."

"Remind me why we're doing this?"

I put my pen down. "I'm leaving in three weeks for a month-long fishing trip. I would like to know my two dear friends are going to be happy before I leave."

Hannah gives me a Just-How-Dumb-Do-You-Think-I-Am? look.

"And besides." I shrug. "It's fun."

"Aha!" she gloats. "There's the real reason. I need to make a note.

Find a guy and marry him during the month of March. I'm scared to death you'll turn and do this to me."

"Hey! That just gave me an idea."

"Lauren Holbrook!"

Chapter Nineteen

"Did you know there's not one river around here that has white-water rafting in January?" I say this as I walk back into the lobby after photographing an older couple.

Hannah looks up at me from her desk, twirling a pen. "I did not know that."

"And it's too cold to hike in the mountains right now?" I lean on her desk. "And, I called the two homeless shelters in the area and neither one of them needs any help for the next three months."

Hannah grins. "Is this the end of Ruby and Nick?" she says in an announcer tone. "Tune in next week to find out!"

"Is she here, by the way?"

"Nope. She ran an errand."

Brandon comes in the door, humming. "I have that dumb song from that stupid commercial stuck in my head," he says to me. He smiles at Hannah.

"Hey, Brandon, you need to sign these checks." She starts scrambling through the papers clogging her desk.

"We need to find a dolphin they can save together," I say, staring out at the big, chunky, perfectly proportioned snowflakes filtering down from a gorgeous gray sky. "Or a country they can protect together. Something like that."

Hannah purses her lips as she thinks. "They could adopt a street."

Brandon scrawls on the last check. "What's going on?"

I roll my eyes at Hannah's suggestion. "Very funny. Don't we have any orphans who need help? Or a marriage-minded mother who needs to be satisfied?"

"Remind me on that last reference?"

"*Pride and Prejudice.*"

"Oh right, right, right." She takes the checks from Brandon. "You have the worst handwriting in the history of the free world," she tells him.

"Thanks. What's going on?"

"Maybe an alien invasion they can fight against? Or a family of ducks they can teach how to fly?" I scoot onto the desk.

"Nick and Ruby," Hannah explains to Brandon. "We're trying to come up with ways they can get acquainted on a deeper level."

"A deeper level?" Brandon rubs his cheek. "Hey! They could dig to China and save the fortune-cookie industry."

"Good-bye, Brandon," I say.

"Travel to the tropical rain forest and plant banana trees."

"Leave, Brandon."

Hannah's smile is ear to ear as she laughs. Fuel to the fire as far as Brandon is concerned.

"Raise poodles and travel around the world doing dog shows together. Toss grapes to seals in an Australian zoo."

"Seals don't eat grapes," I interrupt.

"Bake biscuits and hand them out to the orphans as they backpack across Russia."

"Brandon!"

It is too late. He is rolling; Hannah's on the floor with laughter.

"Create a reality TV show about life as a doorbell installer."

I cover my face.

"Drown tadpoles as they institute a free community for flies of every color."

Hannah snorts she laughs so hard. Brandon grins broadly. I heroically try not to smile.

"Save the pinky fingers! Find a cure for the fear of marshmallows! Bring back the mullet!"

"Enough!" I screech, my sides heaving with mirth.

Brandon laughs. "Or, they could just go to a movie, get popcorn, and head to Vizzini's afterward."

"Go to your office!" I command, wiping tears from my face.

"Fine." He fakes a pout, winks, and goes down the hall.

Hannah pushes herself off the floor. "Oh boy. Mascara is running down my face, I'm sure." She swipes at her cheeks.

"You two are a pair." I pause. "What should we really do, Hannah?"

She opens one of the desk drawers and pulls out a small compact. "How about a blind date?"

"What are you talking about? They already know each other."

She wipes the mascara off her cheeks with a tissue. "Not Nick and Ruby. Split them up. Help them realize they're meant for each other, or whatever you said this morning."

I hold up a hand. "That would be skipping the first step, you know."

"We could just swap those two."

I nod. "Okay. Deal. Who are we setting Nick up with?"

"I'll go. Set me up with him." There is a strange mixture of sheer evil and plain delight gleaming in her eyes.

My brain denounces the plan.

My mouth, sadly, is faster. It's a problem I'm working on.

"Okay," my mouth says.

No! my brain screams.

"Good." She is rubbing her hands together like Scrooge contemplating the loss of Tiny Tim's supper. "Set it up for Wednesday before Bible study. Then they'll see each other that night and realize the truth."

I'm wary. "What are you going to do to him, Hannah?"

She smiles wickedly. "Wouldn't you like to know?"

"Yes, actually, I would."

"Who are we sending with Ruby?" She employs the ask-another-question technique.

I let her get away with it. "There's a scarcity of good men in this town."

"Trust me. I've noticed."

"Gee, thanks." Brandon comes down the hall.

"You're welcome," I tell him.

"Hannah, I need the last few bank deposit slips we've made. What are you guys talking about?"

"Who we can set Ruby up with," I say casually, tossing my hair over my shoulder. It's actually fixed today, so this makes a nice effect.

Brandon frowns. "I thought we were setting her up with Nick."

"Not anymore. We decided Ruby wasn't pastor's wife material. She's too . . . prompt." Hannah waves her hand. "So we're back on the hunt."

"But . . . you . . . wait," Brandon stutters.

I blink innocently. "Yes, Brandon, dear?"

"I don't think this is such a good idea, girls."

"Why?" Hannah asks, just as innocent.

"Why?" Brandon parrots, incredulous. "Because they're perfect together! Nick's crazy; Ruby's steady. Nick's late everywhere he goes;

Ruby's always on time. Nick's a great teacher; Ruby's a great listener. What is the matter with you two?"

I look at Hannah. "Sounds like a lot of confrontation."

"Absolutely. Bad for marriages."

"What?!"

"And," I continue to Hannah, calmly ignoring Brandon, "their kids would be screwy with all that opposite attraction stuff going on."

She nods. "I agree. They'll end up with total lunatics for children."

I rub my chin. "I'm thinking Ruby needs someone more intellectual."

"Right. Scientific, thoughtful, calculated."

"On time," I add.

"You two are nuts!" Brandon shrieks. "A guy like that would bore Ruby to tears!"

"Maybe a calculus major," Hannah muses.

Brandon throws his hands in the air. "Fine, you know what? Fine. I give up. You two want to ruin two people's lives, it's on your heads."

He stalks down the hall and slams his office door.

Hannah collapses into giggles. "Oh, Laurie. That was cruel."

"Yes. But he deserves it. Can I have a Milky Way?"

"Sure." She digs into the drawer and pulls out two. Hands me one. "Okay, so, really. Who can we use for Ruby?"

"Needs to be someone we know and trust." I unwrap the candy bar. "The point isn't to woo Ruby away from Nick." I rip off the wrapper completely and take a caramel-filled bite. It's a scientific fact that massive amounts of chocolate stimulate brain waves.

I'm pretty sure it's a fact, anyway.

I chew for a minute, thinking about the guys in the study. A few of them would work perfectly at making Ruby run to Nick, but they'd probably get hurt in the process.

Hannah chews thoughtfully for a minute. "Did you ever see *How to Lose a Guy in 10 Days*?"

"Yes, see? That's exactly what we need. Someone to completely destroy her faith in any male other than Nick."

Dr. America's face fills my brain. *Hmm.* "Hey, Hannah? What about Stephen?"

Hannah's mouth drops. "Are you insane, Laur? Stephen's gorgeous. We're going for someone pathetic, right?"

"Not necessarily. Stephen could play it up, I think." The more I consider this, the more excited I get. "Hannah, this will be great." I grin. "Stephen can be trusted, and I think he'll have a blast. He acted in high school. Plus, his conscience will be soothed because he'll know it will make Nick happy, and he and Nick are good friends."

Hannah bites, chews, and then waves her hands excitedly. "This will be hilarious!"

I finish the candy bar and then decide. "Excellent," I tell her. "Wednesday night, then. Hand me the phone."

I call Stephen first.

"Hello?"

"Hey, Stephen. It's Laurie."

I hear a smile in his voice. "Hey, Laurie. How's it going?"

"Good. Very good. I have a proposal for you, and you're free to say no, but it will be at the cost of one of your best friend's future happiness." Better to load on the guilt now.

He starts laughing. "Oh no."

"Can you be a blind date for Ruby?"

"Ruby. Ruby Palmer? Isn't she Nick's girlfriend?"

I am impressed. "Very observant, Stephen. And well, she was, but we've, uh, I mean *they've* hit sort of a block as far as moving forward, and so I'm attempting to push them back together."

"With a blind date."

"Yep."

"Why?"

"Well, remember when you played the Cowardly Lion in high school?"

He moans. "I had almost gotten that image out of my mind, Laurie. Thanks."

"I need you to act as boring or disgusting as you possibly can on this date."

"I don't know, Laurie." Skepticism is reigning in his voice. Hannah raises her eyebrows at me, wanting to know what's happening. I roll my eyes.

"Stephen," I say soothingly. "Just one date. You get to be absolutely revolting so Ruby will go running to Nick as fast as her Slim Fast–filled legs can carry her. If you don't want to do it, I understand. I'll just have to find someone else who may not act as well as you do and she might fall in love with him instead and he'll fall for her because she's officially beautiful and Nick's poor heart will be crushed into a quadrillion pieces and he'll move to a lone lake in the middle of Minnesota and spend his days crying into a root beer and staring at cod."

He's laughing again. "Okay, Laurie, okay! I'll do it." He sighs. "Good grief, girl, did you not ever take punctuation classes?"

"Thanks, Stephen." I grin and give Hannah the thumbs-up.

"When? Where?"

"Vizzini's. Five o'clock on Wednesday."

"I'll be there."

I have to make sure. "And you'll come revolting?"

"Yes indeed."

I smile again. "Great! I owe you."

"Just start using commas, and I'll consider myself paid off." He hangs up.

Hannah's laughing as I push the off button. "Oh, Laurie, you're terrible."

I smile and dial again.

"Nick Amery."

"Hey, Nick. It's Laurie."

"Hiya, Laurie. I was actually just thinking about calling you. Bible study for the junior high girls starts next week."

"Ruby told me. It's on my calendar."

"Well, that's Ruby for you." I don't miss the way his voice warms slightly when he mentions her name. "So what can I do for you?"

"Well." I clear my throat. "I have been thinking."

"Could be good or bad."

"Funny. Anyway, I decided that you've been single way too long and I'm going to send you on a blind date."

"Whoa, Laurie . . ."

"Wednesday night," I continue. "Before Bible study."

"Laurie."

"Don't worry, Nick. No strings attached. Just a casual dinner."

"Yeah, but—"

"If you hate it, I won't hold it against you."

"Well, who's it with?"

"Thus the term *blind* date, Nicky. So. Wednesday, five o'clock at Vizzini's work for you?"

"I don't know."

I let my voice soften, a sad lull to it. "Nick, I think you need to find someone who complements you—you know, who has different strengths and weaknesses. It's just one date. One date. Think about everything I've done for you, Nick. I brought brownies, I come to your Bible study every week without fail, I let you rope me into teaching middle school girls, which is something I'm completely nervous about, by the way. Can't you do one thing for me?" If I were any more pathetic, I'd be whimpering.

He lets out a long breath. "Fine."

"Good! Bye now." I hang up and turn to Hannah. "I am so good at guilt trips."

She applauds.

Ruby comes through the door. "Hey, girls."

"Hi, Ruby," Hannah and I chime together. I send Hannah a side-long grin.

Ruby sighs at Hannah. "When's my next appointment?"

"In twenty minutes."

"Okay." She's back to staring out the window.

I look outside. It's dark, dark, dark with low-riding clouds. The snow that fell all morning has let up for a moment, and black ice streaks across the parking lot. The trees are bony, and the grass is brown and covered with icy frost.

It's a gorgeous day to me, but Ruby has always been a summer-oriented person. Maybe this is a another reason she's so depressed.

Hannah makes a face at me behind Ruby's back.

"Ruby," I say businesslike. "I have a proposition for you."

"Oh boy," she says, rolling her eyes.

"A little more enthusiasm would be appreciated."

"Oh boy!"

"Thank you." I launch in. "I think you've been single too long."

Ruby lowers her chin and gives me the classic look I got all through elementary school from my teachers. It's the look that says, *Lauren Holbrook, you have an ace of spades up your sleeve.*

"I'd like to send you on a blind date," I continue, pushing my sleeves up to my elbows to prove her wrong.

Her eyebrows angle toward each other. "Laurie . . ."

"We met this great guy at Bible study on Wednesday, and we think you'd be a perfect match." Sure, let's give Hannah half the blame.

Ruby frowns. "Oh?" I can tell she's replaying the last two dates in her mind. I must establish doubt about Nick.

"Oh," I affirm. "We're setting it up for Wednesday night at five at Vizzini's."

"Laurie, no. I don't want to go on a date." She shakes her head vehemently. "The last two dates may not have been good, but at least they were with Nick."

I watch her still shaking her head for a few minutes. The time has come to play dirty. "Ruby," I say slowly, drawing out her name. "I think . . ." I sigh here. "I think just based on what you told me about the dates, . . . probably you and Nick have . . . well, nothing in common, to put it bluntly. You said it yourself."

She nods miserably.

"I know you like him and all, but don't you think communication is kind of an important thing to have?"

Her expression is pitiful. "Yes."

"So see if maybe you have it with someone else. Nick's not the last guy in the world, you know. And it's not like you couldn't go on the date and then go back to Nick."

She doesn't answer for a minute, looking out the window, eyes big and sad. "Okay, I guess. I guess I'll go."

"Good!" I grin brightly.

"What's the guy's name?" She's chewing her bottom lip.

I shake my head. "Can't tell."

"Have I met him before?"

"Maybe," I say mysteriously.

"Wait a second." She freezes. "Who's we?"

"What?"

"You said 'we' met a guy at Bible study," she points out. "Who's we?"

"Me and Hannah." Hannah waves from behind me.

"Oh dear."

"More enthusiasm, Ruby," I remind her.

"Oh dear!"

Hannah laughs.

"You'll have fun, I promise." I cross my fingers behind my back.

She's pinning me with a stare. "And if I don't?"

"Then I'll make it up to you."

"Oh really?" She leans against the wall and crosses her arms over her chest. "Now I'm curious. How would you make it up to me?"

"Another blind date?"

"Laurie!"

I hold my hands in a peace gesture. "I don't know. Something nice."

"Nice," she says dubiously.

"Perfume. Flowers. Those little gourmet chocolates. A puppy."

She walks past me to Studio One, shaking her head. "I just don't know what to do with you two."

"Love us and hug us and give us Twinkies and take us shopping," Hannah bursts out in a little-girl voice.

"Yeah, right!" Ruby yells from inside the studio.

I grin at Hannah.

Brandon comes out of his office and storms to the desk, not looking at either of us.

"Home wreckers," he mutters, grabbing a chunk of sticky notes from

Hannah's desk.

"That's a little harsh," I say.

He narrows his eyes at me. "In my office. Now."

"But—"

"No excuses. Get in there."

I sigh. "Hannah, when they get here, tell the Macys I might come back, and if I don't, I'd like a walnut coffin because I'm allergic to pine."

"Uh . . . okay."

I amble down the hall, Brandon close on my heels, into his messy office.

He closes the door behind him with a vengeance.

I'm flinching. "Is there going to be bloodshed? Because I'd rather not watch if it's okay with you."

"What is the matter with you? You scheme and scheme and scheme for weeks to get Ruby and Nick together. You even bake doctored brownies, and you hate to cook!"

"Brandon?"

"You trick them into eating together and talking to each other. You even have Ruby bake something against her will!"

"Brandon?"

"You've meddled with their emotions and their lives, and I have held my tongue long enough!"

"Brandon?"

"What!" he yells.

"It's a ploy."

He lowers his hands and looks at me. "What is?"

"The blind date. It's all to get Ruby and Nick serious about each other." I say this in the nice, soothing, "Okay, kids, time for bed" tone of voice that Mary Poppins perfected.

He closes his eyes and leans back against his desk. "A ploy." He rubs his hands over his face.

I nod. "Yep."

"Lauren Holbrook . . ."

"Yes?"

"I'm going to die earlier because of you."

I step over and put my arm around his shoulders. "Ah, no you won't. Just think what great shape your heart is in now." I pat his chest.

He shakes his head as he stares at me. "You've got to stop it, Laurie."

"Stop what?"

"Matchmaking. You're wrecking my employee's life."

My mouth opens in protest. "I am not!"

"You are too!" He pokes a finger in my face. "You're meddling!"

I smack his finger. "I'm *helping*. There's a difference. Ruby and Nick are positively perfect for each other, but they're so awkward that neither of them is ever going to make the second move, *obviously*, since she's thirty-three and he's thirty-four and they've known they liked each other for this long!"

He frowns at me. "That was quite a run-on sentence."

"So see? Without me, none of this would be happening."

"You promise you won't cause mental problems in either one of them?"

"Scout's honor."

"You were never a scout, Laurie."

"But I ate the cookies, so that sort of counts." I smile at him. "Don't tell, please, Brandon? Believe me, it's under control."

He puts his arm around my shoulder. "Remind me why I keep you around."

"Because you love me."

"Mmm."

"Because you can't live without me."

He rolls his eyes.

"Because life would be boring, gray, and dull, and you'd sit in this office every day twiddling your thumbs."

He straightens and walks me to the door. "You've got a client waiting, Laurie."

"Promise you'll keep your hands out of it?" I ask as he shoves me out the door.

"Fine."

Slam!

"Hey," Hannah greets me when I turn from waving at my clients as they leave.

"Hey."

"What are you doing for lunch?"

"I don't know. Can you hand me my wallet?"

She digs around in my backpack and emerges with it.

I open it. Three dollars. *Wow.* All the money I have to my name. At least in cash.

"I only have three dollars," I tell her.

"'Are we very poor, Lizzie?'" she asks, opening her purse.

"'With Father's estate entailed away from the female line, we've little but our charms to recommend us,'" I reply, tucking the bills back in my wallet.

Brandon walks up, making a face. "What?"

"Can I have a raise?" I ask.

"No."

"Oh. Well, can I have five dollars?"

"Why?" He pulls his billfold from his back pocket.

"Because I'm poor." I sniff sadly. Blink a few times.

"'Poor and perfect. With eyes like the sea after a storm . . . ,'" Hannah quotes.

Brandon hands me a five-dollar bill. "You guys watch too many movies."

"Thanks." I tuck the money in my back pocket.

Hannah grins at him. "You can learn a lot about life from movies."

"Like what?" His voice is filled with unbelief.

"Like how to survive the Fire Swamp." She grabs her purse. "Bud's, Laurie?"

I shrug. Grease, batter, and more grease? "Sure."

"Hey, bring me back a hamburger," Brandon calls.

"Do you have money?" My palm is extended and open in the gesture of mercenary friendship.

"Lauren." There's danger riding on his tone.

"Acts 4:32. And I quote, 'All the believers were one in heart and mind. No one claimed that any of his possessions was his own, but they shared everything they had.'" I smile.

"I wouldn't push it." Hannah pulls me out the door into the intensely cold air. "That's a Bible verse?" she asks.

"Yep." I admit I'm rather thrilled I could recall that verse so easily. My devotions are paying off. And not just in my memorization skills. The more time I spend in my devotions, the more the tight feeling in my stomach fades.

"So the blind dates are ready to go, I think." I change subjects and shove my arms through my coat sleeves as we hurry down the sidewalk. The atmosphere is glacial and seeping into my bones.

"You do realize that we sent them to the same place," Hannah says slowly.

My teeth are shivering. "Oh, Honey." I yank my collar up to the crown of my head. "You are *such* a novice."

"Why did we send them to the same place?"

"Because then they have the pleasure of staring at each other out with a different guy or girl for the evening."

Hannah opens the door to Bud's, a welcome rush of warm, greasy air overtaking us. "You're brutal."

I accept the comment for the compliment it is. "I need to call and get their tables arranged."

Mikey comes from around the back and smiles at us. "Hiya, Laur. Hannah."

"Hey, Mikey." I stare up at the menu suspended above the counter.

Mikey follows my gaze. "What are you looking at?"

"The menu."

"*You're* looking at the *menu?*" he asks, dubious. "Why?"

"To see what I want, Mikey. Isn't that what a menu's for?"

Mikey looks at Hannah with his brows raised. Hannah shrugs at him.

"Yeah, but, Laurie, you come here every day," he says slowly.

"Good for your business, I suppose."

He spreads out his hands. "Haven't you memorized the menu by now?"

"Fine, fine, fine. I'll have two hamburgers, two Dr. Peppers, and two orders of onion rings."

"Tack another burger and a drink on there," Hannah says.

He does. "Eleven bucks."

"Even?" My mouth drops.

"Yep, we started adding tips into the order. Too many customers were skimping on them."

I roll my eyes, and we pool our money to pay. "Such service."

"Such customers." He grins at me and hands me a greasy bag. "See you tomorrow, Laurie. Bye, Hannah."

I step back into the frigid outdoors and thank my father's DNA for making me an indoorsy person. The cold seeps between the stitches on my coat and into my flesh. I shiver uncontrollably. I can feel my fingernails ice over, and I know I'm morphing into that acorn-loving creature from *Ice Age*.

Hannah, meanwhile, is completely oblivious to the fact that she is now outside and the temperature has dropped from a comfortable seventy degrees to a hypothermia-inducing twenty-eight.

"So you were saying?" She pulls one of my onion rings from the bag, slowly sauntering down the sidewalk.

"A . . . b . . . o . . . u . . . t . . . w . . . h . . . a . . . t?" I shake through my chattering teeth.

"About getting the tables arranged?"

"W . . . a . . . i . . . t . . . a . . . m . . . i . . . n . . . u . . . t . . . e."

I run the rest of the way to the studio, throw open the door, drag Hannah inside, and shut it.

"BRR!" I yell, hopping around while trying to keep frostbite from forming on my toes.

Hannah's mouth is halfway open, a wrinkle between her eyebrows.

Brandon pokes his head out of his office. "Laurie, shut up!"

His door bangs closed.

Hannah pushes me around her desk, sits me down in the chair, and turns on the portable heater by my feet. "Sit still," she commands.

Five minutes later I'm assured my toes did not contract frostbite and I will live to see another day.

I'm telling you, miracles happen.

"Okay." Hannah sits on top of her desk and pulls out lunch. "About arranging tables." She peeks back at Studio One. The door is closed. "Think it's Ruby in there?"

I nod. "I'll call JACK from Vizzini's," I say in a whisper. "He owes me anyway."

Hannah waves her hamburger at me. "Good idea, Laurie."

Ruby comes out of Brandon's office, yawning. "Hey, girls." She flops into one of the chairs in front of Hannah's desk.

"Hey, who is in Studio One?" I ask.

She glances at the closed door. "Ty, I think."

"Oh." I take another bite. "I didn't know he was in today."

"Just got in, actually. He had a lot of snow at his place." She squints out at the weather.

"Oh."

Ruby eyes the hamburgers enviously. "It is lunchtime, isn't it?"

"Yes, ma'am." Hannah digs into the bag. "Here."

Ruby takes Brandon's hamburger with a sigh of relief. "Thank you."

"Um . . . but . . . uh," I stutter, trying to swallow.

Hannah shoots me a look that says, *Be quiet!*

Apparently she is going to make Brandon walk outside, brave the weather straight from *March of the Penguins*, and get his own hamburger.

I bite back a smile with my burger.

"Can you at least give me a clue about who the date is with?" Ruby wipes the corner of her mouth with the back of her hand.

"Nope," Hannah says. "Hey, have you ever seen *Pride and Prejudice*?"

Ruby shakes her head slowly. "No, but I've heard Laurie quote it enough."

I shrug. "'Well, it is a truth universally acknowledged that a single man of good fortune must be in want of a wife.'"

"'What a fine thing for our girls!'" Hannah shouts excitedly.

"No more, please," Ruby says.

"You asked." I smile at her. She is eating a hamburger—not a Slim Fast bar—for lunch! If anyone is in doubt that love changes people, they need only look at Ruby.

The bell over the door chimes and the three of us reenact the *Little Women* scene—we all look up in unison to see who could be calling.

Ryan grins at us. "Grease is on today's menu, I suppose." He holds up his own bag from Bud's. "Can I join you?"

"Please." Ruby smiles for the first time that day, motioning toward the chair beside her. "Haven't seen you today, Honey. How are you doing?"

He settles into the chair, cradling the bag. "Oh fine." He winks at me.

Unexpectedly, my cheeks begin to heat.

Darn that heater. I reach down and turn it off.

"Hey, Laur." He smiles cheerfully at me.

"Hi, Ry." I nod toward the bag. "I hope there's two burgers in there."

"You are in luck. I bought enough for everyone."

"That was sweet," I tell him.

Little-kid-on-the-monkey-bars smile appears. "Why, thank you."

Brandon comes down the hall. "Got my burger, Nutsy?" He rakes a hand through his hair. "Oh hey, Ryan. These finances are slowly killing me."

I make a face at Ryan. His eyes twinkle. "Here you go, Brandon." He hands him one of the greasy lumps from his bag.

I like this guy better every time I see him.

"So what's up?" I ask Ryan, picking an onion off my burger.

"Lunch break. Thought I'd eat somewhere where I knew the heat would be on." He strips off his leather jacket. "It's bitter cold out there."

"Straight from the South Pole," I tell him.

He smiles at me. "South Pole, huh?"

"I heard Mexico is buried in avalanches."

"Poor little *niños*." Ryan grabs a burger for himself.

I dig around until I find an onion ring in my bag.

Brandon frowns. "Didn't you just take an onion off your burger?"

I take a bite. "Yeah. So?"

"So now you're eating an onion ring?"

"Observant," I praise him.

He exchanges a glance with Ryan, who shrugs. Brandon pats his shoulder. "Hope you know what you're getting into, Ryan."

"I don't think he does. Better keep patting," I say.

Ryan closes his eyes.

Ruby is back to staring at the scenery outside. Ryan watches his sister, frowning in confusion. He looks at me, eyebrows slightly raised.

I smile outright then. Ryan has not been told of Friday's encounter, it seems.

I will have fun embellishing!

Chapter Twenty

"So then he kissed her." I lean over the table.

Ryan's mouth drops open. "He *kissed* her?"

"Yep."

"Wait, wait." He waves his hands. "I thought you were eavesdropping through the door."

"We were."

He frowns. "So how do you know he kissed her?"

"There was this big, long silence, and then both of them gasped and he apologized."

"What do you know," he mutters, mouth open again in shock. "Nick Amery?"

"That's the one." I nod proudly.

We sit in Vizzini's waiting for our dinner, having already consumed the entire basket of breadsticks.

JACK comes by with the water pitcher. Holds it with two hands as he refills our glasses.

"Could we get more breadsticks?" Ryan asks him.

"Sure." He leaves as fast as he came.

"Just once?" Ryan asks suddenly.

I blink. "Just once what?"

"He kissed her just once?"

I shrug. "I don't know. Right there is when she found us. We ran to Bud's."

"Like the brave girls you are."

"Yeah, well."

He fiddles with the cranberry-colored napkin. "So he could have kissed her again."

"Yeah, sure he could have. That's the good news. Apparently the two dates they've had since then have been duds. But don't worry. It'll work out." Best if Ryan doesn't know about my meddling streak right now, I think.

"Hmm." His mouth is in a straight line, his forehead creased.

"Ryan." I tap his arm. "It's okay, you know. Nick's a good guy."

"I don't know him, though."

"So get to know him."

"How?"

JACK brings the basket, gulps, and leaves.

"I don't know." My expertise does not extend to male bonding. "Go play something with him."

His mouth curls. "Play something? Like Frisbee?"

I glare. "Like basketball."

"Laur, it's twenty degrees outside."

"They make indoor courts, you know."

He frowns as he thinks, pulling a breadstick from the green cloth holding the heat in. "Guess we could do that."

A girl in a red shirt comes out with two plates. "Spaghetti?"

"Here," Ryan says.

She sets my ravioli in front me. "Anything else I can get you?"

"Don't think so," Ryan answers.

"Have a nice dinner."

Ryan holds out his hands. "Want me to say the blessing?"

"Sure." I take his hands.

He prays a short prayer, smiles, and squeezes my hands. "Thanks for coming to dinner with me, Laurie."

"Thanks for asking."

I begin hacking into the ravioli, checking the filling inside each pastry square. Ryan is apparently watching. "What are you doing?" he asks.

"Making sure they gave me the cheese ravioli. One time they messed up and gave me the spinach. It was yucky."

He twirls his fork on his plate. "You ate it?"

"One or two pieces."

"Why?"

"I didn't realize it was spinach."

Ryan starts choking on his spaghetti. "Oh, Laurie."

"What? I thought maybe the cheese had molded."

He stares at me, disgusted. "Remind me never to eat your cooking. Ever."

"Hey, I'm learning." I fork off a bite. "For example, expiration dates aren't guesses. They should be obeyed."

Ryan's not listening. "So Nick's a good guy?" he asks again.

I have to laugh.

Ryan drops me back by the studio an hour later. "Have a good night, Laurie."

"See you." I unlock the Tahoe. He lets me drive ahead of him out of the parking lot.

Dad is waiting when I get home. A fire roars in the fireplace. He sits in his favorite chair, feet encased in moccasins, a book open on his lap.

I sink into the sofa across from him. "Hi, Dad."

He smiles at me. "Did you have a good time, Laurie-girl?"

"Yeah, I did." I shed my coat and drop my backpack on the floor, stretching. "We went to Vizzini's."

Dad closes the book, marking his place with his finger. "What a surprise," he says dryly.

I grin at him. "Three weeks until the fishing trip."

"Two and three-fourths weeks."

"Have we made a list of what to bring yet?"

Dad picks up a yellow legal pad lying on the table beside him.

"What a surprise," I parrot, smirking.

"You need to learn to respect your elders," Dad says and grins.

I take the pad from him. *Blankets, tea, socks, small heater, several mugs.*

The list goes on for two pages. "Very thorough, Father."

"Thank you, Daughter." He leans back in his chair. "I suppose we'll need to bring the cell phone since you will want to keep in touch with Ryan."

I can tell he is prying. Dad's not exactly what you would call *subtle*.

"The cabin doesn't have a phone?" I ask.

"No."

"Yeah, I'd bring the cell. If only for emergencies. You know. An attack by an angry codfish and the like."

"I guess you and Ryan could always write letters."

Here's what I am: Blatantly merciless.

Poor Dad.

"We may not have to." I stretch again. "Over dinner we talked about just eloping and being done with it. So if that happens before the end of this month, then I guess Ryan will just go with us."

Dad blinks several times. Opens his mouth and closes it twice.

"Laurie—"

I start giggling. "Gotcha, Dad!"

He sinks lower into his chair. "What did I do?" he asks the ceiling fan.

I decide I will leave Dad and the fan blades to figure it out.

"I'm going to bed, Dad. Good night. Love you." I stand and wrap my arms around his neck in a hug.

"Love you too, Laurie-girl."

I trip up the stairs, throw my backpack in the direction of my squishy chair, grab my pajamas, and head for the bathroom.

Twenty minutes later, I fall onto the bed with a moan. Dragging my Bible over, I flip it open. I finished with Ephesians, and I'm almost through Philippians. I start reading at chapter 4. Verses 4 and 5 catch my attention: "Rejoice in the Lord always. I will say it again: Rejoice! Let your gentleness be evident to all. The Lord is near."

I frown slightly. Gentleness. Not one of my strong points. And why does it follow the command to be gentle with "the Lord is near"? I bite my bottom lip as I consider it.

Maybe it has something to do with the Ephesians passage about living not as unwise but as wise, making the most of every opportunity.

I close my Bible and I'm halfway asleep when I have another daydream.

Brandon smiling . . . eyes twinkling . . . at Hannah.

I suddenly come awake and sit back up. Brandon? Hannah? The thought isn't new, but I'm wondering now if it may have potential.

Hmm.

Come to think of it, it was the *two* of us, plural, who came up with the Ruby and Nick blind-date thing. And Brandon knew that. Yet did he get mad at Hannah?

No.

And he always has a special greeting for her. I get, "Mmph, Laurie."

Hmm.

I lie back down and pull the covers up to my neck. *Brandon and Hannah Knox.*

It has possibilities.

First, Hannah isn't so bad. He can marry her and still be friends with me. Hannah won't care.

And she's been very interested in God and church. Lots of questions. I predict a new Christian in our midst by next month.

She's pretty. Brandon's nice enough looking. Their kids could be cute.

I drift to sleep thinking of Little Brandon and Little Hannah.

The morning comes much too early.

Nothing new here.

Dad is at the table with paper, vitamins, and high-fiber cereal in front of him when I come downstairs. "Morning, Honey. Sleep good?"

"Mm-hmm."

"Good." The paper rustles as he sets it on the table. "Honey, do you think you could get off a little earlier tonight?"

"Sure, Dad. Why?"

He smiles excitedly. "I thought we could go pick out our fishing poles."

I get my coffee. "Okay. Sounds good. What time?"

"I'll pick you up at five?"

"Works."

"This will be so much fun, Laurie."

I sit opposite him and plan the day.

It will go as follows:

(Scene: The Brandon Knox Photography Studio. Morning. Laurie walks in.)

LAUREN: Morning, Hannah. Where's Brandon?

HANNAH: Hello, dear Laurie. I believe Brandon *(said with a blush)* is in the back, reading financial statements with his forehead creased, his elbows on the desk, and stroking his chin *(blushes again)*. But that's just a guess.

LAUREN: You like him, don't you?"

HANNAH: *(covers her face)* What can I say?

LAUREN: The truth.

HANNAH: Yes! Yes, I like him! But I cannot. Not yet. I need to call Nick. I need to learn how to become a Christian first. Then . . .

LAUREN: Then what?

HANNAH: Then I want to marry Brandon.

Seems easy enough.

I kiss Dad's cheek, promise to behave, and set off to work like the good career girl I am.

Hannah is sitting down at her desk when I walk in.

"Hey, Hannah."

She rubs her cheek wearily. "Hi."

I frown at her appearance. Her hair is half-curly, half-straight, and to the untrained eye could look like an attempt at the beachhead look. I know it's sheer laziness and lack of time spent with a blow dryer. This is how I know: She's wearing a fuzzy sweater and jeans.

Everyone knows that fuzzy sweaters and jeans are the outfits of extreme exhaustion.

"What's wrong?" I ask her.

"I didn't get to bed last night until two thirty." She pulls her extra-large coffee closer, yawning hugely.

I shove my backpack in the cubby. "Why?"

"Promise you won't laugh?"

"Uh, sure."

"They were showing an . . ." She clears her throat and looks away. "An Elvis marathon on TV last night."

"You didn't." I make no effort to hide the laughter.

"I did." She groans and lays her forehead on the desk. "Look at me! I am pitiful!"

"Hey, could've been worse. You could've been watching *The Three Stooges*. Then there would be cause for worry." I pat her back. "So cheer up."

Brandon walks in. "If I sacrifice you to the god of money, do you think I'll finish these financial forms faster?" he asks me.

"Pagan. Read Romans 1," I tell him.

He ignores me. "Good morning, Hannah."

She moans, head still on desk.

He frowns with concern. "Hannah?"

"Mmm?"

"You okay?"

"Mmm."

I grin. "That means yes."

"You look like you have a hangover," Brandon says. How he decides this, I'm not sure, because he still hasn't seen her face.

"Mmph."

I interpret. "That means she wasn't drinking, but her hips hurt."

Hannah starts laughing.

Brandon stares at me. "Why do her hips hurt?"

"Because she—"

Hannah jerks her head up, long blonde hair flying. "Don't you dare," she threatens me.

"Hannah?" Brandon asks.

"And her knees hurt." I skip into Studio Two. "Better ask her, Brandon. She might need to go home."

"Lauren Holbrook!"

I bat my eyelashes at her and close the door. The room, dark, cold, and lonely, does not look inviting.

The point of picture taking is to make the person whose picture you are taking feel comfortable enough to look normal. I find doing impersonations of Disney characters and singing off-key parodies of famous songs can help.

However, in order for *me* to feel comfortable doing that, the studio needs to be comfortable.

I turn on the lights, jack up the heater, and force the computer to come out of hibernation. I open the door to go back out to the front office.

Brandon sits on Hannah's desk, idly twirling a pencil between his fingers. Hannah's talking animatedly, her blonde hair bouncing.

Neither hears me.

I turn back into the studio, quietly closing the door.

Ruby and Nick. Brandon and Hannah.

Ty is married with three kids. Newton got married last summer.

Soon I will be the lone single person at The Brandon Knox Photography Studio.

Couples, couples, couples.

I am surrounded by couples!

I sit on the couch in the studio with a huff. There's Ryan, of course, but technically we aren't a couple. Should something ever come of it, it won't work anyway because of Dad.

Why isn't life more like chick flicks?

I sit there depressed for the next five minutes before suddenly snapping. What is *wrong* with me?

I'm Lauren Holbrook, remember? I'm not interested in dating. I'm never getting married. I don't have these kinds of thoughts.

Confession: I'm having these kinds of thoughts.

I sink farther into the sofa. "Oh boy," I mutter under my breath. The tightening in my stomach I thought I had gotten rid of comes back with a vengeance.

This is Not Good At All. *Lord, what's happening here?*

Someone knocks on the studio door and I yell for them to come in.

A woman with brown hair and green eyes pokes her head in. "Hi, we're your nine o'clock. Sorry we're late." She drags a nice-looking, well-dressed man in behind her.

I stand. "I'm Laurie."

"I'm Kristen. This is my fiancé, Gordon."

The speech rolls off my tongue without the use of my brain. "You'll have three clothing changes . . ."

Meanwhile, my brain is busy. *Lord, I'm seriously counting down the days until the fishing trip.*

Chapter Twenty-One

Kristen and Gordon leave at ten.

I walk them out and then turn to Hannah, who is nibbling at a Hershey bar while clicking around on the computer.

"Who's my next appointment?"

She looks down at the calendar. "Um, Ted Crosby and Stacy Hollings."

I draw a blank. "Do I know them?"

"Well, I don't." She grins at me and shrugs. "Not like I would. I think they're first-timers, if I remember right."

I nod. "Oh. At ten?"

"Ten thirty."

"Okay." I rub my head. "I'll be in the studio."

"Hey," Hannah says. I turn back around.

"What?"

She gives me a long look. "You okay?"

"Just a headache."

She raises one eyebrow. "Really." Her tone does not invoke belief.

"Really."

"You're lying."

"Okay. And I'm tired."

"You weren't earlier."

I sit on one of the chairs with a sigh. "Hannah," I mumble, massaging my temples.

"Laurie." She digs into one of her drawers and retrieves a Milky Way. "Here."

"Thanks." I don't open it. "All my life," I blurt out. "All my life, I never wanted to get married."

Long pause. "Okay."

"Never," I say again, more adamantly. "When I was little, I never pretended that I was a mom or a wife or anything like that."

Hannah cups her chin in her hands. "What did you pretend?"

"That I was an astronaut or a firefighter or a . . . or a . . . a dog sitter."

She smiles at the last one. "Laurie? Do you want to get married now?"

I don't look at her. "Oh boy," I mutter. Grab the chocolate bar, rip the wrapper off, take three bites, and finally look at her.

Hannah nods. "That's what I thought. Look, Laur, what's so bad about that? So you want to get married, so what? It's not the end of the world."

I swallow. "You don't understand, Hannah. I can't even remember all the times I've promised Dad I wouldn't get married."

Ruby walks through the door then, shivering. "Hey."

"Hi, Ruby." Hannah smiles. "I was beginning to wonder if you'd forgotten your ten thirty."

"No, I just . . . what's wrong, Laurie?" Her voice is laced with concern. She sits in the chair beside me. "You don't look well."

"She's making a hard confession," Hannah says.

Ruby puts her hand on my forehead. "You don't have a fever."

"Sick at heart, not in body." Hannah shrugs.

"That sounds very soap-opera-ish," I say.

"What's wrong, Honey?" Ruby rubs my back.

I look at Hannah.

"She wants to get married," Hannah says.

Ruby blinks a few times. "Okay."

"No, it's not okay!" I shriek. "Dad would go berserk! He'd be suicidal! Dad would keel over if I left him!"

"Honey, I think you might be overreacting just a little bit." Ruby keeps rubbing my back while I lean forward, putting my head in my hands. "Who do you want to marry?"

"Tom Cruise," Hannah answers.

I can almost hear Ruby blinking. She and Ryan have a lot of the same characteristics.

I can't help it. I smile.

"Well, that . . . might not be what God wants for you," Ruby says slowly.

I laugh. "Not Tom Cruise."

"Yes, she does," Hannah continues to lie. "She sat right there and told me, 'Hannah, I want to marry Tom Cruise.'" She clutches her hands at her chest and sighs breathily.

I raise my eyebrows to Ruby.

"So then I told her she was daydreaming and to get over it." Hannah shrugs. "But you know Laurie. She never listens to me."

"Don't listen to her, Ruby. She's lying like a catfish."

Ruby's forehead wrinkles. "Like a what?"

"Never mind."

I can feel my old self reviving. Good old Hannah. I might have to keep that girl around. She's good for me.

Hannah grins.

"So you're okay?" Ruby stills her hand on my back.

"I'll be okay."

She nods and stands, pulling off her coat. "I'm glad. I'll be in Studio One, okay?"

Hannah salutes.

"You're a nutcase, you know?" I tell her as I finish the Milky Way.

"That's why you love me. Now get to work."

"Well, fine." I slink into the studio to clean up after Kristen and Gordon and get it ready for the next client.

Lord, what is with this change? If this is Your purpose for me, could it at least have been a subtle change instead of a sudden one?

I'm waving good-bye to my ten thirty when the phone rings. "Laurie, phone!" Hannah yells even though I stand a foot in front of her.

"Thank you!" I scream back.

Brandon's office door bangs open. "Girls!" Slams closed again.

Hannah grins. "Check mark for Tuesday!"

I take the cordless phone. "Hello?"

"Hey."

Ryan.

I go into the studio, away from Hannah and her big ears. "Hi," I tell him. "How are you?"

"I'm fine. I heard you weren't doing too well though."

I frown. "From who?"

"Ruby."

Of course. "I forgot you have an inside connection."

"Something about you marrying Tom Cruise?"

I grin. "Aw, and I wanted to break it to you easy."

"Too late. I just called to say, you know, have a nice life and call when you're in town and maybe we could stay friends."

I laugh. "Actually, I changed my mind. I don't want to marry Tom."

"Oh yeah?" he drawls. "Who do you want to marry?"

"Someone taller."

He pauses. "Yeah, I can see that. You wouldn't want him to have to stand on a step every time he wanted to kiss you."

"Well, I guess that could make marital life interesting."

"What was really wrong?"

I sigh. "I think I'm growing up."

"Then you definitely want someone taller."

"I meant mentally."

"Don't tell me. Someone told you Santa Claus wasn't real, didn't they? Oh, Honey, I was worried this day would come."

I sit on the couch, smiling. "He's not real?" I wail.

"Oh boy."

"Oh this is just great!" I wave my hand, even though he can't see me. "One more illusion down the drain!"

Ryan redirects the conversation again. "How are you growing up?"

I purse my lips. "My dreams are changing."

"Dreams as in nightmares?"

"As in what I want to do with my life."

"Got it. So?"

I don't follow. "So?"

"What do you want to do?"

I lean back, picking at the stray threads on the couch. "Get married. Be a mom."

"Really?" I can't decipher his voice.

"Yeah." I'm quiet.

"Laurie, what's wrong with that? I think it's great."

I frown. "You do?"

"Yes, absolutely. Did you not want to before?"

"No. I never wanted to get married. Until recently," I tack on.

"What happened recently?"

I wave my hand trying to find the words. "I don't know if I can describe it."

"Laurie, that's not the answer."

"What?"

"Didn't you hear me fishing for a compliment there?"

"Now that you mention it, I think it had something to do with this really nice construction worker who brings me coffee." I grin.

"Much better." He pauses. "This reminds me of something I read in Proverbs the other day. Chapter 16, verse 9. 'In his heart a man plans his course, but the LORD determines his steps.'"

I'm silent as I contemplate that. "So do you think this is my plan or God's?" I ask finally.

"I guess time will tell, right? As long as you continue to walk with Him, His plan will become yours."

"Poetic, Ryan." I smile.

"Thank you." I can hear the grin in his voice.

"Hey, want to go out with me tomorrow?" I ask.

"I don't know. Is a justice of the peace involved?"

I feel myself blush. "*No*, Ryan. To Vizzini's. Five o'clock?"

"Why do I get the feeling there is more involved here than just a casual dinner?"

I shrug, picking at the couch again. "I don't know."

"Laurie." He draws my name out. I decide I hate it when people do that.

"Fine. I set your sister up on a blind date." I flinch, waiting for his reaction.

"My sister. Ruby? You got Ruby to go on a blind date?"

"Well, see—"

"Hey! What about Nick?"

"What about him?" I bite my lip.

"Laurie."

"I hate it when you say my name like that."

"What did you do to Nick?"

I'm as vague as I can be. "He . . . might be . . . on another blind date."

Ryan sighs heavily into the phone. "Let me get this straight. You set Nick up with someone and Ruby up with someone and, just a guess here, they're both going to Vizzini's at five, right?"

"You're good." I'm very impressed.

"I've been around you too long." He sighs again. "I'm beginning to understand your madness."

"Will you come? Please?"

"And watch my sister get tortured? Who'd you set her up with anyway?"

"Stephen Weatherby. And don't worry, she'll be more repulsed than tortured."

"Stephen. The guitar guy? Why would she be repulsed? He's fairly nice looking, isn't he?"

"Oh. He's *very* nice looking," I say. "That's a perk to make Nick jealous. Stephen's in on the Nick and Ruby thing. He's going to make the date a miniature Pit of Despair."

He stops for a moment. "What's your middle name?"

"I'm sorry?"

"Okay, that's a weird middle name, Lauren I'm Sorry Holbrook. Fitting, however, considering the circumstances."

I roll my eyes. "Ha ha. It's Emma."

"Lauren Emma Holbrook?"

"It was my mom's name."

"Oh." He is quiet for one minute before yelling, "Lauren Emma Holbrook!"

I jump. "What?"

"That's for the blind dates. And sure, I'll go to dinner with you."

"Thanks." I smile. "You called me Honey."

"What are you talking about now?"

"When you were babbling on about Santa Claus. You called me Honey."

I can hear his smile. "Good-bye, Laurie."

"Bye, Ryan." I hang up and rake a hand through my hair.

Is it possible that . . . ?

I stand and walk into the lobby.

Hannah sits pristinely at her desk, hands clasped in her lap, smiling at me. I close my eyes.

"How much did you hear?" I demand.

"What are you talking about?" She is serene.

"Hannah."

She shrugs. "Just your side of the conversation."

"You know, Brandon thinks I corrupted you, but you're worse than I am."

"I resent that. You would have picked up the extension and listened in. I merely listened at the door."

"Eavesdropping either way, Hannah."

She waves her hand. "Semantics. Hey, here's your paycheck."

I take it grudgingly. "You're trying to soothe me over with money."

"Yep. Is it working?"

I open the envelope and look at the amount. "I guess so."

"Good." She clicks something on her computer. "Hey, in like an hour or so do you want to go to the bank and then grab something for lunch?"

"Where?"

"I was thinking Merson's."

"Did you have to ask?" I hand my paycheck back to her and she sets it on my backpack.

A young couple holding the hands of two ironed and starched little kids comes through the door, the bell chiming.

"Hi," the man says. "I'm Travis Easling. My wife, Tracy, and our kids, Trevor and Trina."

And our dog's name is Triscuit and our cat is Trixie.

I smile at the thought. "I'm Laurie. We'll be in Studio Three."

"Two, actually," Hannah calls from behind me. "Newton's got dibs on Three."

"I'm Laurie." I grin. "We'll be in Studio Two."

Travis Easling laughs. Tracy Easling smiles in June Cleaver fashion. Trevor and Trina giggle.

The family marches into the studio and stands in a line before me like I'm a drill sergeant.

I fight the urge to put my hands on my hips. "Right. So. You want a bunch of family prints, right?"

"And a couple with just the kids," Tracy says.

Trevor groans. "I hate smiling."

I bend down in front of him. "You know what makes smiling easier?" I ask him. He shakes his head. "Putting Vaseline on your teeth."

Trevor blinks. "What are you talking about? I love smiling. Smiling is my favorite thing to do."

"Good boy." I slap his shoulder. "Let's start with the family poses."

I take great pleasure turning off my alarm clock tonight. Tomorrow is Wednesday and I have the day off.

I flip my Bible open on my lap, rubbing a hand through my extremely curly hair. It must be humid tonight. Where had I left off in Philippians 4?

"Do not be anxious about anything, but in everything, by prayer and petition, with thanksgiving, present your requests to God. And the peace of God, which transcends all understanding, will guard your hearts and your minds in Christ Jesus."

Anything would probably include marriage. I half-smile at the Book.

Thanks, Lord.

I wake slowly Wednesday morning, lie in bed for about half an hour, and then start getting a caffeine headache. Dad isn't anywhere to be found when I get downstairs, but there's a note taped to the coffeepot:

Laurie-girl, the store called and our bedding sets are in. Will be back from picking them up about 10:20. Love, Dad.

Bedding sets.

I pour the coffee wondering what is wrong with the thirty spare sheets we have stowed away in Laney's old closet.

The phone rings and I answer.

"Hi, Baby."

"Lex." I yawn.

"You're still home? Good. I had a question. Do you want to meet me for an early dinner tonight before your Bible study? Nate's got some shindig at work, and we haven't talked just the two of us in . . . well, days, at least."

"Mmm. Can't."

"Really?"

Wincing at the innuendo in her voice, I gulp a big mouthful of coffee. "Yeah. Sorry, sis."

"Any particular reason why?"

"Plans."

"You already have plans or you're making plans?"

"Already have them."

"With who?"

"Could be a what, you know."

"Are you having dinner with Ryan?"

"Maybe."

"I see." I can hear her delight. I drop my head onto the table. "What was that?" she asks suddenly.

"What?"

"That thud. I heard a thud. You're not trying your hand at cooking again, are you?"

"I hit my head."

"On what?"

"The table."

Long pause. "I'm not even going to ask. Okay. Maybe I'll call Laney and see if Adam can watch the kids tonight."

"Sounds good, Lex."

"Have a nice day, Honey. Tell Ryan hi for me." She hangs up before I can respond.

I hang up and pour another cup. My plans for the day include watching a movie, eating chocolate, and, if I feel like it, Perhaps Playing Ping-Pong.

Heh, heh.

I pull on my favorite winter outfit. It doesn't match, and I got it in seventh grade. Black and pink striped fleece pants and a Christmas tree sweatshirt. I pull my hair up and go downstairs to park myself in front of the TV.

Brandon is in the entry.

"Aren't you supposed to be working?" I greet him.

"Yeah, but I knew you were off and you'll be gone a month, so I decided to hang with you today."

I stare at him. He wears nice jeans that haven't faded yet, a button-down shirt, and loafers. His hair is gelled and spiked.

Exasperated, I point to his outfit.

He looks down at his shoes. "Sorry," he apologizes.

"You cannot *hang* in that."

"Sure, I can. Better yet, I'll go stroke the fire." He strides off.

"I think you mean *stoke* the fire."

"Whatever." He marches to the fireplace, where just the smallest orange glow hangs onto a log for dear life.

"Hey there, little fella," Brandon says to the flame. "Want me to get some of that ash out of the way for you? Hey! Laur! Look, it nodded at me!"

I curl up on the couch. "Careful, Brandon, it might want to go home with you."

There are probably some very good scientific names for the fireplace tools, but I've always called them the poker, grabber, and shovel. Brandon pulls the poker out and shoves a few logs around.

Swish! The flame finds another one.

Swooosh! They multiply and replenish the fireplace.

Biblical fire. Who would have thought?

Brandon puts the poker away and joins me on the couch. "So

what movie is it going to be?" he asks, flicking my hair. "Nice hair, by the way."

"How'd you know I was watching a movie?" I turn my head so he can't keep pulling my hair. "And this is my day-off hairstyle."

"And those are your movie clothes. What movie?" he asks again.

"*While You Were Sleeping.*"

He shakes his head. "How about *The Fugitive?*"

"*The Count of Monte Cristo?*"

"Done." He finds the movie. "I know why you like this movie, by the way."

I spread out my hands. "The cinematography, obviously."

"And it's not the action sequences."

"Of course not. I like the soundtrack."

"I'm putting my money on Jim Caviezel." He gestures at me with the DVD case.

I blink innocently. "Jim who?"

He picks up the remote. "You get very excited at the end."

"Well, he's shaven then."

"Simple minds, simple pleasures."

Chapter Twenty-Two

The doorbell rings. I skip down the stairs and swing open the door before the chiming stops.

Ryan is on the front porch, hands shoved in his jacket pockets, his eyebrows raised. "You are way too excited about this."

"Am not." I grab my coat.

He sticks his hand out suddenly. "Hold it." He turns me around.

I bite my lip.

"Oh . . . my . . . gosh," he says, slow and drawn out.

"Okay, now before you get mad—"

"Lauren Emma Holbrook!"

"Which I suppose has already happened. I didn't—"

"You made a T-shirt for this." Accusations ring in his tone and reflect from his brown eyes.

I try pulling an Ethel Mertz. "Weeell . . ."

His mouth is open in shock. "'Just kiss her,' Laurie?"

"Hannah thought it was funny."

Ryan's shaking his head. "You made a T-shirt for this," he says again.

"But I'm wearing my coat over it. See?"

"Why did you do this?"

I shrug. "Hannah dared me."

He covers his face. "You two are a pair. Come on. We'll be late."

I follow him to his truck and smile sweetly as he opens the door for me. "Thanks, Ryan dear."

"Just get in." He groans.

I climb into the passenger seat and he closes the door after me. A second later, he slides in. "Hey, Ryan?"

"Yeah?"

"Thanks for taking me."

A smile sneaks onto his face. He sighs. "Not fair, Laurie. I can't stay mad at you."

"I'll try to do something really bad next time so you will."

"There's not going to be a next time."

"Mmm, maybe."

He shoots me a look.

I grin.

We drive in silence for a few blocks.

Here's what I hate: Silence. I try looking out the window for something to comment on, but talking about the weather is lame and there is nothing interesting going on outside.

"Hey, Ryan?"

"Yeah?"

I decide to take him into my confidence. "What do you think about Brandon and Hannah?"

He shrugs. "They're nice."

"I meant together, Ryan."

He presses his lips tight and stares out the windshield. "Brandon and Hannah?"

"Why not?"

He appears to be thinking about it. "Guess I don't know them that well. No setting them up, Laurie."

"How come?"

He sends me a quick glance. "If God wants them together, He can orchestrate that much better than you can."

"Gee, thanks."

"And I'm pretty sure God's not in the market for assistants. So back off, Susan."

I look at him. "What did you just call me?"

"Susan. The little girl on *Miracle on 34th Street*. Ruby made me watch it this past Christmas. I thought it an appropriate reference."

"An appropriate reference to what?"

"You. You and Susan have the same little conniving brain."

"Again, gee, thanks."

He grins at me. "You're welcome."

He drives into the parking lot and finds a spot near the back. "There's Ruby's car." He points to her little red Honda.

I look around. "I don't see Hannah's."

"Hannah's coming?"

"She's Nick's date."

He unbuckles his seat belt. "I feel like we should say a prayer or something."

"For what? Success?" I ask, climbing out.

"For safety. All this meddling is going to bring a lightning bolt on your head."

"Just don't touch me and you should be fine."

A much too skinny girl in tight black pants and an untucked white shirt opens the door for us. "Welcome to Vizzini's."

"Thanks," Ryan says.

"Party of two?"

"Actually, I have reservations," I tell her. "Is JACK here by any chance?"

The girl scuffs around the desk. "Yes. What's your name?"

"Laurie."

She looks down at the desk again, twirling her hair around one finger. "Okay. Follow me, please."

She grabs two menus and leads us around tables, chairs, and the big water fountain in the middle and finally points to a secluded table behind a bunch of plants.

"This it?" she asks.

"Yes." I sit and peer around a particularly large green, waxy-looking plant.

Ryan sits opposite me, and the girl shoves menus in front of our faces. "JACK will be your waiter."

She scuffs back the way she came.

Plants of all shapes and sizes are clustered around our table like they had just witnessed a murder scene right before. Ryan inhales. "This part of the place is definitely more humid."

"You don't have to tell me. I should have done my hair curly instead of straight. Not like we'll be able to tell the difference in about ten minutes." I crane my neck, trying to find them.

"What are you—"

"There! There they are!" I clap my hands over my mouth, trying not to laugh too loudly. "He's so cute. I wonder what he's talking about? Remind me to get flowers."

"For Ruby? She'll need them." Ryan's face is creased as he watches Stephen going all for it in his conversation.

"No, Nick can get those. Flowers for Stephen. This is a huge favor he's doing for me."

Ruby and Stephen sit at a table a few feet away. Ruby's back is to us, which is just how I told JACK to do it. Not only does it hide us from Ruby's tortured eyes, but it also gives us a first-class view of Stephen.

He smiles at me over Ruby's shoulder.

I grin.

He's talking animatedly, using his hands, his eyes, his eyebrows, and his torso. Ruby's head nods occasionally. And if it is regular coffee in front of her, she's going to be buzzing all night the way she's putting it down.

Ryan watches her, grimacing. "I hope you know what you're doing."

"Of course I do. Have a little faith." I pat his arm. "Can you see Nick?"

He looks around. "Ah, over there, Laur."

Nick's back is to us. He looks down at the table, tracing a design on it. Hannah sees my wave and takes the opportunity to grin at us.

I mouth, "Has he seen Ruby?"

She nods slightly.

I grin and turn back to Ryan.

"Decided what you want, Ryan? It's on me."

He just stares at me. "I did tell you that you were liking this too much, right?"

"Yes, you did."

JACK approaches the table cautiously. "Did I do it right?" he asks me.

I signal an okay. "Perfect. Thank you so much."

He smiles for the first time since the water-spaghetti incident. "What can I get you two to drink?"

"Coffee," Ryan and I say together.

He scribbles it down on his order pad. "Know what you want to eat?"

"Can I have a piece of your raspberry chocolate cake?" I ask.

Ryan wisely keeps his mouth shut.

"Sure." JACK obviously assumes we've eaten somewhere else. "Dessert for you as well?"

Ryan makes a *harrumph* sound. "No, I'll have the ravioli."

JACK keeps scribbling. "Anything else?"

"A dinner salad. Ranch dressing," I say.

Ryan holds up his fingers. "Two."

JACK nods and leaves.

I look back to Nick and Hannah. Her eyes are big and sad at the moment, her hands moving as she tells a story.

I'm pretty sure I don't want to know what she is talking about.

"What is he doing?" Ryan mutters.

I turn to Ruby and Stephen. He twirls spaghetti around his fork and holds it out to Ruby.

"Oh. Oh now that is just sick," Ryan exclaims. "Oh my gosh, I can't watch." He covers his face, gagging. "She didn't take it, did she? Tell me she didn't take it."

Ruby's back stiffens. She cuts a huge forkful of lasagna and shoves it in her mouth, holding a hand up to Stephen. He watches her, a smile on his face, and eats the spaghetti himself.

"She didn't take it," I tell Ryan, who is busy gulping down the coffee JACK set in front of us. I pick up my fork and attack the salad.

"Thank goodness." He puts his cup down weakly, pinching his forehead. "I don't know how much of this I can stand, Laur."

"Don't worry. Another three cups of that and you'll have the energy."

"When I think about Ruby eating off his fork . . . " He shudders.

"Hey. Relax, kid. It's just a joke, remember? And if Ruby seriously fell for Stephen right now, I would personally take her to get her head examined. He's supposed to be as gross as possible. 'Therefore, strengthen your feeble arms and weak knees.'"

He blinks. "What?"

I grin. "Hebrews 12:12. Found that verse yesterday. Great, isn't it? Sounds like a greeting card."

He finally smiles. "Oh, Laurie. Only you would memorize that particular verse. Whatever happened to the typical memory verses? You know, Psalm 23, Ephesians 5:1, that kind."

"Typical, shmypical." I make a face. "Who wants to be average?"

"You're right. Most people just aim for normal."

"I aim higher."

He laughs at me and changes the topic, crunching a cucumber. "How's small-group prep going?"

I take a deep breath. "Good, I think. It begins this Tuesday. I'm a little nervous, actually. I haven't ever taught anything like this before."

He reaches over and rubs my hand. "My turn to quote the Bible. 'Do not worry about what to say or how to say it.' Matthew 10:19. You'll do fine."

"Sweet boy, thou art. I'll keep you around." I lean over to watch Ruby again.

She puts a hand to her face and tries to look unassumingly over her shoulder at Nick. She's not the best at being subtle. I see it plain as day and so does Nick because he's looking at her. They both jerk back to their dates.

Ryan's still talking. "So, Laurie, fishing trip starts in about two weeks. Ready for nature?"

I moan like I should be in the ER. "I'm never ready for nature."

"And I had you pinned as the outdoor type all this time." He's trying to hide a smile behind his coffee cup and failing miserably.

I look at him. "You know how long our driveway is?"

"Yeah."

"I drive down to get the mail sometimes because it's too long to walk if it's windy or rainy or hailing or snowing . . ."

"I get the point."

I wave my hands. "Even if it's just too sunny, I drive."

"So I guess talking you into a bicycle ride is pretty fruitless."

I tip my head. "What's a bicycle?"

JACK refills my water using both hands. "How're the salads?"

I grin at him. "Great."

"Your cake and ravioli should be out in a few minutes."

"Thanks, JACK," Ryan says.

I check on Ruby again. She grabs JACK's apron as he passes and says something to him. He nods.

"Bet she asked for the check." Ryan licks his fork after finishing his salad.

"Check or an anvil." I watch them for a second. "I think Stephen should get the Golden Globe this year. It's hard for someone that gorgeous to be really disgusting."

JACK sets a black book on the table in front of Stephen. Ruby grabs her purse.

"Poor Ruby," I say.

Ryan's watching his sister with a look of pity. "She'll need therapy after this, you realize."

"Not therapy. Maybe counseling. Poor Ruby."

Stephen sets the twenty dollars I gave him on the book and reaches for her hand, which Ruby shoves into her lap. I watch Nick, who is tense enough to look like he's on the verge of splitting as well.

"Hannah has not stopped talking to breathe for twenty minutes," Ryan says.

I nod knowingly. "She's a superhero. She got bit by a genetically altered shark a few years back and developed gills. It's why she keeps her hair long."

"Made the swim team, I suppose."

"You'd better believe it. Oh brother. Duck!"

I grab Ryan's head and push it onto the table, hiding behind the monster plant probably programmed to eat whomever is stalling dinner near closing time.

"Laurie, I can hold my own head down."

"Sorry." I let go of his curly hair.

"What are we doing?" he whispers.

"Ruby stood up. I didn't want her to see us."

He starts chuckling, eyes sparkling. "You moved from sharks to duck so fast I figured we were covering marine animals as our dinner conversation."

"What's your favorite?" I push my salad bowl out of the way so I can set my chin on the table.

"Sea lions."

"I like otters."

He balances his chin on the table as well and grins at me. "I have to say one thing for you, Laurie. My brain has to work faster when you're around."

"Thereby prolonging your mental capabilities." I smile back. "Is she gone?"

He lifts his head a few inches from the table. "Yeah." He straightens. "She's gone. Both of them are."

"Nick too?" I sit up, glancing around.

"Yep."

JACK appears and sets a gargantuan hunk of cake in front of me and a huge plate of ravioli on the table for Ryan.

Ryan grins as I gratefully dig into the cake. "Eat it quickly, Laur, or we'll be late to Bible study."

We drive onto Nick's street right on time, and Ryan again parks in the dimmest spot he can find.

I stare at him as he pulls the keys out of the ignition. He finally notices I haven't taken off my seat belt or moved when he opens the door.

"You okay, Laurie?

"You parked in the darkest spot possible."

He pokes his head outside and looks around. "There's a streetlight right there." He points up the street forty miles.

"Yes. Barely glowing."

"Don't start with the murderers again. Come on, get out."

I frown, dubious.

"Get out, Laur. I'll protect you. I promise. Come on. Please? We'll be late."

I unbuckle my seat belt. "We have to run."

"We'll run."

I open the door, shut it, and bolt up the street. I beat him to the front door by a good three yards.

"Didn't make the track team either, huh?" I ask him, opening the door.

He huffs. "You never yelled go."

People crowd the tiny entryway, the entire living room, the kitchen, the stairs, and probably the garage. The usual dull roar has been replaced by a four-alarm siren.

Nick needs a bigger house. This is getting ridiculous.

I glimpse a blonde head and a waving hand, figure it's Hannah, and go that direction.

Slowly.

You know that dream where your house is burning down and you're running to get out and the floor turns into Jell-O and you are suddenly moving in slow motion?

Ryan grabs the back of my shirt so he won't get lost, and we slog through the masses.

I try to count the people, but I lose track after thirty-five.

This is a fire hazard.

"Watch it, Laurie!"

I stop and look down. Hannah is on the floor below me. "Hi, Hannah."

She yells at me. "I found it works to just sit, and then they have no choice but to walk around you!"

"What?" Ryan shouts in my ear.

"We need to sit!" I scream back.

I plop down, land halfway on Hannah, and scoot over just as Ryan sits.

Oof!

I push him off and Hannah leans over. "I'll tell you about it later!"

"Okay!"

Nick climbs onto the kitchen counter and waves his hands. "EVERYONE FIND A SEAT!"

Ten minutes tick by as people sit on the couch, the stairs, the banister, in the entryway, and in the kitchen.

Nick slides off the counter. "Whew. This is a crowd."

The aforesaid crowd smiles, nods, agrees.

I crane my head looking for Ruby. She is on the far couch, feet tucked up under her, a kid in a green Adidas shirt and red baseball cap backwards beside her.

She turns in my direction and catches my gaze.

Any thought of a jolly laugh, backslap, and forgetting about the disastrous blind date is immediately obliterated. I feel the optic nerves in my eyeballs singe from the look of pure solder-efficient heat.

Oy.

I grab the back of my hair and elbow Ryan in the ribs as I rip my corneas away. Ryan makes a sound and rubs his chest. I blink repeatedly, making sure I can still see.

Nick makes eye contact next.

I really, really, *really* wish Ryan had parked closer. The murderers hiding on this street have names I recognize and a motive.

Ryan watches Nick for a second and then leans over. "I would avoid going home for a while. They know where you live."

"Well, I can't stay here," I whine softly.

"I'd stay the night with Hannah."

"I was thinking somewhere in Brazil."

"Stephen, take it away," Nick says, the ice in his voice tempered but not in his gaze as he stares at his friend. He sends me another life-threatening look as he sits on the arm of the couch, next to Ruby.

I hope the teaching tonight is on the merits of forgiveness.

Stephen looks around, slipping his guitar pick in his mouth as he tunes the strings. "Hwey, evewybodwy," he says around the plastic disk.

He spits the pick out and smiles. "I was looking over the songs I'd chosen for this week and thought the verse on the top of the song sheets really fits the theme."

Stephen starts strumming softly while the song sheets make their way around the room.

Ryan takes one look at the reference and starts hacking.

Water wells in my eyes, but I can't tell if it is from the damage to my optic nerve or from the continued realization that our sovereign God has a sense of humor.

Colossians 3:13.

"'Bear with each other and forgive whatever grievances you may have against one another. Forgive as the Lord forgave you,'" he reads, gently raking the pick down the strings in the rhythm to the first song.

I drop my head, covering my face, my shoulders shuddering as I suck in my breath, silently laughing.

Hannah makes a weird wheezing noise next to me, and I can feel Ryan shaking.

I peek at Nick and Ruby.

Ruby has a hand over her eyes, and Nick mashes his lips together, trying to cover the smile.

Stephen pauses playing when he finishes reading.

Right then is when Nick bursts.

He snorts loudly. Then he grins, leans forward on his knees, and cries he laughs so hard.

Everyone else in the room stares at him like he finally stacked his last French fry and lost the ketchup.

Ruby keeps her hands over her face, her body trembling, leaning into Nick, which is dangerous because he's about to fall off the couch and land on the three people squished on the floor below him.

Stephen grins at all five of us and then starts the first song.

When Nick gets up to teach, he's collected himself.

He teaches for twenty minutes, and the moment he says the final "amen," the siren-talking starts again and I know one of Nick's neighbors is going to call the cops.

"Hey, see that girl?" Hannah points through the throng to a short-haired redhead. "I heard her talking beforehand. She just got engaged."

I nod. "Goody."

"Guess who her fiancé is?"

"Brad Pitt?" I suggest.

Hannah ignores me. "Her UPS delivery man. That paints a picture, doesn't it? Want to know how he proposed?"

"He didn't ship her the ring, did he?" I look at Hannah. "Oh good grief, he did."

She's laughing. "Hysterical, isn't it?"

"That's just plain corny."

She grins at Ryan. "Think you'll propose with a hard hat?"

"Better." He smiles broadly. "I'm planning on the ring being made from a nail."

I make a face. "Yuck."

"Not a used nail," he says.

"It would rust! Your wife would end up with an orange ring finger."

"Yeah," Hannah joins in. "And then she'd get lead poisoning."

"Or something worse," I say. "And then you'd have mutated children."

Ryan sighs. "One more fantasy down the drain."

"There's chocolate in the kitchen, Honey." I pat his shoulder. "That might help."

"On my way." He stands with difficulty and squeezes in the general direction of the kitchen.

I look at Hannah. "What did you do to him?"

"I didn't do anything to Ryan."

"You know exactly who I mean."

She smiles coyly. "A good girl never tells her secrets."

"Hannah, a good girl doesn't *have* secrets."

She starts shaking her head. "Not true! Sleeping Beauty had a secret, and she was good."

"Sleeping Beauty didn't know she had a secret." I twirl a chunk of hair around my finger. "I wonder if she ever went near a spinning wheel again?"

"I don't know, Laurie. But if I had to guess, I would bet she didn't end up with a career as a cloth maker."

I frown. "Quilter, right?"

"I think the term would be a weaver. Or maybe a textile creator?"

A pair of hose-clad legs stops in front of me. "Hello, girls."

I grimace at Hannah and then smile sweetly to Ruby. "Hi."

"Hey, Ruby." Hannah also wears an innocent expression, blue eyes Bambi-like.

Ruby crosses her arms over her chest and taps one heel. "And what do you have to say?"

I tip my head at her. "Are people who use spinning wheels called weavers or spinners or textile persons?"

She closes her eyes. "Don't know why I bother." She turns to leave. "And they are called textile manufacturers."

Chapter Twenty-Three

I step through the newly cleaned glass door of The Brandon Knox Photography Studio at exactly 8:57 and smile brightly at Ruby, who leans up against the desk with a What-Have-You-to-Say-for-Yourself? look on her pretty face. She's doing a new thing with her eye makeup—a little eyeliner, mascara, and some shimmery shadow that really set off her brown eyes.

"Good morning, Ruby Fair." I set a tray filled with coffee cups on the desk and shed my coat. I hand her one of the cups.

"Unbelievable. You are completely unbelievable, Lauren Holbrook."

"I don't know why. I gave you the black coffee, right?" I check the other two.

"This is to pacify me." She waves the coffee in my face.

"Why in the world would I give someone caffeine to pacify them? If I were trying to pacify you, I would have given you something sweet." I lay my backpack on the desk and pull out a paper sack from Merson's. "Chocolate-covered strawberry?"

She sips the coffee, rolling her eyes. "Fine. You owe me."

I concede with a nod. "I know."

"More than just a strawberry and a cup of coffee. Even though this is a really good cup of coffee."

"It's Shawn's."

She turns the cup around in her hands. "It says Merson's on here."

"One and the same." I hand her the paper sack. "Two strawberries."

She takes a bite out of one, then sets both the coffee and the strawberry on the desk, rubbing her hands together businesslike. "Now that I'm calmer, we can discuss your payment."

I sit meekly in one of the chairs. "Twenty dollars a week for the next six weeks?"

"Honey, that doesn't even scratch the surface."

"Oh come on, Ruby, it wasn't *that* bad."

"Laurie, he seems like a nice enough guy at Bible study. But he talked for forty-five *minutes* about his dog's sinus problems! *Forty-five* minutes! In disgusting detail! Over dinner!" She's making a gagging face.

"Ruby—"

She starts pacing. "I was sitting there staring at the cheese dripping down my lasagna as he talked about a big mucus blockage! It was gross! I'm never eating lasagna again!"

"Would an all-expense-paid date with Nick make up for it?"

She stops mid-rant. "What?"

Hannah comes through the door.

"Hey, Laur. Hey, Ruby." She sets her purse down and notices the extra coffee. "For me?"

"Yep." I look back at Ruby. "What were you saying?"

Ruby's staring slack-jawed at Hannah, who looks amazing in a cerulean sparkly top and brown cords. "How come I got Stephen, who was gross and disgusting, and Nick got Hannah?"

Hannah sips her coffee. "You don't know what I talked about."

Ruby's shaking her head so hard her curls take flight. "It couldn't have been worse than my conversation."

"What did you talk about?" I ask Hannah.

"Flies."

"Flies?" Ruby and I repeat together.

"Yeah." She sips her coffee again. "Did you know that flies develop from an egg to an adult in seven to fourteen days? And since they're usually bred in manure, they carry diseases like typhoid or diarrhea?"

Ruby quits drinking her coffee. "I was wrong."

"Don't tell me you researched for this dinner," I say.

Hannah nods happily.

"Geek," I accuse her.

Brandon comes through the door, slinging his coat over his shoulder.

"It works better if you wear it," Hannah tells him.

"Thanks, Mom. How'd the dates go?" He slings an arm around Ruby's shoulders. She glares at him. "That well, huh?" Brandon asks.

"It was horrible! Absolutely horrible! If all men are like that—"

"Nick's not," I put in.

"I'm marrying Nick, then," Ruby declares.

"You are?" I grin.

She stops, her face turning a brilliant burgundy color. "Well, if he asks."

Hannah looks at me. "So I guess we have a new project, Laur."

"Don't even think about it, girls."

Brandon nods, his arm still around Ruby. "Yeah. Don't even think about it."

"Hey, let go of her, you womanizer." I swat his hand. "What if Nick walks in? Want him to get the wrong idea?"

Ruby blushes. "Laurie."

"Ruby, you know I'd love to chat with you, but my nine fifteen is here. What are the odds?"

"You are one lucky dame," Brandon says in admiration.

The Steeles come in. "Thank goodness it's warm in here," Mrs. Steele says.

My stomach growls as I wave good-bye to my twelve thirty. They run to their car and jump in, probably cranking on the heater.

A pickup pulls into the parking lot and I grin. Ryan.

He comes through the door a moment later. His hair is squooshed underneath a backwards baseball cap, he's got sawdust caked into the creases on his boots, and he obviously didn't shave this morning. I have to smile.

"Hey, Hannah! I've got a live one!" I yell.

Hannah steps out from Studio One. "Hi, Ryan. Sorry about her. She had Coco-Odies for breakfast this morning."

Ryan grimaces as he looks at me. "Coco-Odies?"

"With two extra scoops of sugar." I hold up my fingers like a preschooler to show him.

The grimace hasn't left his face. "Do I want to take her to lunch, Hannah?"

"Please. Then you can deal with her."

"Hey! Let's both step to our neutral corners," I tell her.

She hooks a thumb over her shoulder. "Mine got eaten by Herman."

I peer behind her. It's true. The massive bouquet of white lilies, red roses, and more baby's breath than you see in a hundred nurseries was delivered this morning with a card, which Ruby did not let Hannah and me see. Quite distressing. In rebuttal, we named the monstrosity Herman.

Ruby was not amused.

Ryan lifts an eyebrow but doesn't comment on the name. "So I came to ask you something," he says to me.

"Ask away."

"Want to go get some lunch?"

"Can we get M&Ms afterward?"

"Our stash ran out," Hannah explains for me. "We had to split the last Milky Way."

"Horror of horrors," he responds dryly. "Fine. We'll get M&Ms. Get your coat, it's freezing."

"Ruby's going out with Nick," I tell Hannah. "Make sure Brandon eats, will you?"

She salutes. "I'll do my best."

Ryan opens the door and Cold Wind invites itself inside, offers itself a chair, and then decides to riffle through Hannah's papers.

Hannah smashes the papers down on Cold Wind's icy fingers, and waves. "Have fun!"

"Where are we going?" I ask once Ryan's climbed into the truck after helping me into the passenger seat.

He shrugs. "Vizzini's or Halia's?"

"It's Thursday."

"So?"

"So Vizzini's has their special fried eggplant spaghetti with a side of fresh, albeit fried, vegetables, including squash, onions, and bell peppers, and, for dessert, kumquat."

His forehead wrinkles. "What the heck is kumquat?"

"An orangelike thing, I think."

He turns out of the parking lot. "Halia's."

"Wise man."

Halia's is a good three miles from the studio. We get there in no time at all, Ryan parks, and a bearded male opens the door for us.

"Welcome to Halia's! The best Mexican food on the planet!"

"Thanks. Is Halia here?" I ask.

The man shakes his head vigorously. "Nope. I'm the new owner."

I blink. "You are? What happened to Halia?"

"She retired. Two weeks ago." He's beaming. "Table for two?"

I nod, surprised. The man fairly jumps in his excitement. "Excellent! Right this way, please!"

He leads us through a mostly empty restaurant to a table near the back windows and across the aisle from an elderly couple. "Enjoy your meal!"

"Thanks." Ryan strips his coat.

He waits until the bearded man leaves before leaning over the table. "Odd person. Empty place."

"Yeah." I take off my coat as well. "I wonder why Halia retired. Every time Dad and I came, she always looked like she loved working here."

Ryan looks around. "So Halia is Hispanic?"

"No, actually Halia is Hawaiian. But when she came to the continental U.S., she realized she liked Mexican food much better than Hawaiian, so she created a Mexican restaurant."

"Weird."

"Yeah, well, you'll get used to this town one day." I look at the menu. "I'm getting enchiladas. Halia makes great beef enchiladas." I stop. "Wow. I hope she left her recipes."

"Enchiladas sound good."

A timid-looking girl I've never seen before with big hazel eyes and limp brown hair tiptoes to the table. "C-Can I take your order?" she whispers.

Ryan smiles kindly at her. "Two rolled beef enchiladas, please. And an order of nachos."

"And two Dr. Peppers," I order.

Ryan nods. "And two coffees."

I clear my throat. Ryan rolls his eyes.

"One with room for cream," he tacks on.

The girl scribbles furiously, biting her lip. "I'll have the . . . the drinks right out."

"Thanks," he says.

She fairly bolts out of sight.

Ryan watches her. "No wonder the place is empty."

I frown at him. "Ryan!"

"What? The girl must be hiding a body in the kitchen or something."

"Well, sure! It's what they make the carne adovada with."

He makes a face. "You are gross."

"And you are paranoid. People are probably just crowding Vizzini's to get their hands on the Thursday special."

The old man across the aisle turns toward us. "I heard about that," he says to us, his voice deep and gruff.

Ryan blinks. "Heard about what, sir?"

"The Thursday special. Vizzini's changed it. It's now four-cheese tortellini with a side of buttered broccoli and a slice of cheesecake."

I dab the drool off my lower lip.

Ryan nods. "Sounds good."

"We're going there after this." The old man motions to his wife, who is decked out in a blue-checked dress, blue hair, and matching blue heels.

"I love cheesecake," she declares. Her voice, as opposed to the crusty sound her husband makes, is soft and fluid like I imagine Julie Andrews sounding in about ten years.

"Me too," I say with a grin.

"I just can't eat it," she confesses. "My arteries."

"Verna's had three attacks this year," the man says.

"How tragic," I commiserate.

She waves a blue-veined hand at me that, oddly enough, matches the dress, the shoes, and the hair. "Oh, the attacks aren't the tragic part, Sweetie. It's not eating the cheesecake that's the hardest. Especially when I have to sit here and watch Mr. Smug himself eat it right in front of me." She smacks the old man's arm.

Mr. Smug smirks. "I told you that you should have eaten more vitamins years ago. I did and look at me." He looks at us. "No attacks, no strokes, no cancer."

"You did not tell me to eat vitamins. You told me to eat Brussels sprouts." She sticks her tongue out and gags in a very not-so-old-lady action. "Disgusting things, those little cabbage heads are!"

The man lurches over the table, pointing a bony finger at her. "But they're packed with vitamins! You ate those, you could have had the cheesecake!"

"For heaven's sake, Arnie, I'm eighty-seven years old! Just let me have the cheesecake!"

"No!"

Ryan leans his elbows on the table and covers his mouth, his eyes crinkling.

Verna slams her napkin on the table. "Fine, you old Pop-Tart! I'll go there *myself* and get the cheesecake." She storms off, not sparing us another glance.

Arnie sighs loud enough for her to hear, waits until she gets to the front door, and gives us a grin. "Making her mad keeps life fun." He sets a ten-spot on the table and goes after her. "What did you just call me?" he hollers as he leaves.

I look at Ryan and he uncovers his mouth, grinning broadly.

I giggle.

"Was that a sign of what our married life would look like?" he asks with a laugh.

I nod slowly. "I would say so."

"Their kids must've been a riot growing up."

The girl with the limp hair, who has yet to identify herself, skulks to our table, drops the drinks and a plate of half-cooked nachos, and lights for the back room like a lighter lighting . . . and never mind that analogy.

I try very hard not to gag at the nachos. Well, moderately hard, anyway.

"Blegh." I pull one guacamole-sogged chip from the middle of the plate. "Maybe Halia didn't leave the recipes."

Ryan's nose wrinkles. "I say we skip the nachos."

The chip wilts between my fingers and plunks with a small *glump* back onto the stack.

"Blegh! Yuck, yuck, yucky. Give me a napkin, boy." I shake my hand.

He passes a napkin. "Here, girl."

I shiver, grossed out. "This place has gone way downhill. They used part of the corpse to make that guacamole. The chips are cold."

"You are nasty."

"We've covered this, remember?"

He pushes the repulsing plate to the edge of the table.

"Keep pushing."

"Laurie."

"I'm serious."

"I'm not paying for a broken plate." He swishes his straw around in his Dr. Pepper. "What do you have this afternoon?"

"Appointments at three, three thirty, and four. Then I'm done for the day." I take a drink, my stomach still rolling. "Why?"

The corners of his mouth turn up. He leans over the table conspiratorially. "I can't believe I'm telling you this, but I know what Ruby's card said."

"What?" I shriek.

"Nick asked her out to dinner. Congratulations, kid. Your plan worked. Not that I condone it."

I raise a congratulatory fist. "I'm a genius!"

"No, you're just plain lucky." He lowers my fist and pats my shoulder.

"I don't believe in luck."

"Plucky, then."

"You are patting my shoulder again."

He stops and squeezes the back of my neck. "You drive me crazy."

"I know."

He grins at me, his eyes sparkling. I smile back.

Some of the guacamole spores must have gone through my nostrils and landed in my stomach because I start feeling weird. Sort of a combo of queasy and tingly.

Worse, I can't decide whether it's a good or bad sensation.

The girl squirrels over with the plates and Ryan pulls his hand away. The queasiness stops.

I watch Ryan as he takes his plate and suddenly wonder if . . .

Nah. Not possible. It's the guacamole. That's all.

She sets my enchiladas in front of me, and the queasiness jump-starts back into place.

"Enjoy your meal," she whimpers and runs for it.

Ryan swallows, licking his lips nervously.

I nudge one side of the glob with my fork. "Ryan," I half-whisper, half-shriek. "There's an eyeball in this."

"We're leaving." He pulls twenty bucks from his wallet, drops it on the table, and pushes back his chair. "Get up."

He gets me in the car and drives the few minutes to Merson's. Shawn looks up as we walk inside.

"Hey, guys."

I inhale. Look around. Three-fourths of the tables are filled, Dessert Heaven exists in perfect conformity, and Shawn is already pouring two mugs of coffee.

"Shawn, Shawn, I love you." I grab his spare hand across the counter and kiss it.

"Ease up, Hon." Ryan pulls me back a few inches. "You're scaring the man with the desserts."

Shawn watches me, one eyebrow raised. "Should I be worried?" he asks Ryan.

"No. Just Laurie's unusual way of expressing herself, that's all."

Shawn nods but keeps a wary eye on me. "Here. Coffee."

I take the cup with a grin. "Thanks, Shawn."

Ryan steers me to an empty table, and Shawn comes over, notepad in hand. "What did you two want?"

I look at him. "Do you know how to make tortellini?"

My lamp is glowing like milk left out for four days. I squint at it, scrutinizing it. It may be time to change the lightbulb. It seems dimmer.

I shake my head slightly, trying to get myself to focus. My Bible is open on my lap, but I'm having a hard time not getting distracted tonight.

Possibly the fault of the three mochas I consumed at eight this evening.

Rubbing my forehead, I stare at the words of Philippians 4. "Whatever is true, whatever is noble, whatever is right, whatever is pure, whatever is lovely, whatever is admirable—if anything is excellent or praiseworthy—think about such things."

Paul liked the word *whatever*.

I slide my highlighter under the verse. There's a command here. To think about this list of whatevers. True, noble, right, pure, lovely.

Lovely.

A verse Nick had referred to in his last teaching comes back to me, and I flip to Psalm 50:2. "From Zion, perfect in beauty, God shines forth."

It seems to me, mocha-brained and all, the only thing truly fulfilling this list is God Himself.

I turn the Four-Day-Glowing-Milk lamp off, no longer having trouble focusing.

Chapter Twenty-Four

I get to work just before nine on Friday morning. The studio is dark, cold, and quiet. I get the same feeling in the studio on days like this that I get in a church when there is no one there but me. Creeped out.

I peel off my gloves, stick my backpack in the cubby, unscrew the cap on my thermos of coffee, and turn up the thermostat.

Brandon comes through the door whistling and ends the creepiness. "Morning, Laur."

I swallow. "Hey."

"How'd Ruby's date go last night?"

I shrug. "She's not here. I don't know."

Brandon frowns. "She's not here?"

"Nope."

"It's nine o'clock." He points out the window. "That's the Stewarts getting out of their van. Ruby has them."

I follow his finger and note that he is correct. "Hmm."

"You'll have to take them."

"Brandon, I have an appointment in ten minutes."

He sighs. "Okay. I'll take the Stewarts, you cover your appointment, and if Ruby isn't here in half an hour we're calling the police, got it? This isn't like her."

"Ah, love old."

As the Stewarts walk in, the bell over the door dings. "Ruby couldn't make the appointment, so you'll be with me." Brandon leads them into Studio One.

Hannah arrives just as the door closes behind them. "Hey, Laurie. How'd Ruby's date go?"

"She's not here."

Hannah stops unwrapping her scarf, sets her coffee down, and gasps. "Ruby's not here?"

"Nope."

She stares at the closed door of Studio One. "But that was the Stewarts."

"Correct."

"They're Ruby's clients."

I nod. "Brandon took them."

"Weirdness. I hope she's not home crying." Hannah's eyes get big. "Oh, Laurie, what if the date was horrible?"

"Not possible. Didn't you see them on Wednesday night? Can't you see Herman?" The bouquet had to stay because it wouldn't fit in Ruby's car.

Hannah's advancing to panic mode. "What if it was to soften the blow that he didn't really like her like that?"

"Like what?"

"Like he liked her, like, seriously."

"You lost me after the second like." I smile.

Hannah rolls her eyes, but sighs and giggles. "Speculating does nothing. I say we get to work." She shoves her purse in the cubby and sits authoritatively in her chair.

"Good idea." I take another drink. "What should we work on?"

"When is your first appointment?" She looks at the schedule book. "In exactly four minutes. That gives us plenty of time to sketch out a battle plan."

"A battle plan," I repeat dubiously.

"For when Ruby comes in."

"We'll battle her?" I raise one eyebrow.

"We'll assess the waters and bridge the moat if necessary."

"Mmm. Too much symbolism, Hannah."

She points at me. "You'll see how the date went, and I'll comfort her."

"Hey! How come I have to be the bad guy?"

"You've known her longer."

I open my mouth to protest.

"The Lawsons are here, Laurie."

Rats.

Hannah is sharper than she looks, I'll give her that.

I come out of Studio Two at 9:40 and find Brandon pacing and Hannah wringing her hands. I wave good-bye to the clients and turn to my comrades.

"She's not here yet?" I ask.

"No, and she's not answering her phone. Laurie, what if it was horrible and Ruby went home and—" Hannah stops, but her petrified expression says it all.

"Hannah, she wouldn't do anything *that* drastic. Hand me my backpack."

Brandon stops pacing long enough to watch me pull on my gloves. "Where are you going?"

"To Ruby's house."

"What about your appointments?" he asks, mouth open.

"I just have one at ten, and surely I'll be back before my twelve o'clock. You take the Gordons."

I sling my backpack over my shoulder and march out of the studio, Brandon and Hannah gaping behind me.

Ruby lives four blocks away in half of a cute little duplex. The other half is owned by a fifty-five-year-old spinster named Odella Purvis, who is a workaholic perfectionist and every year plants a line of petunias straighter than a ruler and just about as boring. Ruby once told me she's scared to death she'll never get married and end up like Odella, but I told Ruby she couldn't possibly. Men run from names like Odella. They don't from names like Ruby.

I park in front of the house and jog up the front steps, past the adorable little porch, and knock on the door.

No answer.

I pound the door and ring the doorbell four times.

Somewhere in the back of my brain, Hannah's fear creeps in and I start getting worried, especially when there still isn't an answer.

There is nothing else left to do. I resort to screaming.

"Ruby! RUBY! RUUUUBY!"

I hear a slam and see Odella, dressed professionally from the waist up but wearing designer sweatpants and plain brown functional slippers, march down her front steps, cross her arms over her chest, and glare piercingly at me with eyes that could be soft and brown but at the moment are radiating a steel-like quality.

"What in blue heavens are you doing?" she barks.

"I'm Laurie. I'm trying to find Ruby . . . uh, ma'am."

It seems a little odd to be calling a woman in a blazer, slippers, and curlers ma'am, but Odella fairly radiates ma'amness.

"She's in my kitchen, so for the love of all things quiet, stop yelling like a buzzsaw and get in my house."

"Yes, ma'am."

"And hurry. You made me leave the door open. That's probably a good twenty dollars of warm air I just let out."

She marches back up the stairs. I consider—only for a moment—walking across her grass to get to her front door, see the look on her face, and quickly reconsider. I run down the porch steps, over the sidewalk, up Odella's porch steps, and into her house. The moment my foot hits the beige tiled entry, she slams the door closed.

"For heaven's sake. Couldn't you just call?" Odella gripes, leading the way to her kitchen, rubbing her hands on her arms in an effort to warm up.

"We did call." I'm tripping along behind her like a little lost dog. "We called Ruby's house. Several times. And we never . . . ah . . ."

We enter a living room. That is, I think it's a living room. All I see is beige, beige, beige. On the walls, the carpet, the couches, even the entertainment center.

I think of the scene in *The Ten Commandments* where Charlton Heston is sent to the desert and the sandstorm kicks up and everywhere he looks is just *brown*.

What a depressing color.

No wonder Odella has a moniker like that.

"This way, Laurie," she snaps and thumbs to an old-style bar door. She pushes through it and I follow, blinking.

I stop blinking for just a moment when I step into the kitchen but quickly start again. My contacts are beginning to dry out.

Ruby is crumpled on one of the stools at the kitchen counter, aimlessly stirring a china teacup with something green in it, staring at the oven door. Her hair is a wavy, tangled wreck, she doesn't have any makeup on, and she wears a bright red robe over some flannel polka-dot pajamas. A four-inch mountain of Kleenex grows on the counter beside her.

"Uh, Ruby?" I creep up beside her.

She drags her eyes off the oven and blinks red-rimmed eyes repeatedly at me. "Laurie?"

Oy. I refrain from saying it out loud. She looks like she was trampled by a high school marching band and then dropped into the tuba.

"Hi, Honey," I say, my voice warm and syrupy like Hershey's chocolate sauce. "What happened?" I sit down beside her, wrapping an arm over her shoulders, pushing the strong-smelling, inedible-looking tea out of her reach.

Her eyes fill. "He likes me," she whispers.

Not the response I'm expecting.

"Okay," I say slowly, rubbing her shoulder. "Then why . . . ?"

"He sat there last night and told me straight to my face that he *likes* me!" Her voice is choked and full.

"Ruby, I'm not seeing what the problem is."

"We were sitting there after dinner at this little dessert place and he held my hand and told me he *likes* me and I . . . I . . ." She bursts into tears, covering her face.

I look up at Odella, who stands with arms crossed, leaning against her cabinets. "She threw up," Odella supplies unemotionally.

"Oh, Sweetie." I hug Ruby tighter.

"I can't believe it! I was so *embarrassed*. And I threw up a *lot* too. I felt sick the whole way home and I just couldn't look at him."

"What did he say?"

She waves a hand, bleakly. "He said he hoped I felt better."

"That's it?"

"I don't remember."

"You don't remember?"

She closes her eyes in pain. "I fell asleep in his car. When I woke up, I was here."

"In Odella's house?"

Odella nods. "The man came banging at my door at ten last night, wondering if I had a spare key to Ruby's because he couldn't get her house key to work. Naturally, I don't. I don't believe in having spare keys lying around for every burglar in the neighborhood to break into everyone's house as he pleases."

I nod, only half-listening to her ranting.

Ruby rubs her swollen eyes and sighs. "I botched it, Laurie. The one guy I've ever really liked and I *ruined* it!" She dissolves into yet more tears.

I look back at Odella, who hands me another Kleenex box without a word.

A thought hits me and I feel like throwing up just thinking about it.

"Uh, Ruby?" I cut into her sobs, rubbing her back.

"Wh-what?" She shudders, mopping her nose and eyes with a Kleenex.

"You didn't, I mean, you two didn't go to Halia's, did you?"

She blinks and nods. "Yeah. How'd you know?"

"Oh boy." I pull my hand away and rub my own face. "Ryan and I went there for lunch yesterday."

"So?" Odella demands.

"So they're hiding a corpse in the back. It's what they make the carne adovada with."

Ruby's sobbing gets louder. Odella just stares at me blanch-faced.

"You're not serious," she finally says.

"No, not really. But I do think the restaurant is not cooking things properly."

Ruby begins wailing.

"Oh, Honey, I'm so sorry!" I put both arms around her now and she tucks her head on my shoulder. I feel her tears soak through my shirt. "I just naturally assumed you'd go to Vizzini's. I don't know why, I just did."

Ruby shakes her head vehemently, banging her forehead against my chin.

Ahw. Pain shoots up my jaw and pounds in my brain.

She blows her nose. Once. Twice. A third time and then uses the shredded Kleenex to soak up her cheeks. "You mean . . ." Her voice wobbles. "You mean it wasn't me?"

I'm not comprehending. "What?"

"It was the food? It was the restaurant's fault?"

"Yes, Ruby." My voice is back in Hershey mode.

Fresh tears drip down her cheeks, staining her face red in the meantime. "This is wonderful," she croaks, leaning forward and burying her head in her arms.

I exchange a puzzled glance with Odella.

"What is?" I ask.

Ruby lifts her head. "I thought it was me. I thought I'd gone and gotten a stupid virus or something. Or that Nick telling me he liked me was too much for my stomach and I wasn't built for marriage."

I rub her back, trying very hard not to laugh at her misery.

"But now you say it's the restaurant's fault?" Her voice squeaks like she's in puberty.

I can't decide if that is a question or a statement. So I just keep patting.

Ryan would have been proud of me.

Odella frowns as Ruby keeps crying. "I've dealt with this long enough. Her purse is in the guest room. Her keys are in there."

"Guest room is which way?"

She rolls her eyes like I should know where the guest room is. "Never mind. I'll get it." She stalks from the room, curlers bouncing.

I take the teacup from the counter and set it in the sink, then swipe Ruby's mountain of Kleenex into the trash can I find under the sink.

I see some disinfectant in the cabinet, pull Ruby's head off the counter, and wipe down the whole of it, just in case she has the flu instead of food poisoning.

"What's happening?" She hiccups.

"We're leaving. Come on, Ruby, stand up." She stands and suddenly gasps. I drop the spray bottle and grab her arms. "What? Pain? Where?"

"Work!" she shrieks. "Oh my gosh! What time is it?"

"Ten thirty."

She screams. "I had an appointment! Oh my gosh!" she says again.

"Look, Honey, don't worry about it. Brandon and I covered it. Come on. We'll get you cleaned up and then you can go to work."

Odella reappears with the purse.

I shoulder the bag and smile sweetly. "Thanks for taking care of her, Odella."

"Just make sure it doesn't happen again," she says, huffing. "Men."

Apparently, this one word is the curse-all and end-all for Odella.

I wrap an arm around Ruby, still rubbing her shoulder, and lead her back through the sandstorm and out the front door. Odella follows us and stands on her porch watching as I help Ruby back to her house.

"I would like that robe and pajama set cleaned before she returns it," Odella calls after us.

A sudden realization pinches my spinal column and I look back. Odella has her arms crossed and a sour expression on her face.

"What time do you usually go into work?" I call to her.

She grumpily responds, "Seven."

I smile. "Thanks, Odella." There is hope for the woman yet. Any workaholic who can take a good four hours in the morning to console a wounded neighbor has a good chance of becoming normal.

I unlock Ruby's front door, escort her inside, and point her toward the shower. She goes into the bathroom and I dig through her too-neat closet to find something girly and feel-good she can wear.

I finally find a cute flippy skirt and a bright pink top in the back of her closet.

She comes out of the bathroom in a robe twenty minutes later, looking remarkably better. Her nose and eyes are still slightly swollen, but the redness has receded and her eyes have cleared some.

"I feel horrible." She falls on her bed.

"Not now. Get up, Ruby."

She moans tragically. "I have an awful headache. And I can't believe I spent the night at Odella's."

"You did her a favor by getting her back into the world of the lost and needy. Get up."

She sits, cradling her head in her hands.

I hand her the outfit. "Get dressed and dry your hair."

Thirty minutes later, she looks somewhat professional, and we leave. I drive straight to Merson's and buy us both extra-large coffees while she waits in the car.

"Bless you," she fawns when I climb back in. She pops the plastic lid off and inhales. "Whatever Odella tried to make me drink was disgusting. Tasted like grass."

I park in front of the studio a moment later.

We both stay where we are. I look over at her. Her bottom lip is caught between her teeth and she's staring sadly out the windshield, probably not seeing anything.

"Hey, Ruby?" I say gently.

She jerks. "What?"

"You need to know that if Nick's the right guy, he won't care about what happened." I'm reaching for her arm again.

She sighs. "I keep telling myself that. Let's go inside, Laurie. I'll feel better if I'm doing something productive."

"You can do my laundry for me later if that will help."

She suddenly smiles at me, leans over, and kisses my cheek. "You're the best, Laurie. Ryan's a lucky guy."

"But . . . he . . . we—"

She gets out and shuts the door on my stutter. I'm sure Ryan and I will face grave afterlife consequences for our deception.

I rub my head and slurp my coffee, clambering out after her.

Hannah opens the door for us. "Hi, Ruby."

Ruby smiles bravely. "Hannah."

Hannah's voice is sugary. "Can I get you anything?"

Ruby thinks for a moment and shakes her head. "No thanks. When's my next appointment?"

"In ten minutes."

"I'll just go get the studio ready." She leaves quietly.

Hannah looks at me, eyebrows raised. I smile tersely at her and set my coffee on the desk.

The bell rings over the door just as Hannah opens her mouth.

"Is Ruby here?" Ryan tears into the place. "I tried calling her all morning and she didn't answer at her house and she didn't answer on her cell and when I called here earlier no one answered." He rakes a hand through his curly hair, his eyes frantic. "It's not like her."

"It's okay, she's here," I soothe. "She's in the studio."

He hugs me. Very tightly. My spinal column is protesting loudly and I get a mouthful of his coat when I try to breathe. "Thank God," he says and exhales hard. Stepping back, he levels a look at me. "What happened?"

"Yeah, what happened?" Hannah says.

"Well," I start slowly, milking it, "there's good news and bad news."

"What's the bad news?" Ryan asks.

"Nick took her to Halia's last night."

Ryan closes his eyes. "Oh no."

"She threw up just as Nick told her he liked her."

Hannah shakes her head. "Poor thing! What's the good news?"

"I just saved a bunch of money on my car insurance by switching to Geico."

"Laurie!" Ryan yells, but a grin sneaks onto his face.

Hannah giggles.

"No, the good news is that her neighbor, Odella—"

"Oh. I met her. Scary woman," Ryan says.

"Yeah. Anyway, I think her blood's beginning to warm up, so there's hope for her. She took care of Ruby last night." I lower my voice. "She even let Ruby borrow pajamas and a robe."

"That's really nice," Hannah says.

Ryan melts into one of the chairs in front of Hannah's desk. "Man." He groans, massaging his temples. "I was really worried."

"Well, you're a good brother." I smile at him, feeling sticky. He's slumped over in the chair, his brown hair is a curly wreck, and he's got two-day scruff on his chin. He looks forlorn and little, like the ice cream cone he just bought melted before he got a chance to eat it.

"I think I'll go see if Ruby needs help," Hannah says slowly, looking smugly at me and disappearing.

Smooth, my eye.

I watch her go, shaking my head, and drop into the chair beside Ryan.

He looks over at me from under his hand and smiles. "Thanks for going to check on her, Laur."

I reach for my coffee. "I feel guilty that we didn't tell them not to go to Halia's."

"Yeah. Oh well. Not a lot we can do about it now. Nick's a good guy, right?"

I have to grin.

He answers his own question. "Right. So he'll be nice about it with Ruby."

"I'm sure he will."

Long pause. Ryan's absently stroking his scruff, staring blankly at the desk. "You think they'll get married?" he asks quietly.

I dig into the front pocket of my jeans and come out with a ten-dollar bill, a paper clip, a rubber band, and a couple of loose strings. "I've got all this saying they will."

"Think it'll happen soon?"

"June."

"Why June?"

"Ruby just seems like a June bride sort of person. June lilies and the like."

Ryan smiles at me. "I'm not even going to comment on that. When do you think he'll propose?"

I shrug. Secretly, I hope he'll come in and do it today so I can have a restful vacation in California.

Ryan casually puts one arm around my shoulders like he does it every day and uses his other hand to pinch the bridge of his nose. I pass him my coffee without question.

He tightens his arm briefly and starts guzzling it.

"Slow down, Kid, I want some left over." I'm grasping for the cup back.

He hands it over. "Thanks, I needed this."

"I know."

"You should write a book on the many uses for coffee."

"I'll let you know that I have considered it."

He smiles at me, and suddenly I realize his arm is still around me and we are sitting fairly close to each other.

The weird queasiness starts in my stomach again. Ruby must actually have the flu and I caught it.

His eyes flicker and I look away. He clears his throat.

"Uh, Laurie?"

I bite my lip, staring at my hiking boots. "Yeah?" I must have turned the thermostat too high this morning. It is stifling in here.

Brandon marches out of Studio One just as Ryan opens his mouth. Brandon's lips are mashed together, but he charms his expression as he turns to face the five kids and two adults behind him. "Thanks for coming. Hannah will have the prints ready tomorrow." There is enough sugar in his voice to manufacture fifteen bags of Tootsie Rolls.

"Thank you, Brandon," five little kids chime. Their parents hustle them out the door.

Brandon waits until the door closes behind them before the smile slides from his face. He moans. "I'd forgotten why I like managing this studio so much more than actually working at this studio." He groans again. "I'll be in my office. Listening to the silence."

"OOOOOOHHHH, LA LA LA LAAAAAAA!" I start screaming.

Brandon's door slams.

"Check mark for Friday!" Hannah yells from inside Studio Two.

Ryan grins, squeezes my shoulders, and stands. "I should probably get back to work."

I stand as well. "Okay. Well, be careful. Don't nail your thumb to the house or anything like that."

He's fingering his keys, grinning. "I figured you'd say don't fall off the roof."

"That too. But your balance seems to be okay. It's just your need to pat that worries me." I pat his arm, grinning evilly. "And that's bad when using a hammer and nails."

"I'm never going to live it down, am I?"

"Not while I'm breathing." I walk with him toward the exit.

"Then I hope I don't live it down for a good long time to come." He stops by the door. "Thanks again, Laur."

"Anytime."

I'm turning away from the door when he abruptly leans down and kisses my cheek.

"Bye, Laurie." He steps out the door.

I think he freaked us both out. He strides to his truck and I stare after him, not sure if I should be frowning or smiling.

So I stand blank-faced like a dumbstruck idiot and watch him whiz out of the parking lot like the whole place is quarantined for the Black Plague. The insides of my fingers are itching.

Never a good sign.

Hannah clears her throat behind me, and I close my eyes.

"How much did you see?" I demand, whirling, scratching my fingers.

"All of it," she says airily.

I turn back around, my face burning. "Just so you know, it was staged. We knew you were watching us."

She smiles haughtily. "Liar."

"I'm leaving."

"You like him! You know it!"

I hightail it to the studio like the bad actress I am. "Good-bye, Hannah."

I close the door, flip on the lights, and collapse onto the sofa.

What just happened?

My stomach feels like a tank full of baby guppies has been transplanted there. My cheeks burn and I can't catch my breath.

I cradle my head in my hands and inhale hard.

It could just be I've caught something from Ruby. My face is hot because I turned the thermostat too high. And I can't breathe because I ran from the room when Hannah caught me.

Yeah. That has to be it.

I brush my hands back through my hair and stand. Take a deep breath.

I walk back out of Studio Two. Hannah balances the phone between her shoulder and her ear, typing briskly as she talks.

I sneak down the back hallway to Brandon's office and open the door. Brandon is at his desk, reading a few papers in a folder.

"What's up, Nutsy? And how's Ruby?" He leans back in his chair, closing the folder and smiling at me.

Odd. The guppies must have passed through my system.

"She's fine. She was just upset about her dinner with Nick." I tell Brandon the story and he *tsks.*

"Tough luck. Has he called her yet?"

"Who knows? She was at her neighbor's when I went and got her, and apparently she turned her cell phone off."

He yanks papers out of the way as I take a seat on his desk, suddenly feeling very tired. And it is only eleven o'clock.

I sigh.

"What's wrong, Nutsy?"

"Hmm? Oh. Nothing."

"Don't give me that. I saw Ryan was here. He worried about Ruby?"

"Mm-hmm." I fiddle with the glass paperweight Laney gave him for graduation. What is the use for a paperweight? Nothing. I have never used a paperweight in my life. Especially a glass one with some kind of blue liquidy stuff inside. Laney should have just given him a picture frame. Just as useless, but at least you can then have some faces looking back at you.

"Laur?"

Maybe I should give Brandon a picture frame. I could put the cute picture of the two of us in second grade standing by the swings in there. He'd like it. You can use a frame just as easy as a paperweight to hold papers down.

"Laurie?"

It would have to be a wooden frame because Brandon's notorious for knocking things over. The glass paperweight has been spared thus far, but I'm not holding my breath on that one.

"*Lauren!*"

I startle, nerves making the jump to light speed. "What?"

Brandon stares at me with the wrinkle between his eyebrows, his arms crossed. "Are you okay?"

"I'm fine. Why'd you yell at me?"

He half-laughs. "That was the third time I'd said your name!"

"I didn't hear you. Speak up next time." I take a deep breath and reassure my nerves the place isn't on fire.

He watches me fiddle with the paperweight and grins.

I put the paperweight down. "What?"

His self-satisfied expression is seriously bugging me. "You tell me, Nutsy," he taunts.

"There is nothing to tell," I say adamantly.

"Uh-huh."

"There isn't!"

"Remember who you're talking to, Laurie." He lifts one eyebrow at me. "It's me. Brandon. Lifelong best friend, remember?"

I'm reaching for my collar. "Is it hot in here or what?"

"It's not hot."

"Yes, it is."

"No. It's not." His eyes narrow. "Are you going through menopause early?"

"Maybe that's it." I exhale.

He leans back farther, shaking his head. "Holy cow," he mutters, drawing the words out, grinning like a fool. "Hannah was right."

"About what?"

"You." His smile gentles. "You really like him, don't you?"

I rub my hand down my face. Bite my lip. Let my breath out. My stomach now feels like I swallowed a canister of open safety pins. I look at Brandon and half-laugh, half-sigh. "Oh boy."

He grins outright. Reaches over and takes my hand. "He's a great guy, Laurie."

I shake my head and yank my hand away. "It wasn't supposed to be like this!" I jump off his desk, pacing the floor.

"Whoa, Laurie, what is going on?"

"It was just a joke! A hoax! We were just going to pretend to date so maybe Ruby would get a move on it with Nick!"

Brandon's expression is pure bewilderment. "You weren't really dating?" He stares at me, mouth open, tone incredulous.

"No!" I shout. "At least, not in the beginning. Maybe not even now." I flounce into one of the chairs in front of his desk and bury my head in my hands. "I don't know anymore."

There's a long period of silence while my best friend is putting two and two together. I keep my face covered.

"So you like this guy, but you think he's just pretending to like you," Brandon says, his voice filled with an *ahhh* sound.

I nod into my hands, miserable.

Brandon chuckles. I look up.

"Don't be so stupid, Laurie. Ryan would have to be blind and deaf not to like you. Relax. Okay? *Relax.*"

I take a deep breath. "Yes. Relax. Exactly. That's what I need to do."

He nods. "Good girl."

"It's not like anything could come of this right now, anyway. Right? I mean, I'm leaving for a month soon." The safety pins are starting to disappear.

"Right."

"So I just need to pull myself together and remember that I am *still* Lauren Holbrook and I don't need a guy to be happy."

"Very good."

"So I'll just go out there and take pictures and go home and pack my bags without a care or worry in the world."

He grins. "Well, packing that attitude could be difficult."

I glare at him. Then I smile. Walk around the desk and give him a hug. "Thanks, old friend." I meet his brown eyes.

"Anytime, kid." He chucks my cheek lightly. "Now get out because I need to actually work today."

"Work?" I gasp, old self back. "You work back here?"

"Out, Laurie."

"And all this time we thought you sat back here brooding all day."

"Laurie."

I open his door, smile, and leave.

Hannah covers the phone with her hand when I come back down

the hall. "Hey, Laurie, Lexi on the line. Wanted to make sure you were still on for painting tomorrow."

I take the phone from her. "Hey, Lex."

"Hi, Baby. How are you doing?"

"Okay."

"Make sure you're not working too hard."

"Heh. Right. What's up?" I watch a minivan pull into the parking lot.

"Are we still painting tomorrow? Nate called Ryan, and they're going to finish the porch."

I nod, even though I'm on the phone. "Sure, we can still paint."

"Great! I'll go get it mixed today."

"Lex?" A family of five walks through the door.

"Yeah?"

I wave the Just-a-Second sign to the family. "Don't get beige," I tell her. "Or sandstone, actually. Get like a cream color."

"Why?"

"I was at a woman's house today who had brown everywhere. Rather spoiled my taste for it."

Lexi laughs. "Sure, Sweetie. We can do cream. See you tomorrow morning. Love you, Honey."

"Bye, Lex. Love you too."

I give the phone back to Hannah.

"Painting?" she asks coyly as I grab a pen from her desk.

"Painting," I affirm.

"Porch building?"

"Appointment waiting." I point to the family. "You guys ready?" I ask.

Hannah shakes her head as I lead the family into the studio. "You, Lauren Holbrook, are really something else. I'm not sure what. But you're definitely something."

Chapter Twenty-Five

I finish with my last session at six. Hannah's desk is empty, and Brandon's car isn't in the parking lot. I'm in the middle of the nightly ritual of pulling on my coat, gloves, and scarf and digging my backpack out of the cubby when Ruby opens Studio One's door and waves good-bye to a cute blond couple who could have been siblings.

They leave, the door dings, and she huffs, raking her hands through her curls.

"Engaged," she mutters, either to me or no one since I'm the only other person still there.

"Those two?" I ask.

"Can you believe that?" She sulks, flipping off the light in the studio. "Eighteen and nineteen years old. And *engaged*." She sticks her tongue out as she pulls on her coat. "Makes me sick."

"They look like they could be from the same mother."

Ruby makes a face. "That's gross, Laurie."

"Just stating the facts. Hey." I shake my gloved finger at her. "Remember what we're reading in the Romans study. God's sovereign. You have nothing to envy, Ruby Fair." She smiles at me. "You heading home?" I ask.

"Yeah. You?"

"I don't know. Dad has a meeting at church tonight." I smile at Ruby. "Want to go get something to eat?"

"Sure. Not at Halia's." She's shaking her head vehemently, her hair bouncing.

"Never again."

"Good. Vizzini's, then?" She takes her keys out of her purse.

"Let's carpool."

"My car?"

"Fine." I follow her out, turning off the front room lights and locking the door behind me.

Ruby drives a cute little red Honda that, truth be told, could fit in the back end of my Tahoe with the back seats still in the upright and locked position. She unlocks the car and slides in with the graceful talent that comes from years of driving little cars.

Dad has never owned a little car.

Neither has Laney, Lexi, or Brandon.

Even Ryan drives an SUV.

So my step-and-slide moves are way out of whack.

"Are you okay?" Ruby asks as I get one foot in the Honda and the other underneath it. My rear end, confused, lands somewhere in the middle and begins chastising my common sense.

"Fine, fine," I say with a grunt, lugging myself over the bottom rim of the car door and onto the seat.

She watches me close my door and turns the key, pressing her lips together in a pitiful attempt to not smile.

"Go ahead and laugh."

She does. Long and loud. "Laurie, that was so funny! When was the last time you rode in a car? Before Kraft Mac 'n Cheese?"

"Somewhere around there."

She drives to Vizzini's, and ten minutes later we're seated with menus in front of our noses.

"I want soup," she declares.

"They make good meatball soup."

She wrinkles her nose and flips the menu over. "Anything not Italian related?" She reads for a few moments, her mouth moving without words coming out. "Ah!" she suddenly yells and points. "Clam chowder."

I'm craving carbs. "Does it come with bread?"

She checks. "Yeah."

"I'm getting it too. And mozzarella sticks."

"Yuck, Laur."

"Not yuck. Yum." I close the menu and set my elbows on it purposefully. "Tell me about Nick."

She innocently twirls a curl around her finger. "What about Nick?"

"You like him."

She doesn't deny it. "So?"

"So he likes you."

She shakes her head. "I can see the little cogs clurking in your head, Laurie Holbrook. Lay off."

I grin. "Clurking?"

She sighs. "Great. This is just great. Your word fetish is beginning to rub off on me. Lovely."

"So he hasn't asked you yet?"

She looks at me blankly. "Asked me what?"

"To marry him, of course! Good grief, woman."

She blushes. Rolls her eyes. Opens and closes her mouth a few times. "Not that it is *any* of your business, at all, but *no*, he has not asked me."

"Ruby, you need to show more of what you really feel 'in order to secure him.'"

"Don't tell me. *Pride and Prejudice*?" Her eyebrows angle up.

I'm very proud of her. "Wow, and the first try!"

"The English accent usually gives it away."

"Take my advice, *amiga*."

She leans forward, mocking my position. "So, Dear Abby, have you asked Ryan how he feels?"

I trace a picture of a plate of spaghetti on the menu and try playing dumb. "Asked Ryan how he feels about what?"

Ruby doesn't buy it. "Nice try."

"That's different," I protest, looking up at her all-seeing brown eyes. "Nick is going to marry you."

She cocks her head. "How do you know?"

"Because you two were born and bred for each other, that's how."

"Sounds awfully Laura Ingalls Wilder."

I lean back in my chair. "Didn't her aunt marry her uncle?"

"What?"

"I think she did. Laura's mom married Pa, and I think Ma's sister married Pa's brother."

"Completes the family circle, I suppose. So if Nick and I marry, that would mean Ryan would have to marry Nick's nonexistent sister." She grins. "Want to see if Nick's parents will adopt you?"

I flip my hair behind my shoulder. "I'm perfectly happy with my father, thank you."

She changes the subject. "So middle school Bible study in four days."

A sad groan is my answer. "Why am I even starting to teach, Ruby, if I'm leaving after two weeks?"

"Acclimation. Then you'll have gotten over the original fear and will be able to share all the revelations you received on the fishing trip."

"Such as how to get a Bite of Bass for Breakfast?"

She nods. "Good alliteration."

"Thanks."

"I was thinking spiritual revelations, though. Like you pointed out earlier, sovereignty."

I'm still thinking. "Or how Praise Perfects Prayer?"

She laughs then. "Where do you get this?"

"My mother was said to be a mental case."

"I can believe it."

Officially in Colossians. I plop my Bible on my lap and grin. I think even if I weren't a Christian and weren't falling head over heels for Christ, I'd still love the feel of the pages and the floppiness of the leather.

"He is the image of the invisible God, the firstborn over all creation."

Now, *that's* a cool thought!

I wake the next morning to electric guitars, tired and a tad depressed. My second to last Saturday in my own sweet bed, and I have to wake up to an alarm.

Blegh.

Dad is at the table when I plod downstairs. The scent of lemongrass tea permeates the kitchen.

Double *blegh.*

He looks up from his paper. He's fully dressed, belt and everything. "Morning, Honey. You're helping Lex paint today, right?"

"Yup."

He frowns at my choice of paint clothes. "Laurie," he starts. Stops.

I pour my coffee. He's obviously deciding whether or not to give his grown daughter advice on her clothes.

"Laurie, isn't that the sweat outfit Laney gave you for your birthday?" He goes for it.

I look down at the sky blue velour track pants and matching jacket I'm wearing. "Yeah, my fifteenth birthday."

"Still, you really want to get paint on those?"

I add sugar to the coffee. "I'd rather not get paint on anything."

"And you're wearing your hair down?" Dad's *tsk*ing.

I swipe it back behind my ear with my left hand, my right hand stirring my sugared and milked coffee. "Planned on it. At least until we start painting. Keeps the cold air off my neck."

Dad's fear of sickness keeps him from arguing with that one.

I join him at the table. "What are you going to do today?"

"Lex asked if I wanted to meet you four for lunch."

I brighten. "That'd be fun."

"Think so?" Dad's cautious.

"Yeah. You should come." I sip my coffee, looking down at the table. "Then you could get to know Ryan a little bit."

He fingers his cup of tea. "You like him, don't you?" he asks, not looking at me.

I bite my lip. "Maybe," I say quietly. I can't explain it. Ryan's doing an awfully good job of popping up in my thoughts and prayers lately.

"Are you going to marry him?" Dad sips his tea, his fingers shaking slightly.

Poor Dad.

"Not anytime soon," I soothe.

The doorbell rings. I stand. "See you at lunch, Dad." I kiss the top of his head and go to the front door.

Ryan is there grinning, holding two take-out cups from Merson's. I feel myself getting sappy.

"I like you," I tell him.

"Hi there." He smiles.

"Hold on a sec." I turn to get my coat, but he catches my sleeve and hands me one of the cups.

"For your dad."

I give him a look and pop off the lid.

The aroma makes my eyes water. "You brought my dad lemongrass tea." I smile, even more syrupy.

"You should have seen me trying to talk Shawn into making it."

I raise my eyebrow, replacing the lid. "Funny?"

"Hilarious. The man now has his door open trying to get the smell out."

I take the tea back to the kitchen and give it to Dad. He inhales and smiles.

"Nice boy," he comments.

I nod. "Yeah."

"Laurie?"

I stop on my way out. "What's up, Dad?"

He lifts his cup. "You can marry him."

I blink. "O-okay."

Stumbling back to the entry, I find my coat and gloves. Ryan is still outside, holding the other cup and staring at the overgrown rosemary bush by the door, the only thing still green in our yard.

"Ready?" he asks, handing me the coffee. "Here. Happy Valentine's Day."

"Thanks!" I smile and follow him to the truck. He opens the door and I climb in.

"Hey, Ryan?" I say when he's safely buckled into the driver's seat.

"Hey, Laurie."

"Your sister is in love."

He rolls his eyes. "Gee, really? Who with?"

"I think Nick will ask Ruby to marry him."

He looks over at me, offering a challenge. "What if I don't think he's good enough?"

"Then you're a dimwitted numbskull and I'll have to ask you to pull over so I can get out."

He grins. "Why?"

"Because I'm not allowed to ride with dimwitted numbskulls."

He laughs. "I can just see that as rule number twenty-one on your list."

"Actually, it's twenty-eight. Twenty-one is to avoid toxic substances at all costs." I grin up at him. "So we're painting today."

He smiles at me. "I noticed your clothes. But your hair's not pulled back. You'll get paint in it." He pokes at it in emphasis.

I wave my hands. "Trust me, Ryan. Lexi will make sure I don't. She's a stickler about my hair."

"Good."

I start up the sidewalk. "Thanks for the coffee."

"You're welcome." He crinkles his eyes at me and walks beside me to the front door.

Lexi opens it before we knock. "Hey, guys."

"You're a peeper," I accuse her. She is decked out in ripped jeans and a sweatshirt that says, "A TRUCKER HONKED AND I FLATTENED HIS CARCASS. ROUTE 66. 1996." A bright polka-dot bandana covers her hair Aunt Jemima style.

"And proud of it too," she answers me. "Hi, Ryan," she croons. "Good to see you again. Thanks so much for doing this. Nate's been practically hopping he's so excited."

Ryan laughs. "I hope I don't let him down."

"Honey, the fact that you actually showed up is enough to make his day." She touches his shoulder as she talks to him. Lexi has always been very touchy-feely.

"He's out back?" Ryan asks.

"Yeah."

"Have fun painting," he tells me. Winks and leaves.

Lexi waits until the back door closes behind him. "He's a keeper," she declares.

"You know, Lexi, sometimes I wish you'd just come right out and tell me exactly what you think of people." I go into her living room, which has been attacked by plastic sheeting.

"I'll try to do better." She grins. Almost immediately, the grin is replaced with a frown. "You are not ready to paint."

I kick off my shoes and spread out my hands. "Yes, I am. Look, I've got my old sweats on. Got my shoes off. Set my coffee down."

"Your hair is not properly protected. You will get paint in your hair and won't be able to get it out for a week." She puts her hands on her hips in lecture mode.

"I couldn't find anything other than my lucky Goofy baseball cap at home."

She sighs dramatically. "There's another handkerchief on my bed."

"Ha! I knew you'd look out for me."

"What are older sisters for? Go get it so we can start. The boys are already sawing their hearts out."

I ponder whether or not that would make a good song as I go down the hallway to Lexi's blue-and-white-checked room and swipe up the purple and silver bandana, tying it gangster style on top of my head, only covering my forehead and the hair above my ears. There's a huge bouquet of red roses and daisies on her bureau. *Aw!*

"How's this, Lex?" I ask, going back into the living room.

She turns to look and rolls her eyes. "More than half your hair is hanging out the back."

I fluff my hair, which is curling out of control because once again I skipped the hair fixing in favor of sleep. "See, but that adds feminine appeal. You've already caught yourself a husband. You don't need to have appeal."

She frowns. "I don't think that was a compliment."

"Me, neither, actually."

She picks up one of the heavy-duty cans and swings it around in an odd little dance I think is an attempt to mix the paint. "And I think the kid outside with my husband would find you appealing even if you were in a toga with an olive branch on your head." She wrinkles her nose. "And the sap from the branch dripping down your forehead."

She uses both hands now, turning in a huge circle, twisting the can up and down, up and down, barely missing the crammed together, plastic-swathed furniture in the center of the room.

"A toga?" I question, grinning.

She giggles and smacks the can on the plastic-covered couch. *Oogumph*, the can gurgles.

"Honey! You made me throw off my balance." She comes to a stop.

"That is probably a good thing. You looked ridiculous."

She giggles again. "Ah, but I've already caught myself a husband, so I can look ridiculous anytime I want, right, Baby?"

"Right."

She *schlumps* the paint can to the floor and produces a screwdriver from the back pocket of her jeans. Deftly she plugs the business end of the screwdriver into the lip of the paint can and yanks down.

Rather than hearing the *squwaksug* sound a paint can makes when opening, we hear absolutely nothing. She pulls down farther, eye level with the floor now.

"Uh, Lex?"

"HushI'mconcentrating," she says through gritted teeth.

"Lex, it's not opening."

"Shutuporyou'regoingtodothisnext." Her veins stand out in her forehead.

"I'm sure that one of the guys could do this easily."

She lets go of the screwdriver, huffs out her breath, and backhands her unsweaty forehead. "You would make a very bad suffragette."

"Lucky. 'Cause I'm not one. I don't understand that movement. If someone can do something for me so I don't have to do it, I'm willing to let them." I step to the back door and open it, letting in a jet stream of cold air. "Hey!" I yell. Nate and Ryan each have one end of a plank. They both look up.

"Need something, Laur?" Ryan asks.

"Can one of you come get this paint can open?" I rub my arms, trying to keep them from getting frostbite.

"Sure!" they both say at the same time.

I go back inside.

Lexi stands frowning at the paint can, screwdriver in one hand.

"Trying to open it with the power of your brain?" I ask. "That only works in *Star Wars*."

"No, I'm lecturing it."

"Silently?"

"In paint-speak." She narrows her eyes. "Glug-glurp-blug-blug," she exclaims, shaking the screwdriver at it.

I fall over and conk my head on the plastic-coated love seat.

Lexi grins.

The boys come in, breathless. Ryan frowns at the tears rolling from my eyes. "You okay?"

I nod, my lungs hurting from laughing so hard.

"She just had a bonding moment with the paint," Lexi says. Then she chuckles. "Get it? Bonding? Paint?"

Nate and Ryan exchange glances that say, *Are these women crazy, or have they simply reverted into mindless acts of near catastrophe and should we leave them in this state of being?*

Then Nate shrugs, takes the screwdriver from his bonkers wife, and cranks the paint can open.

Ryan kneels on the floor beside me as I sit up, heave a breath, and swipe at my cheeks.

"What happened?" he asks.

"Do you think a song titled, 'I'm Pining for Maple Syrup by Sawing Your Heart Out' would make it on CMT's top ten?"

He blinks and looks back at Nate and Lexi. Lexi goes into gales of laughter with me, and Nate shrugs again.

Ryan pats my shoulder in his annoying yet kind of cute way. "I wouldn't get my heart set on it."

"'Would You Love Me If My Wood House Would Sing'?"

Ryan grins and leaves me on the floor. "Nate, I think we should get out of here fast."

"I'm with you, bro."

They hightail it out the door and in two seconds flat have the plank back in their hands.

Lexi snickers. "Great songs, Pumpkin. How about this one?" She gestures toward the guys and sings the title. "You Built Me a Board Deck and Then I Decked Your . . . Sword."

"Awful, Lex."

"Yeah, you're right. Come on, let's paint."

By lunchtime we have the cranberry wall finished and two of the cream walls done. Half a wall and the trim over the kitchen counter remain.

Lexi sets her paint roller on the tray and puts her hands on her hips. "Guess we should get lunch ready."

I use my wrist to rub the itchy bandana. "Uh-huh."

She marches into the kitchen and starts scrubbing her hands. I collapse on the couch, my arm sore from rolling and my toes sore from gripping the ladder rung with them.

I hate ladders.

The back door jerks open and Nate and Ryan come in loudly, accompanied by cold air and sawdust.

"Wow, girls, looks great!" Nate exclaims, waving to the walls.

"Thanks!" Lexi yells back, though they are two feet apart.

"Yeah. Thanks."

"Hey, Ryan had a great idea. We're taking you two out to lunch," Nate yells. The boy has the biggest lungs I have ever heard. He can't whisper to save his life.

"Aw, that's so sweet, Ryan!" Lexi squeals. "I'll call Dad."

Lexi can't whisper to save her life either.

Suddenly I find myself praying fervently that any children the two of them have take predominantly after Dad. Or I am never babysitting.

Ever.

"Let me get my coat." I yawn, standing.

"Better not, Laur. You've got paint all over you," Ryan says.

"I do not! I was careful!"

He comes over and swipes his finger over my shoulder blade and shows it to me. Cranberry covers his fingertip.

"Told ya."

I moan. "Lexi Holbrook Kennedy, did you paint my backside while I was on the ladder?"

"Come on, kids, I think Nate's starving." She calmly ignores me, following her husband through the laundry room to the garage.

I send a glare her way.

Ryan smirks. "Sisterly love."

"Ah, yes."

He points. "It's on your face too."

"Well, that was my fault."

"How'd it get on your face?"

"I was pretending the brush was a microphone and it hit my cheek."

A wrinkle appears between Ryan's eyebrows. "You were pretending the brush was a microphone and—you know what? I think I'd just rather not know."

I smile at him. He has sawdust caked into the creases on his jeans and filtered through his hair. He uses two fingers and pushes me toward the garage.

I twist, trying to see the back of me. "I'll get paint on the car."

"Where does Lexi keep her paint rags?"

I frown. "I don't think she does."

"Does what?"

"Keep her paint rags."

"She buys new rags every time she needs to paint or change the oil?" he asks incredulously.

I bite my lip. "I don't think she does that either."

"Buys rags?"

"No, changes the oil."

He slaps his forehead, not realizing the cranberry paint on his finger hasn't dried yet, and gets a nice bullet-looking dab up there. "Women," he mutters.

I grin at him. Widely.

"What?"

"When did you get shot?"

"I beg your pardon?"

I touch his forehead. "You have blood. Figured you'd been shot."

He looks at me, at his finger, back at me, and sighs.

"Does Lexi have a towel we could mess up?"

I nod. "She keeps Barbie towels in the garage to dry Muffin off after she's had a bath."

"Barbie towels?"

I laugh at his tone. "Oh come on. It will be a new experience."

I open the garage door and find Nate spreading the aforesaid towels all over the backseat of his Nissan.

"I wouldn't want my wife sticking to the seats." He pinches the cream-colored back pocket on Lexi's jeans. She yelps.

"So you'd rather my rear end stick to a towel with Barbie's big-busted figure instead?"

Nate kisses her. Probably as a way to get out of explaining his true reason for coating the entirety of the back end of the Nissan with towels.

Lexi pushes away. "You just don't want your precious leather marred up."

"Aw, now, Honey, it's so cute when you're mad and use a word like *mar*."

"Oh, go be smug in the driver's seat."

We pile in, girls in the back, guys in the front. Nate turns the key and grins at Lexi in the rearview mirror. "You know what they always say, pookums. Behind every great man is a great woman." He waves to us in the backseat. "Physical proof, wouldn't you say?"

Lexi crosses her arms and tries unsuccessfully to bite back a smile. "Just drive, Nathan."

He backs the car out of the garage.

"And don't ever call me pookums again."

Ryan snorts in the passenger seat and then tries to cover it with a cough. "Uh, right, um, so where are we going?"

"Subway. Oh, and Sweetie, I called Dad and he's going to meet us there," Lexi tells me.

I make a face. "Oh boy. I'm going to get a lecture about getting toxic chemicals on my face."

Ryan starts laughing. "Rule twenty-one?"

I use the corner of a towel with a particularly cheeky Barbie to try to rub the paint smear off. Nothing happens. It must have already dried.

"I'm toast!"

Lexi leans over and checks her face in the rearview mirror. "It's on my face too, Butternut. You're not the only one in poor sorts with our father."

I'm scrubbing now, panic rising in me. "But you don't live with him." One time I was cleaning the bathroom without gloves and Dad nearly grounded me because of it.

"Very true," she concedes. "Here. Let me try." She licks her finger and rubs my cheek. A little comes off on her thumb. "I'm going to run out of saliva before I'm done."

Ryan watches us and gags. "Lexi, Lexi, Lexi. Stop, please. Look." He grabs a water bottle from the front cup holder. "Wet the towel with this."

"We're here," Nate announces, pulling into a parking space.

"Quick, Lexi," I fret.

She's got her bottom lip between her teeth. "I can't get the bottle open."

"You must have really done well in Phys. Ed." Ryan grins. "First the paint can, then the bottle." He holds out his hand and she gives it back to him. He breaks the safety ring easily.

Nate turns off the engine and hops out. Ryan gets out and then opens my door.

"Let me have one of those extra towels," Ryan says. I give it to him. He soaks the corner of it, closes the bottle, and tosses it over the car to Nate, who stands beside Lexi's side, ready to do the same.

"Look at me," Ryan commands.

He holds my chin with one hand and drags the towel over my face with the other. I can feel my heart starting to beat faster and I don't look at his eyes, sure he's laughing at me.

He finishes scouring a minute later and bends down, smiling into my eyes and tightening my bandana. "You look like a home girl."

"Thanks." I take a breath, trying to be nonchalant, but doggone it, it's hard with him standing three inches away and tying something around my hair.

"Heavens, woman, did you get any paint on the walls?" Nate bursts.

I sneak another breath.

"A few flecks, I think." Lexi twists away from the towel he holds. "You're scraping that down my face! Babe, Dad's going to think you dragged me across the parking lot with how red my face is."

Ryan's eyes twinkle as he finishes with the bandana and moves so I can slide out.

Air. What a marvelous thing!

"Okay, okay, okay, that is enough!" Lexi yells, pushing Nate's futile towel away and jumping out of the car. "Dad will just have to get mad, because I don't care anymore."

"But then he'll suspend your allowance, and what will we use to buy the new table saw?" Nate whines.

She laughs and smacks his chest. "You are nuts! I married a cashew!"

Ryan closes my door and leans down next to my ear. "Are they always this crazy?"

"Since the day they were born," I whisper back. "God help their future children."

"Amen."

I spot Dad's car in the parking lot, and he already has a table for us when we walk in.

"Over here, kids!" he says and waves.

I step around the tables and chairs and smile at him. Dad wears a nice but casual sweater and slacks.

The other people in the restaurant probably think he's a nice older man who has compassion on a bunch of street hoodlums. And my bandana isn't helping matters.

"Laurie, you have paint all over you," Dad chides, his frown lines creasing on his forehead.

"Yeah, well, blame your middle daughter for that one." I am good at shifting blame.

He raises his eyes to his middle daughter. "Lexi?"

She is immediately running for the counter. "Uh, we should probably order before they run out of cucumbers. Can't have a good sandwich without cucumbers, Dad."

Got to hand it to Lexi. She's a smooth one.

Dad stands. "We should save this table. The girl who works here told me every hour on the hour a huge group from the gym next door comes in and crowds the whole place up." He looks at his watch. "We've got ten minutes."

"I'll stay, sir." Ryan touches my elbow. "Hey, order me a ham with lettuce, tomatoes, peppers, onions, and cucumbers. And oil and vinegar on six-inch wheat."

I nod. "Okay, so a turkey sandwich with cheese, jalapeños, and honey mustard on white."

He sighs.

I join the others at the counter and give our orders to the annoyingly perky sandwich maker.

We beat the crowd by a good four minutes. Two bites into our sandwiches, the door bursts open and easily thirty people push and squeeze their way into a semblance of a line.

Dad watches them, finishes chewing, and clears his throat. "Hmph. Girl was right."

Chapter Twenty-Six

I glance at the clock on the dashboard as I climb out of the Tahoe. Six forty-five.

Precariously balanced in my hands are my Bible, my notebook, and my ever-present coffee. Ruby told me to be about fifteen minutes early for small group on Tuesday so I can be here when the kids come in.

It is Tuesday. I'm fifteen minutes early.

I walk through the glass doors leading to the youth side of the church and find Ruby and Nick.

Their backs are to me. His arm curls comfortably around her shoulders, and her head leans against his chest as they study a poster stapled to the wall.

Do I interrupt? Do I clear my throat and make them see me? Or do I try to slip past unnoticed?

I purse my lips as I debate the pros and cons, the stack in my arms getting heavier by the moment.

Nick leans over and kisses the top of Ruby's head, then lays his cheek there.

I am definitely going to sneak past unnoticed.

Here's what I am: A Klutz to the Kore.

I have one foot carefully around the corner, my back rubbing up against it, when my notebook slides out from the middle of the stack and my coffee shudders.

I *knew* I should have bought the texture-covered notebook. It wouldn't have slid so easily.

I grab for the coffee and catch it.

The problem is that in the midst of catching the coffee and saving the church a carpet cleaning bill, I drop the books and they crash to the floor with an unearthly loud *boom*.

I detect an echo. And yet our church does not have a basement.

Or so I thought.

Like most churches, we have a newcomer's class for the people who are on the church hop and trying to see what we're all about. My church puts their pictures up on a bulletin board outside the sanctuary's door.

And yet never once have I seen any of those people around on Sundays.

How would the apostle Paul put it?

"I became convinced that what I once thought, that the newcomers went to a different service time, was not true; in my flesh, I assumed all men, in particular our senior pastor, had the best interests at heart for the newcomers, and yet now I see clearly that all men, in particular our senior pastor, are sinful, fleshly creatures who have only their own interests in sight, not the interests of others."

In other words, I think my senior pastor is hiding the poor souls who go to the newcomer's class in a hidden basement and making them physically act out the five points of Calvinism.

But I digress.

Nick and Ruby whirl when they hear my books.

"Laurie." Ruby breathes, hand to heart. "Good night. I thought someone was trying to break in."

"You said to be early." I sheepishly gather my stuff.

"Yes, I did," Ruby says and nods.

I stand back up, once again precariously balanced. Nick hasn't let go of Ruby. They've just turned in one accord, like Siamese twins.

It is cute in a disturbing way.

"Hi, Laurie," he says.

"Hey, Nick," I answer.

"Excited about tonight?"

"A little confused," I say.

"About what?" he asks.

"Why am I teaching if I'm leaving in less than two weeks?"

Ruby smiles. "Acclimation, Laur. Didn't we already cover this?"

"I wanted to hear it from Nick."

"Acclimation, Laur. Didn't you two already cover this?" He grins cheekily.

I shake my head. "What classroom?"

"Third on the right," Nick directs while Ruby's phone starts ringing.

She pulls it out of the pocket of her jeans, reads the caller ID, smiles, and answers it. "Hey, Honey."

Nick shoots me a look. "Who's she talking to?"

I shrug casually. "Oh, it's probably just Trevor."

He frowns. "Who?"

"Trevor. She hasn't told you about Trevor? Old flame. Comes by every couple of days or so."

Ruby waves her hand, glares at me, and says to the phone, "Hold on, Sweetheart, she's right here." Passes me the phone and a doctored Scripture: "Six things the Lord hates, seven the Lord detests: A lying tongue being one of the top."

I take the phone from her and smile sweetly to Nick. "Hi, Honey."

"An endearment? Her true feelings come to light!" Ryan shouts.

I grin. "What's up?"

"I tried calling your cell phone."

"I turned it off, seeing as how I'm at a Bible study." A subtle way of saying, *Why are you calling me?*

"Not for another thirteen minutes."

I walk into the classroom, again precariously balanced. "True," I say, putting my Bible and notebook on the table in the middle of the classroom and sipping my coffee.

"So you leave for your fishing trip in a week and a half," Ryan starts.

"Yeah."

"Well, before that time we should hang out." He clears his throat. "A month is a long time."

"Yeah, it is." My voice is quiet. I change the subject. "Hey, your sister is letting a strange man put his arm around her," I tattle.

I can hear his smile. "What should I do?"

"What any good brother should do. Come over here, take him outside, and knock his lights out."

"Uh-huh."

I finish my coffee and toss the cup in the trash can. "And I'll cheer from the sidelines and Ruby will gasp dramatically and then when Nick gets a swing in on you, I'll nurse you back to health."

"That part sounds nice, but what happens to Ruby and Nick?"

"They move to Alaska. Raise five kids on a fishing boat and teach them all how to crab."

"A crabbing boat," he says.

"What?"

"It would be called a crabbing boat."

I frown. "I didn't know 'crabbing' was a word."

"I saw a special on *National Geographic*. They're called crabbing boats."

Long pause. "Hey, Ryan?"

"Yeah?"

"You have way too much time on your hands."

He starts laughing. "Says the woman who can quote *Pride and Prejudice* verbatim."

"But I can do that with an English accent."

"So?"

"So *National Geographic* has the same man doing all the voice-overs." I make a face. "A man with a really boring monotone. You'd put me to sleep if you quoted *National Geographic*."

"Wow. Compliment."

I distinctly hear kids in the hall.

"I'd love to keep the compliments coming, Ry, but my doom approaches."

He laughs. "Laurie, you're going to have a blast and you know it."

"I'm nervous."

"Relax. It'll be fine. I'll give you a call later on."

I smile tightly. "Bye, Ryan."

"Bye, Laur."

I close the phone, leave my stuff, and walk into the hallway. A dozen or so girls mill around, talking, laughing, sitting, smiling.

I hand the phone to Ruby and look around. "I can do this," I mutter quietly, gathering my courage.

She grins at me.

Faster than you can say, "Uncle Walleye ate my trout," thirteen big-eyed junior high girls sit in a circle, with Ruby and me at one side of it.

"I think the first thing to do would be to introduce ourselves. I'm Ruby Palmer. I'm a photographer along with my friend Laurie here, who will introduce herself now."

I clear my throat. "Right. So. Uh, I'm Laurie, like Ruby just said. Um." Might as well be honest. "And I'm a little nervous because I've never taught anything before."

The girls smile together.

A little Hispanic girl with gorgeous brown eyes raises her hand. Ruby nods to her.

"I'm Tawnya. And I'm just wondering what you guys think about pre-destination and election. My mom said those are big topics in Romans."

I start blinking. This class might be deep.

Ruby nods. "They are big topics, Tawnya. We'll be covering that as we go along. Particularly how they relate to God's sovereignty." She stops and looks at the group. "Who knows what sovereignty means?"

A dark-haired girl who is built like a soccer player answers. "Doesn't it mean, like, God's in control over everything?"

Ruby looks at me and I start nodding. "Mm-hmm, that's right. Good, bad, ugly, God has ordained all of it." I see a few frowns. "Ordained means designed, basically." I look at Tawnya. "Does that answer your question?"

She nods.

I let out a small breath of relief.

Ruby and I take turns teaching on apostleship, and after we pray, smile, and dismiss, I have to admit it went better than I could have hoped.

Ruby nudges my knee with her foot as the girls leave to go find the chocolate chip cookies someone brought.

"Good job." She replaces the cap on her pen.

I close my Bible. "Same to you. I think it went well. This should be a good year. The girls are really cute!"

"Confidence restored?" She grins at me.

"For the most part. Predestination?"

She stands and stretches. "They grow up younger now. We'll have to be on top of our game."

I stand as well. "Guess I know what I'll be doing on my trip."

"Studying?"

"You got it." I start gathering my belongings. "So, heading home?"

She nods. "Probably."

We step outside and Nick catches Ruby's arm. "Hey."

She dimples. "Hi."

"Want to go get dinner with me on Friday?"

She stares into his eyes for a moment before answering. She must have seen something because she ducks her head, blushes, and nods.

"Good," Nick says softly.

Ping! Ping! Ping! My brain screams.

I look to the left of the two of them and there it is. Big, neon lights. CUPID WINS!

I watch Nick kiss her cheek softly and then go back to his pastoral duties. Ruby stares after him, twisting her bare ring finger.

Friday.

Nick is going to propose Friday night.

Do I scream? Jump up and down? Dance the Hokey Pokey?

"Excuse me for a second," I mutter to no one in particular. I walk into the empty women's bathroom and pull my cell phone from my pocket. *Bee-bee-beeee-beeeee!* it sings as I turn it on.

I dial quickly. "Ry?"

He laughs. "I was wondering how long it would take. Forty-five minutes? Come on, Laur. You could have done better than that," he chides.

"Nick asked you?" I'm fidgeting and my heart is racing with excitement.

I can now officially hang up my matchmaking cap. My work here is done. Besides, God is sovereign. He can orchestrate events much better than I can.

"He asked forty-five minutes ago," Ryan says. "Why are you echoing?"

"I'm in the bathroom."

"Why?"

"'Cause I didn't want Ruby to hear. He asked you? If he could propose?" I am shrieking.

"Yep. *Forty-five* minutes ago."

"Will you get off that?" I pace the length of the three sinks, grinning like an idiot. My nose itches and I can't decide if I should burst into tears or laughter. *Lord, this is so amazing!*

"He's asking her Friday," Ryan says.

I wave my hand. "I already knew that."

"How?"

"Nick asked Ruby in front of me."

I can almost hear Ryan shaking his head. "You'd think the man would be brighter than that by now. Maybe I should've said no."

"Do you know where he's taking her?"

"Halia's?" he drawls.

"Funny."

"He said something about the restaurant at the Marriott. The Land Down Under, or something like that."

"It's The Golden Sea, Ryan." I giggle. "What are the odds?"

"Of what?"

"Him proposing in a room called The Golden Sea right before I go fishing for a month?"

Ryan clicks his tongue. "It's a sign."

"I'm telling you." I wait for a second. Ryan doesn't say anything. "So," I start. "Are you going to ask me or do I have to invite myself?"

"To what?"

"Ryan! The Golden Sea? Friday night?"

He pauses. "You . . . cannot . . . be . . . serious," he stutters.

"I am very serious! I helped arrange this marriage! I want to be there when he proposes." Call it finishing what you start.

"You're kidding!"

"I assure you, dear man, I am not." I wave my hand to my reflection in the mirror. "I was there when Nate proposed to Lexi, and I helped arrange that marriage. It would hurt my track record if I weren't at Ruby and Nick's engagement."

"You are the most devious, conniving little meddler I have ever met!"

I grin. "Well, thank you."

He groans.

"Oh good grief, Ryan. We'll be invisible! That's a huge room."

"You've been there before?" His voice is incredulous.

"Sure." I am matter-of-fact. "That's where Nate proposed."

"I can't win," he mutters.

"No, you really can't. So either ask or I'll go by my lonesome, but I'll be there regardless."

He sighs loudly. "Laurie."

"Yes, dear?"

"Do you want to go to The Golden Sea on Friday?"

"Sure! I'd love to. Thanks, Ryan." I grin.

"I'm going to regret this, aren't I?"

I laugh. "Bye, Ryan."

I hang up and lean over the counter, grinning at myself in

the mirror.

God's sovereign. Divine ordination of everything. Even my match-making tendencies. *Wow, Lord, this is so neat!*

Nick and Ruby. Definitely a physical show of His sovereignty.

Friday morning dawns bright and sunny. A perfect day for an engagement.

I skip down the stairs and kiss Dad on the top of his head. "Morning, Dad."

He looks up at me, smiling ear to ear. "Excited about the fishing trip, Honey? Me too."

I pour my coffee and join him at the table. A yellow legal pad is in front of him, a pen in his hand. "What are you doing?" I ask.

"Checking off supplies. I think I got them all."

I nod, sipping. "Good."

"We leave in a week, so in six days I'll get the food for the drive over."

"Sounds good." As long as there are M&Ms, anyway. I look over at Dad eating his organic whole-grain cereal. Probably won't be M&Ms. The last trip we took he brought candies—and I use that term loosely—made from all-natural ingredients and vitamin-fortified. They tasted like grainy cough drops.

He's still talking. "I called the cabin rental place, and they've got us ready and confirmed."

"Swell."

"Oh, Laurie, this will be so much fun." Dad smiles, his eyes lighting in a way that I haven't seen since before Mom died. Maybe Dad needed a trip like this all along.

I squeeze his hand. "Yeah, it will."

Ryan rings the doorbell at a few minutes before six. If you're male, The Golden Sea won't let you in without a jacket and tie. If you're female, a dress and some major heels are required or I've heard they'll feed you to the piranhas in one of the fish displays.

I recycled the dress from Lexi's wedding.

Ironed, of course.

I open the door and Ryan's eyebrows go up. "Wow, Laur. You clean up nice."

"Same to you, stud. You mean you've had a comb this whole time?" I feel my eyebrows climb on my head. He's wearing khakis, a white button-down, a navy blazer, and a tie that I'd bet money he bought today.

He fingers his combed-down hair and grins. "I think I used too much mousse. Feels like plastic wrap on my head."

He walks me to the car, opens the door, shoves my dress in, and goes around. "So I've done a pretty bad thing." He turns the key.

"Time for confession?" Mentally I'm reviewing my list of things to confess: I arranged the disastrous blind dates; the shoes I'm wearing are Lexi's and I borrowed them three years ago; I hid M&Ms in my pillow case.

Ryan keeps talking. "I invited Brandon and Hannah to go with us." He winces. Smacks his forehead. "I think I suffered a momentary lapse in judgment."

I grin. "I think it's great. Really? Brandon's coming? And Hannah?"

"Well, I figured my excuse to Ruby will be that the four of us are doing some kind of send-off before your trip."

I pause. "Won't she wonder why she wasn't invited?"

Ryan nods. "Yeah." He clears his throat and grins sheepishly. "Which is why I'm going to do this."

He pulls his cell phone out of his pants pocket and dials, one hand on the steering wheel. "Hey, Sis. It's me. Uh, it's about two thirty or so, and I guess you're in with a client or something. Anyway, Hannah, Brandon, and I are taking Laur out for a nice dinner tonight before she has to eat bass for a month, and we were hoping you and Nick could come. So give me a call back. Love ya." He hangs up.

I shake my head slowly at him. "You sad little liar, you." I smirk. "Wait a second, you're taking me out to a seafood restaurant before I have to eat bass for a month?"

"Pitiful, huh?" He parks in front of the Marriott, looks over at me, and grins. "You were right, Laurie."

"Yeah, I know. About what?"

He rolls his eyes. "Funny girl. About this. It'll be interesting to watch my sister get engaged."

I stare out the windshield, feeling sappy. "A June wedding."

"You don't know that she'll get married in June."

"Sure, she will. I'll help coordinate the wedding."

Brandon's car pulls into the parking lot and we watch as he goes around and helps Hannah out. Brandon's all spiffed up in a navy suit. Hannah gets out and I feel my jaw drop slightly. She looks amazing in a powder blue long drapey dress. Her hair curls gently down her back. Even from this far away, I can see that Brandon is completely smitten.

He opened her door, for Pete's sake!

"Hey, Ryan?" I say slowly, a smile spreading on my face. Forget whatever I said about hanging up my matchmaking hat.

"Yeah?" He looks over at me, follows my gaze, and immediately starts shaking his head. "No, Laurie. Resist it."

I point. "Brandon and Hannah look really cute together."

"Just say no, Laurie."

I tip my head, watching her hold his arm as they walk across the parking lot. "How could we get them engaged?"

"I've failed." Ryan is moaning.

I pat his arm sympathetically. "Happens to the best of us. Let's go inside."

He opens the door for me, and I wave at Brandon and Hannah.

"Iron your dress, Laurie?" Brandon yells as they join us.

"Lay off, Knox." I grin. "Hannah, you look beautiful. Doesn't she look gorgeous, guys?"

Hannah blushes. Brandon blushes. Ryan smiles, nods, and then pinches the back of my arm.

I yelp.

A man in a white tux and a frown stares at me, and I smile apologetically. "Sorry," I whisper. "Heels."

"Name, please," he says stiffly.

Ryan steps in front of me. "Ryan Palmer."

Frowning Tux checks his book and then nods. "Right this way, please."

He leads us to a table behind a large aquarium holding a school of orange fish that blink at us.

"What kind of fish are those, Laurie?" Hannah asks as we sit down.

I give her a look. "How should I know?"

"You're the one going on the fishing trip."

"Oh yeah, right. Okay. Let me think." I tuck my dress down in my chair. "These are the dreaded Citrus Husk Fish. Resembling an orange peel, they float along the top of the water and trick people into picking them up."

Ryan and Brandon roll their eyes. Hannah grins. "What happens next?"

"They eat them."

"The people eat the fish?" Ryan asks, feigning seriousness.

"The fish eat the people, actually. Gang up on them. Ant that ate the elephant kind of thing."

Brandon grimaces. "Could I restrict all conversation to work, family, and Ruby and Nick?"

"Where are they?" I crane my neck, trying to see. I see aquariums. Fish in the aquariums. And fish on a platter.

Ryan touches my arm and points. "Right there, Laur."

Nick and Ruby sit toward the middle of the restaurant at a romantic little table lit only with two candles.

"Aw." Hannah and I sigh together.

"They are perfect together." I smile.

Brandon looks across the table at me. "You did well, Nutsy."

"Wow. Brandon. I'm flattered."

"Yeah, well, don't get used to it."

Ryan holds up a hand. "Wait, quiet, folks. It's happening!"

Nick leans over the table and hands Ruby a small box.

She blushes.

"Open it," Nick mouths.

She does and blushes darker. "Oh my," she mouths back.

He slides out of his chair and cracks his knee hard against the floor. Ryan winces along with Nick.

"That had to hurt." He hisses this in my ear.

Ruby erupts into giggles. Nick laughs. Then he turns his head and we can't read his lips anymore.

"What's happening? What's happening?" Hannah screeches.

"Shh," I whisper.

Ruby nods. Vigorously. Nick stands with difficulty, leans down, and kisses her.

"Yay!" Hannah and I yell. Ryan and Brandon grin, laugh, high-five. Hannah and I hug over the table.

Someone clears his throat over our table.

I look up.

Uh-oh.

"Nick." I smile. "And . . . Ruby."

Hannah shoots me a What-Are-We-Supposed-to-Say-Now? look.

Ryan covers well. He stands, shakes Nick's hand, and envelops his sister in a hug. "Congratulations, you two."

Brandon and Hannah join them. I stay at the table, watching.

Hannah and Ruby swipe tears. Brandon and Ryan smack Nick's shoulder, congratulate him, and smack him again.

My father once told me there comes a time in every woman's life when she desperately desires to be married.

No offense, Dad, but I think you were wrong.

I think there's more. *Most* women desire matrimony—but with the guys God has created for them. My job is to be still and wait, knowing He is God.

And occasionally pushing a couple together. Just now and then, of course. I smile at Brandon and Hannah.

What does that verse in Colossians say? "And whatever you do, whether in word or deed, do it all in the name of the Lord Jesus, giving thanks to God the Father through him."

I watch Ryan hold his crying sister and grin at her. Matchmaking is a deed, right? *Thanks, God.* Ryan winks at me and then mouths, "Please come take her."

I slip my arms around Ruby and hug her tight.

"I'm so happy for you, Ruby. Now, what do you think about June?"

a lauren holbrook novel

erynn mangum

REMATCH

About the Author

ERYNN MANGUM is a twentysomething single who still lives at home and has no immediate plans to leave. She has been published in *Teenage Christian Magazine*, has completed the two-year apprenticeship course given by the Christian Writers Guild, and recently completed the one-year Journeyman course. While *Miss Match* is not autobiographical, let's just say that Erynn can relate. This is her first novel. Look for the sequel in stores in September 2007. To learn more about Erynn, visit her website at www.erynnmangum.com.

MORE GREAT READS FROM THE THINK FICTION LINE.

IN BETWEEN

Jenny B. Jones

ISBN-13: 978-1-60006-098-4
ISBN-10: 1-60006-098-6

With a mother in jail and a missing-in-action dad, Katie has never known what it's like to truly be loved. And after falling in with all the wrong people at school, things go from bad to really bad when she takes the blame for vandalizing the local performing arts theater. But in the midst of a dark situation, Katie finds light in the most unexpected places: through her new friendship with an eccentric senior, the commitment of her foster family, and a tragic secret that changed them forever.

MOON WHITE

Melody Carlson

ISBN-13: 978-1-57683-951-5
ISBN-10: 1-57683-951-6

Heather has recently begun studying New Age ideas, but her newfound curiosity is alienating her from others, including her narrow-minded best friend, who has written her off as a witch. Isolated and lonely, Heather encounters fellow seekers who are far more accepting and encouraging than her Christian friends. Yet she soon learns that her "harmless" spiritual journey is anything but.

BAD IDEA

Todd and Jedd Hafer

ISBN-13: 978-1-57683-969-0
ISBN-10: 1-57683-969-9

Griffin Smith is making his first interstate road trip, an adventurous rite of passage that will take him from his Midwestern home to his freshman year at college in Southern California. Soon his journey begins to take random detours as he experiences a bittersweet reunion with his biological mother, confronts a terrible betrayal, and encounters one angry coyote.

To order copies, visit your local Christian bookstore, call NavPress at 1-800-366-7788, or log on to www.navpress.com.
To locate a Christian bookstore near you, call 1-800-991-7747.